DESIRED BY SHADOW

Immortal Warriors Paranormal Romance

CYNTHIA LUHRS

I

644 - Edinburgh, Scotland

A WHISPER MURDERED THE LEGENDARY PIRATE, BLACK BART.

He'd outrun every ship, evaded every customs officer, and made a name for himself only to have his entire life's work destroyed by *her*.

As an example to the people against the vagaries of pirating, Robert and his crew were scheduled to hang in an hour. The watered-down sun rose from its sleep as throngs of common folk gathered, staking out the best seats in the house. People loved a good hanging. Sounds of bagpipes and fiddles reached his ears. If the weather held it would be a festive event with beer, whisky, and meat pies sold by roving street vendors. Children would sit on their parents' shoulders or find a spot with a good vantage point. Everyone attended.

"Robert Bartholomew of Wales or shall I call you Black Bart or was it the Prince of Pirates? You go by so many names it's difficult to know which one to use. The infamous pirate and his crew here in my dungeon at Edinburgh Castle. Not much of a bloody legend now, are ye?" Captain Rawlins Huntington of Her Majesty's army stood before him dressed resplendently in his redcoat and shiny black boots.

"Don't care what you call me." Robert yawned. "Sounds like a large crowd out there. There's bound to be plenty of mayhem and confusion, what say I give you half my fortune to slip me the keys and look the other way while my men and I abscond from this dreary place? You'd be rich beyond your wildest dreams, Captain."

"Yer friend Lord Colin made me a similar offer and we both know how that turned out." The Captain brushed dirt off his scarlet sleeve before looking at Robert. "I don't want your gold. Hanging you and your miserable crew is worth more to me than gold. I'll be remembered as the man who brought down Black Bart. Anyway a breakfast banquet has been prepared and I do so hate to waste a good meal."

Robert sighed. He could almost appreciate the Captain's flair for the theatrical if only it wasn't his and his crew's necks in the noose. Seeing his crew shackled brought a lump to his throat and hatred rose like a sea monster from the depths of the darkest oceans. The crowds brought nasty bits of rotten food to throw as the prisoners shuffled towards the platform. On the bright side, 'twas the largest turnout he'd ever seen, even with the cold air whistling and moaning through the square. Robert quietly addressed his makeshift family. The noise of the crowd would preclude the good English Captain from overhearing. "'Tis been my pleasure serving as your Captain these many years. I make a vow and swear before you—I will find a way to provide for your families. We will have our revenge."

The crew answered back with shouts of "Aye, Cap'n" and "Death to the English buggers." Walking up the platform steps behind them, Robert searched the crowd for a friendly face, for some indicator they might still be saved. "Stay strong lads."

There were six ropes swaying in the wind but there were

twenty-five men including himself. The bastards made it so his crew would have to watch their mates die. Blackness filled him. He looked for a way to escape and destroy those who would harm what was his.

Robert flinched with the loss of each man. Twenty-four good men dead.

Rawlins purposely left him for last. The noose was tightened, the pronouncement read as Robert braced his legs and the drumroll started. Rawlins leaned in close, breath warm against Robert's ear. "Rot in hell, Prince of Pirates."

The force of his anger swelled, filling the air. "Fuck you. I swear I will find a way to haunt you to the end of your miserable days and beyond." Robert ground out in low, measured tones. "Let it be quick." The platform shook. The bang registering as the trap door opened and the rope jerked, pulling tight, cutting off his air supply as he fell through the opening.

Vaguely as if in a dream, he noted his legs twitching and a roaring filled his ears. Like the sound of his beloved mistress, the sea, it crashed through him, pulling him under. His final dying words bubbled up from the depths. "Vengeance shall be mine."

The waves parted, shrinking back from the shadows swimming in to envelop him, pulling him under. Robert's soul screamed in frustration and sadness seeing his body swinging from the hangman's noose. Waves crashed over him and still the shadows held tight. Yet in the watery depths, Robert saw flashes of light, like a lighthouse beckoning in a fierce storm.

Reaching out, he heard a deep voice coming from within the light—offering him another way.

2

HER OLD LIFE ON THE STREET SEEMED TO BELONG TO SOMEONE else. Maggie Wallace finished wiping down the tables at the Merry Maid Tavern thinking about how much her life had changed over the past year. Orphaned at age seven and not having any other family, she was sent to a sad, depressing home for children. At fifteen she'd run away, preferring to take her chances on the street. She'd survived for nine years, finding odd jobs, crashing at friends' places for a week at a time, paying to stay at hostels when she could scrape the cash together, sleeping in abandoned buildings when she couldn't. Other than infrequent odd jobs, this was the first real job she'd held. The tavern owner had seen her on the streets and one cold night last year offered her a job when she refused his charity offer of twenty quid. Other street kids called her stupid for not taking money from strangers, but she had to earn her own way, no matter what. Waitressing paid decently. She had a roommate, Josh, and they'd found a tiny, reasonable flat close to work. Was it only four months ago they'd moved in? Seemed like a lifetime. Her own place, a good friend, a steady job—what more could she ask for?

Why did you always think about your life when the end of the year drew to a close? Shaking her head, Maggie bid the barkeep goodnight and headed out into the clear, cold night. Stepping off the curb, Maggie jumped back falling on her ass as a white van screeched around the corner, an odd thumping sound emanating from inside.

Getting up, she dusted her coat off, checking for damage. Maggie purchased the coat when she'd received her very first paycheck. It had been an extravagance, but she loved the soft wool and beautiful deep-blue color. Tugging her hat down, she set out for the twenty-minute walk home.

Home. Smiling for no reason, Maggie bounded up the threadbare stairs of the worn building to the fourth floor. There were six flats lining the corridor. Hers was at the end of the hall. Turning the key, she called out, "Josh, I'm back."

No answer. He worked as a hospital orderly and took whatever hours he could get. Hanging up her coat, she put the soup on to warm. The flat was small. A large room with a miniscule kitchen and living area which led to a bath built for fairies it was so tiny. There were two bedrooms large enough for a twin bed, nightstand, and chest at the foot of the bed. Shades of gray and blue decorated hers while Josh had done his in boring brown. Rummaging in the chest, she pulled out an oversize sweater, leggings and thick socks.

Changing, she padded out to the kitchen, poured the soup into a bowl and poured a glass of milk from the icebox. There was no dining table so she ate in the living area. Josh had found two overstuffed chairs put out for the trash in a nice part of town and convinced one of his mates to drive them back. The chair was covered in an ugly print with monkeys cavorting in the jungle, but it was comfortable and large enough to curl up in.

Throwing a blanket over her to ward off the chill, she ate the soup, content.

She woke to a quiet flat. Guess Josh was pulling a double-shift. Maggie took a quick shower. If she lingered the meager hot water would run out and she despised cold showers. Reminded her of life on the street. Eating Wasa crackers and cheese, she finished off the milk, making a mental note to pick up a jug on the way home from work.

Locking the door, she looked at everyone as she walked. It was mid-morning, and most people were already at work. The few out and about, she studied, wondering what each of them did for a living and jumping when the person she was watching disappeared in front of her eyes. No one else ever registered the fact that one second a person was walking across the street and the next, poof, gone, vanishing into thin air.

Like magic.

It had been happening since she was five. The first few years she was afraid. But she'd stopped being scared when she realized these ghosts couldn't hurt her. And now she was simply curious as to why she could see them when others couldn't. Maggie had told Josh her weird secret. He cautioned her not to tell anyone else, said the men in white coats might take her away for being crazy. A good friend, he asked her all kinds of questions about what she saw and how her ability worked. He seemed to believe her and not think she was a freak.

Daydreaming, she ignored the warning in her gut. Crossing the street, the sound of metal on metal had her turning in time to see a white van bearing down on her. It had the same dented side door as the one that had almost run her over yesterday. Sounds faded, time slowed and lengthened like a piece of glass heated and stretched from end to end before shattering. Maggie froze like a mouse cornered by a cat. The door gaped open, hands reached out, grabbed hold of her arms, and pulled her in, slamming her to the floor of the moving vehicle. It happened so fast she didn't have time to scream. The doors banged shut as the van screeched off down the half-empty street. The breath knocked out of her, she rolled to her side, taking shallow quick breaths.

Damn it to hell. All the time she'd lived on the streets, she knew better. Knew to always pay attention to her surroundings to watch for those who preyed on others. She'd grown complacent, lazy, living in her cozy flat. Now she'd made the dumbest mistake of all—letting down her guard. Able to breathe, she looked at the men. There were two in the back of the van and one driving. None of their faces were covered and that frightened her more than anything.

To make herself heard over the music, Maggie's voice came out harsh to her ears. "There's some kind of mistake. I don't know who you are, but you've got the wrong person. I was on my way to work. Let me go." *Good. Sound braver than you feel.* Lessons from the street came back to her. Show fear and you'd end up hurt—or worse, dead.

The man driving spoke. "No, Maggie. It's you we're after, and now we've got you."

How does he know my name?

Ice-water ran down the back of her shirt, and goosebumps broke out on her arms. The men in back laughed. Lunging for the door handle, she saw stars when the man with black hair backhanded her. Tasting a warm, coppery fluid, she gagged and retched, wiping the blood from her lip. Tensing her legs, she tried again, kicking out at her captors. Steel bands encircled her arms as the other man with spiked brown hair, wrenched her arms behind her back, securing her wrists with zip strips. She managed a solid kick to the ribs of black hair before the same was done to her feet. He punched her in the gut and for the second time that morning the air whooshed out of her.

"Try it again, and I'll cut you from ear to ear." His breath was putrid, smelling of coffee, cigarettes, and decay.

Huffing, Maggie willed oxygen into her straining lungs. "What do you want with me? I haven't done anything."

The driver spoke again. "It's not what you've done, it's what you *can* do. Jim, tell the lass what she cost us."

Cost them? A sick feeling settled in her stomach.

The one with spiky hair, Jim, laughed. "Three hundred quid, ducky. You better to live up to what he promised or you'll find yourself at the bottom of Leith Harbor."

"Who promised you? I don't know what you're talking about. I won't call the authorities. I'm going to be late, and I really need this job. Let me go." Her voice sounded shrill, uneven to her ears. There had to be some kind of mistake. She couldn't do anything. The only skill she had was waitressing and no one would pay three hundred quid for a waitress. Hell, you could hire one for a paltry sum, especially in today's employment market. What the hell was going on?

Black hair leaned in close and she held her breath not wanting to inhale the stench.

"Yer lousy boyfriend, Josh, that's who, you twat."

"Josh. No, you're mistaken. He's my friend—he wouldn't hurt anyone." A numb heaving sensation filled her, growing into a writhing mass of hurt and anger, threatening to claw its way out of her insides.

An ugly loud sound filled the van as the men laughed. The vehicle bumped over potholes in the uneven street, jarring Maggie's teeth.

"With friends the likes 'o him, you'll be better off with saintly fellows like us. Wake up, ducky. No one has friends anymore. In this world you do whatever it takes to survive." Jim grunted and leaned back against the narrow bench seat.

Maggie's brain processed the words she'd heard. The thought of Josh betraying her didn't make any sense. They'd been friends for three years. Three years was a lifetime nowadays. They looked out for each other, helped each other to survive. Nothing made any sense.

The van slowed. Maggie twisted around straining to see out the front window. The vehicle pulled into an alley behind a stretch of posh townhomes. Looked like they'd been converted for business use by the signs on the back gates. No idea where she was other than it was a nice part of town by how well kept everything looked. The engine shut off, the driver jumped out and opened the back door. The men gagged her so she couldn't yell for help. Struggling earned her a savage blow to the head and she passed out.

Coming to with no idea of how long she'd been out, Maggie was sitting on a sofa with the two thugs on either side of her. The driver was nowhere to be seen, but another man sat across from her.

"About fucking time you're awake, sleeping beauty. I'm Bruce. You've met a few of my men. Welcome to Dante Import/Export, your new home. Do what yer told, don't cause any trouble, and life won't be too terrible bad."

As she wiggled to sit up, Bruce motioned to his men. The straps binding her hands and feet were cut, the gag removed. Rubbing sore wrists, she appealed to him. "There's a mistake. I don't know what Josh did but I don't have any skills. I'm just a waitress."

Bruce tilted his head to the side and snorted. "Right. And I'm just a dishwasher." He leaned forward in the chair. "We put up very specific advertisements, mainly in hospitals offering cold hard cash for certain information. Your friend Josh called. Said you met the requirements, that you told him you saw ghosts. He needed the entry fee into a high-stakes poker game. Said it was a sure thing." Bruce tsked. "Idiot. Now you work for us. Jim will get you settled and explain your new duties." His mobile rang and he motioned for them to leave.

The men pulled her to her feet. Looking for a means of escape, Maggie stopped struggling when Bruce covered the phone and said, "If you try to run, we'll hunt you down and kill you—slowly and painfully. Enjoy your accommodations."

She'd been kidnapped, and Josh was responsible?

Her only friend in the world had done the unthinkable.

Three hundred quid was a fortune to someone as poor as they, but still, how could one human being do something so heinous to another?

Stumbling up the stairs, Maggie kept going over what she knew, looking for answers. What exactly did she know? She knew Josh had a gambling addiction. Always looking for the easy score, stealing from tourists as they bumbled down the streets of the city. Quick money with little or no work, that's what he was all about. Grateful for a friend after so much time alone on the street, she'd overlooked his problems, ignored the ugliness of the things he did. Turned a blind eye when he came home beaten up because he owed somebody money and couldn't pay.

The guy never had the rent money, but she let him stay, feeling sorry for him, believing he had her back. How wrong she was. What he'd done was unforgivable. These men paid money for the identities of those who had died and been resuscitated. But why? Did they believe in ghosts? And what did it matter? The ghosts she'd encountered never hurt anyone. Heck, most people walked right through them. She had to find a way to escape. Josh—he was dead to her. When she escaped, she'd kick his ass for what he'd done.

If she escaped. These were dangerous men. A sour thought took hold...guess it was good to know what your life was worth.

Jim roughly pushed her into a room and locked the door. "I'll be back later to tell you what yer duties are. Try and leave, and I'll gut you without blinking." Turning, she saw eight women ranging in ages from fifteen to forty staring at her with haunted expressions and dead eyes.

Prisoners. What was this place?

❧ 3 ❧

After being thrown across the alley to kiss the side of the dumpster, Robert got up, rotated his aching shoulder, rubbed his jaw, and cursed the offending piece of metal. "Don't know why you're laughing, last I checked I've killed two and you're still screwing around with that miserable bastard." He pointed to the Day Walker writhing on the ground. Looking around for the mobile he dropped when he went flying, Robert glanced over at Jasper, his comrade-in-arms.

Both of who just happened to be ghosts, well Shadow Walkers was the correct term if you wanted to be particular.

"That lovely mademoiselle in the tan coat with the cream-colored scarf could see us, and you frightened her, *mon ami*. Why she might have been *the one* for you." Jasper wiped his hands off on his black wool trousers, frowning at the dirt left behind. Shrugging a very Gallic shrug, as only the French could, Jasper cut his eyes to Robert and ripped out the Day Walker's heart, stabbing it with gusto. Jasper leaned back, dispassionately observing the degenerate disintegrate into gold dust, blown away on the icy winter wind.

"Three of our enemies dispatched. A damn fine day." Momentarily distracted by the area next to the Scottish Writers'

Museum, Robert read the plaque. Called Makars' Court, there were inscriptions on the stones paving the courtyard. He examined a few, holding back a burst of laughter as he knelt, reading the stone to his left, "It's a grand thing to get leave to live, by Nan Shepherd." Tightening the queue keeping his dark hair in place, he stood. "So right you are Nan. Sure Thorne didn't whisper this one in your ear?"

Grinding his palm into his eye socket, Robert thought about it. One woman. Wincing at the thought of only making love to one woman for the rest of eternity, he thought it would be like eating steak three times a day, every day forever. He liked steak, but come on, everybody craves a little variety.

"Most women would run away screaming. None would risk becoming involved with the likes of us. There's about as much chance of that happening as there is of getting struck by lightning and bitten by a shark in the same day." Robert chuckled and rolled his eyes. "I love my life. I'm never giving it up to shackle myself to one woman for all eternity. Think of all the poor, lovely women I'd be depriving of my charming self."

The Frenchman inclined his head. "Until next time." Robert clapped Jasper on the back and dematerialized to his ship while Jasper vanished to his home in Paris.

❧ 4 ❧

O ne Year Later - Wednesday, November 1ˢᵗ - Edinburgh, Scotland

ROUGH HANDS YANKED MAGGIE OFF THE SAGGING COT, startling her from a restless nap. "Get up, you lazy bitches before I knock your teeth out." Mr. Nasty yelled.

Yawning, she pulled her boots on, the rusty bedsprings squeaking when she leaned down. "All right, I'm up. No need to shout, sheesh." Never knowing when they'd be summoned, she and Jean tried to catch a few winks whenever possible. Sleep helped the hours pass so you might forget at least for a few brief moments the hell you were living.

The leader—Bruce, stood blocking the doorway to their room. She and Jean were taken out to spy for their cruel captors, acting like bloodhounds after a fox, pointing out people others couldn't see. When any of the prisoners identified a super ghost as she'd come to call them, they pointed the being out, and once back at the prison wrote up a description. Bruce and his men were afraid of one called Robert or usually they referred to him as "the Pirate." He was rumored to be a ferocious fighter, and she'd heard him mentioned numerous times.

"It's cold out. I'd rather stay in bed." Gloria whispered, pulling on her coat.

"No kidding. Let the super ghosts and Bruce fight their petty little wars without us." Maggie snorted. She didn't know why they fought; didn't care. All she wanted was to survive to live another day and pray that one day she'd be freed. "What time is it?"

"Bit after ten," Jean whispered.

"Come on, ladies. Quit yer yapping and get a move on," the ugly weasel hollered.

"What's his name again?" Jean wrinkled her nose.

"Alvin, I think," Maggie answered sounding distracted. If Solien and Rawlins were leery of this Robert guy, he must be seriously scary. She hadn't seen him, but Jean had encountered him a couple of times and gushed over the guy's good looks. Maggie sent up a prayer every time she went out to never run into the guy.

Bruce and his men didn't have the ability to see the super ghosts so whenever the prisoners were sent out to a club or pub or shop, their job was to look around for these super ghosts or Shadow Walkers as Bruce called them. And Maggie and her fellow prisoners were to tell Bruce or his men when they spotted the enemy. Then the men called Bruce who called his boss. These guys were super ghosts too but called themselves Day Walkers. Enemies to the Shadow Walkers. Locked in some kind of crazy war most of the world couldn't see and probably wouldn't care about if they could. The sucky thing? If a prisoner didn't tell Bruce or his men when they spotted one of these beings and somehow Bruce found out? The prisoner was beaten or killed on the spot. Of course, Bruce and company couldn't see their bosses any more than they could the enemy unless one of these Walkers willed it.

Kept in the dark upstairs attic, there were ten men and only three women remaining, the rest never returned from their forays into Edinburgh and surrounding areas. The only time the men and women interacted was during meals. While they ate, they whispered amongst themselves when the guards changed or weren't paying close attention. The group talked about themselves, figuring out what commonality tied them together. They came from different backgrounds, races, and circumstances. Some kidnapped, some lured to the house by a warm meal or drink, and kept against their will. But all were survivors.

It didn't matter what they had survived only that each and every one of them had been declared clinically dead before being resuscitated. The types of accidents were varied: smoke inhalation, drowning, car crash, knife and gunshot wounds. All the prisoners could see people no one else could. None of it made sense to Maggie. Why didn't they *recruit* the captives instead of holding them against their will? Maggie knew some of the prisoners would have gladly worked for Bruce simply for a roof over their head, food and water. Wouldn't it be easier? What did she know? Deciding not to worry about something she couldn't change, Maggie finished pulling on her gloves.

"Need your eyeballs tonight, ladies." Bruce motioned to the three of them.

Maggie, Gloria, and Jean were shoved out the door into the hallway. Guess none of the men were joining them. The women wore their clothing to bed since the nightgowns provided were little more than flimsy threadbare hospital gowns, gaping open and leaving nothing to the imagination. It was humiliating. Maybe that's why the prisoners were all given the robes, to keep them cowed. And they quickly learned the men would watch them dress if they slept in the gossamer wrappers. Disgusting cretins.

Two men led the way while the other three brought up the rear, ensuring the women couldn't escape as they walked down the stairs to the back hallway and tunnel. The women were split up, Maggie going with three of the men, Jean and Gloria with the other two. Bruce stood with arms crossed, watching them go through the tunnel. It led to a garage behind the house. Too bad it was padlocked and guarded at all times. Otherwise, she might have made her getaway.

Climbing into the white Hummer, Maggie thought about last time someone tried to escape this circle of hell called home. A year she'd been held here, and during that period several men and three women ran away. To no avail. Always caught and brought back to the elegant townhouse overlooking the park.

From the outside, it looked like a normal business with a discreet black sign stating "Dante Import/Export." The neighboring businesses didn't have a clue what went on underneath their noses, or maybe they simply didn't care.

The memory was clear as the mirror in the hallway. Two of the men had been executed. Bruce made each captive walk by and look at the dead men. Three gunshots to the head with the eyes cut out. It was a gruesome sight she'd never forget. The other men and women were brought back alive but soon would be praying for death to take them. Her stomach heaved thinking back on their fates.

The really scary guy in charge, Solien, had come out of nowhere, gliding to a stop in front of them. Maggie heard Bruce talking about the man. Bruce was low man on the totem pole, reporting up all the way to something way more frightening than Solien who was terrifying in his own right. Heaven help them if they encountered whoever was Solien's head honcho. Solien looked human except for the fact he was six foot eight with black eyes, and midnight blue hair. A few months back, she'd seen him get angry with one of Bruce's men. *Minion* was the word Solien used. If she hadn't seen it with her own eyes she'd never have believed it...big black leathery wings sprouted from his back and his skin turned green.

She'd known she was losing it when a part of her brain thought the varying shades of green sliding across his body were beautiful, like the ocean or a spring meadow. Solien disappeared and appeared at will; it was freaky and disturbing on so many levels.

Maggie had watched as he took her four friends down to the basement. No one knew what was down there. Bruce said goblins, but she assumed he meant some kind of animal or said it to keep them all in line. Come on. There was no such thing as goblins. Some conspiracy nut would have uncovered it by now if it were true, right? In keeping she and her comrades cowed, no one tried to escape. The screams from the basement carried throughout the townhome. She never saw the four of them again.

When Solien came up from the basement he had blood on his shirt and pants. He'd told all of them that defying the men was defying him. After that awful night, resigned to his or her fate, no one ever attempted to slip away again.

After all she'd seen, Maggie wasn't sure anything could faze her anymore. She was numb, detached. Focused only on living another day. No longer fantasizing of escape or freedom. Accepted her fate and made the best of it. The ability to adapt was how she'd survived on the streets all those years.

The Hummer hit a pothole pulling her away from the morbid thoughts. Almost there. *Please let me make it through tonight and live to see another day*, she prayed to whomever might be listening.

Maggie wished she didn't know the truth...things that go bump in the night actually existed, and they sure as hell weren't kind fairy godmothers.

5

A knock on the door woke Robert. Stretching, his foot encountered a warm thigh accompanied by a giggle from the blanket. Opening his eyes, he smiled at the three women in his bed. They'd had quite a day of down and dirty sex, just like he liked it.

Getting up, he glanced out the window to see the stars winking across a clear midnight blue sky. Pulling on jeans, he admired the view. Women. He adored each and every one. All shapes and sizes, and colors of the rainbow. Delightful with their quirks that made each of them unique. They were all glorious to him. Running a finger along an olive-skinned foot, he let his eye roam over the beauties. A dark goddess, a porcelain redhead and a saucy Mediterranean brunette lay sleeping in a pile, like puppies after an afternoon of play.

Gods he loved his life. With a last longing look at the bed, he turned from the vision of loveliness and opened the door.

"Sorry to disturb you Captain but 'tis nightfall. I brought tea and whisky for you and the ladies." Ian stood at attention awaiting Robert's orders. He resisted the urge to laugh. The boy was desperately trying not to goggle at all the flesh on display.

On the ship, he was sovereign over all. They were all fiercely loyal to him. A sense of pride ran through him.

"Pour me a whisky, lad, and when the ladies wake, make sure they've had a bite to eat before sending them on their way."

Ian was fourteen. He'd been with Robert since he was seven. Same age as Robert when he worked his first ship. The boy had run away from abusive foster parents. Robert found him trying to steal food as it was being loaded for the next journey. Rather than sending him to the authorities, he hired him as a cabin boy. Tossing back the remains of his drink, he sauntered out the door naked and down the hallway to shower. He'd never admit it, but he took in spurned kids, pulled strings behind the scenes and provided gainful employment, either at one of his many houses, on his ship, or in another of his many ventures.

Fresh from a long, hot shower, Robert felt the pull as he stepped into the cabin. The ladies were still sleeping.

Damn, not yet. He materialized clothing, draining another glass of whisky before he was taken. He'd tried to describe it once, the sensation of someone pulling on your arm, electricity dancing through every vein before your whole being was forcibly ripped apart. Your entire essence scrambled. Sent through a meat grinder and poured out to ooze back together.

When you dematerialized by choice, it was a buzz of energy, a tingling sensation but not unpleasant. He'd guessed it was another way for the gods to make sure he knew who was in control. He wouldn't give up the Shadow Walker life for anything on this earth, but this relive your death anniversary bullshit Thorne made them go through each year reeked worse than week old fish.

THE HUMMER CAME TO A STOP IN OLD TOWN OUTSIDE OF Velvet. Maggie had never been inside the infamous establishment.

The three men who worked for Bruce were dressed to impress, at least in their minds. Maggie wrinkled her nose; they looked like aging, smarmy guys out on the hunt for a quick lay. Garbed in shiny suits, white silk shirts, gold chains, and pointed shoes, she imagined this was what it was like to be trapped inside of a disco ball. Not to mention the cologne. She'd breathed into her sweat-shirt on the ride over, trying to keep from retching at the stench. She guessed their mantra must be—bathe in and own it, baby.

The bouncer frowned as he looked over her attire. Scowling he lifted the velvet rope and motioned them to enter the exclusive club. The guys must spend stacks of cash here for the bouncer to allow her in dressed like a street urchin. The interior was dimly lit by sconces along the walls. Adequate light to find your way but not nearly enough to notice everything that was going on in the shadowy corners and at the high-backed booths. The only other light came from the backlit bottles behind the bar and the flashing lights on the dance floor.

Leaning against the dark wood, the men motioned to the bartender and ordered vodka on the rocks and a glass of white wine for her. They always let her have a drink though she was never left alone. Even a simple trip to the bathroom had one of the guys standing guard outside the door to make sure she didn't try to run. As if. After Mr. Scary had shown them what would happen. She'd rather be breathing and miserable than dead.

Monsters. Anyone she tried to enlighten, the cops, for instance, would lock her up for a psych eval quicker than you could say goblins three times fast.

Thinking back on her old life, the events leading to her kidnapping, and her present circumstances, Maggie sighed. Since she'd been abducted she kept her head down, keeping to the shadows, not drawing any unwanted awareness her way. She did her job and existed. Survival was all that mattered.

An elbow to the side brought her back to the present.

"Oy, pay attention bitch. Drink your vino and get to work, you know the drill. Jones will be right behind ye."

Maggie nodded. Picking up her wine, turning away from the long, polished glass bar to survey the patrons, she caught a smile from the bartender. "Anything else, miss?" He looked to be in his twenties with short black hair and dreamy blue eyes.

She stuttered, "No thanks. I need to be going." If Jones or one of the other men saw the enchanting guy being friendly to her, it wouldn't go well for the bartender. Giving him a small smile, she caught sight of herself in the mirrored wall above the bar.

Nice. I look like a homeless urchin. She dispassionately took stock of her reflection behind the bottles. Long fire engine red hair up in a ponytail, green eyes with purplish-looking circles under them, pale skin and an average if curvy body. Average about summed it up. When she'd waitressed, Maggie thought she looked pretty good. Not beautiful but pleasant to look at. She'd finally been happy—maybe too happy—and it had been snatched away in the blink of an eye. Truth be told, she looked at least ten years older than her twenty-five years, but given the current circumstances she wasn't surprised. The past year had aged her. Made her relinquish the hopes and dreams that had sustained her for so long. Her mouth turning down at the corners, Maggie turned away from the mirror and looked over the crowd.

The music was giving her a headache. Hours had passed, and she hadn't seen anyone out of the ordinary. Most nights she didn't. The guys took full advantage and partied until whatever club, pub, or other rattrap they were in, called last call and closed down for the night.

A loud pop sounded near her ear. Instinctively ducking, she looked around to locate the source of the noise. Maggie saw one of Bruce's men fall to the floor. Screaming broke out as the patrons of Velvet realized shots had been fired. Guns might be illegal in the United Kingdom, but the criminals got hold of them easily enough. Pandemonium ensued and guests fled, stampeding towards the exits.

Pushed against the wall, she stayed out of the way to avoid being trampled. Jones grabbed her arm, his hand slipped out of hers, and he fell. He was thrashing, desperately holding his throat as blood spread across the scarred floor. He'd been cut from ear to ear. The wound was nasty, gaping open as blood drained like spilt wine on the floor.

"That'll teach you to cheat me at cards." A man stood over Jones with a broken beer bottle in his hand, another tucked in his belt, and an ugly snarl on his face. He looked at Maggie and advanced towards her, the jagged glass raised, blood dripping onto the black-and white-tiled floor. No escape. There were too many people. It was like wading through glue. The murderer was gaining on her. Jones's two counterparts were nowhere to be seen.

"Ow!" Maggie clutched her shoulder where she felt a sting. Her hand came away bright red. He'd cut her. Fear drove her, giving her strength to pull out of the man's grasp. Adrenaline fueled her to push and shove her way outside. Exploding out of the exit door, Jones's partner, Donald grabbed her, roughly shoving Maggie into the waiting Hummer. They sped off back to the townhouse. A small hiccup escaped as she imagined her blood dripping in time to the frantic beating of her heart.

"Bruce is going to have my ass." Donald chewed his thumb-nail, looking worried. Back at the house, a shower helped process the surreal scene she'd witnessed. Wincing from the pain, she changed into the only other clothes she owned, pulling on fresh jeans, a tee shirt, and a thick navy hoodie. With only soap and a washcloth, she'd cleaned the wound as best she could. Donald had handed her two aspirin as she went upstairs and told her to keep quiet, he was in enough trouble already. Her shoulder was throbbing, the cut deep. It really needed stitches.

Good luck with that. They wouldn't take her to a doctor, and no way was she letting one of them put a needle through her skin. The shoulder would have to wait. Back in her room she noted Gloria and Jean's cots were still empty. It was unusual for both of them to be out later than her. Worried, Maggie tossed and turned, groaning when her shoulder made contact with the lumpy mattress before falling into an exhausted, fractured sleep.

Waking up, she rolled over. Big mistake. She saw little goblins dancing in front of her eyes, bile rose up, and her stomach threatened to revolt. Swallowing several times, she waited for her body to realize she didn't need to flee. The feeling remained. Voices screamed in her head—not safe, run. What was happening?

There was a shadow under the door to the room. Maggie listened, trying to decipher what woke her. Voices.

"Jean didn't point out one of those slippery bastards tonight. The bitch let him kill Frankie. I saw him when he made himself visible to talk to the pub owner and pay for the damage, otherwise she would have gotten away with it. Gloria lied for her, saying she didn't see anyone either." Shaking his fist, Bruce continued, "They won't be working with us anymore. I took them both to the basement."

Donald's voice sounded weak and reedy when he chimed in. "I lost Jones. Some bloke he cheated at cards. The freak said she didn't see anyone tonight, hasn't for the past month. Maybe the ability wears off after a time?"

"Maggie's lying, or she's useless. Either way, it's time. Take her to the basement then grab a few hours' sleep, you look like you've been on a three-day bender."

The men shut off the hall lights. Maggie stayed still as a statue, listening to the footsteps receding down the corridor. Her thighs shook, muscles clenching, the salvia pooling in the back of her throat as she fought not to retch.

Gloria and Jean were dead.

She was next.

❧ 6 ❧

T hursday, November 2nd

THE NEXT THING ROBERT KNEW, IT WAS EXCEEDINGLY EARLY,
the sun was barely awake, and his blasted powers were gone. He
was in a cell he was very well acquainted with—the dungeon of
Edinburgh Castle.

Dank, filthy, and dim. He shook his head, it was bad enough
to relive it, couldn't the gods at least let the bloody floor be
clean? Sighing, he lifted his foot as a rat scurried across the straw
and ran into a cell next to him.

Grimacing, Robert consoled himself with the thought it
would all be over in twenty-four hours and he could go back to
his life. Every year unless the unthinkable happened, Shadow
Walkers relived their death anniversary and were powerless for
the twenty-four time period surrounding the event. Then it was
over until the next time. Good thing. There was a particularly
valuable shipment of artifacts he was to pick up and deliver to
Wales. The black market thrived and the more things changed

the more they stayed the same. Though he never thought he'd live to see the day England and Scotland would be physically separated. Towards the end of the nineteenth century there were catastrophic weather events, the tectonic plates of the very earth shifted, causing incredible change and damage. Now there was a channel between the two countries and while devastating for all who lost their lives, it was a godsend, time wise for sailing. Instead of going all the way around, he simply went across and took care of business.

During his first life as he liked to think of it, vices prospered while regular folk struggled...whoring, gambling, drinking and smuggling. The same debauchery was still popular and even more profitable today.

"Ready to hang, pirate?" Captain Rawlins Huntington stood at the door to his cell.

"Robert will suffice. My offer stands. Simply leave your post unattended for a few minutes, ensuring the cells of my men and I are unlocked, and I'll make you rich as kings. What say you?" He would gladly give his entire fortune to free them all.

"How it must rankle the great pirate to be brought so low by a mere woman. If only you could keep your wick in your breeches, you might still be sailing the seas. Though I'm sure Her Majesty's Navy would capture you soon enough. I don't need your bloody fortune. It will be celebration enough when the lot of you hang."

How the whole death-anniversary thing worked he hadn't a clue other than the twenty-four hours. It was as if that day was overlaid on the current moment in time. No one but those who were present could see it or experience it. For Robert it played out the same every year, it couldn't be changed—and he'd bloody well tried, hundreds of times over the ensuing years. Well, there was one way...hell no, not going to happen, so forget about it. Bollocks.

"Suit yourself. I'm ready; shall we?" He adjusted his clothing. It never ceased to amaze him how he could be wearing jeans one moment then be back in his pirate attire every year. No mobile phone, keys, wallet, nothing. It was all exactly as the day he died. Made getting home a chore. You couldn't dematerialize as your powers were gone for a full day so you had to find another way. Robert usually had one of his men waiting at the castle to retrieve him. After hundreds of years, he had this bloody inconvenience down pat. Stretching, he stood and moved to the door of the cell.

Walking out into the early-morning light, he blinked after the darkness of the dungeon. He'd relived this hundreds of times yet every year he got a lump in his throat seeing his men all nod to him. Afterwards, he'd done the best he could to take care of the families, providing them with gold and employment as needed. There had only been one family he'd lost track of and couldn't find. To this day, he had descendants of those same families working for him. It was a sick joke of the fates to have Rawlins still in the picture causing trouble, and as a Day Walker no less. He wondered—was the man standing before him the same jerk of today? He didn't think so but it made his head hurt to try and figure it out. If he ever had a civil conversation with Rawlins before he beheaded him, he'd ask.

Day Walkers were the darkness to the Shadow Walkers light in the fight for humanity. They existed to destroy humanity. He and his brethren were sworn to save every last person. The enemy was ruled by Dayne, a god and a mean sonofabitch to boot, and while Robert also reported to a god, at least the guy wasn't quite as unpredictable. Robert swallowed hard. Every year on the anniversary of his death, he had to relive it to signify his rebirth as a Shadow Walker. Fuck me, couldn't Thorne have simply had them light a candle or say a prayer of thanks? Thorne was the god of shadows. It was he, in the darkness of the Shadow realm, who offered Robert the choice to become a Shadow Walker. Wanting to take care of the families his crew left behind, wanting revenge, he gladly made the bargain, accepting the curse, swearing to protect humanity from the Day Walkers and became immortal, keeping his soul—for the soul is the energy life force within. It is all that remains behind if we refuse to move on to the next realm.

The crowds jeered, screaming obscenities, throwing lettuce and other less savory things at him as they marched him to the scaffolding. Looking around, he was always pleased to see such a large turnout. Get through this next dodgy part, and it will all be over. He hated being hanged, the feeling of suffocating; it was a terrible way to die. Casting a look heavenward, he said the same thing he did every year, "Let it be quick."

The platform shook. The bang registering as the trap door opened and the rope jerked, pulling tight, cutting off his air supply as he fell through the opening.

Maggie moved her leg, wriggling her toes. The pins and needles feeling slowly dissipated. She'd lain rigid in bed for hours, waiting, planning. It was really early or exceedingly late depending on how you looked at it. For a few minutes she stayed motionless, listening to the sounds around her. The house silent. Satisfied everyone was still asleep she rolled off the cot cringing at the squeaking noise. Crouching next to the bed, Maggie held her breath. When no one appeared after a few minutes she pulled her shoes on and grabbed a small backpack. There was nothing to take with her other than a toothbrush, hairbrush, and a couple of ponytail holders. The only other set of clothing she owned had been ruined earlier that night. There was no one else in left in the women's dorm-style room to alert the guards she was trying to leave. Donald had been angry and distracted and had forgotten to lock the bolt on the door. Maggie retrieved the bobby pin she'd had hidden under her bed for almost a year and popped the lock. With a loud click, it swung open. Again she waited, hoping no one had heard the sound. Slipping out the door, Maggie softly pulled it closed behind her and pushed the lock in again.

A week ago any thought of running away would have been

unthinkable. Knowing she'd be taken down to the basement, never to return, made her desperate escape attempt the only viable option she had left.

Creeping down to the kitchen Maggie stayed to the edges of the hallway to avoid the creaking wood floors. Turning the corner, she looked into the room they used as a makeshift living room and saw one of the guards dozing on the sofa, the TV tuned to a cooking show. Tiptoeing, careful to step over the couple squeaky spots in the linoleum, she crossed the room to the pantry. Opening the door, Maggie was grateful the bulb over the oven provided enough dim light to see what she needed. She took fresh bandages for her shoulder, a mini-bottle of aspirin, toothpaste, bottled water, crackers, and a few bananas to tide her over. It was a small enough amount not to be noticed but enough to keep her going for a couple of days. Disposable hand-wipes were already stashed in her bag and most important—twenty quid she'd picked up at the club.

Some drunken partygoer must have dropped it and she'd snatched it up fast, hiding it in the pocket of her jeans. Popping a couple of aspirin, she washed them down with a glass of orange juice. She'd miss her favorite beverage. It was getting harder to find things like juice and produce at the grocery stores, and when you could the cost of the items was astronomical. People had begun planting gardens again. Shoving a sandwich in her mouth she checked on the guard, who was softly snoring.

Moving along the hallway, she kept close to the walls stopping every few feet to listen. Satisfied no one was following her, Maggie took the back stairs to the first floor.

No one would be up at this hour. Bypassing the hallway leading to the underground garage, she made her way to the storage room. The garage was always guarded. But cleaning supplies, in some dusty old room? Why bother? Heartbeat loud in her ears, she wiped a sweaty palm on her jeans and opened the storage room door, willing it not to squeak.

Mopping the floors was one of her assigned chores. The

room was damp and dirty, but if she remembered correctly, there was a storm grate in the wall and it wasn't locked.

Moving the boxes piled on the floor, Maggie looked over the grate. The last time she'd cleaned, she noticed the grate had hinges at the top. Lifting it, a horrible, screeching noise had brought the guard running to see what she was doing. Maggie told him she'd bumped it with the cleaning cart. On the rare occasion she let her fantasy of escape play out, she utilized the storm tunnel. Though who would have thought she'd ever have the courage to put the plan into action? Guess desperate times and all that rot.

"Maggie? What are you doing here?"

She jumped three feet in the air, heart beating out of her chest. The voice came from behind her. Damn. Someone was already awake. Whirling around, a finger to her lips to silence him; she stood face to face with dear, bumbling Ned.

"Quiet, or you'll wake the monsters."

"You're not supposed to be cleaning at night." The guy scratched his head looking perplexed. Good-looking but dumb as a box of rocks...that was Ned.

"No, I'm not cleaning."

Ned embraced her, hastily letting go when she didn't return the hug. Nothing personal but she didn't trust anyone nowadays. She had to act normal. "How long have you been working here, a week?" *Play it cool, Mags.*

"Yeah. Some guys offered me a job last week. The hostel closed down, and I couldn't find work. They promised a roof over my head and food. That's enough for me. The guy in charge, Bruce, said I'd be helping to take care of everyone here. It's not like you said it was. The people here need help."

He didn't even realize this was a prison. Didn't believe her when she told him she'd been kidnapped and held here against her will. The guy actually believed the stories Bruce and the others told him, that she and the other captives all had mental disorders and he was helping to care for them. Idiot.

"Ned, believe me, you have to get out. These guys are really bad news. You've no idea what you've gotten yourself into. Like I told you before this place is not what it seems." Grabbing his arm, she wanted him to understand the danger. Stupid, yes but he wasn't a bad guy.

"Mags, it's harsh out there. Things will be better here, they said so and I can help you get better." Confusion filled his eyes. "I remember Bruce saying no one is to be up after lights out. What are you doing?"

In one of the hostels she'd stayed in there was always the sound of trickling water coming from their laundry room. Ned, who worked there part-time, told her it was a storm grate. The tunnel fed into the old sewer system and ended at Edinburgh Castle. Smaller tunnels led to the larger main tunnel. Theoretically once you made it to the large artery all you had to do was follow it all the way to the castle. Ned had seen it on an old map some tourist had but never tried it. Newer homes didn't have these grates. Many older places boarded up the openings, covering them with wallboard. No one had gotten around to boarding this one up. She pointed to the grate.

"You gave me the idea a while ago, back at the hostel. I thought I'd go exploring." Crossing her fingers behind her back, she waited.

"It's probably filled with sewage and other nasty stuff. Why not go out the front door if you want to walk around?"

A pleading note entered her voice. "The front door is guarded. No one can know I went out. I'll be back before everyone wakes. Don't tell anyone, okay?" This had to work.

He shook his head, "Are you sure you're okay to be outside on your own? You know—in your condition?" She nodded and gave him her most innocent smile. Satisfied, he patted her shoulder. "Be careful. If you're not back in the morning, they'll come looking for you. Don't forget, Mags, life on the streets is hard."

"I should get going." Forcing herself to hug him, she smiled into his trusting face.

"See ya in the morning." Ned turned and walked down the hallway, leaving her there. She wanted to think he believed her. If he were on his way to raise the alarm, her captors would catch her before she escaped. It had to be now.

Deep breath. You can do this.

The spray lubricant was sitting in the corner of the cart. Quickly she sprayed the hinges and sat back on her heels to listen for any sign Ned had turned her in. Convinced no one was coming, she took one last look around. Steeling her spine, she carefully lifted the grate cover, damn it was heavy, and wriggled through. Gently closing it so as not to make a sound, her arms strained from the effort, a small ping was the only indication something wasn't as it should be.

She waited a moment, listening, and then reached through the grate, pulling the cart back in place, hiding her escape. It was almost morning; she'd be discovered missing at breakfast. She had to move fast. The plan was to get to the docks, find a ship, and get the hell out of Scotland. Somewhere safe. A place where there weren't men who could disappear, a place where she could feel normal again. She could clean, cook, and sew. Would offer her services in return for passage out of the country. Didn't matter if she had to stowaway, whatever it took.

Ugh, it was wet and smelly in the tunnel. Crawling, Maggie moved forward, inch by inch. It was dark, the walls and floor damp. As she crawled, she could hear voices as she passed under one of the townhomes on the street. Coming to a larger opening, she looked around. Water was flowing steadily now and the reek of sewage was getting stronger, invading her nostrils. Here's hoping Ned was right. He wasn't kidding; the main tunnel was a lot bigger. She could stand up without bumping her head.

Maggie's shoulder was throbbing, the blood a slow trickle down her arm. Once she was safe, she could have it tended. In the meantime, safety was the only priority.

Walking faster, the water up to her knees in places, she kept going. Just a bit further. Teeth chattering and chilled from her wet clothes, she kept moving. Once she surfaced, she'd have to steal a coat or she'd risk freezing to death if she couldn't find a place to hide and dry her clothes.

A couple of hours later, she could see the early morning light filtering in, casting muted patterns on the filthy water.

Heaving a sigh of relief, she looked around for a way to get to the top. Spying rusty metal rungs in the wall, she placed her hand on the first one and stopped. Did she have the right place? The only indication was an EC painted on the wall but that could mean anything. If this was indeed Edinburgh Castle it sounded like some kind of event was taking place. It was way too early for them to be open to tourists. Quickly climbing as her shoulder throbbed and burned, she peered up through the grate.

It looked like a wooden structure of some kind was set up. Maybe left over from Halloween? It would shield her from the people she could hear though she couldn't make out what they were saying.

Pushing up on the grate, it wouldn't budge. She couldn't see any type of lock. It probably hadn't been opened in a hundred years. Not now, not when she'd come so far, so close to freedom would she be stuck in this filth beneath the ground. Climbing up one more rung so she was crouching, she put her uninjured shoulder against the grate and pushed hard. Her thighs straining from the exertion as the grate moved. With a mighty shove, the grate gave just enough for her to shimmy through.

Gasping like a fish out of water, she rolled to her side, scuttling backwards when she noticed there was no back to the wooden structure. Anyone could see in. Taking deep, gulping breaths of air to calm her nerves, she was grateful the roar of the crowd covered the clang of the grate as it slammed shut.

A scuffling sound pulled her attention up. Dirt was falling through cracks in the wooden boards above her. There were people walking around up there. A drum roll started. Crossing her fingers the noise and whatever scene was taking place would shield her from prying eyes; she crawled across the cobblestones to the open end of the platform, wanting to stay low to the ground in case anyone happened by.

When the trap door above her head banged open, Maggie jumped at least a foot in the air. She had to cover her mouth to keep from screaming when a man fell through, bag tied over his head, booted feet kicking, seeking a foothold.

What the hell, someone was actually being hanged. Civilized countries didn't hang people anymore. Had things changed so much in the past year they were hanging criminals? What if Solien or Bruce had found her and it was one of the guards assigned to watch her? It couldn't be, not yet.

A whump and the crack of glass made her jump. Pieces of a bottle fell down between the boards landing on her shoulders and head. One nicked her chin. More glass hit the stage above her as the tinkling of broken glass rained down on her. People were throwing bottles? Had a riot broken out? This was not acceptable, she needed to act, couldn't allow anyone to hang because of her. Her hand landed on something cold, smooth. It was a shard of broken glass. Without thinking, she took the sliver and sawed at the rope.

"You have to stop moving so I can cut through it." Maggie yelled over the din.

The man went still at the sound of her voice. She hoped it was because he'd heard her and not that he was already dead. Wetness trickled down her palm as she frantically cut through the thick rope. Putting her arm around his legs, she grunted supporting his weight to keep him from dying. She'd seen enough death to last a lifetime.

Crap on toast he was freaking heavy. Adrenaline fueled her as she cut the remaining strand, and he fell hitting the stone with a thud. It was quiet. She no longer heard the crowd. It was as if everyone simply left at the same time. Looking up, she couldn't see anyone on the platform. This morning was getting stranger and stranger.

Maggie moved to his bound hands and cut him loose. It was

hard to saw through the rope and the blood from her palm made the glass slippery. Detached, she looked at her hand; it was sliced open. It would have to wait. First, she had to free him. No one else was dying on her watch.

"I'm almost finished cutting the binding on your hands. Stay still so I don't cut you, 'kay?" The reply was a mumble. The man's throat had to be raw, injured from the rope. He was tall, maybe six feet with a heavily muscled body. She could see jet-black hair hanging out of the hood. His clothing was odd. He had on a white linen shirt, suede pants and black leather boots, like a left-over costume from Halloween. Must have been a hell of a cele-bration if he was still wearing his getup two days later and swinging from a freaking hangman's noose.

The guy was having difficulty breathing. Coughing and wheezing. As the rope fell away he sat up and pulled the hood off.

Maggie was at a loss. Breathtaking, feral, hot, the words kept flowing through her mind. Indigo blue piercing eyes, super white teeth, and his face...wow, maybe he was a model and the shoot went wrong somehow? He gave off a magnetic force field that drew her closer until his angry tone stopped her cold.

"You must be bloody kidding me. This can't possibly be happening. Why did you interfere?" His voice was gravelly. He sounded pissed she'd helped him.

"Um, last I checked, you were the one dying and I saved you. How about a little gratitude, buddy? Not like any of your model friends stuck around to save you." Who did he think he was? What a jerk.

"You've no idea what you've started, what you've put into motion. Get out. Leave." The words were punched out. He narrowed his eyes at her. "What on earth have you been doing, rolling in a gutter? You reek of offal."

Maggie was speechless. She'd saved him from hanging, and he was angry at *her*? Not to mention he'd called her smelly, like it was her fault she'd had to crawl through sewage. What a pig.

The man stood, straightening his clothes. He looked annoyed

but leaned down to help her up. "I can't fucking believe this. The gods must be laughing their heads off."

"Would you rather I had let you die?" Incredulity filled her voice at his ungrateful response. She'd just saved this life and this is how he acts?

Jerk.

Looking her over with a look that told her he found her lacking in every way, he seemed to come to some decision. He growled at her, "It would have been easier than what's coming in the week ahead. What's done is done, there's no going back now." He ran his hands through his hair, anger radiating off his body.

"Allow me to introduce myself; I am Robert Bartholomew of Wales, lately a guest in the dungeon of Edinburgh Castle, at your service, Madam. You may call me Robert. I mean you no harm. Shall we abscond from this dreary, dismal place?" His teeth were clenched and the muscle in his cheek was twitching as he raked a glare over her, lingering on her breasts.

She gasped. No, it couldn't be, this was not happening. Not today of all days. Standing in front of her was the infamous pirate, a terrifying Shadow Walker, legend among Solien and his men, feared by all. Did he know what she did? How Bruce made her betray his kind? Didn't matter it was against her will, not with what she'd heard about him. He'd kill her on the spot. She had to get out of here now, before he realized she worked for his enemies.

Stepping backwards, Maggie turned and ran as fast as her feet would carry her, ignoring the pain in her shoulder and hand as she fled.

❀

ROBERT'S LAUGH WAS A HARSH COUGH. HIS BREATHING SLOWLY returned to normal. The irony of the Fates.

The woman who intervened, who was destined to save him,

to be his soul mate according to the prophecy, ran from him as fast as she could. This was hilarious. He could hear Colin and Jasper giving him hell now.

Usually women ran *to* him, not away from him. Though in this instance he didn't know whether to laugh or shout. How could this happen? Another Shadow Walker shouldn't have had a chance at a soul mate for at least a hundred years. Bloody hell. He loved his life, didn't want this. He grumbled as a new thought penetrated his angry brain.

What was she doing hiding under the scaffolding? She smelled like she'd been swimming in a slaughterhouse. He grinned. Even smelling like the back of a butcher's shop she was a pretty little thing. Her hair was the red of a fiery sunset, her eyes the color of emeralds, and her curves, well, those were meant for a man to hold on to while they made love all night long.

Shadow Walkers were cursed. When reliving their death anniversary every year. If by some sick twist of fate, a human woman, not just any woman, but one who had died and crossed into Shadow and back, intervened, then the countdown started, no way to stop it. He had a week to break the curse and in so succeeding would tie himself to her for all eternity. Even worse, he was powerless for the coming week giving Day Walkers an added incentive to try and take his head. He was rather attached to his head, thank you very much.

If this rubbish was true, Robert had a limited time before he'd be trapped forever. For if he failed, he would be cursed to wander the in-between, not living or dying, sentenced to eternal suffering in limbo, gray, and empty, doomed to walk the shadow realm as a wraith. The woman would pay a price for her altruistic act—if she failed, she would never find true love, destined to live the rest of her brief life alone, knowing she had destroyed him, and dying utterly alone. It didn't matter if during that week she perished in an accident, was murdered, or any other harm befell her. Once started, the sands of time couldn't be stopped.

Now the quandary. Did he let her go and the curse be damned? He wasn't sure he believed in the outcome. Yes, Colin and Emily had found each other but they didn't fail and experience the aftermath of the purported curse. Maybe there weren't any repercussions, he might not turn wraith. Could be it wasn't true at all. A ruse to keep the Shadow Walkers in line.

Why didn't she run like most normal humans? Why did she have to help him? If she'd gone on her merry way, tomorrow his life would be back to normal instead of completely cocked up. He spotted the grate. Investigating, he lifted it up. The smell rose to meet him. Yep, that was the scent of his lovely lady. What was she doing down in the sewer? What modern-day woman would willingly crawl through raw sewage...unless she was in some kind of fearsome trouble?

Bloody hell.

These were dangerous times; he couldn't leave her alone if she was in danger. Swearing a blue streak, some rather inventive curses he'd learned at sea, he answered his own question. No matter how angry and pissed he was she'd interfered, he wouldn't leave a damsel in distress.

He'd find her and help her. They'd break the curse. No way was he turning wraith, he loved this life. Robert would simply bargain with Thorne for everything to go back the way it was.

Give up his immortal life—not bloody likely.

8

The damp cobblestones threatened to trip Maggie as she ran blindly down the street. The temperature had dropped. A fine sheen of ice formed in patches making her slip. The trainers she wore weren't meant for ice or snow. The sky was growing darker, a dusky gray, shutting out the weak sunlight. The wind whistled through her ripped hoodie and wet jeans, chilling her to the bone.

Of all the horrible luck in the world. How could she run into, let alone save the man who scared her as much as her captors? Even worse, her stupid body was too busy being attracted to him to be frightened. Remembering the incident, her head screamed warnings to run while her insides turned to liquid chocolate when she touched him. Why couldn't he be one of the good guys? Someone she could trust to help her? And what would it be like to kiss him? There wasn't time for thinking about Robert, not while she was in danger. Maybe she'd truly lost her mind. Wanting to scream in frustration as her brain agreed with her body, Maggie appealed to a higher power.

"Whoever's listening up there, great sense of humor you've got, thanks for nothing."

A nice, warm bed and a cup of tea would be lovely. Banishing the thought, she couldn't stop now. If she didn't get out of the country, her captors would find her. Side aching, she slowed to a fast walk, breathing deeply, taking in her surroundings. Finally, almost to the Leith docks. Funny, she didn't remember making the last two turns. Maybe her subconscious directed her feet to find sanctuary.

On an empty bench ahead of her...she moved closer. Thank goodness. A dark wool coat, forgotten or left by someone. Not caring, she put it on. It was too big but no matter, would keep her from freezing. Maybe someone above was listening.

The first ship she came to was some kind of container ship. The crew was adamant there was nothing for her unless she had ten thousand quid on her. It was hard to smuggle paying customers without passports aboard and most had no use for a mere woman wanting free passage.

Transportation was becoming difficult. Airports had severely slashed the number of flights going in and out of the country and travel documents were scrutinized for any signs of forgery. Maggie didn't own a passport. As a kid in the system, then out on the streets, she wouldn't have the faintest idea how to get one. Listing a townhouse full of killers for her address would get her shipped off to the asylum by the men in white coats.

The second was a private yacht. A man who looked to be in his late fifties, wearing a white uniform was loading food onto the ship. Maybe he could help.

"Hello there, I was wondering if you might be hiring? I'm looking for passage out of Scotland in exchange for work. Whatever you need—I can cook, clean, and sew."

"Oy there, Miss. Do you have your papers?"

"Um, no, I was hoping to work under the table. Look, I really need to get out of here." She finished lamely.

"Now you know we can't take no chances, and we don't want no trouble, be off with you." He waved her away. Standing there watching her to make sure she left.

Beyond disappointed, Maggie looked to the last ship in dock

as her heart sank. It was some kind of historic ship with actual sails. There was a lot of activity, crates being loaded, men coming and going but something about it made her nervous.

Resolving to put her worries aside, nothing on that ship could be worse than the fate waiting for her back at the town-house; she squared her shoulders and approached a grizzled man in canvas pants and a navy pea coat.

Giving him the same spiel, she was dejected when he turned her away. A bench beckoned, and she made her way there, sitting, staring at the water, trying to decide what to do. A huge raven caught her eye, cawing as it flew over the ship, hovering near an open hatch.

Maggie jumped up, looking over her shoulder to make sure no one was paying any attention to her and walked to the port side of the ship. It looked like some type of gun or cannon should be there, ready to fire on the town. Didn't matter what belonged in the opening as long as she could use it to get inside.

There was a rope hanging down, lightly banging against the side of the ship. Today was the day, her luck was changing. Backing up, she ran and jumped, grabbing the rope, her heart pounding out of her chest, hand throbbing. Banging her injured shoulder hard against the hull made her stomach heave. Nausea threatened to overtake her, the pain of her injured shoulder and hand causing her to see spots in front of her eyes. Waiting a moment to settle her stomach, she reached up, pulling her body up the rope.

Shoulder burning, blood seeping through the makeshift bandage wrapped around her hand, she stopped to rest a few minutes, swinging in time to the rocking of the ship, exposed in the cold air. Her hand hurt so badly she thought she was going to pass out. Reaching deep within, Maggie found the place inside where she went whenever things were bad. Closing her eyes, she gave herself over. As her stomach settled down, she opened her eyes, set her jaw, and pulled herself up the rope.

Halfway there; she was going to make it. Maggie's teeth were chattering, her hands and feet numb. The rope had red stains on it from the cut on her hand. At least she was so cold it only throbbed, the pain gone. Some part of her brain yelled out, warning her she was on her way to freezing to death if she didn't get inside soon. Thankful for her years on the streets, she let the wind pass through her, telling her body it was a warm summer breeze instead of a biting wind. Nothing mattered except getting inside. *Keep going; you're losing the feeling in your hands and if you fall you'll land in the icy, unforgiving water and be dead in minutes.*

The last several feet were excruciating as she pulled her tired body onto the platform. Hearing noises below, she scooted the rest of the way in and scuttled out of sight. The interior was dark, the faint bulbs casting strange shadows on the walls. One of the crates was open and yes, that was some kind of gun on the floor. Huh, must be a really good replica. Too tired to care or to shrug out of her wet clothing, she staggered to a corner. There she pulled a canvas tarp over her head and fell asleep, exhausted.

Briefly, she came to, feeling the motion of the ship gently vibrating through her bones. Heaving a heavy sigh of relief, she didn't care where it was going, hoped somewhere far away. Only cared they were finally moving, and neither Solien, Bruce—or anyone else—didn't know where she was. The gentle thrumming of the ship sent her back into a dreamless sleep.

"FIND HER. KEEP IT QUIET, I DON'T KNOW WHAT KIND OF trouble she's in, but it must be bad to crawl through the sewers in winter."

Robert snapped his mobile shut frustrated he hadn't found his rescuer yet. The men were checking homeless shelters and hostels thinking she'd turn up. The rain had turned to ice, and with the temperature dropping fast, she wouldn't stay out on the streets and chance freezing. If he didn't have to be in Wales, he would have stayed behind and looked for her himself instead of getting ready to set sail. Never would he forget the look of terror in her eyes. Staring at him like he was Satan himself come up from Hell to take her soul. Puzzled, he tried to figure out why. The lass wasn't afraid when she rescued him. It was only after he'd introduced himself that her pretty face drained of color and she bolted like a rabbit with a hungry fox on its trail. Women loved him.

The more troubling question was who had made her so afraid?

He was offering a bonus to any of his men who found her. Ringing Monroe, he'd asked him to have the cops in the city on the lookout for her. But not to publicize it; he needed to keep this quiet. Maybe 'twas his fate to have this contrary woman run *from* him when all other lassies would run *to* him.

Turned wraith all because one woman didn't find him pleasing. Bloody fucking lovely.

9

T he tarp was thrown back, startling Maggie out of what could only be called a dead-to-the-world slumber. Couldn't believe they'd caught her unaware. Hard to remember the last time she'd slept this soundly. She had to talk fast.

"What have we here, lads?" The seaman leered down at her.

"I can explain. I needed to leave Scotland. I want to work—cook, clean, sew, whatever. Please, don't turn me in."

"Lass, you're on a smuggler's ship, and the captain frowns upon stowaways. You can tell him the tale shortly."

A smuggler's ship? There were still pirates sailing the seas? Maybe this was a nightmare? The sailor helped her up as she blindly reached for the small backpack. Couldn't be without it, the pack and its meager contents meant a fresh start. Pain radiated down her shoulder and her hand was swollen and throbbing. Maggie stumbled, seeing four blurry men when there were only two moments ago. Hands reached out, steadying her. "Thanks." The words were garbled, her throat dry and fuzzy.

"Take the wee lass to Captain Robert."

No way. What were the odds? There were plenty of men named Robert. Had to be just as many who were pirates named

Robert, right? This couldn't be *his* ship. Bruce called him "the pirate," but certainly this was coincidence. If Maggie got out of this alive, she was having a serious talk with the Universe about what she'd done to piss off the fates.

The turns twisted and meandered around until they reached the end of a passageway and the sailor knocked at a closed door.

"Enter."

The voice was warm, sexy, and masculine and made her want to curl up inside it, safe and sheltered from everything bad. The door swung open and Maggie was shoved into the room. Shapes came slowly into view in the dim light as her vision cleared. And what did she see but long, jet-black hair framing a model's face.

His face. Freshly showered, kicked back in a chair drinking a cup of tea looking none the worse for wear other than a raw rope print around his neck. The dangerous man she'd rescued at Edinburgh Castle stalked towards her.

Fate had a seriously twisted sense of humor.

DANTE/IMPORT EXPORT WAS IN CHAOS. "WHERE IS SHE? HOW the hell did she escape?" Bruce yelled at his men gathered in the kitchen. Maggie had been discovered missing at breakfast. The door to her room still locked from the outside. His men searched the townhouse from top to bottom without finding any clue to her whereabouts. Solien would be furious. Bruce quailed, thinking about what would happen when the demon found out. She was supposed to be dead by now.

"Uh, sir? I think I know where she went."

This statement was uttered by a timid voice behind him. Turning around, his gaze landed on a new recruit.

"Who are you?"

"Uh, Josh, sir. I'm new."

The recruits were getting worse and worse if this one was any indication. The criminals were good choices, but these boys always ended up being a waste of space and resources. He smoothed his hair back. Simple solution, send the rookies out first, if the buggers were killed, no big loss, he'd recruit more. The boy called Josh couldn't have been more than twenty-six or - seven. He was short, and painfully thin with greasy brown hair and a sneaky look permanently etched on his face.

"Well, come on, lad, I don't have all day. Where the hell is she?" Bruce stood glaring, arms crossed.

The little bug stuttered. "Ned and I were talking at breakfast this morning and he told me he saw Maggie leaving late last night when he was doing his rounds." The boy pointed to the one called Ned. Bruce wanted to scream in frustration. He wanted strong men not these boys cowering before him. These two not only would never last as minions, due to this treachery their life was forfeit, unbeknownst to either of them.

Turning to Ned, Bruce leveled his most ferocious look at the kid. Before he could say a word, Ned jumped in. "She wanted to go for a walk, swore she'd be back by morning. I'm not sure Maggie is mentally ill. Seems pretty normal to me."

Eyebrows raised, he glared at the kid. "All the patients here are disturbed, some less than others but still, they have issues. The front door is bolted shut she couldn't have used it."

The boy stuttered. "Uh, she wanted to explore the tunnels."

Motioning with his fingers to get on with it, the recruit told his tale.

"I was checking to make sure everything was locked up before I went to bed last night. I heard a noise coming from the storage room. Maggie was in there. There's a grate in the wall behind the cleaning cart. It goes to the sewer system."

Narrowing his eyes, Bruce wanted to haul off and smack him. "How do you know this, and *where* is she?"

Gulping, eyes twitching, Ned answered. "I used to work at the hostel where she'd crash sometimes. There was a similar opening in the laundry room. I told her how you could basically get all around Edinburgh completely underground by using the tunnels. The main tunnel leads to Edinburgh Castle. Maggie said she wanted to explore, so maybe she went to the castle. From there she could go anywhere, but she's probably holed up in a hostel or an abandoned building."

Josh sneered. "Stupid idiot. Who lets someone go out through a grate in the middle of the night? You had to know what she was up to."

"We're Maggie's friends."

"Friend?" Josh sneered. "I'm not her friend. She was dumb enough to let me live with her. She deserved what she got."

Without warning, Ned turned and slugged Josh, sending him to his knees.

"Ow! What the hell, dude?" A few of the men broke it up before Ned could land another punch. Josh looked like he was holding back tears, his face blotchy and red.

Nodding at his men, two of them grabbed Josh, and two took Ned who had murderous intent written all over his face. "While I appreciate your telling me, you should have immediately told whoever was on guard duty as soon as it happened. Hold Josh." Stepping up to the scarred kitchen table, Bruce selected a sharp knife from the locked drawer. "Ned. Place your hands on the table."

The kid turned pale as milk. "Please, don't hurt me. I told you everything I know. It was a mistake, I won't make it again."

"No you won't. But stupidity will be punished. We must always remember to keep our residents safe." He brought the knife down hard on the kid's right hand taking off his ring and pinky finger. The crunch of steel meeting bone was loud in the silent kitchen. Ned screamed in agony as blood ran down the table, dripping on the floor. The boy's eyes were glazed in pain, tears streaming down his face as he faintly struggled to pull away.

"Take him upstairs to the doc and have him cleaned up. Ned?" The boy looked at his shoes unable to meet Bruce's eyes.

"There will be an extra helping at dinner for you tonight. Rest and heal. I need every man I can get. Are we clear?"

Ned nodded. Softly sobbing he let Bruce's men lead him away.

"Now Josh, Ned volunteered information while you..." He trailed off as the scared kid threw up all over the floor.

"Great. Throw a towel down before we all puke." Disgusted, Bruce continued, looking at his men and noting the pale faces. Scared. Good. He wanted them afraid. "Josh, do you have anything to say as to why you didn't come forward earlier with the information regarding our dear Maggie?"

Josh mumbled incoherently, breaking down and crying. "Please, don't hurt me. I didn't do nuthin'. Please, don't."

Bruce yawned. "Let this be a lesson to all of you. I will not tolerate letting anyone escape or not coming forward with information in a timely fashion. Understood?" He met every man's eye as they nodded one by one. "Take Josh down to the basement. Then find Maggie. We'll make an example of her to the others." As the men left, he called out. "And find me some new blood. Too many empty beds upstairs." Bruce scratched his head. He had to think about how he could spin this to Solien without blame falling on him. Pointing at two of his men, "You two. Go check the hostels and abandoned buildings where she used to hide out. I don't have to tell stress the importance of finding her. Failure is not an option." He glared at the men.

"Failure is not an option pertains to what, may I ask?" A silky, venomous voice made Bruce's balls shrink up.

This was not good. Not at all. Solien was here. The guy scared the piss out of Bruce. The thing wasn't human. If he remembered his old Sunday school lessons, this thing had to be some kind of demon. Solien could do all kinds of crazy shit like shooting fire from his fingers and incinerating people on the spot. The man usually looked human, well, if you could call seven-feet tall with black eyes, human. Except when he got angry, then big black leathery wings unfolded and his skin turned green. He disappeared and appeared at will; it was downright freaky.

Bruce told his knees to stop shaking. "The last woman, Maggie, escaped last night, sir. I'm preparing to send out a search party. We'll find her and bring her back."

"You only noticed her missing this morning? Seems you've become rather lax with your security."

His men were frozen, faces drained of color. Afraid to draw attention to themselves. Bruce knew how they felt, imagined he looked the same way. When he'd looked in the mirror that morning he'd noticed his once thick black hair getting notice-ably thinner, graying. His face looked hollow and drawn. Before he could answer, Solien spoke again.

"Yes, you will find her. I'm sending someone with you to ensure you stupid humans don't screw it up."

Bruce's ass puckered as Solien named the newest addition to their search party. Fury. Fuck me. He'd never met it, only heard unbelievable stories from others. A fucking savage if the rumors were true. He could only be thankful it wasn't him searching for Maggie with that beast tagging along. He'd be lucky if any of his men returned. The monster would likely murder them all for the fun of it.

Solien made a moue of distaste, noticing the vomit on the floor. "Have this cleaned up, I can't abide a filthy kitchen." With that, the boss man disappeared.

The door banged open. Bruce's man, Martin, skidded to a stop in front of them. "You better get out here Bruce. There's a giant-ass, three-headed, talking dog in the living room and he's asking for a keg of beer."

10

"Oh hell, it *is* you."

Speak of the devil. Before Robert could retort, his mysterious runaway fainted, landing in a heap at his feet.

Catching her as she fell, the corner of his lip twitched. Now this he was used to—women falling at his feet. Warm in his arms, he laid her on the bed and placed his hand on her forehead. She was burning up.

"Cold water. Now." Barking out orders, he sent his men scurrying to do his bidding.

The men left as Robert undressed her. What was her name? Who was she? When he removed her hoodie he noticed the tear in the shoulder. Looking at her tee shirt he noted the blood. He'd missed it on her dirty, stained sweatshirt. The blood blended in with the grime coating the filthy garment. Lifting her up to remove the hoodie, unconscious, limp in his arms, it was like undressing a dead man.

The bra and panties she wore were basic white and dingy. No lace, silk or satin for this one. Strange, he never thought he'd find such utilitarian undergarments sexy but on her, he had a hard-on looking at her. The mystery woman was all lush curves with bountiful breasts a small waist and wide hips like some ancient fertility goddess. Women's bodies were a majestic sight. Telling himself it was wrong to lust over her when she was unconscious, he threw the clothing in a pile to be burned. It stunk so badly, the smell would never come out in the wash. A skunk would run from this stench. The bed sheets would have to be burned as well. But first he had to tend the wound.

In the past he'd had to throw out bed coverings after they'd been ripped to shreds during lovemaking but never from someone stinking them up. The corner of his mouth lifted and a chuckle escaped thinking how horrified she'd be to know he thought she smelled, women were funny that way.

Robert covered her with a sheet. Stink and all, he wanted to know her name, her thoughts, why she'd helped him. Shelving the thoughts for another time—wasn't like he could bloody well ask her, he bent back to her injuries.

Leaning down to inspect her shoulder, he stiffened. The wound was about six inches long, and bleeding profusely. A knife wound from the looks of it.

Bellowing for his cabin boy, Ian came running, breathless as he waited for Robert's orders. "Bring me bandages and salve from the infirmary."

The woman's face was clenched in pain. The circles under her eyes standing out like hard-won bruises. Pouring a whisky, knocking it back, he rested his chin on his palms, elbows digging into his knees, deciding what to do with her. Still angry she'd interfered, his chivalrous self warred with his hedonistic, selfish side. The wench didn't know she was doing the worst possible thing for him by cutting the rope. She thought she was saving his life when in fact she'd ruined it as far as he was concerned. Gods, he loved women, but the repercussions from this simple altruistic act were bigger than any foe he'd ever come up against. Robert cursed, kicking a booted foot into the bedpost.

What was he to do? Backed up against the wall, the enemy was advancing with nowhere to turn. If he climbed the wall to escape, he'd turn wraith in a week. That wouldn't do at all. The world would keep changing and he planned to live forever, watching it, enjoying the immortal life. Fighting, drinking, gold... and women. What else was there?

If he stood and fought, he'd have to figure out how to break his bloody curse. Couldn't deny he felt a pull but whether it was fate or his normal love of all women or something more disturbing, he didn't know.

There'd been countless ladies over the years, he'd lost count of how many women he'd loved for a night or a few weeks. But never had he spent more than a few months with one woman. Yes, Colin and Emily had found each other, broken Colin's curse but he didn't believe it would happen again so soon. It'd only been a year.

All the Shadow Walkers were talking about what had happened. None of them would presume another of them might be saved or damned, depending on how you looked at it.

Blowing out a frustrated sigh, he stood up from his slouch as Ian entered with what he'd asked for.

"Captain, I've brought what ye needed. And some clean clothes for the lady." Ian stood there gawking at their unconscious guest.

"Aye, thank ye lad."

"Um, Cap'n?"

"What is it?"

"The lady smells awful bad, even with the window open. Shall I have a bath drawn?" His cabin boy screwed up his nose in distaste.

A grin touched his face. "Aye, the stench is worse than the back alley of a butcher shop. Draw a bath and once I'm done, burn her clothing and all the linens or they'll stink up me whole ship."

Ian agreed and went to fetch the tub. Robert focused on his unwanted guest. There was another avenue...maybe this was simply some kind of measure of loyalty to Thorne. Fine. All he had to do was play along and be nice to the woman but he wasn't telling her about the curse. Let the week run its course and see. If at the end of the week, he was doomed—cue the foreboding music, he'd parlay with his commander and make a new bargain. The way he looked at it, the god needed him for the war that was fast approaching. In the meantime, he'd get to know the lass, love her for the time they had together as he'd loved so many before her. A strangled laugh broke free from his throat. Damn the fates and damn Thorne for fucking with him. No way was he falling for the wanker's little game or test or whatever they called it. No one bested him—after all, he was Black Bart, the most fearsome pirate who'd ever sailed the seas, and he'd be damned to hell and back before he let Thorne win.

Of all the times to be without his powers this was the worst. Swearing under his breath, Robert grumbled. Would have been so much easier to heal her and send her on her way but he was stuck with her and he'd make the best of it. Wasn't her fault she was drawn into Thorne's little game.

Alas, he could do nothing for her suffering thanks to her starting the bloody clock ticking. Powerless for a blasted week. Had to rely on whatever skills he'd honed prior to becoming a Shadow Walker or what he'd learned since. The fever would have to run its course, the wound must heal on its own.

While Ian was doing Robert's bidding, he moved closer to the woman. Normally he had a doctor on board but the man's grandfather had passed so Robert gave him leave to attend to the funeral and other details. Not to mention the thought of someone else touching her made Robert uncomfortable. So instead he'd tend her and call Doc Jones to find out what else to do for the lass. Robert pulled the water from the heat, dipped a washcloth and gently cleaned the wound. Washed it out, finishing it by pouring whisky over it. Did the same to the cut on her hand. Stirring, she moaned but didn't wake. He should have a helicopter pick her up, take her to hospital but he knew as sure as he knew the sun would rise, this woman would not want to be taken to a hospital or have the authorities involved in any way. Blasted injury was still bleeding, he'd have to cauterize it. Thank the gods she was unconscious. The toughest men usually screamed like babes when hot steel was applied to skin. On the bright side, the stench of burning flesh couldn't possibly smell worse than the foulness currently assaulting his nostrils.

Pulling a dagger out of his boot, he poured whisky over it and placed it in the fire that was already burning to provide the cabin with warmth. Taking a large swig of whisky, he studied her face, remembering the look of shock when she saw him.

A warrior, no, a Celtic goddess, that's what she looked like with her long fiery curly hair and those emerald eyes of hers—sad, yet wise beyond her years. The lines on her face attested to a hard life. Wrinkles around her eyes and mouth added to her strong, fierce beauty. Those same creases would vanish, filling with happiness when he plundered her body, made her scream her release. Mentally scolding himself, he pulled the dagger from the fire.

It was now or never. This was going to hurt like a bitch. Hating to cause pain, he took a deep breath and readied himself. 'Twas the best way to seal the wound.

Pouring more whisky on the blade, the droplets hissing as they hit the steel, he splashed her shoulder once more for luck. Without a moment's hesitation he seared the skin. The smell of burning flesh hit his senses causing him to swallow hard. The skin popped and crackled, turning red and blistering as the wound sealed together. Screaming, she thrashed, trying to escape from whatever demon was tormenting her. Robert held her down and as her eyes rolled back in her head, she passed out again. Before she woke he did the same to the palm of her hand. Sweat beaded his upper lip and brow, his arms were shaking. *Gods, don't let her scream like that ever again. I'd do anything to spare her pain.*

Before he could dwell on the thought, he finished tending her before she came to again. Robert opened a jar of salve. It was made in France by a woman who practiced natural medicine. The crew swore it was magical and could heal anything. Who knew what was in it? Shrugging, he put a dab on the rope burns around his neck. Couldn't hurt and if it helped him not to flipping ache then all the better. Carefully spreading the ointment over her wounds, he bandaged them, careful of the raw skin.

Skimming his hands over her feverish skin, he admired her form. 'Twas the palest color of rose, the faint, blue veins standing out in contrast to her fair coloring. The bruises sustained during whatever had caused her to crawl through the sewers, blooming across her shoulder, arms, thighs and torso. Someone had done a number on her. What had happened?

Sitting back in the chair, spent, he drained the whisky and called for Ian to bring him another bottle.

"Is she better, Cap'n? The lady's bath will be ready by the time you finish eating." Ian looked anxious standing there.

"Soon, Ian. Thank you for bringing food. I'll give the ointment time to work then bathe her and you can clear this mess away. Burn it." He flung his arm out encompassing the bed as Ian left the cabin.

Robert ate, not bothering to change. Cleaning up could wait until after taking care of her. While he filled his belly, his eyes never left the woman in his bed. So many questions to be answered.

Ian came back, cleared away the dishes and addressed Robert. "I've brought clean clothes for the lady and the bath is ready."

Robert inclined his head, distracted. Pushing open the sliding door that separated his room from the dining room, Robert saw the copper tub set up. Steam rose off the water. Towels and soap had been placed on the dining table next to clean clothing for the woman to wear. Had to quit calling her 'the woman'. Going through her things, he turned the pockets inside out, looking for any clue as to who she was. Nothing. A lump under a chair caught his eye. A filthy, dirty backpack. He sniffed and almost retched. The bag smelled as bad as she did. Within he found twenty quid, wet bandages and a few toiletries. But no identification. Interesting.

Robert threw the backpack and contents onto the disgusting pile that used to be her clothes. Testing the bath water, he nodded to himself. A few steps back to the bed, and he was looking at his unconscious goddess. Bending, he scooped her up. The chit didn't weigh much, he could count every rib. Lowering her into the bath, mindful of her shoulder, he kept the bandage away from the water. She murmured something as her skin hit the water but didn't wake giving him time to soap her body.

By the gods, she was filthy. The sewage had seeped through her clothing, coating her from head to toe in the noxious sludge. The soap lathered in his hands, and he kneaded the tension out of her neck and uninjured shoulder as he scrubbed her clean. The woman needed to eat more. Muscles flexed in the water as he ran soapy hands down her arms and legs. No softness to her at all, she was lean and hard with small but nicely formed breasts. There were faint scars dotting her torso.

Ah, she was born a redhead. Washing her, he cleaned away the muck and grime from her toes, he squashed the urge to take her little toe into his mouth, to nibble on the arch of her foot and make her smile. Did she ever smile? Soon she would wake, and he would find out her name and what had happened. While not willing to tie himself to her for eternity, he was more than ready to tear apart whoever had hurt her. Men who ill-used women were the lowest of scum in his book. Every man who'd marked her ivory skin would die by his hand.

It was difficult to bathe an unconscious woman. He kept worrying she'd sink under the water. Strange, he'd been in tubs with women, relaxing as they washed each other or made love but never had a comatose woman in his bath.

Why was she so afraid of him? It seemed she knew him though he couldn't remember ever meeting her. Laying before him was a puzzle waiting to be solved. At least it would take his mind off the fact he was powerless for the coming week. A feeling he hadn't felt in hundreds of years bubbled up—helplessness. Was this how Colin felt? No wonder he was so cranky when he met Emily. Now Robert had an inkling of what must have been going through Colin's mind.

Shifting her so he could wash her hair, he cursed. It wasn't going to work. The tub was slick and she kept slipping, worrying him the bandage would get wet or he'd lose his hold and she'd sink under the water. Blast it. There was no way around it, he needed assistance.

A growl rumbling from his throat caught him by surprise—he didn't want anyone else touching her, looking at her. Robert thought for a moment, smiled and called out, "Ian!"

The lad was never far. Was always underfoot wherever Robert went on the ship. The door opened. "Wait, do not enter. The lady is in the bath. Fetch Jaime to me. Quick now."

"Yes, Cap'n."

He supposed he could climb in with her but if she woke, he didn't want to frighten her further by finding herself in a bath with the man she was terrified of. Instead he put his arms around her, mindful of her injuries and held her. The door shut with a soft click as Ian went to find the small boy Robert had recently taken in to his employ. Little Jamie...his thoughts drifted back to finding the lad this past summer. Discovered in a barrel of goods Robert was transporting to England. It seemed the gentleman in question had a fondness for young boys. The boy had been bound and gagged. The crew would have never suspected what was in the barrel except one of the cats on board kept pawing at a crack in the wood as it was waiting to be taken down to the hold. A sailor was curious and opened what supposedly contained cigars. Instead they found young Jamie looking up at them with fearful eyes and a tearstained face.

The kid was five years old. His parents had given him to the gentlemen with such distasteful tastes in exchange for forgiveness of their debts. At least he was an only child; no others for the parents to use. Robert delivered the rest of the goods to the Englishman, less one small boy. When the man had the temerity to demand the little tyke, Robert's impetuousness got the best of him, and he backhanded the man so hard, the crowing rooster left an outline in the wall. He told the rich bastard if he ever used Robert's services again, he'd end up feeding the fish. Thorne's silly rules be damned. The boy found a place with his cook and learned more every day. The men called him Sweet Jamie for the pies and cookies he liked to bake.

The click of the door drew his attention. "Cap'n, you called?"

"Ah, Sweet Jamie. Come in lad. I require your assistance with a damsel in distress."

The lad's eyes grew large as he took note of the lady in the bath. "What happened to her? Is she dead?" He inched closer for a better look. "Why she's no wearin' any clothes!"

Robert chuckled. "Aye, she wouldn't take a bath with her clothes on, now would she? No worries, she's not dead, just suffered a bad cut and now she's sleeping."

Seemingly satisfied, the boy looked to Robert for his orders. "Do ye want me ta bake her a cake?"

"That would be very nice but first I require your assistance. You see the bandages?" Seeing the lad nod, he continued. "We cannot let them get wet but we must wash her hair. Do you think you can protect her wounds from the mighty water?"

The boy stood up straight and looked Robert in the eye. "Aye, Cap'n. I swear I won't let a bit o' water get on the lady's Band-Aid."

He smothered a chuckle at the solemnness of the vow. "Come then." As Jamie supported her shoulder, Robert washed her hair, carefully pouring the water over her stunning red hair.

Sweet Jamie wrinkled his nose, "Something stinks. Smells like poop." The lad leaned over to sniff near the woman's hair. "Ugh, it's her. She reeks."

This time he couldn't help it, the ridiculous situation, the bloody week ahead...he lost it and threw back his head roaring with laughter. "You've got that right, Sweet Jamie. The lady stinks to high heaven. Me thinks she crawled through the sewers. We'll get her cleaned up, won't we?" He reached out, ruffling the boy's dirty blond hair.

"We will, Cap'n. Then she won't stink no more." The youngster screwed up his face in concentration. "Why was she in the sewers? Was a bad man after her?"

Robert's voice was quiet when he answered. "I'm not sure lad. We'll find out when she wakes, but she's safe now, just as you were. Don't worry, I'll protect her too."

Bloody hell. He meant it. The thought startled him. She'd unwittingly ruined his entire existence, but he'd be damned if he'd let some lowlife hurt her. Sweet Jamie nodded, biting his lip in concentration as he held a towel over her bound shoulder to keep it dry.

The only sounds in the dining room were the sound of water tricking down the edge of the copper tub, splashing back into the water as he finished washing her hair. Sitting back on his heels, Robert rubbed his throat. It was still raw and sore from the noose.

"Alright lad, help me get our lady out of the tub." The boy handed Robert towels to wrap her in as he lifted her out of the gray, grimy water. He carried her back into his room. Jamie preceded him bringing the borrowed clothing. While they were in the bath, Ian had stripped the room clean. There were fresh sheets on the bed, the window closed against the cold night air and a pot of water simmered above the fire. Vanilla and cinnamon filled the room to banish the odor from the cabin.

Jamie put a towel on the pillow for her wet hair as Robert finished drying her off. 'Twas rather a challenge to dress an unconscious woman. He was used to undressing women, but had never dressed a woman. Usually he was leaving their chambers before dawn or they managed on their own. His lip quirked...the lady in question would probably be mortified to know he'd stripped her, washed her and clothed her all whilst she was dead to the world. He was amazed she hadn't woken yet and a bit worried if truth be told. But her breath was even, her pulse steady so he felt certain she'd come to when her body had healed enough of its own accord.

"Jamie lad, ye did well. Go ahead now, off to the galley for something to eat. I thank ye." Robert was born in Wales but spent so much time in the UK and sailing to exotic ports, his accent was a mishmash of all the places he'd been. He scrubbed a hand over his face, tired.

Jamie blushed, "Thank ye, Cap'n. I'm going to bake a cake for our lady so she'll have a sweet when she wakes. She will wake, won't she?"

"Aye, she'll wake. Oftentimes the body shuts down the mind so it can heal. Like when you sleep at night. Be off with ye now." The little lad scampered out of Robert's room, off to tell Ian to remove the bath from the dining room.

'Twas well past midnight and Robert was hungry again. A soft knock on the door drew his attention. Ian came in laden with a tray. It smelled delicious.

"Thought ye might want a bite to eat, Cap'n."

His stomach rumbled in reply. "Aye Ian, thank ye, kindly," The lad left the victuals, closing the door behind him. Robert barely tasted the food, he shoved it in his mouth so quickly. Normally Shadow Walkers didn't need to eat except during their death anniversary when they were powerless. Food tasted so much better, his taste buds seemed increased tenfold. Each bite burst with flavor. And the ale and wine, oh, he could sing an ode to those who first created the beverages. But tonight the meal was tasteless. His thoughts consumed with worry for his guest. Taking his plate to the galley, Robert returned to his cabin.

Stripping off his clothing, Robert sauntered nude down the narrow hallway to the bathroom. It barely contained a shower, toilet and sink but was large enough for his needs. He showered, letting the hot water sluice over tired muscles, standing there until the water ran cold.

Thinking about *her*.

Opening the door softly so as not to disturb her, he pulled on soft faded jeans and a V-neck navy blue cashmere sweater. He never bothered with underwear, didn't really see the point. Leaning down, Robert placed a hand on her brow. She was fevered but not as hot as when she first arrived. The bandage was seeping so he changed it. The wound still an angry red but the salve seemed to be working and it was no longer bleeding. The injured hand looked good. It would heal with only a faint scar as a reminder. Content she was cared for, he dragged the chair from the fire over to the bed, sank down, put his feet up, leaned back in the chair, and watched his lady.

Firelight played off her skin, shadows dancing along, casting eerie images on the walls and ceiling. As the fire crackled, his body sore, throat raw, he drank a cup of tea and honey Ian must have brought when he straightened the room. It was liberally laced with whisky, and after a few minutes, the ship lulled him into a dreamless sleep.

❧ II ❧

F*riday, November 3rd*

ROBERT WOKE WITH A START. IAN HAD BUILT UP THE FIRE
sometime during the night. He stood, and stretched, working
the kinks out of his back, absently rubbing his throat. Padding
over to the bed, he checked on his guest. Fever still held her in
its hold. She murmured but didn't wake. He changed the
bandage; the wound looked a bit better. Satisfied, he left his
cabin to clean up and shave. A hot shower would help him face
the day. Then he grabbed a quick bite. It was a terrible annoyance not to be able to dematerialize to Colin and Emily's.

"Ian."

"Yes, Captain?" The boy seemed to appear out of nowhere.
"Stand guard over our lady. If she wakes, give her some water and
broth but she needs stay abed."

"I'll take care of her, Cap'n."

"I know ye will lad. Now, let's gather a few of the boys to take
me ashore."

Rowing the short distance to the pier where a car was waiting to whisk him to Ravensmore; he made a quick call. "Oy, Monroe. How goes it? Listen, you'll never believe the missing lady I told you about? She turned up on my bloody ship. Hidden away. What are the odds? You can call off the search." He paused, listening. "I've taken care of her injuries. She'll be okay with rest and time. Once she's coherent, I'll let you know what I find out. Take care, mate." Technology was a wondrous thing. He loved mobile phones and modern transportation though sometimes it was nice to enjoy the old ways. He settled back into the plush leather seat of the Mercedes and thought about his guest. The trip was uneventful. When he arrived Worthington met him at the door.

"I was told I'd find you here, milady." Robert strode through her lady's solar to where Emily stood at a window looking out on the castle courtyard.

"Robert, welcome." Emily turned, shifting Colleen to her other hip to kiss him on the cheek. Motherhood suited her. She had a happy, contented glow surrounding her.

"How old is she now?"

"Can you believe already three months old? Remember my friend, Kat?"

"Aye, milady how is the spitfire?" How could he forget the feisty female. Her personality was as loud as her clothing.

"I talked to Kat this morning. Her baby is already six months old. Time flies doesn't it? Makes me wonder how I'll deal with not aging while she does..."

"Ah, that's a worry for another day."

Seemed like only yesterday that Colin met Emily. Robert never thought any of his fellow Shadow Walkers would ever break their curse, especially the warrior he'd known for so long and called friend. Colin had been closed off to the pleasures of life, existing only to slay the enemy until Emily came stumbling into his world and turned it upside down. Together they'd broken the curse, married, and had been blessed by the goddess

Terya with twins, unheard of since all Walkers were unable to have children. Yet here the two of them stood with two screaming babes. Emily had been gifted with immortality and helped the cause by gathering information all in the name of saving humanity before Dayne and the Day Walkers destroyed the world.

"Where's the little monster? It peed on me the last time I was here." Robert screwed up his face in distaste remembering getting too close as Emily changed the tiny bugger and Robert swore the lad aimed straight at him on purpose, ruining Robert's favorite scarlet silk shirt.

"Naill's out with Colin. Please, sit. Would you like some tea? Meg brought it in a few minutes ago. She made those lemon bar cookies you love..." Emily led him to a comfortable sofa, poured and handed him the plate. His mouth watered. Emily had shown Meg how to make the sinfully delicious treat. Normally he didn't need to eat but being a blasted human for a week, now he required sustenance. Though truth be told he enjoyed the ritual of dining and had somehow over the centuries developed a fondness for sweets.

"I'd love some though you better take one now before I eat them all."

"That's why there are two on my plate. Mine. So hands off." Emily giggled as she checked on the baby in the crib and curled up in a chair. "What were you asking me? Oh, right. Naill's only three months old, and he can't control his aim, contrary to what you believe." He narrowed his eyes at her when she covered her mouth with her hand. By the shaking of her shoulders he could tell she was trying her damnedest not to laugh. It wasn't working very well.

"I'm sorry. I don't mean to but the look on your face...you were so affronted, it was really quite hilarious." She arched an eyebrow, "Anyway, can you believe Colin has little Naill out at the stables? He thinks it's time his son started riding and learning to carry a sword."

The disbelief in her voice made Robert bust out laughing. Gesturing at the baby he told her, "Milady, be happy it's only Naill. My guess is Colin will have little Colleen out there next."

"Oh no, he's not putting Colleen up on one of those huge scary horses."

"Before I head out to talk to your husband, I heard a few foster kids are coming to live at Ravensmore." Robert couldn't keep the surprise out of his voice. He thought twins would be bad enough. Crawling all over, crying and needing constant attention. Facing Fury would be preferable to taking care of children any day. At least the hellhound would most likely eat him quickly; children would suck the life out of him slowly, making Robert wish to be banished to one of Thorne's infamous torture chambers.

Emily's smile lit up the entire room. "Yes, we're starting with seven children. Five boys and two girls." She patted his shoulder. "Don't look so horrified Robert, we won't ask you to babysit."

"I'd rather face every circle of the darkest realms than spend an evening taking care of children." Disgust filled his voice. "What on earth made you do it?" He was curious why they would want children around. Weren't two enough? He hoped Colin had bargained with the Fae to ward Ravensmore or they might as well hang out a flashing 'OPEN' neon sign for the hungry goblins and Day Walkers.

"For a big bad scary pirate, you sure are afraid of little humans."

"Wait a minute; did I hear 'starting with seven'? Is Ravensmore turning into some kind of foster home?"

"Don't look so terrified." She set her tea on the table, shoulders shaking from laughing so hard. Wiping her eyes, Emily looked at him, a light seeming to radiate from within, making her seem ethereal like some avenging angel swooping down to protect the little munchkins. "Your hearing is fine. This past year things have gone downhill so quickly. We have a huge home and wanted to help as many as we can so we're going to fill Ravensmore to the rafters."

Watching her, Robert was happy for Colin. He'd found someone to love who loved him back just as fiercely. Emily paused, leaning over to check on the babe before turning her attention back to him and her news.

"The Day Walkers have to be behind the missing persons abductions but why would they prey on children? There's no punishment harsh enough for those to prey on helpless animals and children."

"We agree, Emily. 'Tis part of the reason I'm here. Monroe's been looking into the disappearances and claims of Virus. With the influx of new Day Walkers we've all had our hands full keeping them from destroying the city. He'll let us know what he finds."

The door banged open, startling Colleen who cried out in her sleep before settling down and softly snoring again. "Hell, did I wake her?" Colin asked.

Crossing the room, he clapped Robert on the back as he passed and leaned down to kiss Emily. "Naill is going to be a fearsome warrior, he almost picked up his sword today." Colin grinned at his child looking like the proud parent.

"Yes, dear."

"Glad to see you're in complete control of your household, Highlander." Robert teased him. Colin grunted in reply as he put his son down to sleep beside his sister.

"What brings you here today?" Colin sat on the sofa close to Emily as he shoved two lemon bars into his mouth. "By the gods, these are amazing."

"Hey, Meg can make them whenever you want, hands off my cookies, Colin." Robert mock scowled as Emily playfully swatted Colin's arm.

Sitting up straight, a serious look etching his face, Robert leaned forward to tell them the latest news. "Aberdeen and Dundee are empty." Before either of them could interrupt, he held up a hand. "I popped over to take a look around. It's as if everyone deserted the cities overnight. There are mass graves all over. Full of old folks. No one under eighty. The same as we've seen here. This is Dayne's handiwork. His Day Walkers are out of control preying on humans this openly. He must be paying off the media to keep it quiet. There hasn't been anything more than the missing persons reports." Robert stopped speaking as the solar door opened and he jumped up to help Meg with the tray.

"Thought you might be getting hungry so I brought lunch." The housekeeper fussed about, handing out food and drinks.

Bless the woman she had ale for him and Colin and, of course, a cold Pepsi for Emily. Colin's wife was southern born and bred, from Charleston, and she adored cold Pepsi. No one else could abide the beverage, but Colin made sure the castle was fully stocked for his woman.

"When the babes wake, ring and I'll feed them." Meg told Emily as she left, softly closing the doors behind her.

A thoughtful look on his face while he chewed, Colin answered Robert. "Thorne hasn't responded to any of my calls. No one's heard from him in weeks, so we can't count on him to talk to his bloody brother."

"In Paris, Jasper said he killed a Day Walker who confessed to plans to turn or drain the entire population. At least now we know why we're seeing an increase in the bastards." He blew out a breath he didn't realize he'd been holding. "It's good you're taking in kids. We have to stop this before there are no humans left. I'm going to check in with Monroe see what he's found out."

Propping his booted feet on the table, Colin stretched. "Loathe as I am to admit it, he's been helpful this past year. If his hatred of Day Walkers doesn't get him killed, he'll be useful. Tell him to come by if he wants to discuss anything."

Covering his shock, Robert inclined his head. Colin had hated the cop interfering into Shadow Walker business. Being married had mellowed the cranky warrior. Bidding them good-bye, Robert grabbed a sandwich and the last lemon bar off the plate while making for the door, snickering as he heard Colin curse. He had to get back to the *Revenge II* and check on sleeping beauty.

"Milord, I have a car waiting to take you to the docks."

"Much obliged, Worthington." Gods, Colin had to love having the butler around. Robert's crew was great and all, but someone to look after things would be helpful.

B idding the driver farewell, Robert jumped in the waiting rowboat. Tired, he cursed his humanity again as he boarded his other lady, his ship. Running his hands through his hair, he poured a glass of wine and checked on the patient.

"Cap'n. The lady came to for a few minutes and I gave her some water, but then she fell asleep again and hasn't moved since."

"Good job, lad. Go back to your post, I'll take it from here."

Ian left the room, softly closing the door behind him. Sinking into the chair in front of the fire, he drained the wine, his eyes heavy.

Waking with a start, Robert landed in a heap on the floor. Hell, he must have fallen out of the chair. A moan had him jumping to his feet to check on the woman responsible for his current problems.

She opened her eyes. "Where am I?"

"Rest easy, lass. You're safe on my ship."

Mystery girl shook like a leaf in a strong breeze. "No, I can't be here, the pirate—he'll kill me." Green eyes fixed on his face and she gasped. "Don't hurt me."

"Shhh, no one's going to hurt you, least of all me, though I'd like to throttle you for what you've set in motion. Especially after I've spent the better part of the night tending to you. Want to tell me who you are and what happened?" At her wary silence, he tried once more. "I give you my word. I nor anyone on my ship will lay a finger on a single strand of your pretty hair."

Chewing her lip, she seemed to be weighing her decision. "I'm Maggie. The men I escaped from are scared of you—Bruce and Solien. Those guys are really bad news, and you're worse than them..." Losing consciousness again, her voice trailed off. Maggie. A lovely name, too soft for one as hard as she. He frowned. Hearing her say Solien's name chilled his blood. How did she know the demon, and more vexing, about Walkers? Guess he couldn't shake her awake given her condition so instead he got to his feet pacing, swearing under his breath. Thankful she couldn't hear the foul curses flying out of his mouth.

What was her part in this? Was she some kind of minion? Answers, that's what he needed. There was also the small matter of the bloody clock ticking down for his week to the reckoning. Whatever. That was the least of his concern given this latest development.

❧ 13 ❧

Hours ticked by before she woke but when she finally came to, the fever passed. Watching her roll over to stretch and rub her shoulder, he winced on her behalf. The injury would bother her for a while. Coming to, she flinched, seeing him slumped in a chair. Of course he must look like hell and wasn't like he could wave a magic wand to improve his appearance, not this week anyway.

"Oh, I wasn't dreaming ... it is you."

"I'm not going to hurt you. How are you feeling?"

A wary look filled her eyes. "Better." The words came out scratchy.

"Ian." Robert bellowed. The lad came in, tripping over his feet. "Aye, Cap'n? Oh, Miss you're awake. We've been ever so worried about you."

The incredulous look on her face had him stifling a laugh. Had no one ever told her they worried over her? This one was prickly.

"Please bring some water for our guest along with towels."

Ian scurried to do his bidding while Maggie watched, the covers clenched in her hands, face pale. So wary. Who had mistreated her so?

"Maggie, if you feel up to it, you can shower. The wound is healing nicely."

"I remember now...of all the ships to sneak onto, it had to be yours."

A woman of few words. Most men would kneel down and thank their lucky stars. Suppressing a chuckle so he didn't spook her, he moved slowly so she could see what he was doing. Any sudden move might send her bolting from the bed, out the door, and over the railing into the sea.

A knock saved him from replying as Ian came in balancing a tray of food. There was broth and water for Maggie and tea for Robert. Another crewmate followed Ian in with towels for her as well.

"Thank ye, lads. I'll be up in a bit."

Maggie gave them less of a frown, almost a shy smile. "I appreciate everything you've done for me." They bobbed their heads and shut the door with a soft click.

Robert stood and pulled his robe off the hook on the wall. "Would you like to sit by the fire and dine with me?"

Sinking deeper into the bed and coverings, her already pale face blanched, and he resisted the urge to shout. None of this would have happened if she hadn't ruined his life, putting events into play and yet *he*, the injured party in this damn mess, had to calm her down. "Maggie girl, I won't bite...well not unless you ask me to, that is." In spite of himself, he chuckled. This was hard. Usually the women fell all over him while he enjoyed their charms and sent them on their way with a smile. But Maggie, she was bloody work, no fun at all. "Put on the blasted robe and come sit. I'll give you the poker to keep close in case you want to bash me over the head with it, agreed?"

This time, the corner of her mouth lifted in the tiniest start of a smile. My gods, she was stunning. The worry vanished, transforming her face into that of a beauty. Stirrings of desire snaked through him.

"Turn around and don't look."

"Cross my fingers." He heard rustling as the covers were flung back and a gasp. Turning, he made it to the bed just in time to catch her before she could fall over. "Easy. You've lost quite a bit of blood and you haven't eaten so take your time to get up or you'll fall on your lovely arse." The rigid set of her body as he helped her into the robe told him she was truly afraid of him. 'Twas time to find out what she knew. Helping her to the chair in front of the fire, he kept her arm tucked in his. Sighing as she sat down; her skin was pale and clammy. "Here. If you feel the need to use it, you'll have it close by." Grabbing the fireplace poker, he placed it next to her chair within arm's reach.

"Now, let's get some food in you. Though it's only broth." Robert watched Maggie as she looked at every inch of his cabin. Would she find it pleasing? It was well appointed. The bed was massive and made for making love all night. A good-sized dresser, trunk, and mirror finished the room. The furnishings were from his old life though the bathroom was completely modernized. The fire was a nice touch, they'd figured out how to have them without burning the blasted ship to cinders.

Robert served her more broth and poured tea. Lowering his arm, he discreetly sniffed his armpits. Wouldn't do to offend her.

"It's very good. Are those grapes? Where did you get them? They're so hard to find."

Grinning at the avarice in her eyes, he tossed her a bunch. "Go easy. You haven't had any solid food for a bit so make sure your stomach can handle it. As for the grapes—let's just say I have plenty of connections."

"How long was I out?" Watching her nibble the grapes, he shifted his legs, trying to ease the ache in his balls. Poor girl was recovering, and he wanted to feed her those grapes one by one, nibbling her fingers, kissing her lips, tasting the grape juice on her mouth. Pushing the thoughts away, he answered her. "Over a day. You had a fever from the wound."

"That long? I can tell we're moving. Where are we going? Not that I'm complaining...I was curious, that's all."

Leaning in to refill her teacup, he was frustrated when she pulled back, her hand unconsciously going to the poker, curling around it. He ran his hands through his hair, biting his tongue to keep from saying something snarky to her. It was time to find out why she feared him...after she showered and dressed. In his experience, ladies were always more talkative after they felt better about themselves.

"We're headed to Wales. I have to deliver a package to a collector. We'll spend a day there. Does that suit milady?"

"Wales. I've never been to Wales...that's good."

Odd, she didn't seem curious or concerned as to their destination. Before he delved into that, first things first. Tension gripped her as she finished her broth and tea, but at least she didn't have her hand on the makeshift weapon anymore.

"Right, then. There are towels next to the door. Fresh clothing is hanging on the hook on the wall over there. Would you like a shower? Don't bother looking for your clothes. I burnt what you were wearing along with the backpack."

"Everything I owned in the world was in it..." Her fingers clenched into a fist.

"Maggie. The satchel was beyond saving. I will replace whatever was in there and anything else you may need. Try not to worry. After you shower we need to talk about what you said when you woke—about knowing me and why you would ever think I would kill you when I'm certain I'd remember you if we'd met previously."

A look crossed her face and she tensed. Picking up the poker as she stood, she clutched the robe with her other hand. "Shower first." Resignation tinged her voice. "Then we can talk if you wish." Slowly walking across the room, watching him with every step, she paused and lifted the clothing from the hook. As she reached up, the robe gaped open, providing him a tantalizing glimpse of thigh. "The bathroom is the next door in the hallway to your right. You should find whatever you need."

Hand on the doorknob, she paused. "You know, you look like some old-fashioned handsome pirate. I can almost see you decked out in a puffy shirt, surrounded by mounds of gold, jewels, silk, and the heads of your enemies piled around your feet." With that, she closed the door behind her.

Robert didn't know whether to be offended or charmed by the vision she'd laid out of him. He wasn't a barbarian, he'd never pile heads around his feet. They would smell and who'd clean up the mess? Maybe pretty ladies...he could think of one in particular he wouldn't mind having draped across his lap.

While she showered, he called for Ian to remove the dishes and went above decks to check on the state of his ship.

He returned to his cabin in time to see her wandering around the room. When they arrived in Wales he'd get her some new clothes. The ill-fitting clothing would do until then. "Feeling better?"

She favored him with a look. "I am. Before we talk, could I have some more tea and grapes? I can't remember the last time I had grapes not to mention real honey in my tea."

"Whatever pleases milady. I'll have Ian bring it to you. If you'll excuse me, I'm going to shower so I don't offend with my stench." Sketching a bow, he left the room.

After telling Ian what she required, he stalked to the bathroom. It was steamy and smelled of a spicy shower gel he used when he wanted to feel human, and for him a shower was a very human experience. As a Walker he didn't need to shower, didn't sweat, didn't smell. Strange, he never used it when he showered with one of the numerous ladies he entertained. Usually let them pick some kind of fruity-smelling wash. Well, he could think of many things Freud would have to say about that but instead he lathered up. Soaping his body, he thought of Maggie being in here before him, using his scent, washing her body, her hands running over her breasts, stomach, legs, and that lovely arse. Groaning, he finished, the towel slung low over his hips. Shaving. He couldn't remember the last time he'd actually used a razor.

Stretching, he padded back to his cabin. Entering the room, Maggie stopped mid-motion, the teacup halfway to her lips. "What are you doing? You're practically naked."

He had a suggestive comment on his lips when he looked closer at her face. Great, she was afraid. Damn it to hell. "My clothes are here in the room. If you'll turn your head away, I'll dress quickly so as not to offend your delicate sensibilities." Pulling out his most charming smile, he was disheartened to see her hand curled around the poker in a death grip.

Pulling on a pair of faded worn jeans and a cream V-neck sweater, he approached her as a wild animal, speaking softly. "Maggie. I'm dressed. You can look now."

Glancing at him and then back down to her lap, she set her teacup down. Giving her a moment, he went to the sideboard, grabbed the whisky and poured a liberal amount into her cup. At her look he explained, "To help you relax, nothing more."

Looking at him as if he were a very hungry tiger about to pounce on her, she eased back in the chair sipping her tea. Sitting in the chair opposite her, drinking a whisky he watched her. The flames warmed the room. It was almost dinnertime, the day dark and dreary, casting shadows in the corners and on the ceiling.

"Now, back to the matter at hand. Can you tell me how you know me and what led you to my ship?"

Her hesitation made him want to swear, reach across the space separating them and shake her. Instead, he gripped the arms of the chair, fingers twitching. "Maggie. I don't know what you've been through—but given the state of you when you were discovered on board, I'm guessing it was bad. No matter what you've heard or been told, I give you my word—you are under my protection and I will aid you however I can. No harm will come to you, I give you my oath."

Green eyes searched his face, assessing, considering. Seemingly satisfied, she squared her shoulders, tucked her feet up under her, took a fortifying swallow of tea and a deep breath.

"I'm not sure where to start." Sitting there so still, she looked like an ancient stone goddess of old. The only thing betraying her angst was the fear reflected in her eyes and the slight trembling of her hands.

"Why don't you start by telling me how you came to interfere in my hanging and we can go on from there?"

"Interfered? I saved your life. Though if I'd known it was you, I would have kept going. Anyway, I thought things like you couldn't die?"

"Things? You called me a thing?" Nothing that came out of her mouth could have astonished him more. Too damn bad she didn't let him swing. If she had, they wouldn't be here in this predicament right now. To further deflate his ego, he guessed by her tone she didn't care for him. Well, it made it that much funnier for the fates that she was supposed to help him.

"Excuse me. A Shadow Walker, then."

Now she had his bleedin' attention. "Why don't you tell me how you know that term and what you think it means?"

Maggie shrank back into her chair as if he might strike her. Strike a woman? He was affronted. As if he'd ever strike a woman. Never. And any man who did deserved a painful and bloody death at the end of his sword, gun, blast of energy or maybe all three. Didn't matter he was still pissed about her turning his life upside down, all he cared about was destroying whoever had laid a finger on that porcelain skin or fiery red hair. Ruining those who'd hurt her. Clenching the arms of the chair, he heard them creak in protest. *Calm the hell down, won't do any good to scare her. Keep calm and let her talk.*

"I don't know who or what has hurt you but I would never strike a woman." A knock on the door interrupted him. Ian came in bearing a hearty stew, freshly baked bread, tea, and fruit.

"Dinner has arrived. Do you feel up to eating something more substantial than broth?"

"Are you kidding? I'm starving. Oranges, wherever did you find them? It's hard enough to get orange juice let alone the real thing." Maggie looked like she was going to knock Ian over and devour the orange globes.

"Easy now, there's plenty. I've a hothouse at my home in Wales and they're grown there. We keep oranges along with lemon and limes stocked on the ship. Would milady like a glass of lemonade?" The poor woman was ready to start salivating. Hmm, fresh fruit seemed to be the way to get Maggie to drop her guard. He made a mental note.

"Ian, if you would be so kind? That will be all."

The boy left them to their supper. "Shall we continue our conversation? I am most interested in your tale. Eat as many oranges as you want. We've plenty onboard and can restock when we reach Wales in a few hours."

With a wary eye on him, she stood and fixed a heaping bowl of stew, two heavily buttered slices of bread, three oranges and refilled her tea. A good strategy was half the battle. His was simple...he'd ply her with food to get her to drop her guard and open up.

Waiting until she settled back in to her chair, he stood and with deliberate slow movements, made his own plate of food. What would it be like to serve her? To feed her piece by piece, watching the pleasure fill her face? A groan of pleasure filled the room as Maggie dug into her food.

"Take care, lass. Your stomach may not handle the food so well."

With a mouth full of bread, she mumbled, "No, I'm used to not having food for a few days and then eating. I think my stomach is made of cast iron."

It was stated so matter of fact. In this day and age to think someone wouldn't have enough food, it was unacceptable.

Schooling his face into a pleasant expression, he nodded around a bite of stew, motioning for her to continue.

"I don't actually know you, I'd never laid eyes on you until Edinburgh Castle but I knew your name and what you looked like. The people I...worked for, were very interested in you and those like you."

Spoon dangling from his fingers, he nodded, leaning forward in the chair. "Solien?"

"Yes. What a horrible creature. And when I heard him talking to Bruce and Rawlins about you. Well, they sounded afraid. So naturally I thought if they were worried, you had to be terrifying." That lovely full mouth of hers formed an O of surprise as if she realized what words had left her mouth and she shrank back into her chair almost spilling the stew.

He stayed his hand before he reached out to her knowing she'd take it as aggression not concern. "Maggie, 'tis fine. Do you know what the people you work for are?"

"Some of them are human, like Bruce and his men. They report to what I used to call super ghosts but now I know they're called Day Walkers. The Day Walkers answer to the most frightening creature I've ever encountered. His name is Solien and he's something more than even the Day Walkers." Composing herself, she went back to eating her stew. After finishing the bowl, she ate the bread, saving the precious fruit for last.

"Tell me the rest. I'm guessing it has something to do with how you ended up on my ship?" He was careful not to look at her except for stealing glances. Instead he directed his attention to the meal and ate, looking down at the plate to put her at ease.

Sighing, she broke off a piece of bread, heavily buttered, stuffed it in her mouth and chewed. The lass was stalling.

"Maggie, I shall say it until you stop shrinking away from me. Nothing has hurt you since you've set foot on my ship and I will not hurt you. Confide in me. I can help you."

"There are others like me, still at the house. Bruce and his men—they can't see you or your kind...but...we can."

Based on their auspicious meeting at Edinburgh Castle, he knew that. But others? This was interesting. "You are unusual, but I've encountered others like you. Those who have wandered into shadow and back. This Bruce character, he uses you to see us. Then what?" It was brilliant he thought, leaning back in his chair. Recruiting those who had the ability to see the enemy so the minions could try to kill them. Grudgingly he admitted to himself—they had something.

"The men take us out and when we see someone like you we write up a description or sometimes we tell them where you are standing and they shoot at you."

At his look she paused. "Solien told us Shadow Walkers are trying to destroy the world, killing humans and bringing creatures to live in our cities and eat the children." She shuddered.

This was really too ridiculous for words. They were the bloody heroes. "Allow me to set the record straight, may I?" She nodded, peeling an orange and he continued. "We, Shadow Walkers, that is, are the good guys. Solien is a demon and Rawlins is a Day Walker. They are allied in the quest to destroy humanity. On the other hand, we protect all of you. And unlike the enemy, we're forbidden to drain humans dry." Pausing, he let her take it in, watching the emotions play across her face. Had to admit, it was easier talking to someone who already knew about them and the "other" creatures. Not like she'd run shrieking from the news.

"You both profess to be the good guys. I'll make up my own mind, thank you. I've seen what Solien and the others do. Cruel, awful things." Voice breaking, she reached for the cup of tea. "Robert? Are all Day Walkers demons like Solien?"

What the hell had they done to her? It was appalling.

"No. Only Solien. Day Walkers are like us in the sense we were all mortal at one time. Then we died and some of us took one path to protect. Others took the road to destruction and embraced a different existence. Have you met Dayne? Solien reports to him."

"No. If Solien answers to him, I don't want to. So you're what, some kind of ghost?"

"An apt enough description. How did you come to work for them?"

Did she have to bite her lip? It made him think of bedding her. He wasn't supposed to be thinking of sex, well not until after he found out about her and helped her. Or maybe found out, then sex thoughts, then help her, then more pleasurable thoughts. Glad she couldn't hear what he was thinking, he grinned inside.

Maggie squirmed in her chair clearly uncomfortable with telling him. He'd wait. The silence stretched. "I guess it doesn't matter if I tell you. My supposed best friend told Bruce about me in exchange for three hundred quid. I was kidnapped on my way home from work over a year ago. It wasn't just me; there were others in similar situations though now there's only a few left. Some tried to escape and were killed. I thought I'd die there."

"I'm sorry, Maggie. What happened to make you risk your life escaping?"

She exhaled hard, unconsciously hugging herself. To give her a moment, he got up to pour tea. At that moment, a knock sounded on the door. Ian had brought chocolate brownies and lemonade.

"We'll be docking in an hour, Cap."

"Much appreciated, lad."

Instead of pouring her more tea, he served them, making sure to put two of the chocolaty goodies on her plate. Yep, she was watching him like a hawk.

"Don't worry, you can have more."

"Sorry. It's been so long since I've had food like this." A crumb caught in the corner of her lip when she took a bite of the brownie. Before he realized what he was doing, he reached over and wiped it away with his thumb. Green eyes dilated and stared up at him. She was frozen in time; the moment seemed to expand, no past, no present, only now. His body leaned in, meeting her in the briefest kiss before she pulled back looking interested yet distressed. Idiot. Here she's ailing and you try and snog her. Nice. "There was something on your face. It's gone now." Lame. So lame. He mentally scolded himself.

"Um, Anyway, I'd been out spotting for them. I didn't see anyone but there was trouble at the club and I was blamed. Getting ready for bed, I heard Bruce talking. They said I'd been lying to them or my ability had worn off...that I was no longer useful and I'd be killed in the morning."

Robert handed her another brownie and refilled her glass of lemonade, staying silent to encourage her to keep talking.

"I realized they meant to kill me. Escape was my only option. I ran into Ned. I knew him from before when I'd stayed at a hostel he worked for. That's how I found out about the tunnels. Guess I didn't realize the sewage would be quite so awful." A corner of her mouth lifted in what for her would be a full-on belly laugh for anyone else.

"Indeed. I'm afraid you did rather reek. Though it was brilliant to use the tunnels to escape." He hid his anger at her captors. Would only scare Maggie to show it. But he'd take care of each and every one; especially the one who'd betrayed her. Thorne needed to be informed along with the others.

"And that's where I found you, being hanged. Of course I didn't know it was you until I freed you and you introduced yourself."

"I imagine I gave you rather a fright. I'm sorry. I was perplexed as to why you'd run away after risking yourself to help me?"

Fidgeting in the chair, she wouldn't meet his eyes. "You're legend."

He wanted to know more. *Legend.* But Maggie had run out of steam and fallen asleep in her chair, the teacup sliding off her lap. Catching it, he set it on the sideboard and carried her to bed kissing her on the forehead. Summoning Ian, he gave orders to drop anchor in the harbor and spend the night. Would be safer. They'd dock in the morning.

Instinct made him reach for the coverlet to climb in beside her and hold her tight...but she'd be terrified if she woke and found him there. Instead, he made himself as comfortable as possible in the bloody chair...again.

fter finishing off two kegs of beer, Fury was ready to get this party started. The look on faces of Solien's men when he popped in was priceless. He knew what was said about him. The hound was mythical. Midnight black with three heads. Came from one of the deep circles of the Nether realm; loved to tear humans, Walkers, and other creatures to pieces, playing with them before devouring them, preferably with some type of tasty sauce. They said in hushed whispers that the beast had the power to keep you alive so you knew you were being consumed. Worse, the monster actually talked.

All true though he was insulted the puny little humans couldn't wrap their heads around the fact he conversed. What, the three heads didn't bother them, but the talking did? Made him want to tell Dayne to go screw himself, fuck their bargain and amble over to Africa where they worshipped him properly, as a god. Well, demi-god was the correct term, but who cared?

Bruce wanted his men to crawl through the tunnels, see what they could find. He was smart enough not to suggest Fury do the same. The three circles of hell if he was going to stink for no reason. They were to meet at the Castle unless one of the men found something, then they'd call and rendezvous wherever. The silly little humans were petrified of him, not a single one wanted to go with him. Instead of insisting or following them, he preferred to hunt alone. His three heads grinned, showing off massive fangs. If he'd wished, he could have shown up in another form. He had the ability to shapeshift. A raven was his other preferred guise. But rather than showing up as a human it was a great deal more fun to scare them and after all, the three-headed hound was his natural state. Solien and his master, Dayne, had upped their game. Taking over the world? It smacked of a bad sci-fi movie and way too much effort. Grumbling, he padded over the cobblestones at Edinburgh Castle. A startled kid pointed to him and tugged his mother's coat. "Mam, there's a giant monster dog with three heads over there, look!" Oops. The humans would be alarmed seeing him bounding across the court-yard. Before he flashed invisible, one head smiled, one bared fangs, and the third head growled at the child. The boy cried, frantically pointing, "He's going to eat us. Mam! The monster is bigger than the bus dad drives."

"Johnny! What have I told you about making up stories? Stop it right now and behave. Crying doesn't help. Honestly, no cookies after dinner, you're going straight to bed." The frazzled mother yanked the boy by the arm, dragging him across the cobblestones, scolding the entire way.

How insulting. The seven hells he was bigger than a bus. Maybe a large SUV or tank, but no way was he fat. Offended, Fury thought about eating the child—why bother? Not enough meat on the little ones to make it worthwhile. Rather like eating chicken wings. Mostly sauce and bone. He'd wait for tastier fare.

All around the city, missing person's flyers were plastered on building walls, papered in tube stations, and covering lampposts. Was the same all over the UK. Not many fringe elements of society around, and it wasn't because of the cold. Dayne's Day Walkers had been draining them dry. He paused, a discarded newspaper fluttering on the ground. The headline read "Scottish National Party Cleans Up Homeless Problem." Riiiiight. All the politicians were taking credit for what unbeknownst to them, Dayne and Solien were responsible for.

As he was pondering eating the businessmen on the street corner, Bruce's men showed up. He noted with a cock of his head that Bruce wasn't there. The man didn't like to muss his hands. Preferred to let others do the dirty work while he stood by, looking on. Fury wondered if the man didn't have the stomach for it?

The short man addressed him. "Uh, sir? We didn't find her, but looks like she came this way." Fury wrinkled all three of his noses. They smelled of garbage and other nasty things. Splats of brown goo, best not think about what it was, made a plopping noise as it hit the damp stone. His middle head, the one that did most of the talking, turned and stared at them through gold eyes. "I scented her here. My guess would be she headed toward the Leith docks."

The four men conferred amongst themselves. "Me and him will check other tunnels. Paul used to be hunter. He can track most anything." Mr. Short gestured to the other two lack-wits. "They will come with you to help."

A shaggy head, turned brown eyes on the human who'd spoken. "And why doesn't Paul speak for himself?"

"Rawlins cut his tongue out for insolence, right Paul?" The mute shrugged.

"Silence is golden." The head with the red eyes spoke, eyeing Paul with a hungry look.

"Chill boys. Plenty of time for taking care of him later." Fury told the other two heads. Sometimes they wanted to do what they wanted. It was bloody hard having three brains to contend with at all times. Didn't matter he was the dominant head, the other two had strong wills. A thought popped into his head. "Did any of you fine fellows think to bring a picture of Maggie?"

The boy with the missing fingers, Ned, stepped forward. Reaching into his coat pocket, he fumbled and withdrew a grainy photo. The woman had a curvy body and an attribute Fury would recognize anywhere...long, wavy, fire engine red hair. Of course she could have cut if off or dyed it. He sent a mental message to the other two brains to keep a blank look. *But it's her*, the brown-eyed head replied. *We helped her board that ship*, said the red-eyed head. *I know that, but those losers don't. So don't give it away.*

"Seems an attractive sort. Are we to kill on sight or bring her back to Solien to make a snack for him?"

The short man answered him. "We's told to bring 'er back and Solien would deal with her."

Gold eyes regarded the men. This wouldn't do. "Sounds good. You two, continue checking tunnels and the other fine gentlemen here will accompany me to the docks. We'll meet up at the house by nightfall." With that, his heads turned to glare at the humans and spat in unison, "Well, come on then. We don't have all day."

The two men were called Brian and Kevin, whatever. Ought to be called Fat and Lazy. No matter. The dour group parted ways; Fat and Lazy following behind him, looking scared. They'd stay that way if they were smart. At least both men kept quiet as they walked to the docks. He knew which ship she was on, The *Revenge II*. In his raven form, he'd seen the woman, forlorn look on her face and obviously injured, desperately seeking a way out of Edinburgh. No one would assist her. She didn't have any funds and the human males didn't want to be bothered, she wasn't worth the risk to them.

A look of hopelessness in her eyes made him help her. He'd always had a weakness for red-headed women. Drawing her attention to an open hatch allowed her to find a way on board.

Reaching the docks, the heads shook off the rain. Fat and Lazy looked miserable but wisely kept their yaps shut. Wanting time to formulate a plan, he motioned to them to follow him into a pub on the corner. Was rather fun watching their faces turn the color of curdled milk as he transformed into a human male. Fury knew how he must look to them. At six eight with short black hair and gold eyes, well not to mention he was built like a man who spent his entire life doing hard labor. Most men got out of his way as fast as they could.

"What? You thought I'd go in as myself and ask for three pints?" He rolled his eyes. The unlikely trio ordered drinks and sat at a table towards the back of the pub. There was time to enjoy a beverage before paying a visit to the Port Manager's office. A group of bankers had braved the worsening weather and were enjoying a late lunch. He hated bankers. They were responsible for a great deal of the economic turmoil this world was experiencing. And worry combined with hopelessness, made humans taste a bit "off." Fear and anger gave them more of a spicy flavor...

Pondering the situation, his eyes narrowed. Dayne thought he'd gotten the better of Fury in the bargain they'd struck—however, the phrasing was crucial when it came to terms. The demons were masters of properly wording curses and bargains. He'd learned from the best and while he'd lost the bargain, he'd ensured the details weren't as bothersome as Dayne thought they were. While he couldn't eat the god or outright defy a properly worded order for another year, he had a certain latitude in how to interpret the orders he was given unless they were worded explicitly. By the gods, had it been ninety-nine years already? My how time flew when you were being screwed.

In hunting for her, he was obeying the letter of the command. Solien, while a demon, wasn't privy to the terms of the bargain. He thought Fury had been enslaved for a hundred years. Period. Tsk, tsk. He'd let the misconception stand. Nothing said he couldn't *help* her. Smiling, the man on his left quickly moved further down the bar. Guess his smile wasn't very friendly. Since he liked redheads and loved flipping Dayne off, he'd help the human woman. It would make his servitude a bit more bearable. He had every intent of tearing Dayne to shreds when the hundredth year was up.

A few patrons paid and staggered out of the pub into the

cold afternoon air. Likely on their way home to wives or girl-friends. As the door slammed shut, sending the room into near darkness, Fury smiled. The only ones remaining were the bankers, the barkeep and Fat and Lazy. Perfect. Manifesting the rest of the case of wasabi sauce Rawlins had sent him last year, he took note of any potential exits. Two windows up front, a door in back probably leading to an alley and that was it for escape. Was laughable really.

Beckoning Solien's minions to the hallway next to the toilet, Fury changed form. Saliva dripped from the jaws of each head. Brian and Kevin realized a second too late what was happening. Drenched in wasabi sauce, the men were gone in two large bites. Hope he didn't look like an overgrown chipmunk with his jowls stuffed full. Chewing and swallowing, he used his power to mask what was going on by throwing up a mirror image of the corridor sans carnage.

Tasty. The appetizer whetted his appetite. Dropping the mirage, he manifested bars over the doors and windows. The group of bankers screamed. This was going to be quite fun. It was over in thirty minutes. Having three heads came in very handy at times. Licking a few remaining spots off his fur, Fury made a note. Tell Rawlins thanks for the New Orleans wasabi sauce. It was his new favorite.

Burping in satisfaction, he sent forth a mental command and incinerated the pub. The local humans would think a fire destroyed the establishment. They're wouldn't be any bodies inside to be found. Emergency responders would assume they'd all been burned to cinders. A few less bankers in the world—it was shaping up to be a very good day.

Ambling down the street, cloaked in invisibility, he made for the Port Manager's office. Easy enough to find what he wanted as he knew when The *Revenge II* sailed.

This was interesting.

The ship belonged to the Shadow Walker called Black Bart or nowadays he was known by the name Robert Bartholomew.

Fury didn't know him personally, only by reputation. He let out a sharp bark of laughter causing two clerks in the office to jump up in alarm. The woman was with *one of them*. This truly was priceless. Dayne and Solien would have their panties in a wad over this little development...if he told them.

Hmmm, did he care if Walker fought Walker? Not a chance in the seven hells of the Nether realm. The manifest said the ship was making for Wales then returning to Edinburgh. He'd deliver the happy news as to where the runaway human could be found and sit back and enjoy the entertainment. And he'd keep an eye or six on the woman. She wouldn't come to harm on his watch.

Fury dematerialized into the middle of the Day Walker Realm where Dayne resided chuckling the entire time.

❧ 15 ❧

Head pounding, Monroe cracked open a bleary, bloodshot eye and fumbled on the coffee table for his mobile. "What."

"Nice, to talk to you too, get your arse to the station. Did you forget your suspension is over?" Shamus grumbled something under his breath that sounded like pig-headed bastard but he couldn't be sure. Then his partner had the nerve to hang up before he could reply.

Sitting up on the couch, Monroe took stock of his surroundings. He'd passed out on the sofa again. Probably for the best, given he couldn't remember the last time the sheets had been changed. For all he knew, they'd gotten up and walked off of their own accord to escape the filth. Rubbing his eyes, an empty bottle of Glenfiddich lay on its side under a chair with the stuffing coming out of the seat. Another empty on the top of the table.

Suspended for a month over the way he'd handled Emily's case last year. Had to give Shamus credit, he'd helped Monroe cover, but in the end walking into his boss's office in early October, fuck, his ears were still ringing after the dressing down he'd taken from his superior. He thought back. Emily was a Yank whose friend had fallen down some stairs at the museum and broken her leg. Monroe had met them when their hotel room at the Balmoral was ransacked.

She told him what at the time seemed a fantastical tale—now he knew otherwise. Some things were better left in the shadows. She'd gone missing and because he knew her problems were related to his cold case on Alice, he never reported any of it. Broke so many rules he'd lost count and the worst part? Didn't care...all he'd cared about was justice, whatever it took, no line was sacred anymore. Alice. His girlfriend of long ago. Murdered, when he should have been there to protect her. He searched for years until finally getting the mother of all breaks last year. Found the bastard who killed her and then some. Who would have ever believed that all the preaching he'd endured as a child was true—though it wasn't angels and demons...well, there were demons but not that kind. A war was being waged. Every day. Good versus evil. Brewing for millennia and his beloved Edinburgh was in the middle of it all. Monroe had found out ghosts were real during an investigation over a year ago. He'd found Alice's killer. The guy looked human but was not. He was on the side wanting to destroy humanity. Alexander was his name. The guy killed him, well, emergency workers brought him back after three minutes, and now he could see Walkers. Robert had saved his life. Not only that, the guy allowed him to finish Alice's killer off. He'd owe him forever. All Shadow Walkers had some kind of freaky power and a kill-first, ask-questions-later attitude. Monroe also met Colin and a seriously scary man named Thorne. He had Robert to thank for the information download. Rubbing his eyes, Monroe thought about what he knew. Looking around his hovel of an apartment, he scowled. The place had reached a level of nastiness even he was having trouble ignoring. He'd bet he couldn't pay any cleaning service in town to clean it up, be better to torch it and start over.

Rolling off the couch, he groaned, pressing his hands to his temples to stop the spinning. Listing to the left, he staggered to the bathroom, chewed a handful of aspirin and stood under the shower until the hot water turned cold. Toweling off, he picked up clothes off the floor, smelling a shirt here, pants there, searching for something that didn't smell like dead things. Finally a pair of Levis 501s, a black V-neck sweater, black Doc Marten boots and he was sufficiently dressed.

Head exploding with every step to the kitchen, he navigated moldy pizza boxes and take-out containers scattered on the floor. Finally. Relief was contained there in the old, battered fridge. And great. Not much choice other than a partial bottle of mustard, a green piece of cheese, and half a moldy tomato. He grabbed a beer off the counter and swigged it back as he left, shutting the door behind him. Snagging his coat off the chair, he beat feet outside, cranking the tunes in the black Mercedes SUV to drown out the pounding in his head and drove to the station to face the music.

On the way, Monroe stopped to grab a cup of coffee. His stomach rebelled at the thought of food so he decided on a double espresso. Feeling marginally alive, the flat, gray day did nothing to improve his mood. It was raining, sheets of rain, driving everyone away. The streets gave off an eerie vibe, almost deserted. Up ahead there was a lone pedestrian scurrying along, umbrella failing miserably to keep him dry against the gusting wind. At ten o'clock in the morning on a Thursday, he thought there'd be more people around. The cold and wet never kept the city's denizens inside, especially the tourists. Even they had abandoned the streets today. He blew out a heavy sigh.

There had been rumors and whispers floating around with the panic-inducing word "virus." He'd heard it mentioned in hush-hush tones as he walked by a war room at the station. Funny thing, the media hadn't seized on it. Usually they were the first ones to whip everyone into frothing, foaming-at-the-mouth frenzy. He smelled a cover-up.

Gah, he was in a grouchy mood. Pulling into the lot, he parked and jogged in, feeling partially alive. Waving to Shamus as he passed through the open bullpen, he squared his jaw and rapped on his sergeant's door.

"Enter. Monroe sit. Close the door."

Monroe resisted the urge to bark and instead moved a stack of files off the only chair in sight and sat like an errant school kid called into the headmaster's office for some infraction or another. "Hey Sarge, sorry I'm late. Alarm clock is busted. Haven't had time to get a new one."

A rotund man in his mid-forties, with thinning gray hair and tired eyes, looked up from his desk at Monroe. "Really? An entire bleeding month of sulking and you couldn't find the bloody time? From the looks of ye, haven't been able to buy a razor either. My god man, have you been sleeping in the gutter? I was hoping you'd use this time to think about your career, but from the look and stench of ye, I think you spent the entire month soused."

"Nice word, *soused*. Was that in your crossword puzzle today?" Monroe pointed at the open newspaper and cracked his knuckles, full of attitude.

"Watch the mouth, Monroe. I'm no in the mood."

"I'm back, who the hell cares how I look or smell. I want the missing person cases." He tried not to spit the words but flinched hearing his tone, knowing he sounded like a jackass.

"You want? You want? After the stunt you pulled. Years, you've been tiptoeing the line, pushing boundaries; you went too far with the American. Let your personal feelings cloud your judgment same as you did with Alice. For the next three months, you'll be working a desk, doing paperwork until I'm satisfied you can play by the rules and play nice with others, clear?"

Sarge's face was beet red, the veins bulging in his neck and forehead as he stood from his chair, leaning over the desk, shouting at Monroe.

"Leave Alice out of this," he growled at the Sarge. Boss man was still sore over Alice ten years ago...talk about holding a grudge. Course she was a family friend and Monroe had burned a lot of bridges when it happened, guess he couldn't totally blame the guy.

"That's it. I've had it with your attitude. You're working a desk doing paperwork for six months. You will steer clear of all missing person's cases. Piss me off further, and I'll make it a sodding year. Got me?"

Before Monroe could retort. Boss man lumbered around the desk and got right up in his grill, poked a stubby finger in his chest to hammer the point home. "Get your head out of your arse. And quit drinking, admit you're a drunk—get some help."

"The hell I am. Everybody likes to drink, doesn't make you a bleeding advert for some sodding twelve-step program."

"Denial won't help you, son. Alice is dead and gone, God rest her soul. You need to move on. I want you to see the office shrink and start going to AA meetings or I'll have your head. You're an alcoholic. Just like your old man was and look what happened to your mum because of it."

A red rage washed over him. How dare Sarge bring up what happened when he was a child. He was nothing like his old man. Without thinking he struck out, punching his superior in the face. Blood streamed down the guy's nose.

"Get out. You're fired." Holding a handkerchief to his nose, Sarge pointed to the door. "Leave your badge—"

Monroe couldn't see past the anger. He threw his badge on the desk, flung the wooden door open so hard it made the men outside jump at the loud bang, and stalked across the bullpen. He was halfway there when he heard Sarge's voice. "Get some bloody help, you're a pathetic drunk with anger management problems."

Not paying attention to where he was going, he found himself in the locker room. Slumping into the bench, head pounding, he refused to think about any of it. Bollocks. He didn't have either of those issues, he wasn't that cocked up.

Someone clearing their throat had him looking up, ready to take the head off of whoever was interrupting his brooding.

"Are you sure you want to do this, mate? It's not too late. You can sit down, discuss things..." His partner trailed off. They'd been partners for the past ten years. Now Shamus stood there with a look of pity on his face.

"Don't start, Shamus. After everything that's happened, this has been a long time coming." Monroe would miss his partner. But after he'd finally solved Alice's ten-year-old murder case and had his eyes opened to what really went on out there, he wasn't the same, would never be the same. Things that used to be black and white had muddied together into muted shades of gray. A year ago he'd have told you he'd be a cop and a bloody good one, until he retired. That was then, this was now. No sodding use crying about it.

Now if he could get Thorne to welcome him to the little happy Shadow Walker group—who was he kidding? He'd rid his city of all the scum taking up breathing space and killing humans whether Thorne welcomed him or not. Shamus was watching him with a concerned look on his face. Monroe wondered how long he'd been sitting there lost in thought. "It's time to move on. Maybe Sarge did me a favor."

"What are you going to do next?" Shamus was scratching his head, staring at the lockers, not looking at him. At least he had the good graces not to bring up the drinking or Monroe's mom.

"I'm thinking of opening up my own investigative firm. Do things on my own terms. Don't look like you lost your dog, I'll still be needing information."

Shamus snorted, looking relieved to move off the touchy-feely conversation. "What makes you think I'll take your calls?"

They slapped each other on the back as he packed his locker. One lousy box. That was all he had to show for his time on the force. Mumbling under his breath, he headed out into the gloomy day.

❧ 16 ❧

The stygian darkness of Velvet soothed Solien. Reminded him of home. Passing the dance floor, the flickering strobe lights bouncing off his black shades, he headed directly to the bar.

"Grey Goose on the rocks, make it a double with lime." Tossing back the drink, he ordered another, surveying the denizens of Velvet. Dressed in black leather pants, black shit-kickers, a black long-sleeved tee, and a black leather duster he blended into the shadowy interior of the most popular club in Edinburgh. With long midnight-blue hair that somehow enhanced rather than detracted from his looks, he could have been a model. At almost seven feet, he towered over most humans, and radiated evil like some men exuded sex appeal or charisma.

Restless, he zeroed in on two girls, barely legal and high on something from the look of them. Stalking over to the murky hallway leading to the alley, he nodded at the two women never glancing back to see if they followed. The women trailed him down the dark corridor of the club away from prying eyes to a small alcove next to the exit door leading out to the dumpsters. Before he could utter a word, the one dressed in a pink lace bustier gazed up at him with unfocused eyes and reached over palming him through his leather pants.

Shoving the brown-eyed brunette up against the wall, he popped the lacing on her top as her eyes widened. "Oh baby, I like it rough, give me more," she mewed, wrapping her legs around his waist. Opening the bustier, he roughly rolled her nipple between his fingers and she moaned in anticipation. Pushing up what there was of her miniscule skirt; he ripped the pink lace thong off, discarding it on the floor. Solien stopped her from unzipping her thigh high black vinyl boots. "Leave them on, sexy," he growled in her ear. Unzipping his pants, he reached for her, smiling as she let out a small squeak when he took her. As he pounded her into the wall in time with the bass of the music, the green-eyed brunette watched, caressing them while she swayed to a song only she could hear. Turning slightly so his dessert couldn't fully see what he was doing, Solien leaned down to kiss the brown-eyed brunette—the air changed, the scent of an electrical storm filled the hallway as he deepened the kiss, sucking out her energy, her life-force. Brunette hair turned white, the bloom of youth fading to a brown wrinkled rose, discarded on the ground as he shot his wad and drained her dry. With a final gasp the brunette was dead. He propped the girl up in the corner, patting her arm for show. "Sleep it off, love."

A tap on his arm had his head swiveling around to look at his dessert. The girl with the green eyes, pouted as she snorted cocaine from a vial around her neck. "She's sleeping? Her loss. I'm Crystal and it's my turn now, handsome."

"Then let me oblige you with the best fuck of your life. You'll think you've exploded from pleasure." Laughing to himself, he thought she had no idea how true that statement would prove to be. To other humans, it would appear she'd had a heart attack or died from a drug overdose. He loved snacking on humans. Men he killed for the fun of it, the women he screwed and drained. They went with a smile on their faces every time.

Reaching around and picking up Crystal, one arm encircling

her waist, he whipped her about so she was facing the mirrored wall. She arched her hips. He reached around her and cupped her small breasts. Roughly kneading them he moved his hands down to pull up her dress.

"Isn't this a touching Hallmark moment," Kendrick drawled. He raked a glance over Solien who had his junk hanging out, ready to impale a brunette who'd been enjoying some type of illegal substance this evening. "I see you've already finished her friend. What did I tell you about killing humans?"

Solien ignored Kendrick and tried to get back to business, but it was hard to enjoy your dessert when you didn't know if you'd get a sword in the back or not. "Dude, seriously, back off and let me finish here." He spit at Kendrick.

"I cannot allow you to harm the girl, Solien. Now let her go, and we'll take a stroll out into the alley. Come along like a nice, foul-smelling demon." Kendrick languidly leaned against the wall, but Solien wasn't fooled, the Shadow Walker didn't miss anything, he was hyper-alert, clocking everyone in the club, not missing a single detail. Blasted Shadow Walkers, always ruining his fun.

Spoilsport, he thought as Kendrick pushed the girl away. She shook her head and stumbled off. Kendrick had the ability to bend humans' will as Solien did. Party-pooper Kendrick probably sent her home to sleep it off. It was surprisingly easy to manipulate some of these humans, their minds were weak.

Solien finished adjusting himself, and with a glance to the disappearing Crystal, shrugged and headed out the back door into the alley. "You could have at least let me have my taste, Kendrick."

The alleyway was empty except for two large metal dumpsters. The buildings across the way were dark. Some kind of offices, the workers having gone home hours ago. The air blew through the alley and he smelled urine. Disgusting humans, pissing on the walls. They were filthier than most animals. All deserved to die. Kendrick was running his mouth again.

"What, killing one human a night isn't enough for you, demon?"

He laughed. These pathetic Shadow Walkers thought they were a match for him. They were nothing more than dust on his boots. He'd existed thousands of years. A Walker was nothing more than a human with a bit of power—playtime for him.

Kendrick manifested an ice blade. Solien melted it with a thought before it reached his head. "I'm the cat, and you're the mouse. Better run for safety before it's too late," he taunted.

Kendrick kicked out, grazing his side. Solien grunted. He was a decent fighter for a so-called good guy, he outclassed many of the Day Walkers. The Englishman had been around since the 11th-century. He was a Norman, come to sack and conqueror England. The guy loved to fight but his ridiculous honor would be his downfall.

A fist to the face sent Kendrick to the opposite wall of the alley. The man jumped up, ready for more. "Come on, Solien. You're nothing more than a whipping boy for Dayne. Is that the best you've got?"

A lazy smile curved his lips. Yes, he served the god because of a battle he'd lost millennia ago. However, he got to kill disgusting humans, so it wasn't too bad of a deal, all things considered.

"At least Dayne doesn't set silly rules for us to follow. Unlike your precious Thorne. You don't know what you're missing, draining humans. They are simply delicious." Shooting a bolt of energy at Kendrick, he caught him in the knee, sending him to the ground of the dirty, trash-strewn alley.

The Shadow Walker fell to his knees. Solien laughed, on a high since draining the girl earlier.

"Dayne won't win. We'll take you down, one by one." Kendrick pushed back up on his feet.

"Seems to me, we're already winning this little war. Thorne doesn't have a clue what's in store for him. When this world is in ashes, he'll still be crying for his lost love. He doesn't really care what happens to humanity. He's only pretending to help the humans in hope that Luna will one day forgive him. Stupid god. Never let a woman rule you." Solien raked a glare at Kendrick. "I'm tired of playing with you." He took a deep breath, reaching inside himself and before the Shadow Walker could make a move, threw a ball of red energy at him. The red orb enveloped the Englishman. He let out an agonizing cry as his own energy was taken in by Solien's. The air crackled, the sky turned red, as storm clouds rolled in and thunder rolled. The red energy trickled back to Solien, tinged with purple from Kendrick's essence, soaking into his skin. When lightning flashed, his true form appeared, his wings spread wide as he drank in the Shadow Walker's life-force, draining him dry. Solien drew back a black ice dagger, taking two steps toward the Walker who was now on his knees too weak to defend himself.

With a rasp, his foe ground out, "Why do you hate us? Can't you see how bad it will go for you once the humans are destroyed? Why would Dayne be satisfied destroying one race? He'll destroy all the races, one by one until there's nothing left but a barren wasteland."

"Why? Humans are beneath demons, dirt on the soles of our feet. Who cares if they live or die? Let Dayne destroy all that he can. The demons will never be subjugated by one like him. We'll rise up and destroy him if he dares to try and enslave us as he's attempting to do with the fae."

Feebly, Kendrick reached out with a dagger from his boot, swiping at Solien. He laughed and sent out another blast of red energy, paralyzing the Shadow Walker, reveling in his distress. He breathed deeply, inhaling the red energy, now pulsing with color. Blue, purple, silver and green shimmered within the red, Kendrick's life-force. Full of power, Solien reveled in the taste. This Walker had been strong. Drunk on the English warrior's energy, Solien spared him one last glance, "Enjoy being a wraith for all eternity."

The Shadow Walker was no more. Solien heard the wind

change, roaring as thunder rolled and lightning flashed across the ruby red sky. He cared not. As Kendrick faded, his body shimmered, the colors leaching out over the damp, broken pavement, swirling to Solien to lap up. The warrior flashed in the storm and seemed to splinter into the colored dust of his essence. The heavens broke open, rain lashed down as if the very heavens were weeping at the loss. Solien threw back his head and laughed, the leathery black wings unfolding, letting the flame of energy snake through his veins, filling him with power.

Drunk on energy, he stood, spinning in a circle, arms outstretched to the sky. "Thorne, I've destroyed one of your beloved Shadow Walkers, won't you come out and play?" There was no reply from the persnickety god. He tried another tact, itching for a fight. "Terya, I've annihilated one of Thorne's precious warriors, won't you punish me?" She didn't deign to answer him either. Fine. In time, they would learn to heed him.

Voices penetrated his intoxicated senses. A tour group caught in the rain, rushing down the street looking for shelter. An ugly grin worked its way across his face.

How apropos. A ghost hunting pilgrimage. He'd give them a sight they'd never forget. Stepping out of the alleyway, his body softly glowing, as Kendrick's essence churned through his skin, mixing with Solien's red. The colors played across his skin, lending him an otherworldly glow. The sheep were almost to shelter, their salvation lay ahead in the form of a welcoming, dry pub. But it was not to be, not this day.

Today he would destroy. As he appeared in front of them, the group stopped, gaping at his appearance. There must have been forty humans huddled together, miserable with the rain pelting them. Before they could protest or scream, he willed himself to become the rain, dissolving into multi-colored raindrops. The tourists goggled at the spot where he'd stood, mouths agape. Solien burned through them all, stealing energy as their life-force filled him. As each tourist withered away, dropping dead on the wet cobblestones, his power swirled in the air. Sated, he reformed into his human guise. While he despised the humans, he wore the guise—much easier to destroy when you looked the part. The storm was dying down, turning to a gentle mist as the clouds parted and the moon shone on a pile of bodies—grandmothers and grandfathers curled together like puppies. With a snap, his wings lifted him to the air. He headed to Kessock. Tonight he would feast, drain the entire town dry. Let the humans pray, they would find no mercy. On this night the Lord of demons was among them, and his name was Solien.

❧ 17 ❧

Getting canned sucked. Monroe squinted at the blinding light blasting through the broken slats on the blind and pounding into his head like an ice pick. Well, okay it was a normal muted early winter day but to his throbbing head, he was on a greek island in the middle of summer. Cracking an eyelid a bit further, he rolled onto his side. Passed out on the couch again. Empty beer bottles were scattered throughout the flat like confetti and another empty Glenfiddich bottle seemed to be accusing him of being a loser.

What time was it? Hell, what day was it? The last thing he coherently remembered was coming home to his hovel laden with booze and drinking himself into a stupor then imbibing some more.

Groaning, he sat up, head in his hands, willing the room to stop spinning. Maybe some food would help. Staggering the few feet to the small galley style kitchen, he cracked open a cabinet. Nada. Not a can of soup or stale box of cereal in sight. When was the last time he'd been to the market? Damned if he could remember. Didn't even have fucking instant coffee on the counter. The sink was overflowing with dirty, disgusting dishes. Regarding the science experiment, he wondered if he should simply throw them out and start over. The fridge might contain something more promising. Cracking the door, he gagged, praying his stomach would hold it together. Curious, he opened the door wider. There was a Styrofoam container with some kind of moldy slime oozing onto the shelf. The other contender for the stench was what looked like a partially eaten sandwich. It was covered with blue, grey, and green mold. Kind of an interesting pattern. Too bad he didn't need any penicillin, he'd bet there was some incubating on his leftover chow. There was nothing else to eat, not even a bottle of mustard or jar of pickles. Sighing, he ambled down the short hallway to the loo.

If his head wasn't pounding so ferociously he would have high-fived the medicine cabinet. Salvation was at hand. A half-empty bottle of aspirin and a quarter bottle of Guinness on the sink. Washing down a handful, he breathed a bit easier as the flat beer hit his stomach.

Turning the water to hot, he got in, cleaned up and wrapped a towel around his hips. Chanced a peek in the mirror. Nice. Circles under his bloodshot eyes and he'd lost some weight, the hollows in his face making him look ten years older than his thirty-four.

Clothes were scattered across the floor of his bedroom. The bed was rumpled and he couldn't remember the last time he'd changed the sheets or done laundry. Nothing clean in the drawers except two mismatched socks. Sniffing a few shirts, he settled on a black t-shirt with a stain on the front. Rummaging in the closet, he managed to come up with a black sweater. It was faded almost grey but it would do. No clean boxers to be found. Guess he was going commando today. A pair of Levis 501s didn't smell too terrible so he pulled them on. Satisfied he'd dressed himself, he found his Doc Marten black boots under a pile of old pizza boxes.

A sound drew his attention. Insistent. Yep, a knock on his door. Had to be his old partner. Not like he had any other friends...except Robert, but that dude would poof into his living room, not bother with knocking. Wait a minute, Shamus would be on-duty. Maybe his landlord was tired of the aroma of eau du lost soul and was serving him with eviction papers? The rap sounded again, louder. Only one way to find out. The pounding in his head had settled down to a jackhammer—things were looking up.

When he opened the door, he couldn't have been more surprised.

"Hi, I'm Amy from across the hall. You're Monroe right?"

What a stunner. Hazel eyes were framed by short black hair. A pixie face smiled at him and for the briefest moment he wondered if she was a fairy princess, if they even existed. And that body. Made for sin.

"Uh, can I come in or are you just going to stand there with your mouth hanging open?"

Lust surged through him and he resisted the urge to pull her to him. Great, she was shooting him an odd look. Hell, had she spoken again, and he'd stood there like a complete idiot?

"Right, Amy. Sorry. Come in." Seeing his living room through her eyes he cringed. If she were smart, she'd run before mold grew on her too. "What can I do for you?" *Besides nail you on the sofa.*

"I wasn't sure when you worked, and I didn't want to bother you, but I don't know who else to ask..."

"Look, I'm no longer in law enforcement so I'm not sure what I can do for you."

God, the look on her face. Don't let her cry. Nothing was worse than when women cried. "Sit down. I'd offer you something to drink but seems I'm out of everything." A distasteful look was plastered across her face and her nose was wrinkled up as if she smelled something bad—which she probably did given the state of his flat. "Here, let me clear a spot on the couch. Sorry, haven't had time to clean either." Sitting in the only other chair in the room, he gestured to her to continue. "Like I said, I don't think I can help you but why don't you tell me what's on your mind?"

"A few weeks ago my little brother went missing. He's only eleven. Our parents died a long time ago, we'd been living with our grandmother but she passed away last year so it was the two of us. And he's a good kid. Never got into trouble, always came home after school when he was supposed to..." Her voice trailed off. "I'm sorry, it's—"

Damn it to hell, she sounded all choked up. Monroe jumped up from the chair. "Let me get you a glass of water." Practically ran the few steps to the tiny kitchen. Had to wash the glass before he could turn on the water. Maybe she'd have composed herself by the time he finished. If she was crying, she'd have to go back to her own flat for a tissue, he didn't have any to offer her. In fact he'd used the last of the toilet paper this morning. A dirty shirt would have to fill in if she needed to dry her eyes.

"Amy, go on." Hoping he'd cleaned all the crud off the glass, he handed the water to her.

"Thank you."

She drank half in two gulps, and he watched her wipe the back of her hand across her mouth. The pixie had full lips; he could imagine kissing her. It had been too long since he'd been with a woman. At this rate he'd be humping her leg in no time.

"Anyway, three weeks ago today, my brother Mark didn't come home from school. I work two jobs. One in the mornings and one at night so I can be there when he gets back in the afternoon. I figured he lost track of time at the library so I was concerned but knew I'd find him asleep in bed when I got home from work. Only he wasn't." Pausing, she drank the rest of the glass of water.

"Can I get you some more?"

"Oh, yes please."

Fetching another glass, the wish for a beer popped in his brain. Probably wouldn't be very neighborly to ask her if she had any. Thinking about it for a minute, he decided against it.

"Didn't you file a missing persons report? I'm sure the police would be better suited to helping you."

"I did. The nice man said he'd try and help but wasn't optimistic. Said there have been a great deal of missing people and they can't keep up with the cases."

"I'm sorry, but it's true. There are a lot of people missing. Maybe he ran away?"

Wrong thing to say by the way her cheeks turned pink, eyes flashing to a dark grey and she raised her voice at him. Sassy woman pushed his buttons.

"Mark didn't run away! Something's happened to him. Look I don't have much money, but it looks to me like you could use someone to clean this place and pop round the market to pick up some groceries. And do your laundry. You smell. Your flat smells. So what do you say?"

The pixie brat had the nerve to smile at him after she told him he stunk. "Given the fact I was booted from the force and I thought I'd open up me own private investigation firm, looks like you're my first client. Better do something or I might never leave this flat again."

They worked out a small fee. In addition, Amy would clean his place once a week, do the shopping if he left a list along with money and take care of his laundry. Hope she knew where to rent a backhoe, she'd need it along with gloves and a nose plug to clean it the first time. Tomorrow after lunch she'd face the garbage dump known as his place.

"Thank you Monroe. I know you'll find Mark for me. Leave a grocery list and money on the counter, and I'll take care of the shopping first. Then I'll start on the cleaning and laundry."

"I can't promise things will turn out okay but I'll do my best." Walking Amy to the door, he shut it behind her and thought in the meantime he'd better go get something to eat. Screw grocery shopping. Much better idea to hit the pub for a meal and couple of pints.

S aturday, November 4th

MONROE ROLLED OUT OF BED, CRANKED UP THE TUNES AND hit the shower. Hot water cascaded down his shoulders, sliding down his spine to his feet. Yep, the crud was an inch thick in here. He grimaced. Nope not gonna let the disgusting bathroom ruin his mood. After today, it would be livable again. The tiny soap shard gave a last gasp and vanished down the drain. Oh well, he was clean enough.

Shaking the water from his hair, he stepped out of the shower, snagging a semi-clean towel off the floor. A black sweater from the closet, a black tee shirt balled up in the corner by the dresser and a pair of jeans and yep, he was practically in what he thought of as his new uniform. Would be going commando again since all his skivvies were dirty but bonus, one pair of clean socks hiding behind his old university sweater. Shoving his feet into his boots, he banged the few kitchen cabinets open, peered into a fridge that smelled like a garbage dump, pulled the last brew from the counter, popped the top, and flopped on the couch to write out a list for Amy.

Chugging back half the can, he wrote out a grocery list. Slapping money on the counter next to the list, he grimaced at the hazmat location better known as his flat. She'd need a strong stomach to clean this pigsty. Grinning, he downed the rest of his beer, pulled a jacket on and made for the street to find out what had happened to her brother, Mark. *Note to self, stop on the way home, pick up more drinks.*

Glancing at the school photo, Monroe scowled. The kid looked much younger than eleven. Dressed in a clean navy blue uniform, his hair smoothed down—he certainly didn't look like a delinquent.

Monroe jogged to the Mercedes. First he'd start with the kid's school, Tollcross Primary, then the library, friends, hangouts and on from there. But before he ran all over town, he needed sustenance. He grabbed a couple of hand pies, crisps and a Coke from the corner mart to eat on the way. The gray stone building had stood for over one hundred years educating the little buggers. Not that he had anything against kids, just didn't want any of his own.

Shoving the Benz into a parking spot, he took the steps two at a time. The smell of a school never seemed to change. As it invaded his nostrils, he remembered his own illustrious escapades. The smack of ruler to skin was a lesson he and most of his mates never learned. Kids had the day off today, but administration folks were working. Shaking his head, he found the head teacher and enquired after Mark. The classrooms were small, maybe twenty children. He was directed to a cheerful room with Gaelic words posted on the walls. A conservative-looking man in his late forties stood as Monroe approached. He felt like a kid again, in trouble with the teacher. Schooling his face, he stuck out his hand. "Monroe MacDonald, investigator. Wondering if I could have a few minutes of your time, ask you some questions about Mark Weaver?"

"Nice to meet you, Mr. MacDonald. I'm Ailean Ross. Ah, yes, young Mark. Sad story, him missing and all."

The teacher had brown hair liberally laced with gray. Those little wankers would make anyone old before their time. There's a fate worse than death—teaching. Shuddering, he assessed the teacher. The guy had intelligent brown eyes and was dressed in khakis and a sweater with patches on the elbows. Ailean was slender, probably five foot seven and he had the beaten-down look of someone who's given up and is trying to make it through the day.

"His sister hired me to look into the boy's disappearance."

Ailean gestured to a normal sized chair next to his desk, "Please, sit. I'm not sure what else I can tell you. I already told the police everything I know."

Monroe sat, pulled out his notes and began questioning the teacher. After gathering all the information the guy could remember, he stood to leave. "Thank you Mr. Ross. You've been most helpful."

"Of course. I wish you the best of luck finding young Mark. So many lads these days decide to run off and end up on the streets."

And there was part of the problem. Everyone nowadays assumed when a kid disappeared that they'd gotten into trouble, become a delinquent. Hell, he was guilty of the same thinking. But this kid, he should have been an honor student, blowing stuff up at science fairs and winning chess matches, not missing.

Feet tapping on the worn floors, Monroe left the building. He had two good friends of Mark's to talk to, and the library. The kid didn't have any other hangouts.

Punching the button for the heated seats and steering wheel, Monroe stopped mid-motion. Wait a minute. He wracked his brain. Maybe he needed to lighten up on the whiskey he carried around in a flask, it was affecting his memory. In the year since he'd been working missing persons cases he'd found more questions than answers. Though the same Corporation kept popping up. He'd run into one road-block after another digging into them. Somebody had some serious stacks. Now that he was on his own, well, some of those official rules wouldn't hamper his investigations. Shamus had mentioned the name of a foster home last week... *What the hell was the name of the place?* Stabbing the buttons on the mobile, he fidgeted with the radio while waiting for Shamus to pick up.

"Hey mate, how goes it?" Monroe leaned back enjoying the heat seeping into his body. Whoever had invented ass warmers should be made a bloody Saint.

They did the meet and greet, and Monroe got down to business. "Remember that domestic you worked last week? The big place?"

He listened, nodding. "Right. Where was it? I think something strange is going on at some of these foster homes."

"Want me to check it out seeing as how you're Mr. Private Eye now?" Shamus smirked on the other end.

"Naw, I'm good. Going to head over and check it out now."

"Hey mate? You're not official anymore so make sure you call it in if you find anything, you feel me?"

Rolling his eyes, he shot back a suitable reply. "Sure partner. Catch you later."

Disconnecting, he turned his baby in the direction of The Wallace School for Children. Traffic was light. Rolling to a stop in front of the building, illegally parked, he hoped there wouldn't be a ticket waiting for him. Parking wherever he wanted as a cop had been a nice bene.

Taking the steps two at a time, he pushed the doors open and looked around for someone in charge. It was quiet. That was cocked up. Shouldn't there be brats running around making noise? He spotted an office off to the right. The discreet sign read *Administration*. Rapping on the door, he turned the knob. "Hello, anybody there?"

A rustling from behind some boxes had him looking to the

far corner of the room. A woman stood, smoothing her tweed suit and running a hand over her short mud colored hair.

"You startled me. I'm afraid we're closed today, you'll need to come back next week." She stared at him with an expectant look.

"Ms.?" he prompted.

"Mrs. Potts. And you are?" She pushed her glasses up her nose to stare down at him.

Old battleax. "Monroe MacDonald, investigator. It's awfully quiet. What'd you do, gag all the little tykes and lock them in their rooms?"

Mrs. Potts scowled at him. Good. When they were angry, they said more than they should.

She straightened up. "We would do no such thing to our lovely wards. It just so happens we've been very fortunate and don't currently have any children here at the school." She turned, dismissing him, filing paperwork from a huge stack reaching from the floor to his shoulder. If that towering stack fell—what a way to go, death by paperwork. Chuckling at his morbidity, he slapped Mark's photo on the desk. Dust motes floated up in the air, swirling in the pale sunlight filtering in through the curtains. "Have you seen this child? He's been missing for a month now."

The frumpy woman picked up the photo, holding it between her thumb and forefinger. She glanced at it and handed it back to him. "I'm sorry but I haven't seen him. Now if you'll excuse me I have a lot to do."

Reaching into his pocket to hand her his card, he stopped. Something stunk to high heaven here, and if he left his contact information it might tip off whoever was behind everything. "Yes, I'll let myself out. Thanks for your time." The rest of the holdings of this corporation would need to be looked into. He'd stake-out the place to make sure he was right but at this point Monroe felt the wrongness in his gut.

Walking down the hallway out into the frigid cold day, Monroe got into his car and pointed it home. Nailing a parking spot in front of his building, he grabbed the whisky and Guinness he'd stopped for on the way, careful of his purchases.

Opening the door to the flat, he stopped dead in the doorway. *Okay shut your yap before you look like a complete idiot.* Spotless. Maybe he should wipe his boots before walking in. Kicking his shoes off in the entryway, Monroe walked to the kitchen to put away his purchases. Inside various cabinets he found food. Actual, edible things to eat. He opened the fridge and lo and behold, milk, eggs, OJ, cheese, veg, and even a few frozen dinners. Damn. Amy was amazing. Who knew the sink actually gleamed? The counters weren't sticky and whadda ya know, the top of the stove was brown not black after all. Whoa. There on the counter sat a gleaming, sparkling coffee pot. No way. He could've sworn his sludge-filled pot should be labeled hazardous waste. A freshly washed mug, spoon, and hello, coffee all ready for him. How the hell she'd gotten everything so clean was beyond him. Might oughta be a bit embarrassed but naw, he was too psyched over the clean smell to worry she thought him a total slob.

Opening the door to the small bathroom his mouth opened and closed again like a fish gasping for water. She must have used some serious elbow grease to get everything so spotless. He marveled, opening the cabinet under the sink to find it stocked with toilet paper. Yes! Giddy, Monroe beat feet to the bedroom. Again, clean. He could see the carpet. It was gray, huh. The bed was made, freshly laundered clothes stacked on the dresser, wood shining underneath.

This was the best thing that had happened to him in a while. Feeling a bit of a pansy for being so excited over a clean living space, he went out of his flat, across the hall and knocked on Amy's door.

"Amy, I don't know what to say, the place looks amazing and the groceries. Thank you." He grinned at her. "But I have to ask —the coffee pot was green and the sludge was hard as a brick..."

She laughed, running a hand through her pretty black hair, "I bought you a new one since there was some money left over. The change is on the kitchen counter. Leave me a list on the counter and I'll do the same next week." She broke off.

Hell, he was such an idiot. Going on about his clean flat when she wanted to know what he'd found out. Standing up straighter, he got to the subject at hand, "Amy, I don't have much yet, but I'll tell you what I do know."

Motioning him inside, he looked around with frank curiosity. Her flat was the mirror image of his but so different. Hers was welcoming. With girly furniture and paintings on the walls and Mark's stuff scattered here and there. She had pillows on the couch and blankets to pull over you when you sacked out watching the match on the telly. Maybe she'd trade? Swinging his attention back to her as she motioned to the sofa, he noted the slender build, too thin really as if she didn't eat enough. He should find a reason to feed her. Amy perched in a chair across from the sofa, folding her arms across her chest, a hopeful look on her face. The woman had dark circles under those attractive hazel eyes. Shaking his head, he spoke. "I went to Mark's school, visited both of his friends, talked to several folks at the library who remembered him and ended up at a foster home."

She jumped up from the chair, hands on her hips, face red with indignation. "I work three jobs and bust my ass to take care of Mark, I would never in a million years, no matter how bad things get out there, give him up to some wretched children's home..."

Hold up, he gestured with his hand. "The place was something else I'm working on, I wasn't implying anything." He kept his voice quiet when he really wanted to yell back at her.

"Oh, okay." She sighed. "I'm sorry. I didn't mean to shout. It's been a very long day and I'm not sleeping well." Amy sat back down in the chair, the anger draining out of her, turning to resignation.

"As I was saying, he's a good kid. Everyone I talked to likes him. Everything I heard makes me believe he did not run away but that he was taken. Why or by whom I don't know...not yet. But I will find out what's happened to him. You have my word."

Her hand fluttered at her throat and she discreetly wiped a tear from the corner of her eyes. "Thank you, Monroe. I know you'll find Mark."

Standing to leave, he awkwardly patted her shoulder. He sucked at this comforting stuff. If she wanted a quick shag, he could do that but niceness and comfort, he was way out of his depth with her. She was too nice, not to mention she lived across the hall, so he'd not be putting the moves on her anytime soon. "Uh, I'll let you know when I have more information. Thanks again for everything you did today."

❀

BLOODY FUCKING GREAT. RAWLINS HAD BEEN SUMMONED TO Dayne's throne room. He grimaced seeing some poor Day Walker he didn't know chained and opening the doors. Better him than me.

"Dayne. How may I be of service?" He bowed, hiding his distaste.

"I had thought the time you spent doing penance would have been enough of a lesson. Now I hear some human woman has intervened with Robert. What is the meaning of this?" Dayne was sprawled across his throne. Today he was dressed in a gold toga that blended in to the gold ornate chair so he looked like a blob with a head. On his head was a large gold grown studded with rubies. The overall effect was one of a huge sunburst filling the room.

"Milord, the woman is used by the minions to help spot Shadow Walkers. If I kill them all, they will be at a disadvantage when trying to kill something they cannot see."

The god waved a dismissive hand. "Whatever. Robert is weak now—human. Should be easy for you to kill him."

"Consider it done. I killed him once, I'll kill him again.

Though this time instead of hanging, I'll behead him—more fun that way."

"Get it done and don't screw it up."

"Of course, Milord. With your leave?"

The blob, er, god, waved his hand, then spoke before he could dematerialize. "Put a price on this human woman's head. I want everyone looking for her. Find her and we find Robert."

"It will be done." Rawlins nodded and flashed back to his home, Huntington Castle, situated on the English Welsh border to come up with a plan.

❧ 19 ❧

In the morning Robert had to take care of ship business while Maggie ate and dressed. When he returned he found her sitting in a chair by the fire. Replaying the conversation from last night, he couldn't help it. A fully belly laugh burst out. *Legend.* Hadn't heard the term since his pirate heyday. "Sorry. But it is rather humorous."

She blinked at him. "What?"

"Me, a legend."

The lass turned a fetching shade of red. Matched the color of her hair.

"Everyone talks about how many you've killed. They're all scared of you. Even Rawlins and Solien—when they talk about you, there's a grudging respect you can hear in their voices. So why wouldn't I be afraid of you? They're the scariest people I know."

"Point taken."

"You do seem rather normal and you haven't cut me up into pieces yet so maybe you're not as bad as they say. We'll see. Something's been bothering me—I thought your kind couldn't die unless you were stabbed in the heart or something? So why exactly were you at the end of a rope?"

"It seems you are rather well informed. I promise..." He crossed his fingers over his heart for dramatic flair. "To tell you the story of the hangman's noose when we're at my castle in Wales. 'Tis a long tedious tale and will help pass the time. Agreed?"

"Fine by me." Getting up, she stretched. And as she did, her shirt rode up, exposing the creamy skin of her stomach. Gods, he wanted to nuzzle her belly button and lick circles up and down that tantalizing skin. She moved in a tentative manner, like a mouse, afraid she'd be eaten at any time. An awful way to live.

"So, after I ran I looked for a ship. Nobody would take me. I don't have a passport or any money, but I can cook and clean. Each one I tried said no. I couldn't really blame them. It's a big risk to take. Then I came to the last ship in port, yours. Same story. I didn't know what to do. I sat there for a while. A raven was flying around and drew my attention to the open hatch so I climbed in and passed out. Your men found me. Now here I am."

"'Tis quite a tale. What was the name of the one who betrayed you?" So as not to tip his hat, he purposely feigned nonchalance when he asked her.

"Josh. Why?"

"Just wondered what a loser such as he would be named." She looked at him for a few seconds.

"We're docking. Would you like to come up and watch?" At her look, he laughed. "Don't look so surprised. It's not as if you're some kind of prisoner here. You are my guest, and I intend to aid you. If it's a new identity, job, and place to live you're after, I will make those things happen." Damnation. Shock reverberated through him—he meant it and would help her, let her go, and never tell her anything. Doing so would put her at risk. To ensure her safety, she should stay with him. That thought and its implications made him uneasy, almost ill in his gut so he thought about her naked in his bed instead.

"Come on then." Ever the gentleman, he helped her into a

coat as they left the cabin. Robert led her down the passageway and up the stairs.

It was good to be outside. The air had bite. The wind played with Maggie's hair as she breathed deeply and turned her face up to the weak sunshine. She caught him staring at her. "I rarely got to go out during the day. It's nice to have fresh air."

"It is." Was strange to breathe, the sensation felt unnatural. Being made of energy one didn't need to breathe, you simply were.

A shout drew his attention. "Aye, lads, take her in gently."

"So this is Wales? You said something about delivering a package?" The frank curiosity in her eyes filled him with the urge to tell her all about himself.

Wait a minute, you're still mad at her for ruining your life and now you want to be all flowers and candy? Get a grip, man. "This body of water is Liverpool Bay. See those rocks? That's Lady Emily's Tower, part of my estate. Gwrych castle is to the east. Once the lads unload the cargo, we'll go and meet a collector. I'm delivering a piece he's been after for a very long time."

"You live in a castle?"

"'Tis been in the family for generations. No one's left but me so I keep it even though I spend quite a bit of time in Scotland, my heart will always belong to Wales. I'll give you the grand tour when we arrive."

"Isn't it tempting to keep some of these priceless artworks for yourself?"

"Maggie, my lady, you have no idea. In a previous life I was a pirate, as you know and very accomplished at my profession. Nowadays rich collectors trade on the black market and I deliver the goods. Mostly a transport job. Not nearly as exciting as it used to be." He paused to watch his crew. "You'll be safe at Gwrych. Once we're settled in, we can figure out what you want to do and make it happen." The part about killing every minion, Day Walker, demon, and goblin who'd ever spoken a harsh word to her, well, he left that out. There would be a special punishment for good ole' Josh. "In town, we can pick up some clothes for you."

She looked startled. "That's not necessary."

He brushed away her protests. "Maggie, you need them and I'll take care of it. I've plenty of money, it's no bother." That quieted her.

The ship came into port and loathe to leave her side, he let the crew handle everything. On one hand he was furious and wanted nothing to do with her and yet another part of him wanted to keep her close, destroy all those who'd harmed her. What he wouldn't give to see a real smile march across her face not the ghost of one. Still pondering that thought, they walked down the gangplank.

"Maggie, I have a car waiting to take us shopping. Then a stop by my collector and then home sweet home. Shall we?" Holding out his arm, she gave a small start before hesitantly wrapping her arm through his. Poor lass, still had the deer in the headlights look. It would last a while until she felt secure and safe.

"Where are you going, milady?" Maggie was walking straight for a big green Range Rover.

"I don't know, I guess I thought this might be yours. Don't all you guys drive those giant SUVs?"

Pointing to the right of the behemoth, her mouth dropped open as he swept her a bow and nodded to the driver. "If milady pleases?" The Porsche sedan was black as sin, low slung to the ground and almost purred as he helped Maggie in the backseat. Gods, he loved beautiful cars.

"Does it meet your expectations?"

"Are you kidding? It smells amazing, and I think I could sink into the seat and never leave." Silence filled the car on the short drive into town. Hiding in corners, being unobtrusive, Maggie was always quiet. How many times had he wished for a woman to stop talking and now that he had one that rarely spoke, he wanted her to talk. About anything. Everything. But she was over as far from him as she could be. Hell, if someone opened the door, she'd fall out on her head.

The shops on the outskirts of the docks would have what they required. The driver pulled up in front of an upscale shop.

"Let's get you some proper clothes and then I'm burning the rags you're wearing."

As if dreading what was coming, Maggie grimaced. The bell above the door tinkled as they walked in. Watching her out of the corner of his eye, she plucked at the shabby clothes. No matter.

"How may I assist you?" The shop girl simpered over. Maggie stiffened. Interesting. Not as unaffected by him as she claimed. Perhaps he was growing on her.

Maggie was mute. No worries. He'd take control of this skirmish. "We require a wardrobe, top to bottom. Money is no object. I'm going to sit in this comfortable chair while you ladies take care of business.

"May I offer you a beverage?" The chit held out two glasses of red wine.

"We'd love one." Robert took the wine and handed a glass to Maggie. "Darlin' you look like you're about to face a firing squad. Come now, shopping can't possibly be that terrible can it?"

"I've never been shopping..." her voice was barely a whisper and he had to lean in close to hear her.

"Never? Well, there's really nothing to it. The shop girl will bring you all kinds of clothes, shoes, jackets, and undergarments to try on. Simply tell her what you like and what you don't. See? Easy peasy." He smiled to reassure her. "I could help you try on the undergarments if you'd like?"

When she blushed, she turned the most fetching shade of pink. "No thank you. You already took advantage of my unconscious body."

"Well milady, this time you wouldn't be unconscious now would you?"

The shop girl reappeared and saved her from answering.

"The dressing room is this way. I've already picked out a number of items."

Maggie tugged his sleeve. "Yes?"

"How did she know my size? I don't have a clue. This is very overwhelming."

"I find when faced with a situation I'm not sure of to simply dive in and turn myself over to the experts." Her eyes were huge, a look of distress on her face. All resistance fled as he leaned down and planted a quick kiss on her lips. Gods, they were soft. Before he could properly enjoy the velvet skin, she jumped back, a shy smile lighting up her face. "Right. Miss? I'm ready." The clerk giggled as Maggie fell in line behind her.

Robert settled in to the chair, sipping his wine and half watched the news, wishing he had his powers so he could hear what they were saying. Clerks scurried to and fro, arms laden with all kinds of women's things.

Time passed. Another identically dressed clerk refilled his wine and brought him crackers and cheese. Thank the gods. If they took too much longer he'd bloody well starve.

At last, he heard the creak of a door and a flurry of women emerged. Wow, his mouse had been transformed into a beautiful woman. He stood. Dressed in dark jeans, a thick cream-colored fisherman's sweater, black riding boots and a jewel-toned scarf tied around her hair...well, he'd like to peel everything off, one item at a time.

"Maggie. You are a vision. Absolutely lovely. I feel bad we're headed home instead of out on the town to show you off." Standing, he walked towards her, walking around her and lifted the end of her hair. "I like your hair this way."

For the first time ever she shyly smiled up at him. "They're the nicest things I've ever owned." She smoothed her hands over her jeans. The clerk approached, holding a wool coat and soft black leather backpack. The coat was dove gray and brought out the flecks of silver in her green eyes.

"I'm ready to go. Thank you Robert. I'll find a way to repay you."

"A moment lass. You'll need more than what you're wearing." The head clerk was at his elbow before he said a word. "Sir?"

"Were there other things she liked?" The shop girl nodded so fast he thought she'd get whiplash. The smell of a big commission practically had the clerk drooling. "Capital. We'll take the lot. Throw away the clothes she was wearing when we arrived."

"Yes, right away. Of course."

A small hand patted his forearm. "It's too much. I'll never wear all these things."

He rolled his eyes. "You have to be the first woman I've met who'd turn down clothes and frippery."

"Miss, a glass of wine to go as well." Robert handed over his credit card, paid and kept topping off Maggie's glass so she wouldn't hyperventilate when the total cost rang up.

Robert called the driver and they loaded up the car, Maggie protesting the entire time. He pressed the to go cup of wine in her hand. "Drink, you'll quit fussing."

"This is so excessive. I've never owned this much stuff in my whole life."

She tried to hide the gleam in her eye. Ah, now he had her. Food, especially fresh fruit, frocks and what? There had to be something else. He'd figure out what it was. Then he'd start on his plan to kiss her again. Woo her. Get her to come out of her shell.

Bloody hell—he wasn't mad at her any longer. In face, he wanted to make her smile. Do whatever it took to see her blush.

"I think the car is riding a bit low, James." He smirked at Maggie. "Oof." An elbow to the gut shut him up and he rubbed the offending spot, chuckling. Wisely, the driver stayed silent.

"Who is this collector we're going to meet, is he like you?"

"No, he's human. Very reclusive, very wealthy. His estate is on the way to mine. We're coming into view of it now. See? Over there."

"That's a house? For one person? Who needs that much space?" The disapproval in her voice stopped him cold. Goldstein's place was a quarter of the size of Gwrych. Would she think poorly of his home?

"It's been in his family for hundreds of years. I don't think it's a question of does he need it but rather keeping tradition alive." A frown on her face, she looked out the window as the car turned down a long driveway.

"Should I stay in the car?"

"Not at all. He'll be intrigued I've brought a guest. I've never brought anyone with me."

Robert caught her half-smile. She was pleased. He bounded out of the car before James could get to her door. "Allow me." Offering his arm, Maggie exited the car. The driver handed him a small, neatly wrapped package. "We won't be long." The chauffer nodded as he got back in the car and opened up a newspaper.

The door was opened before he could knock. "Welcome, Mr. Bartholomew. If you and your guest will follow me to the study, Mr. Goldstein will be with you shortly. A drink perhaps?"

"No thank you, we're fine." A new Matisse hanging on the wall drew his attention while Maggie picked the chair in the corner of the room, away from everything. Before he could escort her to another, one closer to him, the door opened.

"Robert, lovely to see you again, old chap." Mr. Goldstein rolled in, carried on a cherry red wheelchair. Rumor had it the man was injured during some kind of illegal archeological dig in the Middle East years ago.

Robert stood and shook his hand. "I like the red wheels better than that god-awful hunter green you were riding around in last time I was here."

The big, bass laugh startled Maggie. "And who do we have here?" Rolling over to her, he extended his hand, patting hers.

"Hello, I'm Maggie, a friend of Robert's."

"Now lassie, Rob is a scoundrel so you must keep a wary eye

on him. I smell a story about how you two met but alas, I can tell by the look on Rob's face, he's anxious to get home so it will have to wait for another time. You will come visit again, won't you charming Maggie?"

"I'd love to."

And in that small exchange, he was smitten. A shy, tentative smile put his infamously grouchy client at ease. Someone like that could be useful in other negotiations. The competition would be so busy trying to get her to talk, he'd steal the treasures out from under their noses.

"I suppose you'll be wanting this before we take our leave?" He tossed the package in the plain brown wrapper to Mr. Goldstein who snagged it out of the air. Wheeling over to his desk, he reverently opened it. Maggie inched closer, curious to see what was so important. The client tossed a small bag to him.

Diamonds. Easy to exchange and transport. Maggie's gasp had him turning around. "It's amazing. Didn't I read something about that piece..."

"Robert, my boy, as always, you've delivered. The piece is brilliant, isn't it?"

He chuckled. The necklace was an ornate diamond affair rumored to have belonged to Marie Antoinette, very pricey. "You remember correctly. It came available at a certain auction. Would you like to hold it?"

"No way, that thing is cursed, and I've had enough bad luck to last a lifetime."

"I don't believe in curses." Laughing, he tossed it from hand to hand as she backed away, a look of horror on her face.

Saying their goodbyes, Maggie shivered in the icy air. Buttoning up the top of her coat, he kissed her. Progress. This time she lingered for a few seconds before stepping back from him. Her face flushed.

James was waiting, car running, door open. Sliding into the warmth of the heated interior, she sighed and was it his imagination or did she sit a few inches closer than before?

"Right. I'm famished. Are you hungry?" She nodded. "'Tis a short drive. An early dinner will be waiting when we arrive as it seems we've missed lunch. Afterwards I thought I might show you my home, there is a large hothouse with all kinds of fruit and vegetables growing."

"I'd like that very much." She rubbed her shoulder.

"How's the shoulder, does it pain you?"

"A bit stiff but much better." Twenty minutes later, they turned onto Gwrych estate. She leaned forward in her seat as the castle came into view. "You weren't kidding. It's a monstrosity. At any moment I expect ghosts, not like you, but the ones with chains and sheets to come moaning out of the windows. It's kinda creepy, don't you think?"

"You wound me, milady." He held his hand over his heart in mock horror as he helped her out of the car.

"Gareth. This is Maggie. Without him, the place would turn to a pile of rubble."

"Come in out of the cold and have a cup of hot tea." Gareth took the bags from Robert and led them into the great hall. Maggie's eyes were huge as she took in the size of the place. It did take some getting used to. The place was rather large if you were unaccustomed to it. She stopped dead in her tracks as they passed the library. Ha, he'd found her final weakness—books. Clothes, fruit and books. Now he could prepare a strategy. Everything he needed was right here.

"Better not gape too long, Gareth might think you've gone daft." She scowled at him. "Don't worry Maggie, after you get settled in you can peruse the library to your heart's content before dinner."

"I've never seen this many books. Growing up, I might have had one. It's amazing to see so many books in one place."

Tragic. She'd had a difficult life. He'd fill his home from floor to ceiling if only she'd smile for him. "Let's show you to your room. Gareth lead on." Following his retainer up the stairs to the fourth floor, he walked behind Maggie, watching the sway of her hips as she climbed the stairs. What a fine arse she had. Would she gasp in pleasure if he reached up, grabbed hold and gave a gentle squeeze? Probably backhand him was more like it... though he'd seen her admiring him when she thought he wasn't looking.

They stopped at the second to last room. "Your room, miss." Gareth opened the heavy door, gesturing for Maggie to enter.

"Oh wow. This is amazing. It's huge!" She spread her arms out, turning around in a circle, taking it in. The room was done in shades of purple and cobalt blue. The bed was an enormous four-poster, in fact all the furniture was enormous and made of the same dark wood. Acquired the furnishings when he'd plundered a French ship. Belonged to a King. As Maggie wandered around the room touching and admiring the furnishings, he admired her. Gareth placed her bags by the dresser, nodded to Robert and left, quietly closing the door behind him.

The wretch had gotten under his skin, and he was afraid he was growing to like the itchy sensation, the awareness of her being there at all times.

She entered the en-suite bath and he heard her exclamation. "This is the most decadent bath I've ever seen. I may never leave the bathroom." A large claw footed tub sat apart from a shower that could easily accommodate ten people. There were two sinks done in the same white and gray marble. Gareth had been efficient as usual. A large array of ladies' bath products lined the counter.

"We had a communal shower at the house. I've never had my own bathroom. And in all my life I've always wanted to take a bubble bath. I know what I'm doing after dinner."

Maggie's long red hair trailing over her breast into the bubble-filled water. For the rest of the night he would be thinking of her in there without him. *Nice. Hope I can hold an intelligent conversation with her and not drool during dinner.*

"You can stay in the tub until you're as wrinkled as a raisin if it pleases you. I'm in the room across the hall. Dinner's in an hour. I'll knock on your door to take you down to the dining room. I'd hate to find you a week from now, dead from starvation, in some dusty unused wing of this 'monstrosity' as you called it." He grinned.

"I might have been a bit hasty in my judgment." She said in a prim and proper voice.

He roared with laughter. "If I'd known a simple bubble bath would cheer you, we would have taken care of it sooner." He bowed and let himself out of the room.

here, I'll knock on your door to take you down to the dining
room. Or hide behind your own curtain now freed from staring, in some diary, an end. Why or that? monotonously as you
hadn't. He got up.

"I might have seen a bit later in my judgment," she said in a
firm and proper voice.

He turned with bad joke. "No." Even a simple phone call
would drop you, so would. Take all of care of a scotch." He
bowed and let himself out of the room.

M aggie couldn't believe it. The one person in the
world who terrified her more than anyone else...was
the man she now entrusted with her life. The man
she wanted. The thought sunk in and she sat down hard on the
sumptuous bed, groaning in pleasure. The startling realization
hit her—she wasn't afraid of Robert. He'd been true to his word.
Not only had he saved her but he'd brought her to his home and
promised to help. Unconsciously, her fingers went to her lips.
He'd kissed her. The kiss traveled down to her toes and made her
want to crawl inside him before fear pulled her back. A little
time was all she needed. Yes, she wanted him. At least she could
admit the truth.

It was surreal to be in his home. She rotated her shoulder. It
ached but was getting better fast. Robert had insisted on putting
saltwater on the wound each day. Stung like a bitch but she had
to admit, the seawater had healing properties. In the course of a
few days her life had changed dramatically. The shock of learning
the Shadow Walkers and Robert were the good guys—the ones
working to save humans, it was nothing short of astonishing.
The revelations had rocked her world, turned her thoughts
upside down and inside out. She felt sick to her stomach that

she'd unwittingly helped destroy men on the right side in this hidden war.

Bruce and his men must be hunting for her. Would Ned be blamed? Robert told her she could stay here at Gwrych as long as she wanted. Or he'd find her a job and set her up in a flat wherever she chose. If anyone had made that offer a couple of days ago she'd have jumped at it. Now...well, not being afraid of Robert carried other consequences. Damn it, she wanted to be near him. Charming and old-fashioned in a nice way, she knew deep in her bones he could keep her safe. And her body certainly wanted him. The only question was did he feel the same? The guy was rich, immortal and gorgeous. Let's see what did she bring to the table? Oh yes, she was homeless, jobless, hunted by the bad guys, poor, and average looking on her best day. Why would he be interested in someone like her? *Stop kidding yourself. He's a good guy, he's being nice and helping you and you are a nitwit if you think there could be something between you two. Right. And a tiger could date a bunny rabbit.*

On that sour note, she blew out a sigh, stood and unpacked, her purchases taking up three of the dresser drawers. What did one wear to dinner in an old, moldy, castle? She was wearing nicer clothes than she'd ever owned so with a shrug, she decided not to change. The rest of her stuff, she took with her into the bathroom and placed on the counter. Dragging a brush through her tangles, she shook her head at the reflection. Spying the scarf Robert had used to tie her hair back, she picked it up and deftly fashioned a high ponytail. Didn't help much, she still looked old. Tired and worn. Washing her face, she tried a small smile and jumped at the soft knock on the door and the voice on the other side. "Maggie, dinner's almost ready."

Breathing in deep, she tiptoed over to the door uttering a prayer for strength and opened it. "Great, I'm starved." Good heavens, he looked like a movie star standing there. He'd changed into black wool trousers, a deep red silk shirt and his hair was loose around his shoulders. Revise that. The devil incarnate was more like it.

"You look lovely. Shall we?" As before, he offered his arm and escorted her down the hallway. "Thank you." Walking arm in arm with him made her feel like someone important.

Her stomach clenched at the mouth-watering smells wafting towards them. *Oh my god, I smell citrus. Oranges.* Wiped the corner of her mouth to make sure she wasn't drooling.

"What's for dinner?" She barely noticed the furnishings as they descended the stairs to the second floor, turned down a hallway and came to double doors. Robert pushed them open. "Given your fondness for fruit. Stephan has prepared a few courses. We'll start with grapes and cheese and crackers. May I offer you a glass of champagne?"

"Grapes. Red and green. Oh, yes, I'd love a glass. Sorry I was distracted."

Would he think she was trashy if she dumped the platter of grapes onto her plate? Probably. Instead she only took a few of each color as he poured their drinks. There was a roaring fire flanked by several chairs in the pretty room. It was small but cozy and there were two massive doors on the other end leading to the dining room if she remembered correctly. Stuffing the grapes into her mouth she vibrated with pleasure. The sweetness popping in her mouth. Not caring what he thought, she took the tray of goodness over to a chair by the fire, ignoring his laughter. Scowling she turned to him, hands on her hips. "What? I'm hungry."

The man walked over to her like a model on the runway. Fully aware of his appeal, he sat opposite her. "No need to scowl. I wasn't laughing at you. It's been a long time since I've seen a woman enjoy fruit as much as you do."

"I guess the woman you usually see have plenty to eat. I'm not like them." Frost coated her words and she was surprised they didn't crack and fall to the floor as they came out of her mouth.

"No, Maggie. You're not like any of them. I..." He didn't finish as Gareth entered the room. "Milord, Miss. Dinner will be served shortly." Robert nodded to the man.

"What were you going to say?"

If she hadn't been staring at his face she would have missed the fleeting look of horror before he hid it. "I was going to say, you're not like other women and I'm glad of it. Now finish your grapes and let's eat." Glad. That was a good sign. Maybe he was interested in her? Her inner voice piped up. Quit acting like you're his, he's only doing what he'd sworn to—protect the human. To think she was only a job to him hurt more than she would have guessed.

Swallowing, she stood and said in her best fake cheerful voice. "I'm curious to see what else we're having for dinner."

Robert led the way, pushing the doors open. They had to be twelve-feet tall. The room was cozy with four chairs surrounding a round table. Each chair was covered in chocolate velvet and looked like you could fall asleep in it. He pulled out her chair and took the chair across from her. The table was set with a deep citron tablecloth with some type of jacquard print. There were crystal goblets on the table like the champagne glass she was holding. It looked like real silver though she'd never used sterling flatware so she wasn't sure but it all looked horribly expensive. The dishes were cream colored with black and red and gold diamonds and vines around the border. Don't break anything. These dishes must have cost more than what you made in a year waitressing.

The room was lit by sconces on the wall, candles were scattered across the sideboard and table, this was a room for lovers. Maybe he wanted to keep her out of sight? The thoughts were forgotten as a man came in bearing plates and a mouth-watering aroma reached her nose.

"Stephan. This is Maggie. Stephan is an amazing cook, among other things." The man smiled at her. He looked to be in his early thirties with salt and pepper hair, a pockmarked face and a limp. Maybe five eight. Kind of like her...he looked like he'd lived a rough life. Might Robert be truly able to help her? Might he be attracted to her?

The plates were set in front of them as Stephan withdrew. Roast surrounded with potatoes and carrots. Fresh rolls, butter, and the fruit. Oh, the fruit. Would it be wrong to leap onto the table and snatch the platter like some wild thing? Rejecting the idea, she sat still letting her eyes take in the feast. The dish held pineapple, mango, papaya, pomegranates, and...oranges. She looked up into those bottomless dark blue eyes to find him holding her gaze.

As she dove in, drowning in his eyes, the irises deepened to the color of a moonless night telling her safety awaited if only she'd let go and fall, forget everything that had happened. No longer be afraid.

When he cleared his throat she felt the heat creeping up her neck, catching fire on her cheeks. "May I offer you some fruit?"

"Are you kidding? I might devour the entire plate."

He chuckled and scooted the china platter across the table to her. While she took healthy servings of each fruit, he served her roast, veggies, a roll, and butter. With a longing look at her fruit, she decided she should eat the hot foods first. Well, after a bite of pineapple and mango...hell, after a taste of each. Juice dribbled down her chin and she reached up to wipe it but was blocked by a finger...his finger.

"Allow me, milady."

Chills swirled around her spine hearing the gruffness in his voice. Ever so slowly he wiped the moisture, drawing the tip of his finger across her bottom lip, her stomach doing flip-flops while her brain raced in a thousand directions. Why couldn't she read his face? Did he think she was a slob? It wasn't that kind of look. It was a look of—hunger for lack of a better word.

Hell, it'd been so long since she'd been with a man, she couldn't even decode the signals anymore. Not that she ever could. Whenever a guy was interested it always surprised the hell out of her.

"There. That's better."

Oh my gosh, as he pulled his finger away he put it in his mouth and sucked off the juice. Part of her, much lower south, tingled in anticipation. A tiger. That's what he looked like as he smiled and speared his roast as if nothing out of the ordinary had taken place. A million questions filled her brain. Questions she'd never have the nerve to ask. Instead she picked up a wine-glass he'd filled while she salivated over the fruit and drank, draining half the glass. It was a rose. She didn't know anything about wine except if she liked it or not and this one tasted like summer. Maggie tried not to smack her lips or gulp the rest of it down. Following his lead, she ate her meat and veggies. They were very tasty but simply an excuse to move on to her beloved fruit. Growing up, she'd been lucky to have the odd apple or banana. There was never fruit for the taking.

Pushing her plate to the side, she pulled the fruit platter in front of her and piled the unused butter dish high. The pome-granate seeds, she spooned in a small dish. The small globes were a tart explosion in her mouth, the experience the equivalent of what she thought Christmas might be like. Taking a bite, she almost swooned at the delightful taste. Another sip of wine and she decided to ask one of her questions.

"Can you really help me? Bruce and the others must be looking for me. What if they find me?"

He put his fork down, sat back in his chair and pinned her with his gaze. "Maggie. I will help you. Might you want to stay here for a while?"

No, no, no. Didn't want charity. Would earn her keep. "I can't. I need to pay my own way. I don't want your pity."

"Why ever would you think I pity you? On the contrary. I think you are brave and strong and beautiful and fearless."

Beautiful? Fearless? Her? Were they talking about the same person? "Until we arrived here, I lived in fear pretty much every day of my life. I only ran because I'd rather die escaping than die alone in a dirty basement."

"As I said, strong, brave and fearless. You may feel fear but you overcame it when you took the chance to run. Being fearless doesn't mean not being afraid. It's having the courage to make the hard choice. Something I think you're rather good at."

"Oh. Sorry."

He waved her apology away. "Eat your fruit. To answer your other question, I've put the word out you were drowned in the sewers. If they are still on your trail, I'll take care of each and every one of them. Don't spare a thought for any of those despicable creatures. I will protect you. With me, you are safe."

Could it be true? "Even from Solien?"

"Let the demon spawn try. I'll relish cutting him into tiny pieces and feeding the fish."

Thinking while she chewed, she stabbed another piece of mango. "Can we help Ned? The guy could have turned me in but didn't. I met him when he worked at a hostel I used to crash at when I could afford it. It's how I learned of the tunnels. I'd hate for anything to happen to him because of me."

The look he shot her was razor sharp. "What is Ned to you? Boyfriend?"

Confused, she answered, "No. A friend, that's all. I don't want him to get hurt because he got caught up with them. The guy was never very smart and the offer of getting off the streets, a hot meal, and someplace safe to sleep would have been too good to resist." He gave her a curt nod. "I never finished school so I'm probably not qualified for much but do you think I could help you save others?"

"What do you have in mind?"

"There are other places. Places like where I was held. I've heard Bruce talking. One night, Solien and Rawlins were in the living room talking while I cleaned the kitchen. They kept their voices low but I heard them say there were other houses used to lock away others like me. And buildings where they were experimenting with some kind of farms for humans. What they're doing is wrong and I want to stop them, however I can."

Before he could reply, Gareth came in to clear their plates. The man was older than Stephan, his hair a silvery gray with friendly brown eyes that reminded her of a big, shaggy dog. On his right hand he was missing two fingers. The sun had weathered and lined his face like someone who'd lived their entire lives outdoors. Gareth reached out for the fruit plate.

"You can leave it, I'll finish off the rest of the fruit, thanks Gareth."

"As the lady wishes." He winked at her. "Milord, shall I bring another bottle of wine and dessert?"

"Yes, I think Maggie will be ecstatic when she sees what you've made for dessert."

As Gareth left, Robert had been staring off into the distance. He had a serious look on his face, she wasn't sure what to expect.

"You know Maggie, if any other woman told me she wanted to help, there's no way I would have let her." Holding up a hand, he stopped her as she fumed and sat still, hands under her thighs. "But. You can strike where it would harm them most. I don't want you going into any of these places, it's too dangerous. However, I think you could be a tremendous asset to us in this war...though I have one condition that is nonnegotiable."

Looking across the table at him, she was afraid to ask. What could he want of her that he would look so stern and forbidding? Fear and anger made her voice sound low, broken. "What's your condition?"

"Safety first. Fully protected. Full room and board, a car at your disposal and generous pay—and you will live here at Gwrych. You may have an entire wing to yourself if you so wish. What say you, do we have an accord?"

Stephan brought in dessert, giving her time to think. It was a white mound piled high with...yep, fruit. Blackberries, blueberries, raspberries, and strawberries.

"Enjoy." The plate was set in front of her with a flourish, chocolate drizzled on the white cloud stuff.

"Let me eat my dessert. I won't be able to focus until I do, okay?"

"Woe to the man who stands between you and fruit. Remind me to show you the hothouse after dinner."

Topping off her wineglass with more of the refreshing liquid, her head pleasantly buzzed. The last time she'd been tipsy was when she made her home on the streets. Never again though, it was too dangerous, you had to have your wits about you at all times or you'd end up dead.

The dessert was fantastic. The white cloud was crunchy and melted on her tongue. Mixed with the chocolate and berries. Well, heaven couldn't be much better than this. What was that scratching noise? Oops, it was her, purring as she scraped the plate clean. Hearing laughter, she looked up as Robert slid another plate over to her. "Don't worry I had them make extra." She grinned at him. Why he looked so taken aback she didn't know but couldn't think about it, not with this temptation in front of her. Eve would have sold Adam out in a heartbeat for a taste of this concoction.

A jolt ran through her body. She felt safe enough here with Robert to allow herself to relax. When was the last time she'd been secure? Never. Not until he came into her life. There was her answer. The only remaining question—what would she do if he brought other women home? Even in another wing, she'd be bound to run into them. Clenching her jaw so tight she swore her teeth would crack, Maggie knew without a doubt she didn't want him with anyone else.

Wanted to be his alone. And there it was.

With him she felt safe, secure and cared for. Putting down the spoon, she looked up at him. As always, he was watching her.

"We have an...accord as you call it."

"Gareth." His steward appeared. "The lady and I are going

for a stroll to the hothouse. Cognac in the library when we return." He got up and pulled her chair out. "Shall we, milady?"

Sometimes she thought they were in the past, he sounded so old-fashioned. On anyone else it would be silly or pretentious but it suited him and there was something about being called 'milady' that made her smile and turned her insides all mushy.

The library was calling to her as they passed. So many books. It boggled the mind. For the rest of her days she could be content there, discovering new worlds, letting the world pass by.

"Maggie, I promise, you may spend as much time in here as you wish. And since you'll be living with me, if there are certain books or authors you fancy, say the word and I will have them delivered here for milady's pleasure."

"Living with me" had a pleasant ring to it. There'd never been a boyfriend she was with long enough to consider living with. Other than Josh and not only was he a roommate but it was only a four months so it didn't count. Might be nice to have another person around. Someone you could rely on, to be there, no matter what. Someone who wouldn't get you kidnapped for a lousy three hundred quid.

Maggie turned to him, her hand on his sleeve. "You seem to know all of my weaknesses yet I don't know any of yours."

"I would think it quite obvious." He placed his hand on her back and motioned her forward.

With that cryptic comment, she rolled her eyes and kept walking. As if she was his weakness. Mr. Model could have anyone he wanted, models, actresses, the most beautiful women in the world...why her? Giving up on pondering something she had no answer for, she looked around her new home. A friggin' huge castle with thick, solid walls and heavy doors. Surely she'd be safe here?

Robert's home was beautiful. There were really nice furnishings everywhere and he sure liked his comforts if the silk and velvet fabrics were any indication. After walking down numerous hallways and making several turns, she was lost. Should have brought a piece of chalk to mark her way. Then up ahead, her nose twitched. "Do I smell honeysuckle?"

"Good nose, 'tis indeed honeysuckle."

"But, it's winter." How was it possible to have so many different fruits this time of year? Looked like her answers were straight ahead. Massive wood doors inlaid with carvings of trees, fruit, and bees stood twenty feet high. As she approached to take a closer look at the beautiful woodwork, she could feel the warmth emanating from under the doors. It felt and smelled like summertime...that wondrous summer day you experienced once if you were lucky and then measured all others against it for the rest of your days on earth.

"Costs a bloody fortune to heat. Shall we?" Warm, humid air caressed her face as he pulled one of the doors open. Seagulls? Yep, gulls and other birds were flying around, singing, doing bird stuff. She'd been picturing a small hothouse, the kind you see attached to someone's house or a smallish freestanding structure. But this.

"I may move in to this room. It's bigger than most people's homes." Stepping inside her version of heaven, she relished the warm moist air tickling her skin.

"Good to know where to look for you when I can't find you. This is the tropical room. We have bananas, pineapple, mango, papaya, pomegranates, and of course, your favorite citrus fruits." There were all kinds of butterflies and bees and birds. Huge honeybees, the size of her thumb were darting amongst the honeysuckle she'd smelled when they entered. "We harvest our own honey as well."

"Honey? Ned loves that stuff. He used to put spoonfuls in his tea. I told him he liked a little tea with his honey." Did she say the wrong thing? A scary grimace marked his face as he stared off into the distance. What was his problem? Chalking it up to business matters, she shrugged.

"If you can't find me, I'll be here sitting in one of those chairs whiling the day away with a good book." Maybe now, she'd get a chance to be a sloth for an entire day. The very thought made her giddy. The ladies who lunched crowd were on to something. How she'd looked down her nose at those pampered women but now with the opportunity in front of her to enjoy the same comforts? Never again would she make fun of them as they flitted from shop to shop with nary a care in the world. Coming to the next set of doors, she paused. These were heavy leaded glass and through them yet another oasis. Each of the wondrous rooms had decorative flowers growing as well. Scattered around randomly as an afterthought. The entire place was a magical kingdom come to life.

Robert opened the door for her. "I call it the Berry Room. Blueberries, blackberries, and others." A small bunny jumped across the path in front of her. Had she fallen and hit her head? Maybe it was all a strange dream and she was wandering around some kind of crazy Wonderland? Ahead she could see more rooms. One contained various fruiting trees with apple, pear, plum, and cherries. There were four vegetable buildings, a large structure devoted to flowers and finally a huge storage area. Coming out of the final hothouse, they came to another set of heavy wood doors with the same carvings. They were deposited into a hallway with black and white tile on the floors. It looked unused. "Where are we?"

"We're in the North Wing. It hasn't been lived-in for hundreds of years. If you want it for your own, you could invite Ned to live with you, there's plenty of space." Black boots stomped across the floor sending up small clouds of dust. Ned? Why would she want him here?

"No, I don't want him here. Because I worry for his safety doesn't mean I'd ask him to live with me."

The irascible man ignored the comment. "We could go back through the hothouse to the library but it will be faster to step outside and go around." Leading her to yet another set of doors, he removed the heavy bar and opened them.

"How do you lock them behind you?" It was bracing to say

the least and she shivered violently after the warm, humid air. The cold wind blew through her clothing and she wished for a warm coat.

"No need. No one would dare set foot on my property. If it makes you feel better, I'll have Gareth lock them and have the rooms tidied up for you. Gareth can show you to the storage room. You'll have your pick of furnishings. If nothing suits, we'll go into the city and find whatever you desire."

She could smell the tangy sea air. One minute Robert was nice, the next he treated her like she didn't matter. Made her want to throw her hands up in frustration. "Thank you. I really don't need an entire wing, it's very generous."

Grateful to be back where it was toasty inside the main wing, she couldn't wait to get her hands on the books. Yawning, she stood in front of the roaring fire.

Robert brought her a glass with amber liquid in it. "Cognac. 'Twill warm you."

"What's it taste like? I'm mainly a wine drinker." Mesmerized, she watched him raise the glass to his lips, his neck muscles moving as he swallowed, his eyes never leaving hers. Lost in his gaze, she felt desired for the first time. Desired by a man made of shadow. Deliberately he set the glass on the mantle, still staring at her, his irises almost a blue-black. Rough hands grasped her arms and she let out an involuntary gasp when his mouth captured hers. Maggie couldn't think, couldn't move. Moaning deep in her throat, she opened her lips as his tongue conquered her mouth. Out of breath, she reached up, holding onto him, afraid she'd fall into the abyss. That was a kiss she'd never forget.

Fear crept in. Could she truly trust him? Grasping the crystal tumbler as if it were a life preserver, taking small sips, her hand gripped her stomach as the warmth slid down her throat, pooling in her belly.

As he spoke, she held up a hand and croaked, "Wow. I need a moment."

Wandering around the room, she couldn't pick *one* book. Wait a minute. You're going to live here, plenty of time to read them all. Shoulders relaxing, she turned and saw *Gone with the Wind*. Had heard of it but never read it. Taking it down from the shelf, she settled into a comfy chair big enough for two, facing the fire.

Robert refilled his glass and paced the room. Why couldn't he sit still instead of stalking around? Shaking her head, she went back to her book. The South. The opening page sucked her in, the kiss pushed to the back of her mind to be explored at a later time in the safety of her room, everything around her fell away. The fire crackled, she was immersed in another world.

The hair on the nape of her neck stood up. Was someone watching her? Body rigid, instinct telling her to flee, she breathed in through her mouth, shallow breaths, afraid to look up from the book. In the book's world, she was safe but here, in the library...

"Well, well, well, what have we here?"

Jumping up from the chair, the book fell to the carpet and she dropped the glass of cognac. It shattered on the floor, narrowly missing the beautiful rug. Legs propelling her, she backed up until the stone fireplace met her back. The intense heat buffeted her but no way was she moving.

Odd. There was some kind of silver shimmer in the air.

Oh god no.

Like when Bruce and his men murdered that Shadow Walker. Had this guy hurt Robert? She tried to shrink into herself, disappear. But it wasn't working. He was staring at her as if she were a roach crossing the dinner table.

The accent was British, reminding her of Solien. Where the hell was Robert? Why hadn't she heard him leave the room? Her voice deserted her. Was he related to Solien? Had he come to kill her? How did he find her? Opening her mouth to scream, nothing came out. The man—creature, must have been six foot seven. With long silvery hair, not gray but silver like Christmas icicles she'd seen in store windows as a small child. Hell no, he had to be like Solien. The skin was platinum and on his forearms and neck she could see blue tattoos, changing, slithering across his body. The air smelled of rain and something else...electricity maybe? Was that thunder?

"W...who...who are you?"

The thing arched an eyebrow. "Who am I?" The steel in his voice made her cringe. He stepped forward, his arm outstretched. This was it, he was going to kill her. Had he brought the goblins? In the distance she heard the crunch of glass and before the darkness swallowed her, she thought Robert's voice rang out but it couldn't be...wasn't he dead?

Voices penetrated her consciousness. "Robert?" Something tickled her nose, she reached up to scratch it and grasped hair. Silky hair.

"I'm here, darlin'. Can ye sit up?"

Opening her eyes, she looked into deep blue eyes full of concern. "You're not dead? I thought he killed you." She struggled to sit up. "We have to run. He found me. He's going to kill me." Grabbing Robert's sleeve, she yanked hard.

"Easy, milady. Thorne isn't going to kill you."

"How do you know?"

"I work for him. I called him to tell him what's been happening, thanks to you."

The sound of thunder swung her attention to the chair across the room. *He* was sitting there, legs casually crossed, holding a drink.

"My apologies for scaring you. Though how on earth you might ever think I was anything like that demon spawn is beyond me. Rather insulting really." He brushed lint of his black dress slacks, sniffing.

"You're not going to kill me or have the goblins kill me?" Still not sure if he was telling her the truth, she held on tight to Robert, thankful he was alive.

"Goblins are nasty creatures and I certainly don't need them to do my dispatching for me. If I wanted you dead, you'd no longer be breathing. Though I must admit you were right, Robert. The lady smells intoxicating. I wonder..." He shook his head. "I do thank you for bringing this matter to my attention. Dayne has rather a few things to answer for."

"You're scaring my guest, Thorne."

"Hmm, am I?" Icy blue eyes regarded her. She wanted to curl up into a ball and whimper. The power coming off him was like standing in the middle of a tornado. Not that she'd ever stood in one but she'd seen them on the telly and it looked like what she was experiencing. "You're the one who changed Robert's fate."

What the hell was he talking about? "His fate? No, I saved his life when he was being hanged." The scary guy threw back his head and laughed. Maybe he was demented?

"Saved his life. That's rich. Oh Robert, you've not enlightened dear Maggie have you, boy?"

"What is he talking about?"

"Maggie, it's late. Thorne and I have a few things to discuss. We'll talk later."

She arched an eyebrow at him. What was he hiding? No matter, she'd find out once his boss was gone. Not like she wanted to have a conversation with him looking on anyway. He might say he wasn't going to kill her but she didn't trust him as far as she could throw him. "Fine." Grabbing the fallen book, she stomped out of the room, Thorne's laughter mocking her as she fled to the stairs.

✤ 21 ✤

The clock was ticking and not the bloody alarm clock. Head pounding, Monroe stumbled to the shower, detouring to the kitchen for a Guinness to kick-start the day. Smacking his lips, he at least threw the can in the bin instead of on his now clean floor. Amy had done a great job, and he'd try to keep it tidy, but she'd be fighting a losing battle.

Was nice to have proper soap in the shower. He let the hot water cascade down his tight shoulders, down his back and over his arse. Every muscle ached. Guess passing out in a chair would do that to you when you crossed into your thirties. Stepping out, he dried off and slung the towel towards the hook on the wall. It missed, sliding down the wall and landing in a heap on the floor. Shrugging, he took a hard look in the mirror. Bloodshot eyes with serious circles gazed out at him. Should probably shave... naw, why bother? Death stared back at him. Sighing, he palmed four aspirin and chewed, chasing the bitter taste with the remains of the Guinness. Padding naked to his room, he reached for what he thought of as the uniform. Now that he was an investigator he could dress as he wished.

Worn jeans, a red sweater and his shit-kickers completed his new look. Grabbing grape Pop-Tarts and a cold Pepsi—thanks to

Emily he'd also gotten addicted to her favorite breakfast. It was portable and got you going in the morning, well, the brew probably helped. Not chasing that thought to ground, he snagged his keys and jacket, walking out of the flat and getting into his baby.

Two voice mails were waiting. The first was his old partner telling him the Corporation he'd been looking into was called Mors Omnibusa or 'death to all', nice. Shamus wanted him to be careful and not do anything since he'd been warned off looking into them. Guess spending a boatload of quid made those in charge look the other way.

Robert was his next call and the guy couldn't help him. He was knee deep taking care of his own problems so he had to make a call he swore he'd never make. The guy was such a prick. Punching in Colin's number, he waited, fingers drumming out a beat on the steering wheel.

"Cop."

"Seriously, Colin. I know Robert gave you the deets. You bloody well know I'm no longer a cop so how about using my name—Monroe."

"What do you want?"

Resisting the urge to throw the mobile at the windshield, he took three deep breaths. Colin wasn't worth destroying his phone over. Hell, until his new endeavor took off, he'd have to watch his expenses. He had plenty saved, but nowadays you had to be careful.

"As much as it pains me to say it—I need your help."

"Sorry, I didn't catch that."

Yep, there was a smile in that sentence. "Really, you should get your ears checked. I thought you 'live forever' boys had perfect hearing?"

Silence greeted him. The guy had no sense of humor. "Fine. Colin, I need your help. Okay?" Monroe filled him in. They agreed to meet behind the foster home in the alley. It was a Saturday, and if there were still no kids there, the place should be quiet as a church.

Cutting across back alleyways, he managed to avoid the tourist traffic and make it to The Wallace School for Children in record time. He parked two blocks over, got out, hit the locks and jogged to the alley behind the building. Of course Colin was already there. He was a huge sonofabitch. The guy was six five and built like he could tear your head off with the flick of his wrist. Course he'd heard the big guy in charge had given Colin some kind of power boost when he married Emily so the bastard was even more dangerous. They'd rubbed each other the wrong way from the moment they met. He thought of Colin as a nothing more than a rich, spoiled aristocrat and Colin thought he was a nosy, obnoxious cop. The dislike was still mutual, but he'd try to put his feelings aside if it meant finding Amy's kid brother.

The aristo inclined his head. "Monroe."

Maybe Emily had told the ancient warrior to play nice today. Nodding back, he jumped in. "The kid, Mark, was last seen here teaching some of the kids how to read. Like I said, Mrs. Potts is involved or knows something." He paused to take a swig from his flask, offering it to Colin. He surprised Monroe by accepting.

"Ah, the good stuff. Is it Ravensmore Whisky?" Monroe wanted to smack the grin off his face but he'd probably find himself fried by a bolt of energy.

Grudgingly he admitted, "Your estate does produce the best whisky, in my opinion."

Colin's eyebrows hid in his hairline. "I'll have a case sent over to you."

Now it was Monroe's turn to be shocked. "Appreciate it."

"It's awfully quiet for a foster home. Emily and I haven't visited this one yet."

He couldn't help it, Monroe burst out laughing. "In other words, the little monsters are overrunning the place and you couldn't wait to get away. No wonder you said you'd help me."

"I'll deny it to my last breath. 'Tis nice to be out and about, helping the humans."

And there was the arrogance again. "This 'human' is ready to kick down some doors but let's take a look at the alley first. I'd guess they take the kids from here rather than the front."

Colin had already begun looking around. He raised his head scenting the air. Man he wished he had the abilities these guys had. And Colin walked straight to the dumpster at the end of the alley.

"Blood. Maybe a day or two old." Flipping open the top, he leaned in, swearing. When he turned to Monroe with a sweater, part of a navy school uniform, wadded in his fist, Monroe's stomach hit the cold ground. "Fuck it all. That's the kid's uniform."

Colin's voice was quiet. "Do you have anything of his? So we'll know for sure?" Reaching in his jacket pocket, he pulled out a plastic zip top bag and handed it to the warrior. It contained his hairbrush and a pajama top. Opening the bag, Colin inhaled. He gave it back to Monroe while bringing the sweater to his nose. The look on his face said it all.

"It's a match. Doesn't mean he's dead, but the kid's hurt."

"Not calling this one in. I'm going to take this place apart."

"I might be starting to like you a bit after all." Colin bared his teeth in a chilling smile. "Shall we invite ourselves inside?"

Colin wrapped his hand around the padlock on the back door in the alley. The air seemed to glow bluish silver and a popping noise broke the silence. The useless lock hit the stone with a thunk. The halls were empty, their footsteps echoing on the worn floors. Leading the way to Mrs. Potts office, Monroe stopped. A tangy copper smell overlaid with burnt electricity hit his nose. Colin grimaced at the same time. "Methinks we're a bit late, aye?"

Blood was spattered on the scarred wooden desk and walls. Mrs. Potts sensible loafers were sticking out from behind. Stepping over her feet, he leaned down. The matronly woman looked about ninety. Drained. "Damn it. We're too late. Why do those bastards get away with killing humans while you're forbidden? It's bollocks."

"I don't make the rules, just enforce them."

He was disgusted. Following Colin out of the office and down the hallway, they came to the stairs. He took them two at a time while the cheeky bastard dematerialized to the top of the staircase. Damn, he needed to get some kind of exercise other than lifting a glass or fork. Catching his breath, hands on his knees, he gave Colin the one-second motion. Walking the corridor, every door was closed, padlocked on the outside. Nice. The kids were kept locked in their rooms. Colin blasted each one. All were empty. There was evidence the children had been there recently. Unmade beds, a shirt or pants left on the floor. The padlock was already hanging open on the last room. Nudging it wider with his foot, his mouth hit the floor. The cell had no windows and was padded on all four sides to silence any noise. He felt sick to his stomach. Colin did his bloodhound thing.

"He was here, recently. Along with at least fifteen others."

Monroe nodded. "Can you track them?"

"Aye. I'll be dematerializing, ye canna follow me. Give me the photo of the boy in case I find anyone. I'll call when I know something."

Nodding he handed over the picture, "All right. I'll be ready —" before he could finish his sentence Colin had dematerialized. The guy might be a pain in the arse but if he could find Mark and the others, he'd do his best to get along with the arrogant aristocrat.

Cranking up the tunes, he listened to *The Peatbog Faeries*, drumming on the wheel, sipping from his flask. Thirty minutes later his mobile rang. "Remember the town where everybody up and left? Some bollocks about the people moving to better places?" Monroe vaguely remembered. "Kessock?"

"Aye. Get out here as fast as you can. There's a farm up ahead. Three men posted as guards, what a joke." With that, he disconnected. Great, bloody fantastic. He'd never make it in time without breaking numerous laws. Sending up a prayer to whoever was listening, he put the vehicle in gear and hauled ass.

COLIN WASN'T GOING TO WAIT FOR THE EX-COP. THE FARM was in the countryside, in a decimated town, perfect cover for all kinds of illicit activities. This reeked of Solien's handiwork. He'd like nothing better than to kill all three of the hired henchmen. Yes they were human but on the wrong side. Therefore, fair game. But maybe a little chat first.

Dematerializing to the northwest corner of the farm, Colin appeared directly behind the first man. He'd just rounded the building out of sight of the others providing perfect cover for what he had in mind. Lifting the man up by the back of his coat, he cranked his other arm around the guy's windpipe cutting off any call for help. "Answer my questions and I will let you go. Nod once if you understand."

The man nodded.

"I want to know about the children held captive here." Releasing his grip enough to allow his feet to touch the ground and for him to speak, Colin waited.

"Yeah, there were kids here. What do you want to know?"

Excellent. Cooperation was a good sign. "Tell me about this place, where the kids were moved to and if you've seen this child in particular." Colin pulled Mark's photo from his inside coat pocket. Releasing him, he faced the minion, pushing the image into his face. "Look closely."

"Aye. I seen the lad."

"Before you tell me about him, answer my earlier inquiries."

The man put his hands on his knees, taking great breaths of air into his aching lungs. "We were sent here to guard the kids. It's a temporary holding location. Once we have a good number they get sent someplace in Edinburgh. That's all I know about this place, I just work here."

CYNTHIA LUHRS

"Of course you're not responsible for anything. Tell me about Mark."

"I didn't know his name, but I seen the kid in the picture. I remember because he and another boy got shot—" Colin punched the man in the gut, doubling him over.

"Not by me!" He gasped. "Was one of the others. Happened yesterday. The kids were hit trying to escape, they're dead. We told Solien we checked but it was raining and none of us wanted to go out in the muck. By the way they fell when shot, was obvious they were gone. Why traipse all over to tell them what we already knew?" He pointed away from the building towards a house in the distance. "Please. I told you everything you wanted to know, let me go."

Minions. He hated them. If he let this one go, he'd tell Solien about this little visit. Couldn't do to have word get out. Colin blasted an energy bolt through the man's spine, killing him instantly. The man's body went rigid, then limp. Dragging him out of sight, Colin dematerialized to the front of the farmhouse where the second man was standing guard. Manifesting an ice dagger, he stabbed the man through the eye, the blade penetrating into the brain, dropping the man like a stone. A mobile rang. Probably the third loser checking on his mates. Ah, no need to go to him, he was headed this way. Not waiting, he shot another bolt of energy, catching the man, lifting him off his feet and slamming him to the ground. With one last look back, Colin sent a bolt of energy to the barn, igniting the hay. The place would burn to ashes, covering the evidence of the three dead men.

Dematerializing to where the first man had pointed about a half mile away, he landed in some kind of small garden. It was surrounded on all sides by a thick hedge. He could smell blood and the stench of infection. Scanning the hedge, he spotted a flash of color. There. Within the bushes he could see the two boys.

"Mark? Can you hear me?"

The boy furthest away from him, moved. "You're all right now. I won't hurt ye, lads."

He heard a muffled cry and a weak voice answered him. "Are you the police?"

"No lad, I'm Colin. A friend of Amy's. She's been worried about ye. Can ye come out?"

The boy moaned as he crawled towards Colin. "Aidan. Can ye follow me? He knows Amy, we're goin' ta be all right."

Moving slowly, both boys wriggled their way out of the hedge. They were filthy, their shirts crusted with dried blood. Neither could stand. Colin caught Mark as he struggled to get to his feet. "Easy lad. I've got ye." Easing the boy to the ground, he heard a car engine. A large Mercedes SUV pulled up next to them, heedless of the bushes crushed beneath the tires. Monroe jumped out, slamming the car door.

"Nice fireball, Colin. Made it easier to find you." Catching sight of the boys, Monroe squatted on his haunches. "I'll be damned. You found him."

Both boys were flat on their backs. Mark had been shot in the shoulder, through and through. The other boy, Aidan, took a bullet in his side. The hole in his back telling Colin the bullet had exited the boy's small body. He cursed. "You were verra brave lads to run away and hide in the hedge. Ye've both been shot, aye? How long have you been out here?"

Mark answered, "Almost two days. We haven't eaten anything. I'm so tired." Aidan simply laid on the ground, his brown eyes staring up at Colin.

"Hold on, we'll get you fixed up." He spoke in a low voice to Monroe. "They've lost a lot of blood, there's no time to get them to hospital. I can heal them."

He wasn't surprised to see Monroe start. He hadn't seen this little trick. Oh well, Robert trusted him, guess he'd have to see what the guy was made of. "I'm going to assume you know to keep this to yourself?"

Monroe scowled. "The fact you need to say anything tells me you're still an arse. Yes, I'll keep quiet. Will it hurt them?"

"Mark. Aidan. I'm going to make the pain go away. I want ye to lie still and think of something you like, okay?"

Aidan' small voice answered him. "Like football? I like football."

"Aye, lad. Football's a good thing to think on. Shall I ring your parents and let them know we found you?"

The boy let out a soft sob. "Me mam and pop are dead. I was living at the home."

"Shhh, Aidan. 'Twill be alright."

Looking around to make sure there weren't any witnesses, Colin took a deep breath. He felt Monroe's eyes on him. He began with the worst injury. Aidan. Raising the boy's shirt, he placed his hands over the bullet wound. It was an angry red, swollen and infected. Silver light spilled out of his hands, illuminating the area around them.

Aidan gasped. "It's so warm."

He concentrated on the torn flesh, willing it to heal. Minutes passed, he couldn't say how long but felt the draining effects of expending a high volume of energy. The light subsided, going dim, then extinguishing. The boy looked into his eyes with gratitude before passing out.

"Is that normal? Should he fall asleep like that? Is he okay?"

Shooting the annoying bastard a nasty glare, "Seriously?" Removing his hands, he heard the guy's sharp intake of breath.

"Wow. It's like he was never injured. His skin looks sunburned but that's the only clue anything happened to this kid."

"If you're done with the commentary, I'll heal Mark." Wisely, the cop or former cop as it was, didn't say a word.

"Mr. Colin? Are you going to make me better like Aidan? He's not dead is he?"

Resisting the urge to laugh, he moved over to Mark, kneeling down beside him and looking him in the eye. "He's sleeping. He's fine and yes, you'll be fine lad. You might feel warm like Aidan and then sleepy. When you wake, you'll be safe. Are you ready?"

The boy nodded, his eyes never leaving Colin.

"Don't be afraid. I'm going to cut your shirt so I can see the wound."

"But it's the only school shirt I have. Amy will be mad it's ruined."

"Dinna fash yourself, lad. I'll see you have a new one." He paused and when Mark shook his head yes, he pulled out his dirk. Cutting away the fabric, he swore. The kid's shoulder was shredded by the bullet. He'd hunt down and kill every last Day Walker and minion he could get his hands on. Breathing deeply, he pressed both hands over the wound and concentrated. Sweat broke out on his brow. Silver light filled the garden, glowing bright as a full moon in a clear night sky. Satisfied the boy was healed, he removed his hands. Yep, the only telling sign was now a small pink circle. The color would fade and no one would ever know he'd been shot.

Standing up, Colin swayed. Monroe was there, a hand on his arm. "Thanks. Afraid I won't be able to dematerialize back to Ravensmore. Catch a ride with you?"

"Of course. Bloody hell, that was fucking amazing." Shaking his head, the guy looked at him with a new respect. "I'll call Amy on the way, she's working so she can meet us in the morning. I didn't think the boy would be found alive."

Too weak to lift the kids, Colin let Monroe put the unconscious boys in the backseat while he clambered into the passenger seat. Once he could recharge tonight, he'd be fine. "Since we've taken in so many children, I've hired a live-in doctor. He can check the boys over."

"Want me to call Emily?"

"No, I'll call her. 'Tis a half hour drive to Ravensmore." He paused. "Thanks."

If Monroe was surprised, he did a good job of keeping his face blank. He shrugged at Colin, "Don't mention it."

On the way, Monroe called Amy. Told her he'd send a car to bring her to Ravensmore first thing in the morning, thanks to Colin. Let her know they found Mark and he was fine. Hanging up, he faced the warrior. "What will she think when he tells her he was shot but there's no bullet hole?"

Quirking an eyebrow, Colin expended the effort to answer. "When I healed them, I took the memory of being shot away and replaced it with one where they heard shots, ran and hid. Easier all the way around."

"Nice trick."

"Aye." He was done talking. Pulling out his mobile, he called his wife. "Emily love, I'm on my way back. Monroe is driving me and the two lads."

"Are you all right? How are they?" He could hear the worry in her voice. Her soft Southern drawl. He hoped she'd never lose it. Shifting to ease his hard on, he answered her. "Both were in pretty bad shape, they'd been shot." He paused as she fussed. "I healed them, they'll be fine. I'll have a car sent to bring the sister, Amy to Ravensmore so she can see for herself Mark is better."

"Colin, what about the other boy?"

"He's an orphan. I thought he could stay with us." He held the phone away from his ear. Gods, she loved kids. Thank Terya he had his business endeavors or he might go crazy from all the noise. "You healed them. How are you holding up?"

"Don't worry lass, I'll be fine tonight." He hung up, still amazed they had managed to find each other. She was his world.

As the boys slept, they drove in silence, lost in thought. The drive took about thirty minutes. Pulling into the castle, he could hear the children playing, laughing, doing all the things kids should be doing.

"Damn, I thought you only had seven. How many of the little monsters do you have running around the place?"

Colin chuckled. "Aidan will make thirty-one." At Monroe's horrified look, he laughed. "You know Emily. She loves kids and wanted to help. We have tons of room so why not?" He shrugged. "I'm teaching the boys to fight with swords."

"Heaven help us all. Just what we need, little Colin's running around Scotland." Monroe was saved a punch to the face by Emily flying down the steps towards the car.

He caught her as they came together, kissing her hard. "Colin? You're pale." Choosing to ignore her remark, he pointed the live-in doctor trailing behind Emily to the car. The man peered in the glass. "Looks like they're awake. I'd like to check them over."

Nodding, he turned to see Monroe hugging his wife. "You look well. Awful lot of kids you and Colin have here."

Her whole face lit up as she told the ex-cop about her plan to help all the orphan children of Scotland. Emily picked up Aidan, and the doctor took Mark. "I'll get them settled in and see you both for tea?"

"Aye, love. We'll be in shortly." Colin turned to Monroe. "Shall we go in for a whisky?"

"Thought you'd never ask."

Colin greeted the kids playing outside in the cold. "Come in soon. Meg will have tea and biscuits waiting." A thunderous roar answered him and he and Monroe stood back as the fifteen or twenty kids ran for the front door.

Once the dust settled, they went inside. He loved his home. Wondered how Ravensmore looked through the ex-cop's eyes. Made of gray stone, the castle sat on the edge of a cliff. Open ground in front of the fortress led down to forest. Behind the building was the sea, the walls had never been breached. Colin absently counted the rooms they were currently using. Still plenty of rooms for more children. He'd have to look into restoring Castle Gloom. After all, wasn't like Hamish needed it. Sweeping thoughts of his traitorous long-dead brother aside, he led Monroe to the library.

"Dude, I'd forgotten the floors were heated. You look like something the cat dragged in."

He waved the comment away. "Ravensmore was built on an old Roman fort. They figured out the heated floors, running water and bathing chambers. My ancestors kept the features intact, cheaper that way." Monroe smiled. "Thrifty bastards."

Handing him a tumbler of the estate whisky, he sank into a chair, catching Monroe's look. "'Tis from expending the energy to heal the boys. I'll be fine tonight."

They sat in companionable silence enjoying the spirits. A timid knock sounded at the door. "Enter."

A girl of about nine or ten came in bearing a tray. She placed it on the table in front of Colin and Monroe. "Milord. Meg sent tea, sandwiches, and molasses cookies. Well, I made the cookies." The lass blushed, looking at her feet.

"You made them? I shall have one first then." Colin took one and handed the platter to Monroe who took a handful. "Delicious, Anne." She turned and ran from the room.

"I think she has a crush on you."

"The kids are cute. You know one of them found the secret passages, and they've had a grand time jumping out and scaring each other and the staff. If my hair could turn gray, I'd have a headful by now."

Quiet descended on the room as both attacked the sandwiches. Colin shifted in his chair, tired. Monroe cleared his throat. "Emily said you've been making wine and cheese?"

He raked a hand through his hair. "Aye. 'Twill be years before anything is ready but 'tis something I've wanted to do for a while."

A few crumbs were all that remained on the empty tray. Draining his glass and pouring another to take up to his room, Monroe bid Colin goodnight. "I'm going to take some of your fine whisky upstairs and turn in. Amy will be here in the morning to pick up Mark."

"Sleep well. I'd like to hear more about this 'death to all' Mors Omnibusa Corporation front for the Day Walkers. But first I need to recharge."

"Colin?" He turned, looking at the guy. "Thanks for the help."

Maybe he was beyond spent or maybe the guy was starting to grow on him. "Glad I could help." And what did you know? He meant it. In the hallway, Worthington was waiting to show Monroe to his room. Emily came bustling from the kitchen. Putting her arms around him, she whispered in his ear. "Come milord, let's get you into bed."

"I have enough energy left to properly bed you before we sleep, lass." He waggled his eyebrows at her, kissing her soundly as they made their way up the stairs to their room, children calling out goodnight as they passed various rooms. The sounds of their voices filling Ravensmore with laughter and love.

What a difference a year made.

❧ 22 ❦

Curled up in the window-seat, Maggie was ready to throw something. But not the wonderful snacks Stephan must have brought in moments ago. The mug was still steaming. Thorne. Yes, he was scary but the guy also pissed her off. Sipping her tea, she opened the book. When was the last time she'd read anything? Maybe during a slow time when she waitressed? Too damn long. The story pulled her in, taking her mind off Mr. Infuriating and Mr. Arrogant. A knock at the door pulled her out of the old South. She was rooting for Scarlett and Rhett to end up together. Standing, she stretched, working the kinks out of her back from sitting still so long.

"How are you? Do you need anything?"

Anger bloomed. "Other than flipping out when someone scarier than Solien showed up in the library, I'm good. What did he mean about me changing your fate and you not telling me everything?"

Robert hedged, leaning in her doorway. He was so flippin' sexy standing there, it was hard to stay angry especially when he ran his hands through that gorgeous hair, mussing it up.

"Thorne believes our lives have already been written out, that everything we do is fated. It's really quite ridiculous. We all have free will; no one makes my choices but me. The 'not telling' is his way of causing trouble. He's happiest when there's discord amongst his fighters. Gods tend to be rather nasty at times. No need to worry."

Scowling at him, she narrowed her eyes. "What aren't you telling me? I don't care if you have secrets, everyone does...but deliberately withholding information is something I can't forgive. Josh did it. Even Ned lied to me, and I thought he and I had..."

"Damn Ned. I'll kiss the bloody bastard out of you." Robert pulled her against him, captured her mouth and kissed her hard, marking her. Flesh met a solid wall of muscle. Warmth spread from her mouth, down her throat to pool in her stomach before heading down to her toes. The man could kiss. What was she angry about? Forgetting, she gave her entire being over to kissing him. Her arms went around him, pulling him tighter as he growled deep in his throat. What would he be like in bed? It had been a long time since she'd been with anyone. Didn't matter she was falling for the charming badass, feelings be damned. Her body wanted him, and truth be told so did her heart.

Breaking the kiss left her adrift, cold. Her knees shook as he let go. Reaching out to steady her body against the doorway, she caught the look on his face. Very satisfied, like a dog with a large, juicy bone. Stalking across the hallway, he slammed his door shut, leaving her there stunned.

Leaning back against the doorjamb, her fingertips went to her lips. They were swollen. Her body was an electrical wire, humming, seeking *him*. Five minutes must have passed before she gathered the will to move. Shutting the door, she found herself in the bathroom with no recollection of how she'd gotten there. Turning on the taps and pouring in bath salts and bubbles, she wandered around the room restlessly picking up objects and putting them back down. Her skin felt too tight, she was jittery and the temperature in the room must have gone up, she was burning up. Stripping off her clothes, she slid down the side of the claw foot tub, sighing in bliss as warmth seeped into her aching body. Resting her head against the edge, her thoughts drifted. So much had happened. She couldn't imagine how someone who didn't know about this crazy other world would handle things. Maggie could barely process it herself and she'd been living it. Sliding under the water, sound fell away. Closing her eyes, she pictured a tropical beach, the waves gently rocking her, holding her in their embrace. Surfacing, she washed her hair. Running the soap over her body, she imagined it was his hands caressing her. Arching her back, her nipples puckered as the cold air hit them. The sensation was almost painful. She felt weightless, boneless, teetering on the edge of a precipice. Feelings she'd never experienced crashed over her, raising the gooseflesh all over her body. She stood, dizzy. Holding on to the edge of the bath so she wouldn't fall, she wound a towel around her hair and another around her body.

Catching her reflection in the mirror, she gasped. Who was this woman? The person looking back was sexy, like she'd been made love to, long and hard, all night long. Eyes sleepy, skin flushed, every pore tingling, she turned away, shaking her head. Dressing in a beautiful emerald silk nightgown, she let the truth surface. *Face it, you want him.* Like a sleepwalker, she moved to the door, watching from above her body, she dimly noted her hand reaching for the latch, raising it, pulling the heavy door open.

Standing at a crossroads.

Across the hall, shadow blocked the dim light coming from under his door. The corridor was silent. The door opened. He stood, silhouetted in the glow, every inch the pirate. Come to plunder, take what he wanted, consequences be damned. The snowy white linen shirt was open to his waist, showing off tanned skin stretched over a chiseled body. From where she stood his eyes were black as night, the very definition of sin.

Slamming back into her body, she hastily backed away...to the safety of her room, shutting the door with a soft click. What was she thinking? This would end badly. No matter how kind, he was a playboy who could have anybody he wanted. Why on this earth would he want a plain Jane like her?

Gareth must have brought wine while she was bathing. Pouring a glass of the golden liquid, she took a long swallow, a few drops running down her chin and neck.

KICKING THE WALL NEXT TO THE FIREPLACE, ROBERT PACED the room as a caged animal in a zoo. The dratted woman made his blood boil. He'd never worked this hard to bed a female in his entire existence. Stopping, he nearly stumbled over his own feet. Bloody hell, she wasn't 'one of his women', she was different. Enchanting yet innocent. Hard as steel and vulnerable. The mass of contradictions named Maggie was so far under his skin he swore she'd become a part of him. Finely attuned to her every movement, he'd lost control when she mentioned that idiot Ned. Raking his hands through his hair, he cursed, reaching for a glass. Scowling at the crystal, he set it down, hefted the bottle and drank deeply. Fire burned down the back of his throat into his gut—still he saw her face. Saw her standing there, fingertips pressed to her delectable swollen lips. It seemed like hours had passed as he walked in circles, staring into the fire and drinking more whisky to obliterate thoughts of her. None of it was working. Damn it to hell.

Stalking to the door, he wrenched it open so hard, the hinges groaned with the assault. He had to have her, Ned be damned. He would stamp his scent all over her, mark her inside and out so all would know—she was his. Not even pausing at the barrier in front of him, Robert took two steps back, lifted his booted foot and kicked the bloody door open with a satisfying bang.

"Bloody door was stuck."

In the center of the room stood an angel of mercy or a siren beckoning him to crash on the rocks, he didn't know and didn't care. The emerald silk flowed across her body, her nipples standing out, two hard points. The flimsy straps begging to be torn to shreds. He crossed the room so fast, for a brief moment he wondered if he was wrong about everything and he'd dematerialized there, had his powers back. The thought was unsettling. To test the idea, he tried to manifest the whisky bottle. No luck. Damn the gods, it was true. Pushing the bothersome thoughts aside, he swept her into his arms and savaged her mouth in a bruising kiss. A growl percolated out of his throat. She tasted of wine. Running his tongue down the corner of her lip, down her pale neck, he tasted more. A few drops must have spilled. What he wouldn't give to be that wine trailing his way down her body.

Her throat convulsed as she swallowed, and he nipped at her neck. Slowly, he slid her down the length of his body. His cock, hard and ready, screaming *take her* while his mind told him to take his time. About to stop, to ask her if she wanted this, he froze as her arms entwined around his neck pulling him closer. Lush breasts pressed against his chest, the silk sliding like water over rock. The pirate within bellowed in triumph. She wanted him, not Ned. Him.

"I...um...I've not been with anyone in a long time." Her green eyes beseeched him. Desire roared through him; he was important to her, a first of sorts.

"Maggie. I don't care. Can't you see how much I want you? How lovely you are?" He guided her hand to his raging cock. It strained up to meet her, seeming to try and breach the barrier of his pants to get to her soft, warm hands. Her mouth parted in an "O" shape while a faint blush crept up her chest, to her neck, and cheeks. "By the gods, you're so beautiful. You steal the very breath from my body." He cut off her protest with a scorching kiss. The daft woman had no clue what he thought of her. Well, he'd show her what it was to be desired by shadow.

Reaching around her, he gripped the front of her gown and shredded it, baring her to him. "You smell like a summer's day." She wiggled, bringing hands up to cover her alabaster skin.

"It's the bubble bath."

His voice came out in a guttural grunt. "No, it's you methinks. Now, let me take my fill." Dropping her hands, standing there trembling before him, her hair caught the light and turned the color of rubies, cascading over one breast. Trailing kisses down her neck to her shoulder. Her eyes were dilated, wild as he leaned down flicking his tongue over her breast, lapping the underside before capturing the nipple with a light scrape of his teeth. A tiny whimper escaped from her lips as her hands stroked his bare chest. She pushed his shirt off, and he shrugged out of it, reveling in the sensation of her silky palms caressing him. Like butterflies, her fingers fluttered around the waistband of his pants. He rumbled low in this throat, wordlessly urging her on. The button popped open, she unzipped him, his erection sprang free, bobbing towards her hand, seeking what he needed.

With a sharp intake of breath, she palmed his cock, running her fingers over the head, feeling the moisture on the tip. Not another second. Bending down, Robert kicked off his boots, shrugged off his pants and in one fluid motion lifted her up in his arms. He kissed her knees, small kisses on her thighs, her belly, her breasts, before reaching that mouth that tasted of honey and wine. She tasted of a warm summer day. Effortlessly holding her, he took one last torturous step, tossing her on the bed, looming over her.

Wrapping his hand around her foot, he felt the waves of tension rolling off her body. "Relax for me darlin'. Close your eyes and enjoy the sensations." He sensed the war within as she debated whether or not to comply. Curiosity won out, and she squeezed her lids shut tight.

Her feet were worn, calluses on her heels and toes. Swearing, he vowed to destroy any responsible for her hard life. Kneeling he leaned forward, kissing the arch of her foot. She arched up off the bed.

"What the hell?! You're on your knees. You can't do that!"

"Why ever not sweetheart?" Pausing, he stood up, went to the table by the fire and poured them both a glass of wine. Well, one glass. The other one was lying under a chair on the floor where she'd dropped it when he surprised her. Shrugging, he brought the bottle over. "Drink, 'twill relax you, Maggie darlin'." Handing her the glass, she drained half, motioning him to refill it. Chuckling, he complied. "Might want another sip as I plan to start with your delectable toes and kiss my way up your entire body."

A gasp filled the room. She leaned up on her elbows looking at him. Smirking, he drank deeply from the bottle of wine before kneeling at the end of the bed. His Maggie needed to realize how desirable he found her. Feathering kisses across the sole of her foot, he nipped her heel. Working his way up, he used his hands to massage her feet while his mouth ministered to her. Taking her little toe into his mouth, he sucked, pulling, kneading the insole. A purr from deep within her bubbled up. He paid homage to each toe, sucking, licking, feeling each suck deep in his balls. Willing his body to slow down, he licked her ankle. Continuing to stroke her calf muscle he licked and kissed his way along her body, lifting her leg and licking the back of her knee. Reaching down, he took another pull of the wine and ministered to her other foot. Caressing and sucking, he moved up to her thigh. The muscles flexed under his touch, her breathing heavy, she was gripping the coverlet, holding on for dear life. "Maggie, my sweet, feel my tongue against your velvet flesh, let go."

"It's, well, no one has *ever* sucked on my toes." Her voice rose in pitch.

"A tragedy of epic proportions. I shall endeavor to make up for all the years you've been mistreated." His fingers kept drawing circles on her thighs, stroking. She might say she was nervous but her body betrayed her. He could scent her arousal and shifted to ease the ache in his groin. Bloody hell, it was easier to control his body when he had his powers. Well, never let it be said he didn't have an iron will, he'd hold out, giving her pleasure before taking his.

Bending his head to his task, he was gratified to hear her whimper as the cold wine from his mouth dribbled down her thigh. Growling in the back of his throat, he licked the droplets from her skin, blowing across her flesh, raising goosebumps. Licking the crease where thigh met hip, she clapped her thighs together.

"Wha...what are you doing?"

"Shh, love." Gently he pulled her thighs apart, watching her unfold as a flower to the sun. Sliding his hands under her ass, he squeezed. Groaning, he wanted to flip her over and nibble each delectable half but not yet. Patience. He kissed her hipbones and then went straight for her core. He licked her, flicking his tongue over her bud. Maggie keened deep in her throat. Smiling, he slid one finger in, feeling her tighten around him. He sped up the motion, back and forth as she moaned. Latching onto her, he sucked, rhythmically, inserting a second finger, thrusting as she thrashed, her body arching off the bed. Replacing his fingers with his tongue, he licked and sucked as her hips pumped in time to his motions. Clenching her thighs tight around his head, her back arched, she came hard. He lapped every drop. Crawling up between her legs, he continued to lick and kiss her stomach. They fit together perfectly. His cock was poised to enter her but still he waited. She'd never been properly loved and he'd be damned before he left her wanting. They had all night to explore each other.

Her hands stilled him. "I want to feel you." She reached down and wrapped her hand around him.

"Ah darlin', your hands are like silk." After a few minutes, he moved upward. If he didn't, he'd take her now, going slow be damned. Her breasts were the perfect size for his hand. He cupped each one, rolling the nipple between his fingers, kneading and stroking. Taking the puckered nipple in his mouth, he sucked. She was panting, her stomach and chest heaving. He licked the underside of each breast and moved to her shoulder. On her right shoulder she had a smattering of freckles. "Did you know your freckles right here look like a smiley face?"

"I never noticed."

He traced each one with a fingertip. Then kissed the same spot. Kissing his way down her arm he worshipped each finger, slowly inserting it into his mouth, sucking and kissing. Kneading her palm, he moved to the other hand and arm, repeating his attentions. As he nipped and sucked the soft underside, he lifted her arm above her head and licked her armpit. She jumped.

"You can't do that, what if I hadn't had a bath?"

Arching an eyebrow, he answered, "I suspect you would taste even more delicious with your natural scent." He chuckled. She had nothing to say to that. He'd bet bloody Ned had never noticed her freckles or licked under her arm. Bloody wanker.

Wanting to mark her, he reached down between them, flicking his thumb across her nub. Faster, faster, until she was arching off the bed. Gripping his arms, she cried out, "Please, don't stop."

With a very satisfied male rumble, he increased the pressure and inserted two fingers, pumping in and out, feeling the tension build inside her. Clenching around his fingers, she dug her nails into his biceps and shuddered, her entire body vibrating with her release.

Positioning himself over her core, he plunged in, filling her as she thrashed and shook her head side to side.

Deeper and deeper he thrust, supporting himself on his forearms, kissing her, thrusting his tongue in her mouth in time with his cock. Feathering kisses and nips across her breasts, she moaned, "Robert, please." Not knowing what she asked. He bit her shoulder and ground into her, hips pumping, he bellowed, taking them both crashing over the edge.

His woman, now well satisfied, let out a purr. Inside he sat up and preened. He rolled her on top of him, keeping them joined, her head coming to rest on his chest. Not wanting to move her, he reached down for the wine bottle offering her a sip.

"Tastes wonderful."

He chuckled low in his throat. "Is milady pleased?"

That fetching blush spread across her bare skin. "You're... well, that was... amazing." Green eyes gazed into his. Trailing a finger over her chin and shoulder, he traced lazy circles around her breast and stomach.

The fire needed to be stoked. He didn't want to get up yet. Looking at her, she had her eyes closed, seemingly to doze. Guilt set in. Fuck it all. Why hadn't he told her? Yes, Colin and Emily broke the curse, were happy together but—what would it mean for him? Thorne had made a comment in passing that it was different for each of them. Seemed like a load of bollocks to him but hell. He blew out a harsh sigh.

His life was perfect. Fighting, being nearly invincible, living forever, what could be better? Sure, he didn't have his own Emily, and maybe, just maybe, he wanted to be with Maggie. Though she was a human, would age and die. Was it better to have her for a short time or let her go? The thought of not having her near—losing her, made his insides clench. Hand trembling, he drained the rest of the wine. Raking his hands through his hair, he gently disengaged from Maggie, slid out from under her and built up the fire for the night. Opening the door, he padded down to the kitchens. Fixing her a plate of her beloved fruit, he poured a pitcher of water and brought it back upstairs.

Strolling back into the room, he pushed the door shut and paused. Maggie was stretched out in his bed, one arm dangling off the edge, the other thrown across her forehead. The sheet was tangled around her waist, baring her breasts and stomach, her hair glinting like burnished copper in the firelight across one shoulder, tickling her breast, drawing his attention to the rosy pink nipple.

He sunk down in a chair next to the fire, drinking her in, pondering.

Telling her, saying it out loud, would make it real.

❧ 23 ❧

S unday, November 5th

MONROE WOKE EARLY. HE'D REVISED HIS OPINION OF COLIN from total Grade-A asshole to a guy he might actually want to be mates with. Of course, the estate's excellent whiskey he'd enjoyed and the case he'd found waiting in his room here at Ravensmore Castle with a note from the Highlander didn't hurt.

After breakfast he and Colin discussed the Day Walker's activities. The Mors Omnibusa Corporation was an audacious move. He wondered what else the Day Walkers were planning and why the hell wasn't the big boss man, Thorne, doing anything? Maybe the other side had more juice in this fight?

The black Maserati sedan pulled up in front of Ravensmore at nine. These guys had more money than they knew what to do with. Robert said they were paid well, and they all had side businesses they dabbled in. Did you have to have money to make money or could a guy like him with a modest nest egg, make some serious paper? Thoughts of acquiring a better lifestyle would have to wait. The door of the expensive car opened before it came to a complete stop, Amy leapt out, running to him. He'd thought about asking her out. Hell, taking her to bed. But in the end it wasn't a good idea. The clean apartment, grocery shopping and laundry...let's just say he respected the expression, 'don't shit where you eat'.

"I knew you'd find him." She threw her arms around him, her body crashing into his, bringing her skidding to a halt. "Where did you find him? Is he OK? What happened to him?" The words came out in a rush.

"Amy, take a deep breath. Mark's unharmed." He wanted to cross his fingers behind his back but technically the kid was unharmed. No need to tell her the boy had been shot and healed by an immortal Shadow Walker. "We found the boy at a farm in Kessock. He and another lad escaped the kidnappers and hid. The boys heard gunshots but didn't see anything. Those men will never abduct another child again." Damn, she felt good pressed up against him. *Hands off, asshole. You want to go back to living in a stinking hovel? I didn't think so. Anyway she deserves better than a guy who can't get through the day without a serious amount of booze coursing through your veins.*

"They're dead?" Steel filled Amy's voice and she gave him a look full of all the things she'd like to do to those who hurt one of her own.

"Aye."

"Good."

Monroe nodded. "Follow me, he's around the corner, playing with the others." He led her around to the side of the castle. It might be the twenty-first century but Colin believed all the boys, and any of the girls who expressed an interest, should learn to fight with sword and dagger. The sounds ringing across the lists made him think he'd stepped back in time.

Out of the thirty, make that thirty-one with the addition of Mark, twenty-three boys were outside swinging wooden swords, yelling like little banshees. Some of the tykes were wearing kilts and staring up at Colin, hero worship in their eyes. The guy did look fearsome and lethal showing the lads how to hold a sword, demonstrating how to thrust and parry. Bloodthirsty lot by the looks of them all.

A nasty thought crossed behind his eyes. Such a difference between the number of boys and girls rescued, why? He sent up a prayer to whatever might be listening that the females weren't being forced into prostitution or other unsavory situations by their enemies.

"Are those swords?" Amy stopped, gaping at the scene before her.

Monroe chuckled. "Colin has a passion for the old ways. Says it's good for the boys. Helps them learn discipline and wears them out. I think wearing them out is the key."

She scanned the kids with worried eyes. "Mark! Mark! Over here!" Running toward the children without a care for getting smacked by a wooden sword, Amy sprinted across the distance, heedless of the mud and muck, arms outstretched, tears streaming down her face.

Her brother, stopped, got a whack on the shoulder and turned, eyes searching. "Amy." He dropped the weapon and ran to her, leaping into her arms. Babbling.

"Whoa. Slow down buddy." She hugged him tight, laughing and crying at the same time. Feigning something in his eye, Monroe swept a hand across his face. Hell, he wasn't choked up, just some irritating dust kicked up by the little monsters.

Everyone stopped what they were doing to watch the happy reunion. The smell of the ocean wafted across the courtyard and the eyes of children all around held naked envy at the scene. Amy looked at Monroe with so many emotions playing across her face, he felt a bit ill. She put Mark down, her hand on his shoulder as if she couldn't bear not to touch him. Reaching out, she hugged Monroe hard.

"I can never thank you enough. Never repay you. I'm going to clean and shop for you for a very long time for free."

He protested, "No, Amy. I'll pay you a fair rate. So many cases end badly, I'm happy this one turned out well. Thank Colin as well, I couldn't have found Mark without his help."

The Scot's eyebrows rose, the corner of his mouth quirked up. Monroe nodded at him. Amy walked over to Colin and hugged him, thanking him, her eyes shining with tears.

Mark held out his little hand. "Thank you, Mr. Colin, for saving me and for teaching me to fight. Do ye think I might could come back and learn more?"

"Aye, lad. You and your sister are most welcome at Ravensmore."

Happy, he ran over to bid Aidan goodbye before scampering back to his sister. Kids were pretty resilient. Monroe hoped neither of them would have nightmares now that they were reunited.

Colin clapped his hands. "All right lads, pick a new partner and again." He inclined his head to Monroe. "Don't worry. Now we know the business name they're hiding behind, we can strike back, hit them where it hurts."

Monroe bid Colin goodbye. "Tell Emily, we're leaving. I don't want to interrupt her with the others. She said she was teaching the girls how to make what she called and I quote 'real honest-to-goodness Pop Tarts.'"

Laughing out loud, Colin smiled. "She's worried with the shortages she won't be able to get them soon. The lass has been trying to perfect her recipe as she calls it. You don't want to know how many batches have gone to the dogs. Now they run when she starts experimenting." He rolled his eyes. "Have a safe drive back."

Monroe showed them to his Benz. Mark carried his toy sword. Colin had given it to him with instructions to continue practicing. He opened the door for Amy. Going around to the driver's side, he got in and as they drove away from the castle, waved goodbye. Mark was snoring before he'd driven ten minutes. Amy looked exhausted. "Hey, try and get some shut eye. He's safe now." She smiled and stroked his arm. He compressed his lips into a tight line. *Keep focused boy. You're not nailing her no matter how badly you need a woman. You just want a warm body to make the loneliness go away for a few hours. Don't fuck up a good thing.* As the kilometers sped by, Amy fell asleep too, a scarf balled up against the window as a makeshift pillow, leaving Monroe alone with his thoughts.

He made good time; traffic was light on Sunday. Amy woke as he parked and cut the engine. Not Mark. The boy was out like a light, exhausted from his ordeal. Monroe lifted the sleeping boy. "I'll carry him in for you."

Amy went ahead, opening the doors to the vestibule of the flat. She preceded him up the stairs, turning the key in the lock. He followed her to Mark's room and put the boy in his bed not bothering to undress the kid. Laying the sword next to him, he turned on a nightlight and left the bedroom door cracked. "Do the kid some good to sleep for a few hours. I left him in his clothes."

"That's fine. He might have woken up otherwise. Listen, thank you again. Would you like to stay for lunch?"

"I appreciate the offer, but I've got a few leads to chase down on the group that's responsible for what's happening to all these kids. We need to stop what happened to Mark from happening to other kids."

She nodded. "Good. You can't let people get away with hurting children. The thought of someone else going through what Mark did...the worry. No one deserves that kind of pain. Those are evil people who would hurt a child." She shook her head. "The usual day all right for me to clean?"

"Sure. I'll leave the list and money on the counter." He let himself out. Before he could cross the hallway into the flat, his mobile rang.

"Hey, Robert. What's doing?" He listened for a few minutes. "Yeah, I'm back in the city, got Amy and Mark settled." Did the listening thing for a bit longer, fidgeting in the chilly hall. "I know the airstrip. Give me an hour." Hanging up, he jogged down the stairs, went to the SUV and brought the case of Ravensmore's finest to his flat. Safe and sound. No way was he taking a chance on someone breaking in and stealing his whisky. He inhaled. It smelled clean inside. Nice change from the usual rotting food and other smells he usually associated with the place.

Pulling a duffel bag down from the closet in case he needed to stay overnight at Gwrych Castle, he quickly threw in clothes and toiletries. Before he'd learned about Shadow Walkers, the closest he ever came to castles were tourist attractions or talking to the aristocrats about some complaint they'd phoned in. Now he was staying at Colin's palatial castle and jetting off in a private plane to Wales and another castle. Knowing what he did of Robert, the place would most likely have gold floors and precious stone inlaid in the bloody walls. He took the time to make a sandwich and shove it down his gullet, washing it down with three Guinness's. Refilling his flask, he took one last look around and locked the door behind him.

Heading back out into the bracing air, he drove out of the city to the industrial park and private airfield. He found the hangar easily enough and saw the Gulfstream jet waiting for him. Parking in one of the marked spots, he grabbed the duffel, hit the locks and strode over to his ride.

"Welcome, sir. Glad to have you aboard."

A lovely lady took his coat and stowed his bag. The inside was all leather and comfort. There were only four seats. They were like small sofas and smelled new. The flight attendant leaned down, showing off her assets. "Can I get you a drink?"

"Whisky, neat. Thanks."

She came back with the amber liquid. He tasted it. Ravensmore. Nice. Settling in, she did the make ready, closed the door and they taxied down the runway. The Captain chatted over the intercom informing him the skies were clear and it would be a short flight. Once they were up and level, his personal attendant, unbuckled and tottered over on long legs. She was a stunning blonde, tan in the winter, blindingly white teeth and no expression when she smiled. She had the youthful, artificial look so popular nowadays.

"How do you like your steak? We're serving a wedge salad, filet mignon with sautéed mushrooms, fresh asparagus with hollandaise sauce, baked potato and pumpkin pie for dessert..." She paused. "Oh, and a Merlot. If that pleases you."

Hell yeah. The sandwich he'd wolfed down was just a teaser that had his stomach demanding more sustenance. "Absolutely. I like my steak rare." Holding out his empty glass to her, "And I'd love a glass of that wine now."

The blonde swayed back to a tiny kitchen area. He heard the cork and she was back with his drink. Settling in to enjoy himself, he half-watched the Barbie efficiently pull the meal together. Idly, he wondered how much it cost to have your own personal plane with pilot and flight attendant on stand-by. Had Robert bedded the woman? Probably, he seemed to have a never-ending supply of women hanging around though what was the deal with this Maggie chick? She was street tough, not his usual model, bimbo type.

Stowing his thoughts as the leggy blonde brought his meal, the aroma preceding her, his mouth sat up and looked around for the food. Now this was living, private jets, fancy food and excellent booze...he could get used to this lifestyle.

The filet melted on his tongue. He propped his feet up and chilled. The hostess or whatever she was called, her name was Mindi or something, was attentive without being intrusive and did a great job of keeping the wine flowing. Finished with his meal, she brought him lemon sorbet and a cognac. "Everything was tiptop, thanks."

Mindi beamed at him and left him alone. His life seemed to flash on the clouds. If he were prone to depression, he'd be feeling pretty shitty right now. As it was, he knew he was a jerk to women, put his job first. Could he change? Did he want to?

Or was it that as much time and effort over the past years he'd invested in solving Alice's death, he never really loved her...not like Colin loved Emily. He remembered Alice's lifeless body, aged and withered, found amongst the remains of St Anthony's chapel within Holyrood Park.

Satisfaction coursed through him—he'd found her killer. It had been one of the Day Walkers, a dude named Alexander. The scene played out in front of him like he was front row, opening night. The dirty bastard kept a memento. An earring he'd given Alice on her birthday. Knew it was hers when he saw the "Love M" carved on the back. Why'd the guy hold onto it? If he'd felt something for her, he could have left her alive. And it wasn't like they'd found any other souvenirs.

Retribution was sweet. As a cop he wasn't supposed to cross the line and mete out justice but the hell with that. He'd crossed too many lines in his career to stop. He wasn't corrupt but he strongly believed in making sure the guilty got what they deserved, screw the paperwork. Guess that's why he wasn't part of the force any longer. *Quit letting this bullshit bounce around in your brain. It's over and done with.*

Hell, he was destined to be an ass. God, this trip down the yellow brick road was ruining the mellow feeling provided by the alcohol he'd consumed. Better to think about the Day Walkers and figure out their plans. In his opinion it came down to one of two things: money or power. Sometimes both.

Plastic Mindi informed him they were on the initial descent. Stowing his thoughts along with his bag, he was interested to see Robert's home. What was with these guys and castles? Okay, maybe a bit of jealous talk, but still. Damn. The sprawling mountain of stone beneath him had to be Gwrych Castle. The aerial view was spectacular. Wonder how much land the estate encompassed? The plane came to a soft landing, taxiing to a gentle stop. Mindi opened the door and shot him a blinding smile. "Glad to have you aboard."

Nodding his thanks, he hit the bottom of the makeshift steps and stretched. There was some uptight looking guy waiting. "Mr. Monroe. I'm Gareth. It will be my pleasure to escort you to the castle."

A butler. So let's get this straight—a castle, a butler, fancy cars, and loads of cash. He was so getting in this circle. Lush meadow bordered the airstrip. He could see sheep grazing. Turning to take in the surroundings, he inhaled deeply. Nothing like the fresh, salty smell of the Irish Sea. They walked a couple of kilometers before reaching the castle. It sat on a wooded hillside, surveying everything around it, daring you to approach.

Had to admit, the pile of stones was damn impressive. The entire place must have stretched almost two kilometers. His eyeballs jumped around taking it all in. Part of it was four stories high and hello, there were nineteen towers if he counted correctly. Shutting his mouth with a snap, he wished his ex-partner, Shamus could be here. The guy would be salivating, getting a chance to poke around history up close and personal. Guess he'd have to remember what he could to tell Shamus over a pint.

Entering the castle he was speechless upon laying eyes on the impressive marble staircase. Gareth led him up the stairs to the second floor. "How many bloody steps up this thing?"

"The staircase consists of fifty two steps. Gwrych has over 128 rooms including the outbuildings."

Must cost a hellacious fortune to heat the place. Who needed that many rooms? What would you do with them all? Gareth spoke, jolting him out of his thoughts.

"If you'll follow me to the sitting room sir. Milord will be with you shortly."

"Sure, great." He'd counted the outer hall, inner hall, a dining room, drawing room, billiards room, he'd like to get a crack at the table in there, a study, library and as Gareth opened the doors, the sitting room. The place reeked of money. Antiques were scattered around with careless abandon, the rug looked old and very expensive and oh yeah, his eye was drawn to the ornate sideboard. There was an assortment of amber colored liquids.

Gareth offered him a drink before closing Monroe into the masculine room. Not a flower covered chair in sight. He sank down next to the fire, sipped his whisky and gazed around the room.

The doors opened with a bang as Robert and the woman stepped over the threshold. He stood to shake Robert's hand. "Monroe. See you've found the drinks. Appreciate your coming on such short notice. How was the flight?"

"No problem. You always have the good stuff. I'd gotten Amy and Mark home so I had the rest of the day to kill. The kid's fine. Colin healed the boy and his friend. Nifty trick. Can you do it too?"

"We all can."

He wondered what else they could do. "Don't think I'll ever want to fly commercial again. Nice plane."

Robert shrugged. "Gets me from point A to point B when the need arises. I've been remiss. Allow me to introduce my lovely Maggie." He pointed to a woman with porcelain skin and long hair the color of sunrise. She stepped forward, meeting his eyes.

He stuck out his hand. "Nice to meet you. I'm Monroe."

She gripped his palm in a firm handshake. "Robert told me you helped look for me. Thank you."

He brushed her gratitude away. Was never comfortable with it, hell, it was his job. Well, ex-job but still. "This place is immense. Do you use all the rooms?"

Maggie snickered. "I called it a monstrosity when I saw it but there's something about it that makes you feel like you've come home..." Her voice trailed off. The way Robert was looking at her, well looked like he'd found another woman to worship him. Though the way Robert was mooning over her...damn. Looked like the feeling was mutual.

"I can't remember. Anyway, in addition to the hothouse there are a number of outbuildings and a generously sized wing for the staff. Maggie is planning to wander the unused wings and see if she finds any treasure lying about." He smiled at the lady in question who blushed.

Stephan came in bearing a tray laden with sandwiches, fruit, tea and some kind of lemon tart. "Late afternoon snacks."

He left them to the food. Monroe thought Maggie was going to knock him over for the oranges and cranberries.

"Sugared cranberries. I think I've died and gone to heaven." She groaned. Robert laughed.

"Better look out, pilfer her beloved fruit and she'll take your hand off."

The lady in question stuck her tongue out at him. "Be nice, or I'll eat all the cranberries myself."

"What are those things? Isn't that the stuff that comes in a can, Yanks eat it at Thanksgiving?"

Maggie's eyes opened wide. "Seriously, you've never had one? Well, in that case, I guess I can share a few with you." She spooned a few of the red globes coated in a white sugar looking like crystals onto his plate and watched him. "Well go on, pop one in your mouth."

He was game. His mouth exploded in flavor. The tart against the sweet of the sugar was delicious. He eyed the dish. Robert roared in laughter.

"Gods, darlin'. You've created a monster. No need to fight over them, I'll have Stephan make some more." Robert looked perplexed. "I've never seen two people so crazy about fruit. Now gold, jewels, paintings...that I can understand. You're daft, the both of you."

"Whatever. Maggie obviously has excellent taste. Now. How do we stop these bastards before they destroy my entire Country?" He passed on the sandwich, still full from his delicious lunch in the sky.

They sat around the fire eating and drinking tea, talking about recent events while Monroe filled Robert in on what he knew and Robert did the same. Maggie told him of her kidnapping, the house where she was held, what went on there. Monroe's blood turned to molten lava.

"Fucking Day Walkers and their crews, kidnapping and killing my Countrymen. I've had enough of this bullshit."

"Good. You're impassioned and angry. And no longer a cop." Robert held up a hand. "I mean no disrespect. On the contrary, you're no longer bound by ridiculous human laws so we can do whatever is necessary to stop these atrocities."

Maggie got up and brought the lemon tarts over. "I want to help." She had inside information and could be an asset. Before Monroe could answer her, Robert jumped in.

"Maggie, you've told us enough to go on. You don't need to do anything else, you've taken enough risks. Stay here at Gwrych where it's safe. Help from here."

He could see the color rise up from her neck to suffuse her face. Her hand gripped the arm of the chair and the other hand shook while she refilled her tea.

"Don't tell me to sit back and write up a friggin' report or some such nonsense. I have as much right, no more right, to help. To make sure they don't keep hurting people. I may not be a man, or an investigator, or a blasted Shadow Walker but I can be useful."

Robert held up his hands. "Easy love. I meant no disrespect. All I thought was with Bruce and his men looking for you, it might be wise to lay low for a while and then take a more active role. If you want to go out in the field and shoot the bloody bastards, I'll teach you myself. Deal?"

So not only did the guy have feelings for her, his lady meant a great deal to him. In the year since they'd met, he'd never seen Robert with the same woman more than once and never with one who had the hard, street look Maggie did. She was interesting rather than pretty. As far as he knew Robert had never brought a woman to his home. This was more than protecting a female, he could see it in the way Robert looked at her, the way he acted around her. Protective.

"We both think you'd be a great asset." Monroe liked her spirit. She'd been through the shite and came out swinging. "I've got to get back to the city. You'll let me know which locations Colin thinks are fronts?"

"Aye. We will. I'll walk you out. Would you like to go back by ship? Unless you're one of those blokes who gets seasick. Maggie, want to come along?" Robert smirked at him.

"I would. I do not, and for that smart ass remark, I'll drink all the whisky on board." Monroe retorted.

"You two go on. I'm going to curl up in the library and finish *Gone with the Wind*."

The pirate laughed. "Be my guest, I've plenty more." He walked over and kissed Maggie. "I'll walk Monroe out and then we can figure out the best way to proceed."

She nodded at Robert, standing to look Monroe in the eye. "You won't regret letting me help."

He patted her shoulder as Robert scowled. "I'm looking forward to it. Here's my number if you think of anything else." He handed her his card.

Maggie touched Robert's sleeve. "A word before you leave?"

"Aye, milady. Monroe, I'll be outside in a moment." He left the two of them and walked out the door catching Maggie's question and Robert's response.

"Since I'll be living here, what would you think about using one of the empty buildings to start a school or provide housing for those we find and rescue?"

"'Tis a wonderful idea. I think we should do both. Have a look around and take your pick of buildings. We can talk more when I get back. I thought I'd drive Monroe to the ship."

Monroe softly walked down the hall and out the door. Yep, the womanizing pirate had fallen for the bewitching redhead and it seemed she for him. Especially if he was going to allow children to run amok.

Robert caught up to him. "I'll drive you to the dock."

"My ex-partner, Shamus will be dying for details. He's crazy for old ships." Robert led him to a black Aston Martin. "Another black car, really? Do you guys own vehicles in any other color?"

Robert turned and looked at him. "Black is classic. Get in. Stop being a wanker and maybe I'll let your friend Shamus board the *Revenge II* one day and have a look around."

Monroe caught movement over to the right, next to the stables. Turning around to look, there was no one there. "Did you see someone by the stables?"

Stopping the car, Robert got out. "There's no one there. It was probably Ben, the stable boy." Getting back in, he turned the beautiful machine away from the castle.

Monroe's vision was playing tricks. Chalking it up to a lack of sleep, he took one last look back before settling into the rich leather seats as Robert gunned the engine turning the picturesque scenery into an impressionist painting.

※ 24 ※

No, you don't want Ashley, you want Rhett, you twit. Curled up on the sofa in the library with an icy cold Pepsi and more sugared cranberries, Maggie was content. Robert had introduced her to drinking cold soda with ice, said it was Emily's favorite. It was delicious and the bubbles tickled your nose.

Content.

The word settled in her mouth and she sat forward, reaching out with a hand to steady the crystal dish of berries she'd almost knocked over. Maggie thought about it. For the first time in her life, she wasn't always looking over her shoulder. Felt like she belonged here at Gwrych. Had come to love this sprawling estate and if she was truthful, had serious feelings for the owner. Sinking back into the cushions, pondering these thoughts it took a few moments before she acknowledged someone was standing in the doorway.

"Stephan. Is that you?" Turning to look, the goblet fell from her fingers, landing with a thud on the priceless rug. "Ned? What on earth are you doing here? How did you find me?"

"Huh, Gwrych Castle. You've moved up in the world. I studied this place when I worked at the hostel. Never thought

I'd see it up close and personal. Did you know the estate is over six thousand acres? There's an area to the west called Cae Gerail or field of corpses from some old battle though I'm guessing it will be aptly named again soon." With that cryptic comment, her old friend wandered around the room, keeping his distance. While he wasn't very smart, Ned had a thing for castles and remembered the most obscure facts. The book lay on the carpet next to the Pepsi now seeping into the rug. Surely Gareth or Stephan had let him in. Opening her mouth to call out, Ned was suddenly standing in front of her, his face an angry purple, the vein in his neck throbbing. Ants skittered up her back and the reptilian part of her brain screamed at her to run. Willing her body to calm, she asked again, "How did you find me? I said I was going to Edinburgh Castle."

He held up his hand showing off the thick bandages. "This is your fault."

"I don't understand. What happened?"

"Because I let you go, they took two of my fingers and took Josh to the basement as punishment." Thrusting his hand in her face, Ned looked unhinged. Why hadn't anyone come to see what the commotion was? Robert should be back soon so she'd stall until he made it back or someone heard and came to check on her.

"Josh is dead?" Was it wrong to feel nothing but relief? Her betrayer was no more. A weight lifted off her soul, she could breathe again.

Ned was shaking, a fine sheen of sweat on his face and neck. Maybe he was on something? "I'm really sorry about your hand. I had no idea they would punish you for me leaving. I truly am." She patted the arm of the sofa. "We can talk about it. Robert will be back any time now and he'll help you. You won't have to go back to Bruce or that wretched house ever again." The plead-ing, sad voice was hers though it sounded strange to her ears.

"Go back? I'm working for Bruce now, one of his soldiers. Said he needs me. Robert is it? Don't you know those guys are evil? They're destroying our planet and we have to get rid of them all." His eyes glowed like some of the IRA fanatics she'd seen on the telly. Great, he'd been assimilated. Icy fingers walked down her spine.

"Ned. You never answered me. How. Did. You. Find. Me?"

"Oh, Mags. It wasn't hard. There's a creature, a three-headed hound from hell, scariest thing I've ever seen. Told us where you'd gone."

Maybe he meant that metaphorically? Not sure her brain could handle another supernatural being. Ned was standing right in front of her, less than an arm's reach away.

"Mags, Mags, Mags. You brought this on yourself by running. We need your special abilities, even if you are crazy. Now I have to prove myself worthy to the cause and then I'll have a home." He pulled out a gun, his arm shaking as he leveled it at her. Anger rocketed through her.

"Cowardly bastard. You're no better than Josh. At least he made three hundred quid. What did you get?" White-hot fury radiated through her core and she sneered at him, the gun forgotten.

"A new life." The sound of a gun cocking shattered the silence of the library. "Goodbye Mags."

There was nowhere to run. The gun was at point blank range. When she closed her eyes it wasn't her life that flashed before her...it was Robert's face. She loved him.

The pressure in the room changed, making her ears pop. A loud crunch and a scream made her open her eyes. Staggering back, her knees hitting the chair, she sunk to the floor.

"I was detained on an errand, then I almost forgot my favorite wasabi sauce and had to go back for it. Allow me to introduce myself, I'm Fury." The largest middle head licked its chops. Ned was curled into a ball on the rug, moaning, blood pooling around him as he clutched a bloody stump where his arm used to be.

"Um, you really are a three-headed hound from hell. I

thought maybe he meant it in the abstract, you know, that you were so terrible or something."

The head on the left swiveled around to look at her. "I think we should be insulted."

"No, she just needs to get used to us." The head on the right replied.

The dog, hound, whatever it was, looked at her. "Give us a few minutes to dispose of the trash and then we'll have a nice chat." Before she could utter anything but a gurgle, the beast drizzled the sauce all over Ned and proceeded to eat him. This wasn't happening. Plugging her ears, Maggie curled up into a ball, pressing her head against her knees, shutting out the gruesome noises around her.

A tongue licked her hand. She thought she'd have a heart attack and scrambled back towards the fire.

"Don't be afraid of me. After all, I'm the one who rescued you."

"Rescued? Ned said you told everyone where I was. Why save me?" The heads were grooming the blood and other grisly bits off the midnight black coat. A part of her detached from reality, noting his fur was thick and glossy, almost a blue-black and each head had different colored eyes. Really rather striking.

"Maggie is it? Are you okay? Looks like you might lose your lunch. To answer your question...I'm bound to work for Dayne for another year. However it's all in the wording so while I had to tell them your location, nothing said I couldn't stop them." The middle head looked at her as if it were the most normal response.

"I...I can't take another 'other being'." Her arms gave out and her butt hit the floor. As blackness took her, she swore she heard the beast chuckle.

M aggie woke from the dream. She'd been dreaming about Lulu. The stuffed cat she'd carried everywhere as a child. In her dream, Lulu could talk. Talking cats? The subconscious was a mystery. Memories swam before her, and she sank down into them, floating and remembering as scenes from her life rolled over her like waves buffeting a rowboat in a stormy ocean. "Please mam, don't leave me." She was seven. Her daddy died when she was a baby or so momma told her. She couldn't remember him. There weren't any pictures.

"I'm going to be late for work. Now do what I told you."

She nodded. Mama would hit her if she didn't do what she was told. She recited. "Don't answer the door. Don't go outside, clean the house, do the dishes and laundry before you get home." She stared at her mother. She looked like she'd been taking too many of her pills again, stumbling around the small, dingy flat. Praying her mother wouldn't bring home another man tonight, she stayed small and still so she wouldn't risk her mam's temper. Her mother fumbled around for her purse and left without hugging or kissing Maggie goodbye.

Locking the door behind her, she traipsed to the kitchen carrying her stuffed cat, Lulu. It was the only pet she'd been allowed to have. The animal was missing one eye and the stuffing from its back leg but she loved her all the same. Going to the tiny corner, she reached up on the counter and got her princess bowl and spoon. She'd been a good girl so mum had bought her favorite breakfast food...frosted flakes. Opening the refrigerator, she sighed, no milk, again. Pouring the cereal into a bowl, she ate it dry. There was no orange juice either so she drank a glass of water. Washing her dishes, she put them in the strainer and wiped down the table. The sound of kids laughing drew her to the grimy window. Looking out she could see kids of varying ages dressed in uniforms going off to school. Smiling and playing with each other. Why couldn't she go to school like other kids? Every year she asked and every year the answer was still no. To stop being selfish, thinking of nothing but herself. If she went to school, who would cook and clean? Her mum certainly didn't have time, what with working three jobs. They owned a telly and when her mother was home, it was on all the time. She usually fell asleep on the couch, the soft blue glow illuminating the shabby furniture. Maggie couldn't stand the noise. The old lady upstairs, Mrs. Williams, would get her stories from the library each week. She'd taught Maggie her numbers and how to read. She devoured books, soaking up the knowledge. Wishing she was elsewhere.

Tomorrow was her birthday. Maybe if she were really good today, momma would bring her a cupcake with a candle. The day passed quickly as Maggie finished her chores and curled up in bed with a book. She was reading *Little Women* and must have fallen asleep. Waking, the room was in total darkness. It was late. She'd slept through lunch and dinner. Her mother would be furious. Though maybe she wasn't coming home. Sometimes she didn't. The worst had been when she'd stayed away for four days. Maggie had run out of food and was hungry, crying when she finally came back and staggered to bed with no explanation as to where she'd been.

A knock made her jump. Afraid, she stayed still and quiet.

The sound came again, more insistent. She could see the shadow of feet under the door. *Please let them go away.* She scrunched her eyes shut tight, praying. It seemed like hours had passed when she heard a gentle tap and Mrs. Williams' voice. "Maggie lass, open the door. 'Tis all right child."

Opening the door, Mrs. Williams stood there with a man in uniform and a mean-looking lady. Had they come to take her away? Her lip trembled.

"Let us in, honey." They sat on the sofa with the stuffing coming out and the springs that poked you in the rear end.

If she didn't say a word, maybe it would all go away. The officer with kind brown eyes spoke. "Miss, there's been an accident. Your mum fell at the station today. The train couldn't stop. I'm sorry but she's gone."

Her voice deserted her. This was because she'd fallen asleep without completing all of her chores, it was her fault momma was dead. If she'd been good enough, maybe her mum would be here now instead of these strangers.

"I want my mum." The sound was scratchy as if dredged up from the bottom of the ocean and full of sand. Tears welled up in her eyes. Mrs. Williams patted her hand.

The mean lady spoke up. "You'll be coming with me, Maggie. There's a lovely home for children like you with no family. You'll have lots of other children to play with. It will be fun."

"Can I go to school?"

"Yes, there's a school at the home. Why don't you run and pack?"

Maggie went to her bedroom. She had one small backpack into which she stuffed her only pair of pajamas and another set of clothing. Her hairbrush, toothbrush and toothpaste and that was it. The clothes and shoes she had on completed the sum total of everything she owned in this world. Coming out of the tiny room, she stood looking around the flat. They'd moved so many times she'd lost count. With her mum gone, it didn't hurt to leave the place.

"All ready to go then?" The lady held out her hand to Maggie. Picking up her stuffed animal, Maggie kept her eyes on the floor and nodded. While she was packing she heard the woman call her an 'orphan'. She hoped the home and school would be fun. Maybe she could finally have a real friend, no offense to Lulu.

The Westerly Home for Children was dark and forbidding. It looked like one of those scary places where children are sad and lonely. She was afraid.

Time passed by. The caretakers were mean. Locking children in the closet for hours at a time. Sending them to bed without anything to eat for the smallest infraction and worst of all, she was no longer allowed to have her own library books. She could read the books the home had but she wasn't allowed to take them to her room. The room was a long hallway under the eaves that housed twenty girls. Each had a bed with a small chest at the foot. The boys had a similar layout. She managed to get by simply by keeping quiet and not drawing attention. The other kids called her 'Mousey Maggie'. As long as they left her alone, she didn't care. Not a single one of them was ever adopted. More children came and the home grew more and more crowded with less food for all.

Over the years she managed to survive. She'd found a nook in the attic wall where she hid her most treasured possession, a book about different kinds of fruit. When she turned fifteen, everything changed. Life was harder at the home, staff came and went. Mr. Brewer was the most recent custodian. He was super creepy. Always skulking around at bedtime, watching them dress. Finding excuses to come into the girls' bathroom when they were showering to catch a glimpse of them. After one of the girls returned from the bathroom, pale and crying, refusing to say what happened other than Mr. Brewer touched her, Maggie knew what was coming. Resolve settled around her like a warm blanket.

She would leave. Tonight.

Maggie crept down and out of the orphanage without anyone

noticing. All she had were the clothes on her back and a sack of food she pilfered from the locked pantry. She'd picked the lock with a bobby pin.

It was still raining. She stood in the doorway, watching the rain fall in sheets. Standing on a precipice, she could see the rest of her life in front of her. The streets looked welcoming compared to the life she foresaw. Squaring her shoulders, she slipped out into the wet night.

Nine desperate years dragged by. Survive or die. She did whatever it took, stealing, hiding in abandoned buildings, always keeping her guard up. A vendor in Old Town was selling kitchen knives, without an ounce of remorse, she stole a small knife, kept it in the stolen boots she had on. Over the years, she'd had to stab a few men in the arm who tried to take what was hers or worse. When she was old enough, she took whatever odd jobs she could find, asking for payment under the table. She made less that way but it was worth it to stay under the authorities radar. Once in a while she'd crash at a friend's place she'd met at a job. Never staying more than a week before moving on. When she saved enough, she'd splurge and stay at a hostel for a few days. Hot showers were a godsend. Otherwise, she washed up in public bathrooms the best she could.

When you didn't have a home and lived in dirty, empty buildings, it was hard to keep clean. Even more difficult to keep clothing clean. As she grew and clothes no longer fit, she had to pay a few quid at a charity shop for something else to wear. Usually, if the person working was old, she'd steal another outfit when they weren't paying attention. Putting it on under what she was wearing. She'd lost the guilty feelings a long, long time ago.

Sounds filtered in. The memories receded, like the tide going out to sea and slowly, she came back to the present. Great, just freaking great. Another day before her birthday and Ned almost kills her, before a talking monster shows up and saves her. Was she cursed? What was with the catastrophe's happening on the day before her birthday all the ever-loving time?

Cracking an eye open she looked into worried, deep blue eyes. Safety.

Her heart fluttered. Robert. Where did he come from?

Movement made her look to the left. The beast sat, all three heads watching her. Was she dead or dreaming?

26

"You rang?" With a puff of air Fury dematerialized from Gwrych Castle to the Day Walker Realm where Mr. Annoying, otherwise known as Dayne resided. He spared a thought for the girl, Maggie. From what Robert had filled him in on, she'd been betrayed by Ned. Made him happy he'd eaten the bugger. The human woman had faced tragedy yet come through the other side. He respected that. Didn't know why he'd helped her find a way on Robert's ship. At the time he wasn't aware it was the pirate's ship. Fate was in play with those two.

Seven hells, Dayne was in a snit.

"Where in the hell realms have *you* been?" The angry god snarled, kicking the chained fae at his feet. "One simple task. Find and take care of the woman. Well? It's taken long enough. Tell me she's no longer a problem."

Fury sat on his haunches. "Yes, Ned shot her. She's no longer our problem. I've taken care of her." He failed to mention the shot never made it to Maggie as he ate the bullet, gun, and Ned. And then he'd tended to her. Dayne didn't ask the right question. Omission fit the parameters of the agreement. Wisely, the other two heads kept quiet.

"Excellent. I will not have dissension amongst the ranks. Breeds problems. Where is this human boy? Perhaps I shall thank him."

Right. Because the god was sooo generous. "Alas, the human died when he turned on me. Though even with extra wasabi sauce, he was rather tasteless."

The red-eyed head chimed in. "We're still picking the stringy bits out of our teeth."

Dayne waved them away. "No matter. There are plenty of other humans. The last thing I need is for Thorne to get wind of my plans and go crying to mommy."

Fury nodded each head. "I'll be going if there's nothing else."

"Wait, hound." Fury tensed. Hated it when someone called him 'hound'. How insulting. Yes, he was a three-headed beast but 'hound' implied a Lab or Dalmatian or some other menial dog. He was so much more. Dayne stood and walked down the dais steps to stand in front of Fury. "I have another errand for you."

Huffing in annoyance, Fury sat and waited while the god laid out what he wanted. He'd kiss the door of each of the seven hells when this agreement was over. This task needed to be dealt with quickly. His gut told him to return and keep an eye on the lovely Maggie.

❧ 27 ❧

After dropping Monroe off, Robert jogged up the steps and took a guess he'd find Maggie in the library. The scene was not at all what he expected. Calling out, walking through the doors, he swore in every language he knew. Maggie was lying on the floor. There was blood on his Aubusson rug, seeping onto the stone floor. Was she injured? Dead?

What was worse, Fury was there. The demon hound worked for the enemy, had he come to kill her? Reaching down, he pulled a gun from one boot and dagger from another. "What the bloody hell have you done?" The roar clawed its way out of his chest.

The beast was licking the remnants of a meal off his fur. "Put your weapons away, pirate. Maggie is fine. Though poor Ned made a rather unsatisfying meal."

Not sheathing his daggers but placing them on the floor within easy reach, he sat with Maggie cradled in his lap waiting for her to wake. It gave him plenty of time to get the story from Fury. Thank the gods the beast was there to save her not eat her. If he'd lost her... "You're fighting for the enemy. Why did you aid Maggie?"

All three heads turned to look at him. The head with red

eyes spoke. "We're not aligned with either side. Lost a bet with Dayne and have a year remaining to play errand boy for Mr. Bossypants."

The head with brown eyes answered next. "We like Maggie. You should be thanking us."

At Robert's quizzical look, the main head continued. "Has dear Maggie told you how she came to be on your ship?"

"What of it?"

"While we didn't know at the time it was your ship, we were in raven form and showed her the opening to gain access. We thinks you should thank us or who knows what could have befallen her—the nasty human, Bruce or Ned might have found and dispatched her before you located her. Then where would you be?"

Robert was stunned. Like a bludgeon to the head, he blinked a couple of times to make sure he'd heard correctly. Damn. The truth was evident in the beast's voice. How would he ever repay the debt? He inclined his head. "Fury, you have my gratitude. Maggie is...different. I would be vexed if anything happened to her. I owe you a boon—"

"Whoo-hoo, we're going to have fun with this." The three heads looked at each other and Robert swore they were smirking at him.

"As I was saying, I owe you a boon. However. Nothing that would have me betray my brethren or my cause. Do we have an accord?"

All three heads nodded. The middle head, which was slightly larger, answered him. "We have an accord. We've not had feelings in eons. 'Tis rather nice to care for a change. There is something about your lady...she understands suffering. Maybe that's why we're drawn to her. Take care, Shadow Walker." Fury paused and the heads spoke in unison. "Should harm befall Maggie by your hand, Thorne himself won't be able to save you from our wrath. Are we clear?"

"Crystal." A harsh burst he didn't realize he'd been holding escaped on a hiss of breath. The beast liked Maggie, was willing to protect her. It was always good to have another at your back. Bowing slightly to Fury, he met the gaze of each head.

"If Maggie requires aid, all she needs do is call out." Robert felt the air crackle, a lavender shimmer swirled around the room before settling over Maggie and when he looked up, Fury had vanished.

"I had the strangest dream. There was a three-headed talking dog..." Maggie's voice trailed off about the time realization set in that she was prone on the floor of the library, head cradled in his lap.

"Darlin', you weren't dreaming. I should have been here. From now on, I'm not leaving you alone. If Fury hadn't shown up..."

She coughed and sat up, holding her head. He called for Stephan. "Could you bring Maggie a cold beverage, some cherries and a bottle of Ravensmore for me?"

"Anything else, milord?" Stephan stood there wringing his hands, a look of horror and failure on his face.

"That will be all."

Helping Maggie to her feet, he settled her on the sofa. Stephan had cleaned up the mess. The only evidence was a wet spot on the carpet. Her eyes went to the priceless Aubusson. "Did I ruin it? It must be horribly expensive."

"Who cares about the bloody rug?" Smiling at her, he felt the warmth of the sun in his chest. This woman had managed to find a way in. When he thought of something happening to her, the breath left his body, paralyzing him.

Soon, he needed to tell her about the curse. But not today.

"Wait a minute. 'Fury'. That was real? I wasn't hallucinating?" Her eyes filled but didn't spill over. "I thought Ned was going to kill me. I heard the click of the gun and then the beast, er, Fury, ate the gun, the arm, and—the rest of Ned." A hardness settled over her features turning her to an ancient fiery goddess, ready to destroy. "I'm glad. He would have killed me. If it makes me a bad person, so be it. All I feel is relief." She shot him a tentative look like she wasn't sure what he'd think.

Leaning forward, he ran a finger down the side of her face. "You have nothing to feel guilty about. I would have ripped him to shreds for daring to point a gun at you. You are not a bad person, don't ever think differently." A growl rumbled out of his body.

She was his. He needed to mark her, to let the world know if they laid a finger on her, they would incur the full import of his wrath.

Reaching out to pull her close, the library door opened. Damn Stephan for his timing. Sighing, he leaned back into the cushions.

"Milady." Stephan served her. She favored him with a tremulous smile. "I've come to love Pepsi, thank you. Sorry for the mess earlier."

"Not at all, Miss. Gareth and I should have known something was amiss. Please forgive us." Stephan trembled picking up the tray still upset over what happened to Maggie.

"There's nothing to forgive."

"Anything else, Milord?"

He shook his head in the negative and his throat closed up. Maggie'd charmed his household, him, and even that beast.

Taking a long drink, she curled her legs under her and faced him. "I feel, I don't know, different somehow. Like my skin is tingling."

"I wasn't sure if you'd notice anything or not. I think I'll start calling you Beauty." At her confused look, he chuckled. "Beauty and the Beast. You charmed Fury and he gave you the ability, if you are ever in danger, to simply call his name and he will aid you." The look of disbelief was almost funny except he'd witnessed it first-hand and knew how she felt. "'Tis true, milady. I think he's quite smitten with you." He put his hand on her thigh. "Do you remember when you stowed away on my ship?" She nodded. "And the raven that flew near the open hatch?" Eyes wide, she shook her head yes. "The raven was Fury. He can shapeshift. And he's not just a big-ass dog but something more. Some say demon, some say demi-god, some say very powerful being. Whatever he is, his aid is a great honor."

"But I thought he was working with Dayne and the others? Isn't he our enemy?"

Robert knocked back a hefty swig of whisky. "He owes a debt of service to Dayne but nothing more. Says he's not taken a side. I think he finds the god as annoying as I do. Do you know what he calls him?" The humor filled his voice. She raised an eyebrow. "Mr. Bossypants." At that a laugh broke free from her, sounding like tinkling crystal. Pure and clear.

"No way. Fury must be powerful to not be afraid of Dayne." She looked thoughtful eating her beloved cherries. "Where did he go? I didn't even thank him."

"Your beast said something about an errand to run and vanished. You can thank him when you see him next. I have a feeling we haven't seen the last of him."

She scooted over and leaned into his side. His arm naturally encircled her, playing with her hair before he leaned down and kissed her, softly. Grateful she was unharmed.

"Maggie. You are a grown woman and fully capable of making your own decisions. It wasn't my place to say whether or not you could work with Monroe. I know I sounded like a chauvinist pig." Robert continued before he lost his nerve. "Monroe would be lucky to have you work with him. The school is a marvelous idea even as much as I despise children, for you I'm willing. Whatever you need to make it happen is yours. Don't worry about the money." He paused. "Promise me one thing?"

Kissing him, she looked at him with those emerald eyes. "Anything."

A crushing weight lifted. "Working with him. Be careful. If I'd lost you..." For the first time, words failed him. He stood, bent over and swept her up into his arms, carrying her up the stairs to his, make that their, bedroom.

hispering into Robert's ear, Maggie entwined her
arms around his neck. "This is like Rhett carrying
Scarlett off to bed. Are you going to ravish me,
milord?"

"Aye, milady. I'm going to worship your delectable body from
the tip of your head to the bottom of your sexy toes." Kicking
open the door to the bedroom and slamming it closed behind
them, he strode to the bed and gently laid her across it like some
pagan offering. A feast for his very soul.

Taking her foot in his hand, he removed her boots and socks.
Next he undid the buttons on her pants and slid them down her
hips, stopping to kiss each delectable hipbone. His fingers slid
under the lace of her panties and with a rip, he tossed them to
the floor, chuckling as she gasped. "By the gods, you are breathtaking." A lovely blush suffused her skin turning the porcelain to
pale pink. Unbuttoning her shirt, she leaned up to help him
remove it, perfect breasts straining to leave their lace confine-
ment. A flick of his wrist snapped the delicate fabric as the
porcelain flesh burst free. Her breath was coming in small pants.
Wanting to take her, he instead quickly stripped, padded over to

the sideboard where a light dinner had been laid out and came back holding a jar of honey.

Dipping into the honey, he drizzled it across her shoulder and down her breast. Lying next to her, he lapped the honey, licking his way down the sweet path.

"Is that honey? I've never, I mean..." A smirk filled his face as she lost her train of thought when he dipped his head, taking the pink bud in his mouth, scraping teeth across before blowing on it and sucking. Moving to her other breast, he drizzled the honey along her stomach, breast, and neck. The smell of summer filled the room. The honey giving off a scent of honeysuckle and pear mixed with the woodsmoke and beeswax candles. Looking around he noted the room was bathed in lavender and golden light, casting shadows across her skin, illuminating and hiding at the same time. Following the shadows, he traced lines across her body using the honey, a map to treasure only he could see.

Her breathing was labored. Arching, she grasped the sheets with her fists, sparks seeming to glint in her hair, catching fire. Pale blue veins showed through skin that glowed like fine marble and he kissed his way down each line. The voice that came out was hoarse, sounding as if it belonged to someone else.

"Milady should be dressed in silks and jewels, worshipped. A lovely jewel. Will ye allow me to honor your body?" No one had ever made him feel thus. As if they were the first man and woman to come together, made for each other alone, for all eternity.

Gazing at him with eyes full of passion, she reached out and stroked his check. Palm soft as suede against his skin. "Please." She whispered on a sigh, running her hands along his chest, raising the gooseflesh.

Capturing his prize, he pulled her to him, holding her close, the last bit of bee's nectar forgotten as it dripped down the side of the bed. Plundering her mouth, she moaned from a wild place within. Tasting and nibbling, his tongue dove in, seeking. She tasted of honey and cherries and a tiny hint of lavender. Welcoming him, twining her arms around his neck, she kissed him eagerly, running her nails up and down his back. Trailing kisses over her eyes and nose, he nibbled the delightful corner of her lip. The spot that turned up when she wanted to smile but wasn't sure if she should.

Firm hands explored his body, running through his hair, combing out the tangles. He pulled them both down so they were on their sides facing each other. Tentatively she reached down to the juncture of his thighs, stroking him. He let her take the lead as she pushed him onto his back and slid down his body between his legs. Seeing her there, looking up at him, fondling his cock, he had to concentrate or he'd lose it before he could properly bed her.

A tremulous smile crossed her face an instant before she bent her head, taking him in deep. Licking the head, she swirled her tongue around, kissing the shaft and then covered him again. The soft rhythmic lapping almost undid him. Pulling her up his body, he kissed her. In the blink of an eye, he flipped her over, earning a startled gasp from her. Had someone mistreated her, taken advantage of her? The thought made him tense, muscles tightening. Men were such wretched things. The tenseness in her body remained, the worry in her touch. Whoever had hurt her, he'd burn them out and brand himself in place. Give her pleasure. Show her how wonderful the act of love could be between two people. Reaching for the tray next to the bed, giving her a moment to calm, he sipped the whisky and took a handful of pitted cherries. Chuckling, he squeezed, dripping the dark red juice on her calf, the back of her leg—that spot he loved on the back of her knee.

"Oh, what is that? It's cold."

Licking the juice from her, he grinned. "Why 'tis some of those cherries you're so fond of, darlin'."

"Don't waste the cherries. I love those." The indignation in her voice had him throwing back his head with laughter.

"Easy, love. We've plenty more. If it will calm you, I promise to build you another hothouse and fill it with whatever you desire so you'll never fear running out of the fruit you love so much."

Maggie grumbled words he couldn't quite catch, her voice muffled by the down-filled pillows. It sounded like she'd said something about a hedonistic pirate but he wasn't sure. "Now, where was I?" He dripped more juice across her arse, stopping to admire the twin globes. Her lovely bum was shaped rather like a cherry. Muffling his mirth against the soft flesh, he licked and sucked, his tongue dipping into the crease as she jumped. This time he did laugh out loud before going back to nibbling her delectable flesh.

Reaching under her, he lifted her to her knees, her rump presented to him, her sex glistening in the candlelight, plump and ready for him. Groaning, he tilted her back and popped the last of the cherries into his mouth. He stroked her with a finger, running it through her folds, stroking her mound, kissing each delectable buttock. Inserting two of the cherry stained fingers, he thrust in and out of her core as she clenched around him. So tight, so wet and ready for him. Continuing to thrust, he stroked and circled her bud. She ground into him, a dance older than time itself. Inserting another finger, stretching her, preparing her to take him, he increased the pressure. She was close. Rolling over on his back, his head beneath her sex, he looked up at the delicate pink skin, engorged, flushed and ready for him. Latching on with his mouth, his tongue thrust inside her as he hummed a wordless tune against her flesh, the sounds vibrating against the hard nub. Her thighs clenched tight against his head as she cried out, her release taking her. She tasted of cherries and honey. The smell of a summer meadow filled the room and if he hadn't known for a fact his powers were gone, he'd have sworn he'd taken them both to a field of flowers with the sun shining turning everything to gold.

Hands on her waist, he lifted her, positioning her over his cock. Long and thick, hard and hot, his member jutted out proud, bobbing, seeking her heat. Lowering her gently to let her body accustom itself to the width and length of him, he slid her down inch by inch until she was fully seated, taking all of him in. Her body was tight around him, slick with sweat. Her hips moved of her own accord, breasts bobbing above him as he pumped in and out. Fingers reached out, cupping each breast, kneading and stroking as she moved faster and faster. Sensing she was ready again, he sped up the pace, pumping into her harder and harder, salvation at hand. With a deep thrust, he bellowed, "Maggie."

She let out a keening sound and shattered, body clenching around him, tumbling over the precipice.

A satisfied male rumble emanated from him as he gathered her close. Stroking her hair, murmuring endearments. A shy smile on her face, she ran fingertips up and down his bicep.

She handed him the whisky and took another sip of her wine. Sighing, looking content as a cat with a bowl of cream. Warm, next to each other, they enjoyed the companionable silence, touching each other, learning the other's body.

He must have dozed off. Turning, Maggie was sleeping and still his body stirred, needing her again...she was his oasis in the desert. Lifting her, she woke when he carried her into the bath. Candles filled the room, a bottle of chilled wine waited for them. Steam rose and bubbles mounded in the deep tub. One of his staff had entered through the adjoining door and prepared the bath for them while they slept. His voice came out rough, new, as he lowered her into the water and climbed in behind her.

"I thought we'd have a bath together. I want to feel the silk of your skin sliding against me when I make love to you in the water."

Rather than answering, she reached down taking him in her hand, guiding him home as the air shimmered around them, settling into the tub, turning the water to molten silver, coating their bodies, turning them both to liquid silver as they came together.

They explored each other until the water turned cold. Water had sloshed all over the stone floor during their lovemaking. Toweling her off, he carried her back to bed. Loved picking her up, holding her close. Pulling her tight against him, she fit perfectly. Wrapping an arm around her waist, the other entangled in her hair, they forgot about dinner and fell asleep. As he drifted off, a wisp of a memory blew by. "Lola." At one time, he'd thought she'd be his wife, before she brutally betrayed him. Being with Maggie, he knew Lola meant nothing. How didn't he see it sooner? Maggie was his future. The one he loved. Somehow he'd deal with the curse and avoid telling her altogether. His lady had enough to worry about. Didn't need to worry about the curse too.

❦ 29 ❦

"What do we have here?" Dayne circled the iron cage peering in at the fae woman. He shook his head, looking at his fae slave, Robard. "Wherever did you find her? I swear she looks exactly like Luna."

"In the winter realm, my king. She has no family left and given the discord between the realms, no one will notice her absence. Or if they do, they will simply believe she's gone to linger among the horrible humans. Lemera is her name."

"Leave us." Standing with his hand on his hip, he stood inches from the bars, thinking. The fae hissed at him, baring her teeth as she hit the bars. Rebounding in pain, she sunk to her knees, face contorted. "What gives you the right to hold me? I owe no allegiance to this realm. Release me at once."

Cocking an eyebrow, he pointed in her direction and laughed as the red energy swirled from his finger, snaked through the bars and landed on her mouth. Well, she no longer had a mouth. "If I want your opinion I'll ask. You will learn to obey me or suffer for it. I have plans for you my pretty and you *will* cooperate."

The beautiful woman glared at him before sitting cross-legged in the middle of her cell. He suppressed the urge to rub his hands together in glee. There were enough "inducements" at his disposal for him to break her in a matter of weeks. This woman would be his weapon. With her he could destroy Thorne and the Shadow Walkers in one fell swoop. Nothing would be left to stand in his way. First the human realm, then the rest would fall. One by one until he ruled them all.

Thorne didn't know Dayne knew all about his dear brother prostrating himself on Luna's tomb, begging her to answer him. Would be easy enough to set the stage, have Thorne see her, well an image of her, wandering Luna's temple. The time he'd spent perfecting that little trick was going to be so worthwhile. Then he'd sit back and watch the fun begin without having to break the girl. Simply manifest the appropriate clothing and hairstyle... she already had the haughty look and stance down. Life was good.

Dayne went about his realm, seeing to the inhabitants. Returning hours later, he stood in front of the cage. "Swear you'll behave, and I'll let you stay in a proper room during your time here."

Scowling, she pointed to her face. Right. Waving a hand gave back her mouth and speech.

"I will not swear but in exchange for proper accommodations, I won't kill those who check on me." The words were spat at his feet.

A shoulder lifted. "So be it." The bars fell away and he transported them to a room down the hall from his. It was opulent. A large bed, silk and fur bedcoverings, velvet drapes and comfortable furniture. The floors were blood-red marble with pitch-black thick wool rugs. The door had a heavy bar to lock her in. Not to mention the enchantments he'd laid over the chamber. "Does it meet with your approval?"

The girl had the temerity to sneer at him. "A prison is still a prison, no matter how pretty it looks on the outside. What do you want with me?"

"In due time." Waving a hand, he manifested the appropriate

clothing and hairstyle. By all the realms, she was brilliant. "Food and drink will be here shortly. Enjoy your stay."

Dematerializing out of the room to his private chambers, he lifted a picture off the wall, revealing a rectangle. It was made of a rare crystal, polished to a mirror finish. Waving his hand over it, Luna's temple appeared. Thorne was so predictable, showing up every month on the day of her death to beg forgiveness. Of course she never bothered to answer. Bitch. Reaching deep within, he pulled on the massive amount of energy he'd need to manifest Lemera's image, placing it inside the temple, looking out at the grounds.

Just in the blasted nick of time. The air shimmered and his perfect brother appeared, face full of shame. Dayne sank into a chair eagerly watching the tableau play out. Thorne approached, looking like a man going to face judgment. Nearing Luna's tomb, he stopped. Mouth open, he stared at the column to the back of her resting place. The shimmer of blue gossamer silk caught his eye. There was his decoy, standing in profile. His brother fell to his knees.

"Luna. Forgive me. I've waited eons to see you. To hear your voice." As he neared her, Dayne motioned and she turned her back as a puppet on a string. "Wait. Luna." The agony was almost enough to make him feel sorry for his brother. Not.

With a laugh he blew on the crystal and the manifestation disappeared. Thorne bellowed her name. Sitting with his back against the wall, he pulled his knees up, crossed his arms and buried his face.

Step one complete.

M onday, November 6th

MAGGIE CRACKED AN EYE OPEN. THE PEACE AND CONTENT seeping out of her body, shivering as a chill blew across her. Robert had said "Lola" before he fell asleep. Did this woman hold his heart? What was she to him? And what did Maggie mean to him? Just as she'd thought he meant everything he'd told her, the self-doubt came crashing back. She stewed, fuming.

Secrets.

Maggie hated the nasty little things. They poisoned and betrayed. In her experience nothing ended well when secrets were involved. She wanted nothing more than to shake him awake and demand answers but instead she would lie there and when he woke, still groggy, then she'd ask about *her*.

The candles had been extinguished during the night. It was like the elves had come. The dishes and food debris cleared away, fire stoked. Yawning, her nose twitched. Looking to the side-board, she almost jumped out of bed. Breakfast had been delivered. Maybe that was what woke her while he slumbered on. Guessed she'd fallen asleep after all. Before coming here, she never used to sleep deeply, starting awake at the slightest sound, always tired from waking hundreds of times during the night, being vigilant. But since she'd been with Robert—she slept through the night, rarely stirring. Didn't take a head-shrinker to tell her it meant she felt safe. Enough to let her guard down, to trust nothing would harm her while she slumbered.

Blowing out a frustrated sigh, she slipped from under the covers, padding to the bath. The elves had been here too. Almost as if it were all simply a pleasant dream.

Turning on the shower, Maggie groaned as the hot water hit her body, easing the tension. No longer worried one of Bruce's men would walk in on her, she lingered, blowing the soap suds out of her hands and watching them float, landing gently on the stone floor to be washed down the drain, erased. When her fingers turned to prunes, she sighed. Time to get out and face him. Stepping out of the bath, feeling slightly better, she slowed, the urge to run hitting her hard.

Breathe through your nose. No more running. You are a survivor, and you will face whatever he has to say.

Drying off, she played out various scenarios in her head, none of them with a happy ending. Hair in a towel, she dressed in jeans and another thick sweater. Comfortable on the plush sofa, she ate breakfast by the fire while her hair dried, ignoring the elephant in the bed.

Robert tossed the sheet aside, sat up naked and shot her a wolfish grin. "I wondered where ye'd got to darlin'. I would have joined you in the shower."

Ignoring him, she walked to the sideboard, poured another cup of tea and sat back down in the chair facing the fire. Not looking at him, hands trembling as the tea sloshed over the rim of the cup, she asked the question. "Who is Lola? What exactly is she to you?"

The next thing she knew he was kneeling before her, heedless of his nakedness. She'd never heard him get out of bed. He started. Then stopped. Oh god. It was going to be bad. Wrapping her arms around her middle, rocking back and forth, the remains of breakfast forgotten, she dreaded the answer. "Tell me."

Robert looked into her face and held her hands in his. "Last night was perfect. You are perfect, in every way. Lola was someone from my past. A long time ago, I thought I loved her but years ago I realized I never did. I didn't even really like her. The woman betrayed me. After the events of the last few days, I guess the past was on my mind and her name slipped out in my sleep. I was dreaming of her betrayal. Because of her, I was captured along with my crew and sentenced to death. I died and yet...I have to thank her because I wouldn't have become a Shadow Walker if she hadn't done the things she did to me. Of all people, I would think you could understand where I'm coming from." He sat back on his heels, waiting.

Maggie slid out of her chair to sit on the floor facing him. "Robert, I'm sorry. After all I've been through my own fears took over, and I assumed you were keeping secrets from me. Involved with another woman. We haven't said anything and I shouldn't presume...I don't have intimate relationships with more than one person at a time..." Her voice was small, her eyes downcast.

He raised her chin to look her in the eye. "*You* are the only woman I am involved with. Since I met you there hasn't been another woman. I don't want anyone else. There's only you." Reaching out for her, he traced her lips with a finger.

A small smile flitted across her face. The picture they must make—her fully dressed and him naked as the day he was born... the man was amazing. Inside and out.

"Though Maggie—there is something else I want to tell you." Her shoulders tensed up. "I've been married. Twice."

She stopped him. "I need to eat. My stomach feels funny."

Helping her to her feet, he settled her and fixed himself a

plate, adding whisky to his tea. "Are you going to put clothes on?"

Blinking, he looked down and laughed. "After. Unless my naked body offends?"

Heat bloomed across her face and his chuckle made it worse. "If you spill tea on your 'jewels' don't cry like a big baby."

Kissing her, he pulled the chair closer to her and sat. Seeing him holding a cup of tea, sitting by the fire naked as if it were the most natural thing in the world; she wondered for a brief instant that maybe Ned had shot her, she was dead and this was some screwed up version of heaven or hell.

THE PENSIVE LOOK ON MAGGIE'S FACE TOLD HIM HOW worried she was. Clearing his throat to get her attention, he bravely soldiered on.

"To finish the tale. The first time I married was to a woman with a title. One I barely knew. Once she found out what I really did for a living, she wanted nothing to do with me. Times were different then and divorce wasn't an option so I did what was common practice and took a mistress. I was at sea when I'd heard she died of pneumonia." Hell, he'd never shared this much personal information with any woman. That lone thought scared him more than anything he'd encountered in his life. Buying a few moments to think, he shoveled food in his mouth. Wiping his mouth, he took a furtive look at her. She hadn't run away in disgust, so far so good.

"My second wife was the daughter of the lord who stole my innocence." Her eyes widened as she took in his meaning. "I was seven when it happened. Years later, the same lord was in dire need of funds. The match was arranged. Of course he didn't know who I was but I could never forget his face. At the time I thought it'd be funny to marry the girl. I was dead wrong. Turned out she spent all her time in prayer, thought fornication a deadly sin. The sea was calling. I left and never saw her again. The chit was perfectly content to spend my money and live a life of luxury. All things considered, we were relatively happy with the arrangement." Maggie refilled his tea, adding a hefty dose of whisky. He looked into her eyes for any trace of pity and found... understanding. Nodding he went on with the rest of the sordid story.

"I met Lola during this time. The first few years we were happy. We had an agreement to see whomever we pleased when we weren't together. Not my idea, hers. Time went by and she became increasingly jealous of the others and the money I'd been putting away. What she never told me was she was also mistress to a Royal Navy Captain. Told him everything about me and played both sides by telling me about his ship that was carrying a large shipment of gold. The wench set me up. During the battle I was struck in the arm by grapeshot and transported to Edinburgh Castle. My entire crew captured. As an example to all against the vagaries of pirating we were hanged in front of a crowd at Edinburgh Castle. 'Tis said it was the end of a legend and the golden age of piracy."

To her credit, Maggie didn't say a word. Simply got up, came over and sat in his lap, threw her arms around his neck and kissed him, running her palms over his bare chest. "Thank you for telling me. All of it. We're not so different. You have my trust."

Fuck. She trusted him. His throat closed up, and his bowels turned to water. What would she do when she found out he was keeping the curse from her?

Would she understand and forgive him, or would she leave him? He was in love with her. Couldn't take the risk she'd reject him. Somehow he'd figure it out, break the damnable curse and she'd be none the wiser.

"If you keep sitting on my lap, we'll never get back to Edinburgh."

She laughed, smacking his ass as he got up and sauntered to

the shower. The nice thing about your own private plane—you were never late. It was cold but clear. The sky a grayish blue, the smell of snow in the air. Maggie wanted to walk to the waiting jet.

"You own your own plane? Why am I not surprised?"

He shrugged. "After you, milady." Settling in, he told her there was one stop he needed to make before they met up with Monroe.

Lola. After all this time, Robert no longer hated her. Now he simply felt indifference. He hated to think on his childhood but Maggie's accusations brought it all crashing back.

Robert had been fighting since he was a boy, carving a fearsome reputation across England, Scotland and Wales. A smuggler by trade, he was good at what he did. After sacking his twentieth ship, he'd earned the name, Prince of Pirates and bought the *Revenge*. Truth be told, he was the most dreaded pirate on the seas before he was hanged for pirating at Edinburgh Castle all those years ago. Out of all his nicknames, his favorite was Black Bart. It was a rather dashing tribute to his midnight black hair, of which he was very fond. Sipping a cup of tea, memories assailed him.

Orphaned at age seven, he survived on the streets not unlike Maggie making a living thieving and working when someone would hire him. Though unlike her, his mum had been a prostitute and he'd been born in a brothel. The ladies all took turns caring for him, fussing over him. As a tot, he'd loved helping the women prepare for their suitors. Running to and fro, fetching water and whatever frippery they required. Truth be told, he'd learned a great deal about women. Thinking back on those paid harlots, he smiled. Who could blame him for loving all women after being surrounded by them from his birth to age seven. Wincing, he remembered his mam's death. The man had eclectic tastes. The gentlemen liked inflicting pain, watching the welts and bruises rise on the pale flesh of his mother and others at Posey's. On that fateful night, the man came in out of the rain, wet and drunk. Continuing to drink, he stumbled up the stairs to the room where his mother entertained. Posey wouldn't let any of them interfere on account of the gentlemen being an important Lord. The screams grew louder, carrying on until he thought his ears would bleed. Three times he tried to sneak up the stairs to help her and each time he was cuffed on the ear by one of Posey's men and sent sprawling. As the candles burned down, the night deepened, and her screams became whimpers. The Lord came down the stairs calling for his carriage, the front of his shirt spattered with blood, his hair mussed and a gleam in his eye.

Robert ducked under the guard and ran as fast as his scrawny legs would carry him. Gaining the threshold, he flung the door wide, calling out. "Mum, Mum, are you okay?" There was no answer. Rushing to the bed, he threw the bed curtains open. Shaking his mother, the tears streamed down his dirty face. "Please, wake up, don't leave me." Dead. Bloody lashes marked her back, the delicate skin ripped to shreds. Masses of bruises marked her thighs and her arms were turned in unnatural positions. Blank eyes stared ahead, no life left in them.

It took three of the ladies to pull him away. There was a small burial in an unmarked plot down the street from Posey's establishment. They'd found him a little black suit and black shoes. Besides him, Posey and the ladies who worked for her were the only ones in attendance. The rest of the week they all fussed over him, feeding him the choicest morsels, letting him sleep with them once they were done working for the night. At the end of the week, Posey summoned him to her study. A large woman with orange hair and an overflowing bosom, she told him now that his mum was gone there was no one to pay for his room and board, but he could earn his own way. Pay her back for his expenses and the funeral expense. That evening, he was given a bath and dressed in a linen shirt and suede breeches. They'd given him too much wine and he was tipsy. The rest of the night, he tried to erase from his memory.

A wealthy gentlemen with a taste for young boys had purchased his innocence. Distasteful memories assailed him—pain and a lot of other nasty things he'd had to do. But being taken from behind by a grown man, he thought he'd be ripped apart from the inside out. He'd cried and the man slapped him until he stopped. Then the man wiped his tears and held him close before leaving the money he'd earned on the table. The worst thing was he'd been given his mother's room. Word spread and others came to degrade and defile him. A year passed.

On his eighth birthday after a particularly grueling night with two drunk lords, he fancied taking his chances on the street. The so-called gentlemen had left him curled up in a corner bleeding. After it was over Robert crept down to the kitchens where Cook fed him a late dinner. Leaving him alone to eat, he waited until everyone was gone then he filled a knapsack with bread and cheese and a bottle of wine. All he had was the rucksack and clothes on his body as he slipped out into the night.

Five years, he'd survived as best he could on the streets. Stealing when he had to, sleeping in boarded up buildings, working for food but always on guard. Time passed and made him ruthless and hard, unwilling to show pity to anyone. When he turned thirteen, he found work on a ship captained by an illustrious pirate. 'Twas hard work but fair and the captain warned his crew off from buggering him. A quick study, he rose in the ranks. After a few years, the crew and ship he was working were captured by another band of pirates. Their captain was marched off the gangplank and the rest were given the choice to join the new captain or suffer being sold as slaves. The very next year Robert was given command of his own ship. Being verra enterprising, he decided the pirate life was the life for him. In the years that followed, he and his crew terrified sea-faring folk for years and made a bloody fortune doing it too.

With all he'd been through he couldn't abide a man getting close to him, but women, he still loved them. Was able to put his suffering in the back of his mind and focus on giving pleasure to the many fine ladies he'd bedded.

His thoughts took another dark turn down the pathways he'd rather not visit, and he remembered Lola's last words. What a jealous, conniving woman. Knowing of the betrayal, as he died, he screamed out for vengeance and was answered. 'Tis said, though he had no recollection of it, the captain wanted to let him die, wrap his body in the sail of his ship and cast it over-board so the *Swallow* might have good fortune on the rest of her voyages. But common sense prevailed and he was taken to Scotland.

Thorne answered Robert's call and in return for vengeance, made him a Shadow Walker. The captain, his crew, and trai-torous Lola all perished by his hand the day he was reborn to a new life.

To this day, he had a hard time trusting, especially women. They would betray you for a bauble or a chance to move up the social ladder. He knew he used sex in place of any real connec-tion, and gods help any woman who placed a finger anywhere near his arse. While not violent, he'd jump out of bed and end the encounter immediately. The rest of the night would be spent in a haze of whisky.

The attendant served them beverages and a light lunch, pulling Robert out of the past. Back to the present. He'd been thinking about doing this ever since he'd helped Colin look for Emily last year when she disappeared. Rubbing his hands together, he turned sideways on the chocolate brown suede sofa and laid out his plan.

"Have you ever been to Rosslyn Chapel?"

Maggie sipped her tea and turned to look at him a question in her eyes. "No, never really had the chance. Why?"

"I'll tell you a tale and at the end if you don't want to accompany me, you can go on to meet with Monroe. But if you do, I think 'twill be a grand adventure."

Tucking her legs up under her, she smiled. "You've piqued my curiosity. Tell me." He relished a good story. Hadn't been on an adventure like this since he was a human. Nowadays there wasn't much call for a pirate. Sure, people smuggled objects but it was all so clean and sanitary, no risk other than the authorities. It wasn't fun anymore.

"Remember I told you about Emily and the time she went missing?" Maggie nodded. "What I didn't tell you was one of the places I searched for her was Rosslyn Chapel. There was a carving of a gargoyle with an apple in its mouth—an old symbol for knowledge. I was tracing the carving when the apple pushed inward and a section of the wall opened." He paused as any good storyteller would. Took a drink and sank back into the sofa.

"You're killing me. Go on." Maggie's eyes shone with interest.

Good he had her. "Right. There was a dark stairway leading down, full of cobwebs and dust. Naturally, I followed it to see where it went. I came to another door made of wood covered with a carving of a huge tree. Apples carved at the base of the tree. There was no handle or keyhole I could see. It didn't work to push any of the apples either. As I'd almost given up, I noticed one of the leaves in the tree had a book carved onto it. Pressing the book opened the door." Again he stopped. Maggie was leaning forward, her tea forgotten beside her.

"Do you want to know what I found?"

She smacked him in the arm. "It isn't nice to tease." Mock frowning, she refilled her cup of tea and waited.

He waggled his brows at her. "The chapel itself is the size of a modest country church. As I walked down the next flight of steps, there was a glass bottle filled with matches. I struck one and lit a wick. Lights flared to life, illuminating the path. The stairway seemed to go on forever. I could see my breath in front of me as the air grew colder and colder as I descended into the bowels of the earth. At the bottom, the floor was marble. Oil ran along the room, and great urns of fire flashed...before me lay treasure. Beyond even my wildest dreams. The room was immense, many times larger than the chapel itself."

He was interrupted by the attendant telling them they'd be landing soon. "Is there anything else you require?"

A glass of wine for each of them and he resumed the tale. "There was dust on the floor but not a single human footprint. The air smelled stale and of something ancient, predatory. It was as if I could sense the being watching me, assessing, though no one was there. Shadows slithered across the walls, the treasure casting ominous shapes on the wall. I swore I could feel ancientness in the room. A low-level song, not loud enough to make out, like a distant memory of the best time in your life, played yet no matter how you searched, you couldn't find the source." His voice dropped an octave and he looked around the interior of the jet. "I swear the Grail was there."

"Wait a minute. The Holy Grail? Of ancient legend...from Jesus and King Arthur and the Knights Templar? That Grail?" She looked shell-shocked and a little disbelieving.

Saying it out loud, the outlandish claim seemed fable or conspiracy. But he swore it was there, felt it in his bones. One thing he knew, he was bloody good at what he did, had a nose for sniffing out treasure where others saw nothing. Oh, yes, it was there. He paced.

"Yes, Maggie. *That Grail*. And I mean to have it—of course there is the small matter of the treasure guardian."

"Let me guess, some kind of monster or terrible curse or other equally daunting task or thing will prevent you or should I say us from stealing the Grail?"

"Now darlin', don't put it in such a negative light. Half the fun of treasure hunting is the finding and taking. It isn't stealing. The original owners are long gone so it falls to the one who claims it. I mean to claim not only the Grail but all the treasure."

"Robert. You're disgustingly rich. How much money does one person, oh excuse me, Shadow Walker, need?"

He laughed. "The fact you ask, milady tells me you've never felt the pull of gold and other treasures." Donning his serious face, he told her, "I didn't have time to search the room, but Colin said a great, ferocious, beast guards the treasure. I believe he used the word 'dragon.'" He turned his hands palm up and shrugged as the pilot announced they were descending.

Maggie looked resigned. "Dragons and treasure. Well things with you certainly aren't boring. This dragon isn't going to eat us is he?"

"'Tis always a possibility, my sweet, but never fear, I'll keep you safe." On that note, the plane landed in Edinburgh at the private airstrip he usually used. They were bustled into a black Range Rover and driven to Rosslyn.

"I've never been here. The grounds are beautiful."

He helped her out of the vehicle. There were few tourists wandering around. The cold and fluffy snowflakes keeping most visitors ensconced in warm pubs and museums. Leading Maggie into the interior, her mouth agape as she turned taking everything in, she almost fell over. Walking backward, looking up to admire a particularly intricate carving, she bumped into someone.

"Oh, pardon me."

Robert glanced over. The man had to be pushing ninety. He looked like a crotchety old guy, stooped over, a couple of tufts of white hair over each ear and the dark brown, weathered skin of a sailor.

"Ach, happy to run into such a pretty lass as yerself." He looked at them with bright, intelligent brown eyes. Robert's nose twitched. The guy had a familiar look, something about his eyes... Before he could place the old-timer, he eyed the portfolio the guy was holding.

"Allow me to introduce this lovely lady, Miss Maggie Wallace." He sketched a small bow. "And I am Robert Bartholomew, at your service, sir."

The man took a step back, grabbing the back of a pew, lowering himself down. "It canna be. Ye have the look 'O him and the name...but that would be daft, 'twas hundreds of years ago." The man rubbed the tuft above his left ear, looking thoughtful. "I'm Angus."

Robert looked hard at the old geezer, the name and the eyes. It fit. "You look like a sailor, Angus."

Maggie sat in the pew in front of them and turned around, taking in the scene. He answered. "Aye. I was for many years. Like generations before me, all the way back to Angus the first. He was hanged with Black Bart's crew. Was a bloody shame." He muttered. "Angus left detailed journals and lad, ye are the spittin' image of the infamous pirate himself."

Out of the corner of his eye, Robert saw Maggie sit up straight.

Robert went down on one knee in front of Angus. He didn't question how he knew but always trusted his instincts.

"Angus, you look like a man to keep a confidence." Angus nodded gravely. "I can't explain, other than to say I was given another chance. After...that day. I tracked down every descendant I could find, offered them work, made it right. Angus' family was the only one I couldn't find. Somehow I lost track. He was a good sailor. I was proud to have him as part of my crew. You have my sorrow for losing him." By the gods, Angus' descendant was sitting in front of him. He'd felt guilt for not helping those who were left behind, those who came after.

Maggie got up and discreetly wandered away, allowing them privacy. Angus looked him in the eye.

"The fates have a plan for us all. Your secret is safe with me, Captain. I feel like I know you. Maybe sometime I could show you Angus's journals?" The man's face was pale under his year-round tan.

"I'd like that verra much. May I ask, what you've got there?" Robert pointed to the portfolio.

"Black Bart, I'll be damned." Angus muttered under his breath. "You gave me such a start, I'd almost forgotten. Found this in a junk shop out in the country. Folks didn't know what they had. I'll turn them in when I'm done exploring. I work at Edinburgh Castle now." Chills raced down Robert's spine. "A police officer located a tunnel leading out of the dungeons coming out near the Black Swan. Why, just a month ago, poking around on my break, I followed another, leading here of all places. Take a look at these maps, Cap'n."

Robert smiled. Angus was calling him captain without even realizing it. Leaning in to look over the parchment. A wolfish grin spread over his face. These would help him. They showed secret passages at Rosslyn.

"Well done, Angus. Though I wouldn't turn them in, there's valuable information here. I'd keep em' for myself."

The man smiled up at him, eyes gleaming with mischief. "Mayhap I'll do that."

Running a finger down his nose, Robert had an idea. "How would you like to help us on an adventure, Angus?" He stopped the guy from speaking with a finger to his lips. "Before you agree you should know 'tisn't strictly legal. Not to mention, it's probably dangerous. However, there's great treasure for our efforts. What say you?"

Angus clapped him on the back. "Do ye have to ask, Cap'n? Course I'm in. What are we after?"

Maggie had made her way back to them and heard Angus. She smiled. "I see he's persuaded you to join in this madness."

Angus nodded at her, rubbing his hands together. "I've dreamed of a grand adventure all my life."

"Um-hm. Well, did he tell you about the dragon guarding the treasure?"

The man's eyes gleamed. "Truly, Cap'n? I never thought I'd encounter anything so interesting in my lifetime. Where is the wee beastie? Let's have a go."

Robert chuckled as Maggie rolled her eyes, throwing her hands up in the air. "You two are unbelievable. We'll be lucky if we aren't eaten or burnt to ash."

33

I n the kitchen of Dante Import/Export, Bruce hit end on his mobile and threw the plate containing his sandwich against the wall. The shattering pottery was as loud as a gunshot, making the three other men seated around the table jump and take cover. "Damn stupid boy." He snatched a drink out of the fridge, draining half of it in one long swallow. After spending a year across the pond, he'd come to love cold lite beer.

The men looked at him, questions evident in their faces. "That was Solien. Even after we taught Ned a lesson, he turned on us. The only bit of good news—at least the boy took care of Maggie but then, the cheek, the lad took a shot at Fury. Of course the nasty beast ate him." He was thoughtful. Ned had seemed sworn to the cause, especially after losing two fingers. The boy was eager to prove himself part of the team. If he'd had to guess, he would never have picked Ned as a turncoat.

The mobile jangled again, jarring him from his thoughts. "Bruce here." He listened, anger spreading across his face. He felt the rage building, starting as a ball of fire in his gut, moving up into his chest and neck. He swore he could feel the blood in his veins boiling, beating in time with his heart. Hanging up, the bile bubbling up in his throat, he swallowed. Cocking his arm back to throw the phone against the wall, he thought better of it and pocketed the offending piece of technology.

Appetite gone, he grabbed the rest of the six-pack and cracked the next one open. Turning to address his men, he pushed the palms of his hands to his eye sockets. "Shit bag Shadow Walkers destroyed our largest locations in Paris and London. If that weren't insulting enough, they took out Edinburgh too. All of our hard work, ruined in a matter of days. And they stole all the kids. I want extra guards at every remaining location. We're sending out full squads. No one goes out alone. Understood?" He shot a look at each man. When they nodded he finished. "They haven't hit the industrial site in Glasgow yet. I've had the rest of the people moved and left a rather nasty surprise there for them. Tell your crews, pass the word. Be glad Solien didn't share the news in person." He cringed. The demon was the angriest Bruce had ever heard and when he was angry...

PARIS WAS BEAUTIFUL IN THE WINTER. THORNE MANIFESTED clean clothing and a rare smile leaked out the corner of his mouth. Dayne had to know by now. Did he really think he could get away with kidnapping and killing humans with no consequences?

His brother thought he was the only one with informants. Thorne had been hearing disturbing reports from his Shadow Walkers and put out feelers of his own. The news wasn't good. He'd been preoccupied for far too long. It was time to take action.

By Terya, it was Luna. Only a fleeting glimpse but she'd manifested in her temple. She wouldn't speak to him but she'd seen him, had to have known how much regret flowed through his veins. Making things right with her—it would go a long way to show her how he'd helped the humans. Gone to such lengths to save humanity. Surely it would present him in a favorable light? Filled with optimism for the first time in millennia, he was in arm's reach to destroy his brother.

The sound of Jasper's voice brought him back to the present. He inclined his head.

"Appreciate the help. Do you have enough men in place to guard both locations?"

"We do. Both locations are ready."

A small mademoiselle, no more than four, approached Jasper, tugging on his hand. "Pardon moi, may dolly have a glass of milk?" Thorne smiled as Jasper knelt down to her level. She was a beautiful child. Blonde hair, blue eyes, innocence still present. Her parents were inside. The family was reunited, bent not broken. Manifesting a large mug of milk, Jasper handed it to the little angel. "For the princess." The girl giggled.

Thorne patted her on the head and dematerialized to London.

The children were settling in nicely and efforts underway to reunite any who still had parents. The rest would be cared for, protected. The workers Kendrick had hired were efficient. A pang hit him hard. The warrior was one of his most favored truth be told. To lose him to the in-between, to become a wraith. His face hardened. Terya, his dear mother, wouldn't interfere. Thorne didn't have the power to do it himself, only she did. But no, she spouted some line about the fates and each soul has a destiny set forth in the stars. He would have liked to see Kendrick's face when the first children were liberated and taken to safety. The Norman knight's hired men were standing in the courtyard of the fallen warrior's castle watching him. He cleared his throat, voice gruff, unused to kindness. "'Tis a job well done. Kendrick would have been proud."

One of the men, a mason, lifted his head and addressed Thorne. "We know Lord Kendrick's body wasn't recovered but we made a stone for him." The man pointed to a newly set stone over the door. Not a traditional headstone, this was in shape of a shield, inscribed, *ille qui nos omnes servabit* or 'he who will protect us all'. 'Twas fitting. Kendrick bravely protected humanity. "Kendrick would have approved." Bidding them farewell, he walked down the street before dematerializing. No need for them to realize he was *more*.

After stopping at a large manor home in the highlands of Scotland to give the worker's the same speech, he dematerialized to visit Terya in her realm. Otherwise known as his mother.

Time for a little chat with her regarding his dearest brother. He called out down the long hallway. The marble floors were made of varying shades of green to mimic the outdoors. The walls a colorful mosaic suggesting trees, flowers, and shrubs. The ceiling soared and was done in shades of blue, white and gray. The colors seemed to shift based on her mood. From stormy to clear. Right now he was in luck. The ceiling showed a clear blue sky with the sun shining, not a cloud in sight. Outside, her realm was a perfect, unspoiled world. Verdant forests and meadows gave way to grassy plains and mountains. There were rich swamps and beautiful beaches. Every creature known and some unknown were afforded sanctuary here with her. The only other beings were his mother's attendants.

His footsteps echoed down the empty hallways. Where was everyone? Thorne turned onto a brilliant yellow floor leading outside to one of her favorite gardens. Pushing open the doors, he stood on the threshold a moment, savoring the sun on his face, the sea breeze rustling his shirt. The sound of waves gently lapping the shore were a balm to his tortured soul. Terya was stretched out in a hammock, dressed in a sheer gown of palest yellow. Her long silver hair laced with diamonds, blew in the breeze, fluttering around her. And one ethereal foot hung over the edge swinging in time to the waves.

"Mother. He's gone too far this time. You cannot let Dayne continue with this folly. When will you punish him for his deeds? I demand my right to challenge him to combat...to the death."

Terya held a hand up across her forehead and looked up at

him with her silver eyes, the color of a winter storm, before answering. "Thorne, how lovely to see you, whatever is the matter?"

Reining in his temper, he tried again. "He is enslaving the humans, turning them into cattle. Allowing his Day Walkers to freely feed and kill them. Kidnapping children. It's outrageous. Why aren't you punishing him?"

A hammock appeared next to hers. Between them, a table held icy cold drinks. Beer for him and honeyed wine for her. Terya motioned to the hammock. "Relax."

She could be so infuriating but if he didn't play the game her way, he'd get nothing from her. Kicking off his shoes with a sigh, he looked down at himself and changed his clothing from jeans and a sweater to a pair of surf shorts and sunglasses. His natural platinum skin glowing under the sun, turning to polished silver. His blue tattoos swirled in the sunlight, changing to various colors of blues, greens, and purples to match the sea around him. Picking up the beer, he drained half of it. Settling himself in the hammock, he forced his voice to come out steady, calm.

"Mother, why haven't you done anything? The humans are yours just as the other creatures who inhabit earth belong to you."

When she answered him, her voice sounded like the water, trickling over the boulders around them. "My darling son, we all have choices to make in life. Choices that carry great power. Power to heal or destroy. There must always be balance. Without sun there can be no rain just as without pain there can be no joy. As you must live your life, Dayne must live his. The choices we make define us and have the power to change humanity's fate."

He pushed out of the hammock and stood facing the vast ocean. Did she want humanity destroyed? Did she even care any longer? Terya used to walk among humans, blessing those she found worthy but it had been a long time, eons since she'd done it. Well, Emily was an exception. Maybe she was coming out of this strange ennui that held her for so long, leaving her content to sit back and watch. Never venturing out of her realm. Letting Dayne do as he pleased. Finishing another beer, he sighed, turning to her.

"So you won't become involved, no matter what? Will you even come see what he's done?"

A graceful hand reached out and touched his shoulder. "I will walk amongst humanity." He thanked her. "Thorne?" He looked down at her. "Talk to your brother, it's time to make amends."

His tattoos flashed an angry red before turning such a dark shade of blue, they looked black against his skin. "Amends. After what he's done. I'll never forgive him. Not even after I kill him."

Instead of answering, she looked at him, seeming to stare into his very core. He looked away first. Her voice was soft when she spoke. "You believe Luna is returned." It was a statement. He paced in the sand, small crabs and sandpipers scurrying out of his way.

"She was standing in her temple as beautiful as ever but she wouldn't speak to me. After all this time, she still won't forgive me." His voice broke at the end. When he left here, he was going back to the temple. She had to talk to him. To listen. To let him make it right.

Terya stood and hugged him tight. He dwarfed her, her head barely coming to his chest. "How can Luna forgive you when you won't forgive yourself?" He didn't have an answer for her. Releasing him, she walked to the waters edge and spoke to the dolphin's playing in the shallows. He almost missed her words. "Living in the past, you never learn to see the present."

And another statement he didn't have an answer to. He lived in the now. If he didn't, things would be much worse, humanity would cease to exist. He kept the tide from turning. Maybe his mother had one thing right—it was time for he and Dayne to have...what did Colin's adorable wife call it? Oh yes, a come to Jesus meeting. His face set in stone, he materialized back into old, faded jeans and a sweater. Best to look like he didn't care. If he showed up in armor, dear brother would know the war was on. Thorne would come at him under the guise of conciliation. Though the only reconciliation his brother would ever get from him was a dagger to the heart. Daggers in the pockets of his coat, Thorne pictured his brother's throne room and decided to pay him a little visit.

✣ 34 ✣

Rosslyn Chapel was closing for the day. Ducking into a secret panel against the back wall, they waited until the last worker locked up and left. "Good thing I brought me maps, they show a tunnel under the chapel. We can use it to escape the wee beastie." Angus was grinning from ear to ear, so excited he was practically vibrating off the floor.

Robert led them to the first set of stairs and on down to the door carved with apples.

"It looks exactly like you described it. Can I look for the leaf with the book carved into it?" Maggie's eyes shone with excitement, like a kid at Christmas. He sobered, wondering if she'd ever had a proper holiday or an adventure. Today she'd get an adventure and he'd make sure she got a holiday in the future.

Working her way through, branch by branch, she started with the leaves carved into the left side of the tree. Not wanting to hurry her, he stood back watching. What would she do if they came face to face with the beast said to guard the Templar's treasure? Would she and Angus stand or would they run? Dragons were supposed to be extinct so he'd only heard stories. But the tales. The fire and scales hard as diamond. Colin said the beast was huge. That it had made its lair here since the Templar's entrusted their treasure to it for safekeeping. Supposedly dragons loved treasure. Colin told him the beast left to hunt, taking a few sheep, horses, pigs, or cattle here and there. Not enough to be discovered but plenty to eat well. Of course, Colin could be getting one off on him...he'd find out soon enough.

"I found it!" A click had the door swinging open. Warm air greeted them.

"That's odd. Last year the air was really cold. I could see my breath." Robert inhaled, taking the humid air into his nose and lungs, tasting it. Was his foe in residence? The matches were where he'd left them last year. Still snug and dry in the glass bottle. He struck one on the bottom of the ridged bottle and lit the wick. As before, the pathway before them was illuminated. Descending down the steps, the air grew warmer. Maggie bumped into Angus who stood stock-still, mouth agape.

"I've never seen such a thing in all me days." The lights had flared to life, displaying the treasure in the immense cavern.

"It smells strange down here. Like a mix of dust, old books and...the ocean. But we're nowhere near the ocean. I don't get it." Maggie shook her head.

Robert could smell it too. Never wished he had his powers back as he did now. Was the beast lying in wait or had it gone out hunting? The warm air gave away the fact it was there or had recently been there. "We should hurry. The dragon, animal or whatever beast it is will most undoubtedly be back soon."

Leading the way, he handed each of them two duffel bags.

Angus looked at him. "Are ye daft, Cap'n? We need ships to haul away this much booty. Two scanty bags won't hold much." Even Maggie looked perplexed.

"The two of you look like it's Christmas and Santa didn't come. Never worry. We take what we can carry and once we ascertain there is no beast, then I bring in the crew to take the full booty away. Work for you two pirates?" He chuckled. They had wide-eyed looks like lads seeing their first haul. It took him back to his first catch when his share had been a handful of precious gems and a gold statue. Riches danced in front of his eyes, the future laid out in front of him full of wondrous possibilities.

"Maggie? Angus?" Questioning eyes turned towards him. "Be watchful. And what you fit in the bags is yours to keep, aye?" Smiles broke out on both faces and Angus went first, like a magpie drawn to bright shiny things. Maggie hung back a moment.

"You're going after the Grail."

"I am. Though make no mistake, I'll fill my bags. Will be good to show the crew what they'll have a taste of. Be off now, find whatever makes you smile." For the first time since they'd met, Maggie looked light-hearted. Seems adventure agreed with his Maggie.

Cocking his head, Robert listened. Yes. He heard it again. The low level song met his ears, soft and the memories flew behind his eyes. Where was it coming from? If he could find the source, the Grail would be his.

Keeping an eye on Maggie and Angus, he followed the music. Along the way, picking up jewels, gold and other treasures as they caught his eye.

"Robert? Can you come over here?" Maggie was hidden by a stack of gold statues. All he could see was her hand waving above her head. He made his way to her and sucked in a breath.

"Wow. That's a lot of paper."

A glazed look on her face, she hugged him. "I know. Can you believe all the books?"

"Wait a moment, milady. Robert reverently picked up a small, leather bound book. The pages seemed to be made out of something other than paper. They were strong and the ink still dark after all this time. Carefully, he opened it. "Bloody hell, do you know what you have here?"

She shook her head. "Old books and I'm taking as many as I can."

"These are so much more than 'old books,' some of these

may be from the lost library of Atlantis if I remember correctly. In a port in Greece, I met an old man who told me a legend passed down through the generations of his family. A long time ago, they were guardians of knowledge and one of them failed and lost the key they'd been entrusted with. He said I'd know any of the books if I ever came across them by the pages. The ink would shimmer and never fade. These are priceless. Well done." Bending her backwards, he kissed her deeply.

Peering into one of her satchels, he smiled. It was full of books. "You can take gold and jewels as well, milady." A teasing noted filled his voice.

"I know. I'll take a few things to sell for the school but the books—those I want to keep."

He gave her a slight bow. "As milady, wishes."

A tinkling sound and smell of the ocean drifted into the cavern, carried on the breeze. The scent filled him from within... wait a minute, why was he feeling air movement?

"Angus?" There was no answer other than a soft chuffing sound. Keeping his voice low, he warned Maggie. "We have company. Hide here in-between the stacks of books until I come for you." She nodded, her eyes wide and darting around the immense space. "Stay quiet." With a finger to his lips, he moved like a shadow, wishing again for his powers. Damn rules.

Robert moved towards the sound, stopping every few feet to listen. Moving past solid gold statues, he saw Angus crouched down, bags bulging. The old man pointed to the wall. Lamplight reflected off something shiny and he could see glittering, like gold coins tumbling in the surf, caressed by sunlight. Scales. The chuffing sound was followed by a puff of smoke. The thing was enormous, much larger than Fury and that guy was the size of a bloody bus. The dragon had two black horns, gold eyes and blue skin. The scales were iridescent in the soft light. Reflecting the colors of the rainbow on the walls, floor and treasure around them. Great claws protruded from each foot, black like the horns. Muscle rippled as wings unfurled. The wings easily spanned a large jet. They too were black and looked like worn leather.

Watching, he made himself still and silent as a great beast of a dragon, climbed the walls, the spiked tail lashing as it disappeared into darkness.

Letting out breath he didn't realize he'd been holding, Robert picked up his booty, quickly filling the remaining bag. Circling back to Angus on his way to Maggie, he hoped they'd escape before they were nothing more than a tasty barbequed treat for the dragon.

Tapping Angus on the shoulder, the man jumped, clapping his hand over his mouth. "You scared ten years off me life, Cap'n."

"Let's find Maggie and abscond with our bounty. We'll come back another day with the crew. No sense taking too many chances today."

Angus agreed and they slowly made their way back to Maggie. Taking a longer, more shadowy route back, Robert spied something. 'Twas jewelry simply laying across a gold plate but—.

There were earrings, a necklace, and ring. His insides knotted, the hair all over his body standing at attention. The exact match to the bracelet he'd given Emily to wear at her wedding. Fate.

A long time ago, he'd had a sister. The gentleman took her when his wife wanted a child and couldn't have one. The wife wouldn't ask where the baby came from or how her husband came by the child. The lord paid his mother well for Susanna with the promise they would never seek her out.

Robert went by the house many times to peer between the iron fence at the large home trying to catch a glimpse of her. They looked so much alike. She had the same midnight black hair and indigo eyes except she was tiny, so petite.

A letter reached him with sad tidings. At sixteen she'd been thrown from her horse, contracted pneumonia and died. Somehow she'd found out about him and had entrusted her lady's maid to get a message to him. Inside the letter was the bracelet. It was her favorite and she wished him to give it to the lady he would wed. Funny, he'd saved it all this time until giving up, he gave it to Emily.

Emily's words came back to him. *Oh, Robert, it's stunning. I would be honored to wear it, to borrow it, but I must give it back, you'll want to give it to the woman you marry.*

A shadow crossed his face, leaning down so only she could hear, No, lass. Tis unheard of for one of us to break our curse, I don't expect to see it happen again. I gave up on love a long, long, time ago.

It looked beautiful on her. Afterwards, she returned it, telling him again she knew in her heart he'd find his other half. At the time he didn't believe her. Now...Maggie.

The bracelet was stunning. Fashioned into flowers and vines. The vines were tiny emeralds, the flowers alternated between sapphires, rubies, and diamonds. He'd never thought there was anything else like it and here in front of him was the rest of the set. Was it a sign from Terya?

Taking the jewelry, he and Angus walked down a corridor filled with chests of jewels and coins, turning the corner of the first stack of books to where Maggie had been hiding.

There was no sign of her. A few tumbled books on the floor the only indicator she'd been there. The footsteps in the dust stopped abruptly and vanished. His gut clenched.

"Angus, head to the left and we'll meet up at the golden doors." He pointed ahead of them. "If you see anything, call out." Angus nodded and moved down a narrow pathway.

Robert started to the right of the footsteps. She had to be here. Maybe she'd wandered off looking at her blasted books. The alternative was something he refused to think on. Time seemed to pass slowly and the feeling of wrongness intensified. He'd made it to the far wall when he heard a whisper. Who the hell was she talking to?

A rush of wings made him lean back as warm air skimmed his face. "Robert. The most amazing thing—."

He crushed her to him. "Where have you been? I thought... Are you unharmed?" Holding her at arm's length, he looked her over for any signs of injury.

The chit had the nerve to giggle. "I was trying to tell you. Draken showed me around and let me fly on his back. It was amazing." She was giddy, breathless.

"Maggie, *who* is Draken? Gods, tell me you didn't encounter the guardian?"

Throwing her arms around his neck, she hugged him, kissing him, her hair was tousled, and her eyes sparkled. A carefree look filled her face.

"Robert. He's marvelous. The knights left him here with orders to guard the treasure and then they never came back. Can you believe they just left him here? All that time? Poor guy. I think he's lonely."

Barely resisting the urge to roll his eyes, really, a lonely dragon? What was coming next? Bringing it home to Gwrych like an abandoned puppy? He caught her sheepish look.

No. Hell no.

"I, uh, told him, he's welcome at Gwrych. We have tons of room. All this time, with no one to talk to, please can he come home with us?"

"Maggie, dragons aren't to be trusted."

She snorted at him. "How do you know? Do you know any dragons?" Well, she had him there. Running the calculations in his head, he'd need to increase the cows, sheep, pigs and horses on his estate in order to feed the beast. Bloody hell, was he seriously considering bringing a dragon home? In a matter of days, she'd turned his household upside down.

Maggie batted her eyelashes at him in an over-dramatic way. "Draken said you can have the treasure, *all* the treasure, if he can come live with us. He'd rather have company. Ask him yourself."

Looking around he spread his hands to show he was unarmed. Was he really doing this? Colin said he'd do insane things for the woman he loved. Guess he was about to find out.

"Sir Draken. May I have a word?" What an idiot he was, talking to the air.

Warm air ruffled his hair, the flap of great leathery wings, signaling the arrival of the beast.

"Black Bart. Even down here, I've heard tale of you. Have you come to steal from me?" A puff of flame mere inches from his face before the dragon dropped his invisibility.

"Please, call me Robert. Black Bart was another life." Bowing, he told the massive creature, "Aye, I'm still a pirate of sorts, here to steal the treasure though I never meant to offend the guardian. My apologies."

Draken's laugh was a deep rumble, shaking the floor, coins spilling down the tall piles, plates and statuary rattling. "You're not the least bit sorry, but as Maggie is rather charming and promised to read to me every day, I'll let it go." What, the dragon could talk but not read? Seriously, did he just say 'talking dragon'? Was he losing his mind? Draken continued. "I can read but it's challenging to turn the pages without tearing them." He sounded indignant.

Ancient eyes regarded him. "So Shadow Walker. The earth is in trouble, and from what I hear, you could use some help."

"I thought you didn't get many visitors here?"

"None. Though I listen when I fly out to eat and sometimes I hear people walking around above talking."

Robert cleared his throat, not believing what he was about to offer. "Draken. Maggie and I would be honored if you would consider living at Gwrych Castle with us. And yes, we can always use help against Dayne and his Day Walkers. What say you, do we have an accord?"

The dragon bent his massive head down nuzzling Maggie before he looked Robert in the eye and answered, his voice deep and solid like the stone around them. "We have an accord. Can I eat as many Day Walkers as I want?"

"Aye, you can. Not to mention the nasty human minions who help them. I'll also add more sheep, horses, pigs, and cows to my estate. The entire North and East wings are unoccupied. Maggie is going to use one for a school, the other is yours. Will that suit?"

Draken chuffed. "Most generous. Shall I fly you there now?"

Angus had been silent all this time, looking as if he wasn't sure what was real and what might be hallucination. "I've always wanted to fly."

Maggie smiled. "Then it's settled. You'll fly home with us." As the old seaman's mouth fell open, her smile faltered. "I shouldn't have assumed. You probably have a place you love. Why would you want to live with us and all the chaos that's about to descend on Gwrych? I'm sorry, Angus."

The man took two steps and with a look at Robert to make sure it was okay, hugged her tight. "Lassie, 'tis the nicest thing anyone's ever done for me. I'd love to live at Gwrych. Think ye mayhap I could help teach the little ones? I've a great love for history."

She had tears in her eyes. "I'd like that very much."

Robert clapped his hands together. "It's settled then. Draken and Angus are come to live at Gwrych. Angus you'll fly back with him, and Maggie and I will drive. I need to make a few calls for my crew to come and collect everything. We're going to need tractor trailers for all this." He rubbed his hands together, understanding a dragon's fascination with treasure.

"I've given up wondering how much treasure one man needs. Anyway, a school is expensive and I'm sure it's going to cost a boatload to feed Draken. So enjoy your treasure, I won't say another word...as long as I get all the books, that is." Winding his hair around her fingers, she kissed him on the cheek, her hand stroking his neck.

Robert helped Angus onto Draken's back. "By the way, do you like to eat goblins?"

Gold eyes turned to regard him. "They taste terrible, but I rather enjoy burning them to ash. Why?"

The beast didn't hear everything. "The goblins have aligned

themselves with the Day Walkers, causing havoc in the human world." The dragon nodded and with a great whoosh took off towards the black ceiling. Angus whooping until his voice was lost.

Whipping out his mobile, Robert called his right hand man, Baylor. Appraising him of the situation, he chuckled at the man's reaction. They could all retire rich men if they chose after this. Hanging up, he looked over at Maggie. The warm light turned her into a goddess. She had suffered, been betrayed and abused and she was still a kind, giving person. As good as she was, he didn't deserve her, not in a million years. Could he be the man she needed?

"I thought my life couldn't get any stranger but I was so wrong." Maggie kissed him. They sank to the floor on an undoubtedly priceless rug and he peeled her clothes off. After all, he had a few hours to kill before his crew arrived to transport the booty. Couldn't leave it unprotected, could he? What better way to while away the time than by making love to his woman.

Maggie dozed in his arms, her glorious hair fanned out across his chest. Would he ever tire of looking at her? His life was turning upside down and he...liked it. She stirred, her breath soft against his skin.

"Did I fall asleep? Has the treasure express arrived yet?" She yawned and curled into his side, sleepy eyes looking up at him. His heart clenched. So this is what it was all about. The moment stretched until he thought he could live suspended like this and be content.

"You were kind to take Angus in."

He waved the comment away. "It was the right thing to do. I failed his ancestor. I won't make the same mistake with him. Now he can live out his life at Gwrych, never worrying. See he hasn't any family left."

"You've become quite the king of lost humans. I like this side of you. Very much."

She was pleased with him. Could hear it in her voice. Now he had the treasure and her. Once he took care of the little curse problem, his life would be perfect.

"Something's been bothering me. Before...I saw others like you disappear, manifest weapons, take people away, all kinds of things. And you guys are basically invincible. So why didn't you use your powers today? Is there anything you're not telling me?"

The question was like a bucket of cold water to his face. He wouldn't scare her. Not now. Not after she slept through the night without starting at every creak. She was like a mistreated animal that was always on guard, never feeling safe or trusting enough to sleep, always vigilant, an ear alert to any sign of danger. Finally she was learning to trust again, he wouldn't take it from her and replace it with worry. The curse wouldn't control either of him. The hell if he knew how, but somehow he'd make sure of it.

So he did what he thought was right. "No. Everything is fine. I haven't recharged my powers and didn't want to deplete them, that's all." After giving him a long look, she shrugged and kissed his shoulder. His mobile rang. "We're here. I'll tell you how to get in. Did you set up the road closed signs to keep prying eyes away?" Blood singing, he finished telling them how to find him. All of it would be his. Well most of it. A generous portion going to his crew, Angus and Maggie. And the Grail. It was here in the treasure. Once it was safe at Gwrych, he'd have plenty of time to listen, and find it, hidden beneath the mounds of loot. Dressing they went to meet the motley assortment of men unaware a traitor lurked within.

✖ 35 ✖

With the treasure safely transported to Gwrych, Robert checked in on Angus who was happily settling into the North wing. He'd taken one of the rooms as his own, waving them in. "You're back. To fly is a wondrous thing. Draken stopped at me flat and I packed up everything I wanted. Once we got here, he decided he preferred the East wing, something about the light so I came here to the North. This bloody castle is huge."

Maggie and Robert laughed. "There's plenty of unused furniture around, take whatever you want. I'm going to check on the unloading of the treasure and give the men their shares." Angus happily waved him away. Turning on his heel, Robert kissed her. "Will you be alright for an hour or so?"

Her cheeks flushed from the kiss, she gently pushed him out the door. "Go. Angus and I have much to discuss for setting up our school. Then I want to check on Draken, make sure he's settled in, and I promised I'd read to him after dinner. I was telling him about *Gone with the Wind*. He thinks it sounds wonderful."

Rolling his eyes, he called out over his shoulder. "Any excuse for starting it over, I'd expect. You know, I thought I was the lord here. I'd better not come in second place to a bloody dragon."

❦

LAUGHING, MAGGIE TURNED TO ANGUS. THEY SPENT THE next several hours discussing how to set up the school, coming up with a plan. He had great ideas and was excited as she to help those who'd been forgotten. Leaving Angus to the plans, she hugged him as she left. "I want to go see how Draken is doing."

"I won't be surprised if all sorts of animals and creatures start turning up here, looking for sanctuary. Seems if people need help, critters will too."

"Guess it's good I'm rich now and the castle is gigantic, we've plenty of room to take in all who seek shelter." Wandering down the hallway, lost in thought, Maggie came to the East wing, the salty ocean tang permeated the air, the dragon's unique scent, and called out. "Draken? It's Maggie."

She heard his welcoming chuff and saw gold eyes in the dim light at the end of the hallway. "Do you like your new home?" The dragon's claws clicked on the stone floor as he came towards Maggie. Lowering his head to look her in the eye, he smiled. Well, it looked like a smile to her.

"I can smell the ocean again and there are people around. I feel their heartbeats as they come and go." He bobbed his head, horns dipping. "This is a good place. I shall be happy here. Though I must knock down a few walls and doors to make it easier to move around."

Biting her lip, she hoped she wasn't saying something she shouldn't. "Go ahead and make it to your liking, Robert won't mind a bit."

Draken motioned her through a wide archway. The room was bare but what caught her eye was the large bank of windows. Rushing to the stone window seat, she clambered up and peered out. "You can see everything. The water looks like molten silver."

Iridescent scales caught the weak winter sun as Draken stood beside her. Eyes closed, he breathed in deeply. "Yes, I will be happy here." Fixing a gold eye on her, he cocked his head. "Maggie. You seem happy with the Shadow Walker. Have you already broken the curse? I've heard said their curses are near impossible to break."

The air whooshed out of her lungs, stomach falling like that first hill on a rollercoaster, and her legs tingled. It was almost dinnertime; maybe it was low blood sugar or some kind of virus? He had to be mistaken. Robert would have told her, he promised no secrets.

"Are you unwell? Have I caused you offense?" Draken was so close she could see the flecks of amber, honey and sunlight in his eyes.

"Robert never told me about any curse. There must be a mistake."

The gold eyes squinted, taking her in, measuring. "On one of my flights to find food, I encountered a Shadow Walker whose name was Kendrick. He kept me company outside of Chillingham Castle in England while I finished my meal. He kept very tasty sheep there." Maggie was looking at him, an anguished cry escaped and she clapped her hand to her mouth. Draken's tail curled around her the spikes retracted, holding her next to him. "Kendrick told me the story of Colin and Emily and entrusted me with the curse all Shadow Walkers live with. I would never have mentioned it except you both seemed happy together so I wrongly assumed you'd broken it. Forgive me for upsetting you."

Tears leaked out of her eyes. Please not him too. I can't take one more betrayal. Her stomach hollow and heart beating erratically in her chest, Maggie rested her check on Draken's side. His scales were warm like smooth pebbled rocks kissed by sunlight. Her voice came out thin, reedy. "Would you tell me what the curse is? I don't know."

The massive beast hesitated, seeming to weigh his words before he answered. "Beautiful girl, you should really talk to

Robert about this...'tis evident I'm out of practice in the art of conversation. I've botched this terribly." He snorted and a small plume of flame shot out. "Alright. Kendrick told me as part of accepting the bargain to become a Shadow Walker, they all bear a curse. Every year on the date of their human death, they relive the end and are subsequently without any of their powers. Usually for just a night and day but—oh, seven hells, if they meet the one and only, their true love, during the anniversary, they are powerless for a week."

Maggie gasped, her entire body trembling. Draken enfolded her in his wings, the warmth keeping her teeth from chattering. "Kendrick said during the week if the curse isn't broken then the Shadow Walker's soul is lost. Trapped forever in-between. Not living or dying but turned into a wraith. They also become wraith if a Day Walker takes all of their life-essence, draining them dry."

Draken shuddered. "The in-between is a terrible place. Dragons know of it. It is a realm of eternal suffering. Gray, soundless, empty. Though I've heard tales of terrible creatures who haunt it." Maggie was wiping the tears away with the palms of her hands but they kept coming as if she'd turned on a faucet and couldn't turn it back off. Draken's body vibrated and a purring sound emanated as if he was trying to calm her. She patted his side, stroking the inside of his wing. It was soft, like the finest suede.

"Tell me the rest." He fanned his wings slightly, sending heated air across her body. It didn't matter, she didn't think she'd ever be warm again.

"Pretty Maggie. You earned the right to know when you aided Robert in some way. What happened?"

Her shoulders tensed, remembering. "Yes, I saved him from being hanged at Edinburgh Castle. Course then I ran away when I saw it was him. Maybe I should have kept running."

The scales shimmered as he shook his great body. "No, Maggie. It was too late. If the curse isn't broken, not just Robert will suffer. You will be doomed. You will live the rest of your life alone, dying without anyone beside you, never finding true love. I'm sorry to be the one to tell you."

"Why would he lie to me after he said he'd told me everything? Promised me we'd have no secrets from each other. I trusted him." The tears were falling freely now. Hitting the stones with a tinkling sound like water on fine crystal.

"Shall I go and eat him?"

She started. Draken looked serious. "No, don't." Anger flared, covering the pain and hurt and she stoked it high. Would need it to confront him. "If you eat him, I won't have the satisfaction of seeing his face when I out him for lying. I'll never let anyone hurt me again. So if the curse is loneliness, well then bring it on, I'm rather friendly with the emotion by now."

"Maggie, loneliness is a terrible thing. Do you know how long I've ached to find one more of my kind? To know if there are any left or if I am the last of all dragonkind? I wouldn't wish desolation on anyone, child." Draken let her go and chuffed. Maggie looked down at the floor. There in a pile on the stones were clear bits of glass.

"Diamonds? What on earth are those doing here?" She hadn't seen them before.

The massive beast chuffed again. "A side effect of being around a dragon. If you cry in a dragon's embrace, your tears turn to diamonds. Gather them up and cast them into the sea and your heartache will go with them." He gazed at her with wise, kind eyes.

Kneeling, she picked up every stone marveling that such beauty could come from so much sadness. "I will. But not today. For now, I want to capture the hurt so the next time I think I might let someone in, I'll touch these and remember." Her eyes were sandpaper on silk, her throat burned from the hurt, and she tasted the bitterness of betrayal in her mouth. After being betrayed three times...by her mother, Josh, and Ned; she thought this one would be a bit easier to swallow. It hurt more than all the past hurts combined. Was this love? A silent, distorted laugh broke out inside her. Then let the curse take her, being alone would be better any day of the week than having to feel her insides ripped to shreds, over and over, again.

Draken didn't say anything.

What was there to say?

❧ 36 ❧

With a heavy heart, Maggie left the East wing, deep in thought. Wandering the corridors, she came to the North wing. A small sob escaped. This was to be her school. Randomly opening doors, she could see Angus had been at work. Some of the rooms had paper taped to the walls. The lists detailed what the room might be used for and what furniture would be needed. A pang hit her and she reached out to lean against the wall. Angus could do this without her. There was no way she was staying, not after Robert's deception. The sound of wood scraping against stone had her turning around.

"Perfect timing. Look what I found." Enthusiasm filled Angus's voice. He had a beautiful desk halfway into the room.

"Let me help." They pushed the heavy furniture the rest of the way in. It looked like it belonged there. "Where did you find it?"

He scratched his head. "I came across a room full to the top with bits and pieces of furniture. There are tables and benches and all sorts of things which would be perfect for the kids to use as desks. Want to help me bring them in? I thought this room could be the history class." He stopped and looked at her. "I didn't want to overstep so I did this one first to see if you might like it." He waited.

"Angus, I couldn't have come up with a better setup myself. You have an eye for this. Might you want to set up the rest of the classrooms?" And with that line, her heart crumbled. "I have to go to Edinburgh for a while and help Monroe. Think you could work on the school while I'm gone? Draken said he'd help if you needed it."

He grinned. "Go. Do what ye need to do. A dragon helping me? Would have never thought it in all me years." He waved her aside, the wheels turning in his head. "I'll have plenty to show ye when you get back, lass."

"A dinner buffet should be set up by now. Don't forget to eat." Maggie gave him a quick hug and fled before the tears could spill over. She ran down the hallway, heedless of where she was going and crashed into a warm wall.

"Pretty Maggie, don't cry. Come with me and you can watch me eat Robert." Draken nudged her with his great head.

Throwing her arms around him, she cried until there weren't any tears left. A small pile of stones lay at her feet. Looking down a hysterical laugh burbled up. "Diamonds from tears, it's really rather perfect." She scooped them up, put them in her jeans pocket and pulled herself together. "No, don't eat him. But might I ask a favor?"

His tail thumped, making the door nearest her rattle. Thank goodness the hallways were so wide, otherwise he wouldn't fit. "Name your boon."

"I'm going to my room to pack, and I realized I don't have any way of getting to Edinburgh. I could borrow one of the cars but I don't want to. I just want to leave. Would you take me to the city?"

Draken brought his head to eye level. "Yes, Maggie. Go and pack. While you do that, I'll eat and be waiting in the court-yard." She turned to go, his words stopping her in her tracks. "Tell him why you're leaving. The pirate deserves to know."

She wanted to explode. Deserves to know, my foot. Counting to ten, she took a deep breath. Maybe Draken had a point. She'd want the courtesy of an explanation if it were her in the wrong. The thought of facing him made her knees weak. She offered up a prayer to whoever might be listening. *Please grant me strength. Don't let me give in.* "You're right. I'll tell him. See you in a bit." Walking slowly, Maggie went to pack. Her room. It was beautiful and she'd miss it.

Miss *him*.

The door shut with a soft click and yet to her ears it sounded like a thundering boom. The imagery of a door closing equating to endings struck her at the same time. Get it together. She squared her shoulders and straightened her spine. You've lived most of your life with no one to rely on, you can do it again. And now, there's plenty of money so at least you won't be back on the streets. Groaning as she hefted the four duffel bags, she made her way down to the great hall. Dropping the luggage on the sofa, she went in search of Robert.

She found him in the kitchens. His hair was windblown and he looked so sexy and perfect standing there smiling at her that she had a moment's hesitation. She could pretend she didn't know about the curse, un-know it. A small shake of her head and she knew she'd never let it go. The hurt would subside... eventually.

Robert filled the room with his presence. "Ready to eat? I'm starving." He went to hug her and she stepped back noting the frown on his face. "What's wrong? Have I done something to upset you?"

She was numb. There were no more tears, no more anger. Only regret. The scent of it—dust and lilies, filled the air, burning her eyes.

"The curse." Maggie watched his eyes widen and his nostrils flare as the words registered. "Were you ever going to tell me? Or let the week pass and see what happened? How could you?"

Stepping towards her, he reached out as she stepped back. "Maggie, I can explain. Let me explain."

"There's nothing more to say. I came to tell you I'm leaving. Going to Edinburgh to work with Monroe." She turned to go.

"Maggie, wait." Hope filled her chest. Would he come clean, make it better?

"I didn't want to worry you. I can handle this myself. And really, no one knows exactly what the curse entails."

He was making excuses. The light within her extinguished without a sound. "At least now I know what Thorne meant when he asked if you'd 'enlightened me'. We said no secrets. What you did is unforgivable. Goodbye, Robert."

She turned and left him standing in the middle of the kitchen amongst the overpowering smell of lilies, looking shell-shocked. He didn't make a move to come after her. She'd been wrong. She loved him but he didn't love her. If he did, he'd never let her walk out.

Opening the door of the great hall and stepping out into the courtyard, she saw Draken waiting. Her soul screamed out at her not to leave. To make it right. This was her home, where she belonged.

Not anymore.

Climbing on Draken's back, they took to the evening air. Don't look back. No matter how much she ached to stay. Instead she clenched her jaw, wrapped her arms around the dragon's neck and shut her eyes tight. Repeating over and over like a benediction, *don't look back, don't look back, don't look back.*

The flight to Edinburgh was exhilarating, the cold air tempered by the heat rising from Draken's hide. They flew above the clouds. With the evening sky darkening to indigo, even if a random pedestrian happened to look up they wouldn't see anything amiss. Maybe a shadow or large bird but no one in their right mind would think 'oh, that's a dragon'. A dragon in the sky. A week ago she would have thought it crazy but now after everything she'd been through, hell, anything could happen or appear and she would no longer be shocked.

The rhythmic whump of Draken's wings soothed her temper. The hollow feeling threatened to consume her. Rubbing her temples to massage away the headache she looked down. The countryside was beautiful. Ribbons of gray and silver, lights shining from the windows of homes. The stark beauty of late fall deepening to winter as if the world were sleeping, waiting for spring to begin again. Maybe she could go to sleep and wake in the spring, renewed and able to start anew. Robert's betrayal was different than her mother's or Josh or Ned. His burned through her, scorching away everything in its path, leaving charred earth behind in place of her heart. Turning her into one of the walking dead. Body alive but the soul and heart destroyed. Usually she could push the feelings down deep and think about them later, but this. His face kept appearing before her eyes. Blinking, she thought of the last thing he'd said when she mounted Draken.

He was standing with one of his new crew members. The one who kept looking at her and the castle as if casing the joint. She didn't trust him as far as she could throw him. They'd finished divvying up the treasure and Robert looked rumpled and sexy as hell. No way was he helping her onto Draken's back. Gareth assisted her as Robert stood stiff as a stone wall, glaring, the corners of his mouth pulling down.

Anger flooded in so easily ignited when she thought of his words. That she'd overreacted. It wasn't really a secret but rather something he was planning to take care of so why worry her? As if he really believed he was in the right.

She sighed. In her book, it was not only a betrayal but also a big fat lie that had the potential to impact the rest of her life and he basically told her not to worry her pretty little head. A snort escaped and Draken turned to glance at her.

"I'm fine, just thinking about taking you up on your offer to make a Robert sandwich." She yelled over the wind. Draken's response was to shoot a plume of fire. Anyone looking up would think it was a jet trail.

Robert told her she could use his house in Edinburgh. She said no, thank you. As if. Like she wanted him showing up whenever he felt like it. No, she needed neutral turf where she felt safe and wouldn't have to see him. It was too difficult. The thought of seeing his face, she was afraid she'd cave and forgive him. That if she did, he'd betray her once again. And she'd never recover.

Part of her was angry he didn't drag her off Draken, tell her he couldn't live without her. Say he would forsake his immortal life to be with her. But this was real life not some fairy tale. In reality you were betrayed, hurt, and discarded. Maggie was a grown ass woman and would no longer hope for the magic of children's stories. It might seem like she'd found her fairy tale—

well the scary beasts and curses—but the charming prince was nothing more than a toad in disguise.

Time to grow up. Fairy tales never came true.

"Hold on, we're landing." Draken's voice was in her head. How did he do that? Nice trick. He set them down with a soft thump in an empty parking lot down the street from Monroe's flat. She'd only had to pull up the destination and show him on a map before they'd left. His internal radar was better than any GPS she'd ever seen.

Sliding off, she made sure she had her gear. A single large bag. The rest she put in Draken's room figuring no one would dare take them. The dragon had assured her he'd eat any who tried.

"You realize I *let* all of you enter the treasure chamber. I could have turned you to ash at any time."

She patted his snout. "I know. I think you were ready to spend time with others. Thank you for not eating us and for the ride." She choked up. Would she ever return home? She'd only met Robert but it felt like they'd known each other forever, that she belonged at Gwrych, had finally found her place in the world. Get over yourself and pull it together.

"Will you go back home?"

"After I have a snack. Is there anything else you need?"

She told him no and bid him goodbye before she could cry again. She'd never cried this much in her life. Maybe she was getting soft.

Monroe didn't know she was coming. In her rush to leave, she'd forgotten to call him and there was the small matter that she planned to crash on his couch. Entering the vestibule, she looked for his name and took the stairs to the flat.

Knocking twice, she waited. A few minutes passed and she shifted from foot to foot. Rapping again louder, relief washed over her when the door was thrown open.

"Maggie. Sorry, I was in the shower. Come in." Monroe stood back to let her in. The flat was clean. She mentally chastised herself but given the way the ex-cop liked to drink she expected a dirty, bachelor pad.

"Nice place. Sorry to barge in on you."

He interrupted her. "Robert called. Said you were coming and might need a place to stay for a few days. Everything alright?" He was looking at her as if afraid she'd crumble to pieces in his living room. She wanted to laugh at the panicked look in his eyes.

"If it's not too much trouble, could I crash on your couch for a couple of days? Just until I find my own flat." She ignored the raised eyebrows and questioning look. "Does the offer still stand to work with you?"

"Sure, you can stay here until you find something and hell yes, I could use the help." He took her bag and put it next to the couch. "There are blankets and pillows in the closet. I'll get you a key so you can come and go as you please...oh, my neighbor across the hall, Amy, comes to clean and do the shopping every week so if there's anything you need put it on the list on the counter." He paused. "Um...everything okay? Do you...want to... talk?"

"Monroe. I'm fine. I don't want to talk about it and don't worry. I won't sit on your couch and cry. There are lots of people who need our help, let's get to work, shall we?"

He looked so relieved it almost made her laugh.

"Sure. Great. Have a seat." He motioned her to the sofa and handed her a beer. "Yell if you need anything. We'll get started in the morning."

She'd thanked him and made up the makeshift bed. Instead of tossing and turning, exhaustion consumed her as she fell into a deep dreamless sleep.

❧ 38 ❧

T uesday, November 7th

MUNCHING TOAST, MONROE SHARED HIS INFORMATION. Maggie added details where she could. She'd slept well, waking before him and starting the coffee before hitting the shower and getting dressed. It was early but she needed to do something. Anything to keep her mind from rehashing the previous events. Work would occupy her and take her mind off him. Monroe laid out three locations he wanted to check out before rallying the troops.

"There's a building near Glasgow. It's the perfect location to hide people. If you don't need anything else, we'll get on the road and scout that one first."

Grateful for immediate action to fill her brain, she drained the coffee. As she jogged down the stairs behind him, she only thought of Robert three times. It was a good start to the day. She'd ask lots of questions on the drive so she wouldn't have time to dwell.

✿

Neil couldn't believe dragons existed and there was one living at Gwrych. Wait until Bruce heard Maggie had a beast protecting her. Hell, he'd flip when he found out she was alive. That monster, Fury lied. If he hadn't been standing there in the courtyard with Robert and seen it with his own eyes, he'd never have believed it.

Slinking around behind the stables, he placed the call. Bruce was very interested in the treasure and they plotted to kill each crewmember and steal their share. The treasure inside the castle would be harder but not impossible with the right distraction. To say he was furious Maggie was alive was an understatement. Neil heard breaking crockery and what sounded like a chair or table turning over before Bruce came back on the line.

"Good job, Neil. I want everyone on board for this. We'll need two large crews. One to hit Robert's men at their homes and another at the castle in Wales. Keep an eye on things and I'll ring once his men are dead. We'll hit them within the hour."

Ending the call, Neil smiled. He'd be richly compensated. No need to bother Bruce about the share of treasure Robert had already given him. As the newest man, he got the smallest share but that paltry amount should bring him several million pounds easy. No, he'd tell Bruce he only got a handful of coins and jewels. Skulking around the stables, he went back inside the old soldier's garrison now turned luxurious quarters for Robert's men who wanted to stay at the castle. He had a diversion to plan.

❧ 39 ❧

Maggie was gone. Left him. Robert wanted to go inside, lock himself in the study and drown in a cask of rum. Draken deserved to be hit with a blast of energy for telling her before he could. Well, he would have... eventually. Once he'd taken care of everything.

He ticked off the accusations—lying, keeping secrets, not trusting her, and betrayal. Okay, he lied by omission and technically he kept a secret from her. But not trusting her. He trusted her with his life. She was someone he'd want at his back. The accusation of betrayal stung the most.

He'd called her mobile a dozen times. The first two times she answered but wouldn't say a bloody word. How could he make it right if she wouldn't speak to him? Realizing she was sending her calls to voice mail, he rang Monroe.

The guy wouldn't even hand the phone to Maggie. He had the nerve to tell Robert to give her time, a few days. Time. That was rich. The one thing out of his control.

Hours passed in a blur. Feeling sorry for himself, he sat and drank. Damnation. He'd return all of the treasure if it would make this right. He tried calling Thorne but got bloody voice mail. At this moment, he hated technology. How could he fix things if the bastard wouldn't answer?

And he had to resolve matters with Maggie. Gwrych was desolate, empty without her presence. How could he tell the bloody stubborn woman he loved her if she wouldn't pick up the damn phone?

Deciding he needed to vary his swear words, he threw out a few choice phrases he'd picked up. Nope, didn't feel a bit better.

Banging his head on the desk, he shouted to the fates. "Thanks a bloody lot. Not like I have a lot of time left here."

Nice. Now he was talking to the ceiling.

The bottle of rum was empty. Squinting at the glass, a smile curved across his face. He wasn't some green lad. He knew Maggie. What made her tick, what made her happy and what made her angry. A strategy was what he needed. Then he'd woo her back. And he'd take care of the curse all in one nice pretty package. He could fix this.

Gareth burst into the study, interrupting his planning. "Milord, I'm terribly sorry to interrupt, your mobile's going directly to voice mail.

He glanced down and sure enough he'd set it on silent. What if Maggie had called? Rubbing his eyes, his shoulders tensed as he noted the look of alarm on Gareth's face. "Whatever is the matter, man?"

"Bean has been badly injured. Three men attacked him on the way into his cottage, after the treasure, they were. Lucky for him the missus wasn't home. He'd have been killed except the authorities happened by and broke up the quarrel. Bean told them it was nothing to worry over and sent them away."

"How bad is it?"

The steward grimaced. "Bad. The men knew about the treasure. As they planned to murder Bean, guess they didn't worry about what was said. All of your crew is supposed to be hit tonight. The orders were to kill the crew and steal the gold."

Gareth paused, swallowing. "Bean heard them mention Solien. There's a traitor amongst us."

Standing and looking out the window over the courtyard, Robert swore in every language he knew. "Neil is the newest addition. The rest of the men...there's no way any of them did this. He came to us from another ship with a story of losing his job and a family to feed. At the time he checked out so either he had some help infiltrating the crew or he turned minion after. No matter." Robert paced the study, planning and discarding until he stopped and spun to face his most trusted man. "Call the crew and warn them. I'll call Colin and Jasper for help. Every last one of those buggering bastard minions and Day Walkers we can locate die tonight." Sweeping his arm across the desk, sending papers and crystal to the floor, rage filled him. The door swung open. What now? Like he needed any more problems.

"Milord, we're under attack."

"Gareth, make the calls." Running out of the room, he checked to ensure he had daggers in his boots, he grabbed the shoulder holster off the table along with extra magazines and bolted for the courtyard. A fight was just the thing for keeping his mind off Maggie.

Thank the gods for voice dialing. "Call Colin." Come on, come on, answer, blast it. A cranky voice picked up. "I'm in the middle of trying to feed the twins, 'tis worse than facing ten Day Walkers with no powers. What?"

"My crew's been targeted. I need you and Jasper to go to each house and check on them. The enemy will be out in full force." He was almost to the great hall. Breathing heavy, he took the stairs two at a time, wishing again for his powers.

"Why are you out of breath?" Colin's voice was laced with suspicion.

"Seems, some of the losers decided to come at me here at Gwrych. Don't worry about it, just get to my men. I can't be both places at once—" Fear gripped him. Maggie was out in the city. "Colin. Listen to me. Call Monroe and warn him. Maggie's with him and I can't go to her."

There was a sharp intake of breath. "Bloody hell. You're powerless. Why isn't Maggie with you? The week's almost—"

Robert cut him off. "Don't say it, get it done. We can talk like little old ladies over a pot of tea when this is over." Ending the call, he threw the great doors open.

Pandemonium reigned. Men filled the courtyard, fighting. How utterly insulting. Not a Day Walker among them. Solien had only sent minions to steal from him? He didn't know whether to be furious or roar with laughter. One of the losers caught his attention. Well, at least the current minion leader, Bruce was here. He wanted that one for himself. Owed it to Maggie.

Jumping into the fray, dodging bullets, he took out two minions as his feet hit the bottom step. Cutting men down, making his way to the center of the melee where his target stood, Robert dimly registered the screams but kept going. Battle lust taking over, sending him onward. Shooting a man point blank in the chest, he came face to face with Bruce. Gratified to see the man pale and take a step back when he saw Robert. 'Twas his undoing. No bullets for this one. Pulling a dagger from his boot, he sliced the guy's trigger arm, hitting tendon as the gun fell from Bruce's fingers and his hand refused to close on its own.

"Bruce, the merry minion leader. I've been wanting to meet you."

The man's eyes darted to the side seeking help. None would be forthcoming as his men were fighting for their lives. There were a small number of men at Gwrych but they were used to brawling, had grown up in the streets or on a ship. Both taught a man to stand up and fight at an early age.

Grasping his injured arm, Bruce backed up a few more steps. "You've stolen my property, pirate." The words were bold but the voice, shaking, reedy, gave him away.

"People are not property. And Maggie is under my protection." Gods, he was sweating. It felt warmer. Shrugging, Robert struck again. The blade cutting through the man's denim-clad thigh like butter. He cried out. His pants leg soaked. Good he'd hit an artery. He wanted this worm of a man to suffer for what he did to Maggie. Wanted to be the one to end his life.

The smell of cooked meat assailed his senses. Punching Bruce in the face, he was gratified to hear the crunch of bone as his nose shattered, blood gushing down his face to soak his shirt. The piece of trash fell to his knees giving Robert time to process what was happening behind him.

Draken had joined the party and was shooting flames from between his massive teeth, roasting minions where they stood. As he watched, Draken snatched one man around his midsection, threw him into the air and as the great jaws snapped shut, he swore he heard the man still screaming.

Turning back to finish Bruce off, a bolt of lightning cracked next to his head missing him by mere inches. The smell of electricity filled the air. What the bloody hell? Had a Day Walker or three arrived late to the party? With all the smoke from burning flesh it was hard to see. A large, shaggy head appeared, followed by two more.

Fury had joined the melee.

Kneeling down, Robert raised his dagger to Bruce's neck. "I want you to remember your men dying, barbequed and eaten alive while you bled out on the ground, unable to help them. Know this. I will raze every holding location, destroy every minion and let Draken eat every goblin in my Country. The Day Walkers will fall and everything you've done will be for naught. Ready yourself to face judgment. I don't think kidnappers will be well received."

The leader of the minions, didn't blubber or cry, he glared at Robert. "Screw you. There's something big coming and you and every last Shadow Walker are going to die while Solien and his goblins feast on your guts."

"Blah, blah, blah. Whatever. Let Solien try." Sliding the dagger across his neck, Robert opened Bruce from ear to ear. He bled out frantically trying to hold the gaping wound together.

Wiping the blade off on his pants, Robert stood and surveyed the courtyard. It was a bleedin' mess. Draken and Fury were arguing over whether or not to put the wasabi sauce on before Draken roasted the bodies or after.

Gareth had minor cuts and bruises. Stephan sustained a bullet wound to the shoulder. The rest of Robert's men had various injuries, none life-threatening. He was proud of them. They'd fought well.

"Colin's in-house doctor will be here shortly. Colin sent him on the jet." Gareth coughed. "Seems we won't need to clean up the bodies." He gestured to the dragon and hound who were making happy chomping noises.

"Did Monroe call? Is Maggie all right?" Please let her be unharmed. If she'd been hurt when he couldn't protect her...he would rather face eternity as a wraith.

Baylor appeared out of the smoke. "She's safe, milord. Monroe and Maggie are in Glasgow investigating a building used in the kidnappings. I've apprised them of the situation. They will take the utmost care."

Relief flooded his system, overriding his legs. He sat down hard on a stone bench in the courtyard, wondering how he came to be sitting. He was standing a moment ago. She was unharmed. Thank the gods. "What of the men? Did Colin and Jasper get to them in time?"

Gareth was sorting the men into groups based on their injuries. Stephan was passing out rum and whisky. The good doctor would be on-site in thirty minutes.

Handing Robert a bandage to wrap his arm where he'd been nicked by a stray bullet, Baylor answered. "Aye. Two of the crew were badly beaten, the rest taking minor injuries. Colin and Jasper killed all thirty minions and three Day Walkers sent after the crew."

Thanking him, Robert sent Baylor to help the men. He stood, testing his legs. Steady, he moved towards them intending to talk personally with each man. Fury blocked his path, his great paws resting on someone.

"Shadow Walker. I heard what was happening, wanted a snack and here I am." The middle head spoke to him while the other two watched the man wiggling on the ground. "You didn't tell me you had a dragon living here. I haven't seen one in at least a thousand years. Gwrych is becoming rather interesting."

Throwing his head back, Robert roared with laughter. The hound thought this 'interesting'? "Mayhap you should share the East wing with Draken. Who knows what other interesting doin's might take place?"

All three heads swiveled to look at each other and then Robert. "When we're in this realm, we'd be honored to make our home here at Gwrych. Though Draken needs to get his own stash of sauce. All my wasabi sauce is gone and we have seven or eight bites left."

Robert schooled his face into what he hoped was appropriate consternation. "I'll make sure we keep a supply on hand. I've a feeling there will be plenty more minions to eat. Welcome to Gwrych." He threw his arms out and spun in a circle.

A grunt drew his gaze to the lump at Fury's feet. "Neil. Bloody buggering traitor. I should kill you but I think instead I'll let Fury and Draken play tug-o-war with you." The man moaned in terror, crying and begging for his life.

Stalking towards the drive to meet Colin's doctor, Robert threw over his shoulder, "Fury. Share with Draken."

❧ 40 ❧

The drive to Glasgow was uneventful. Maggie was grateful Monroe kept his thoughts to himself. She wasn't ready to talk about Robert. Grateful to him for letting her crash on his couch, she'd need to find her own flat soon. Fresh pain ripped through her, she put a hand to her side, pressing hard in vain attempts to push the hurt back. Baylor had called Monroe warning them to be careful. Bruce and his men had come after the crew and shown up at Gwrych.

She hoped everyone was okay...that he was safe.

Restless, she adjusted her seat. These guys and their fantastic cars. His Mercedes SUV was so comfortable she'd gladly sleep in the backseat if needed. Turning the seat warmer up, she tensed. Monroe turned onto Pinkston road. Off in the distance she could see the building. One might think it was abandoned until they looked closer. New fencing surrounded the property, new boards covered the windows. An ideal location, it overlooked the Glasgow-Edinburgh railway line. Her mouth turned down. Perfect for transporting human cattle. The old industrial building was large. How many people would they find held inside, prisoners?

Monroe pulled over to the side of the road. "You drive, I'll take photos. Something might show up when we take a closer look later."

"Are you sure there are people here? I have to hope you're wrong. If you're right...look how big the building is, there's probably hundreds of people inside." She kept the fear tamped down tight. While she'd never lived at one of the holding locations, she'd seen one, once. Bruce had her with him and made her go inside. The conditions were deplorable. People slept on cots or on the floor. They were filthy and many had been beaten. The children were the worst. Vacant, glassy-eyed stares met hers if they would look at her at all. And the shrieking. She could hear them screaming when they were taken to give energy. The place stank of desolation, hopelessness, and pain. She shuddered.

"Maggie, stay in the car. You don't need to get out."

She shook her head. "No. I want to. I've been to one of these places before. I know what to look for."

He nodded, his face set in grim lines. "Drive slowly over to the pile of rubbish. We can use it for cover. Don't see any guards about so we'll have a quick look around. They might have been diverted to deal with the raids on Robert and his men."

Maggie could see the cop in him come to the forefront. His posture changed, his face was hard. Somehow seeing him look the part made her feel safe. She was with a professional. They were simply looking around. No need to worry.

Thankful for expensive vehicles, she exhaled a breath she didn't realize she'd been holding when the door clicked shut with a soft snick. "Maggie, stay there, I'll come around to your side."

Before she knew what happened, Monroe was in front of her, crouched low to the ground. He was fast. "Are you sure you're not one of *them*?"

Chuckling low in his throat, he smiled. "Nope. I'm just that good." Under her breath, she murmured "Arrogant jerk."

"Did you say something?"

She shot him her most innocent look. "Not a word." He didn't look convinced but let it go.

"Follow me. Do what I do and we'll both be fine."

Taking a zigzag path, he led her to the corner of the structure. Still no sign of anyone about. Maybe Monroe's information was wrong. This might be an abandoned building after all. There was a loose board on a dirty window and a large drum underneath it. Perfect for standing on.

Putting her hand on his arm, she stopped him from climbing up. "Let me." He hesitated a moment then put his hands out to give her a leg up. Crouched on the drum, she caught her breath. How did the cops do this every day? Her nerves were going haywire and she swore anyone within a kilometer could hear her heart beating out of her chest.

"Take a deep breath. Steady your stance and slowly stand."

Grateful to him, she did. Rubbing off the grime on the windowpane with her the sleeve of her coat, she peered inside. The interior was dim. Giving her eyes a moment to adjust she took a deep breath, willing the gods of calm to visit her.

Nothing moved. There had been people here. Cots were overturned, pillows and blankets strewn across the floor. It looked like they'd left in a hurry. Pressing her ear against the window she plugged her other ear and listened. Silence. No screams, no voices. She swallowed. Her mouth was dry. Something was wrong here. Every instinct screamed at her to run.

It was cold outside, no wind but why was she sweating and feeling air blowing across her face? It was coming from the building. Reaching a hand out, Monroe helped her down, the concern etched across his face. "What's wrong? What did you see?"

"There were people inside. A lot of people. I think they left in a hurry. The only thing I saw was scattered bedding and overturned furniture. Something isn't right. We need to leave. Now."

To his credit, he didn't say a word but motioned for her to go as he turned and followed her back to the SUV. She heard the sound of something heavy hitting the ground. Looking over her shoulder she saw Monroe face planted on the ground. Gasping, she ran to him. He was shaking his head. "What happened? Hell, feels like I was hit by a train."

Before she could get the words out, one of her worst night-mares came into view. Sauntered out of nowhere, stalking her like a lion to a gazelle.

"Maggie, my dear. How lovely to see you. I'd head rumor you were dead, seems I was rather misinformed."

Ice crackled within, freezing her veins, blooming across her body, she couldn't move. "Rawlins. I don't want any trouble. Please let me go. I promise I won't say a word." A shot rang out, making her ears ring, missing the Day Walker by millimeters. He merely raised an eyebrow and kicked Monroe so hard he went flying into the SUV denting the door.

"I've heard tell of a human cop, oh pardon me, ex-cop, who's been working with the enemy. Monroe, is it?"

Her partner was silent. Oh god, was he dead? "Monroe. Get up." A small groan answered her. Great, just frigging great. He couldn't help her. Somehow she found the strength to look up at Rawlins.

"Guess your friend doesn't have anything to say. I don't have any tea to offer but I believe you and I are long overdue for a chat."

The voice in her head admired the look of him. He was rumored to be a fierce fighter, over four hundred years old. When you first noticed him, he was breathtaking. Easily six three, with a heavily muscled body and broad shoulders tapering to a trim waist, he had short, dirty blond hair and dark brown eyes. But the eyes gave him away. Dead like the sharks she'd seen on the telly. He dressed in designer clothing and today was no exception. His dark gray cashmere coat gaped open showcasing some kind of fancy suit that looked really expensive.

"Let me go. Monroe was helping me find a place to live and we got turned around, ended up here." She put on her most convincing face, hoping the lie would be enough to spare them both.

A beeping noise pulled his attention away from her. He reached in his pocket pulling out what looked like a tiny phone. He sighed. "No fun for me today. Seems to be a theme this year." He raised his hand and hit Monroe with a blast of energy. The cop was still on the ground. Motionless.

She held her hands up in front of her face, backing away. The hair on her arms prickling was the only warning before she found herself flat on her back, staring up at the sky. The clouds were blotted out by a shadow, no make that Rawlins. He knelt down beside her.

"Maggie. If only you'd come to me. I could have taken you away from that dreadful house, kept you for myself." He tsked. "But instead you ran. Have you any idea the problems you caused? Bruce and all of his men are dead, most of our locations have been destroyed, the humans rescued by your new friends. All due to events you set in motion. Now I have to locate replacements. Do you know how difficult it is to find acceptable help?" He stroked her hair. Tears leaked from the corner of her eyes. She couldn't move, could barely breathe. He'd done something to her, paralyzed her or maybe she was dying.

"Rest assured, you won't feel a thing," He held up the small phone. "This place is about to be blown to smithereens and I'm afraid you and Mr. Monroe will be incinerated in the blast." He examined his nails. "I had all the humans moved to a new location. Don't worry, I'll take excellent care of them." His smile didn't reach his eyes. "Being blown up is much better than being eaten by goblins, wouldn't you agree?"

Standing, he dusted off his suit, pressed a button on the phone and dematerialized. She closed her eyes. Nothing happened. Her finger twitched. Could she move? Willing her body to get up, she wanted to scream in frustration but nothing came out. Channeling every ounce of willpower, she rolled to her side. Maggie could see Monroe. Was he still alive? Her hand moved a millimeter.

Hope suffused her.

Dust rose up around her, swirling in the air, filling her lungs, choking her. Her vision dimmed, Monroe faded to blackness. Why hadn't she made it right with Robert? She'd never told him she loved him.

The noise from the blast reached her ears a few seconds later. It was the last sound she heard.

W*ednesday, November 8th*

ROBERT CLAPPED THE DOCTOR ON THE BACK. "I'M GOING TO build a small hospital in one of the buildings here. And then I hope we'll never need to use it. You know any other docs who might want to live here? I'm guessing you wouldn't want to leave Colin's employ?"

The doctor Colin sent stayed up all night tending to the men. Still in good spirits, he laughed. "No. His lordship pays well and I have family in the area. However, I do know of a young doctor, very discreet who would be interested. He was born in Wales and would love to return. Shall I make inquiries?"

"Absolutely." Smiling he moved to check on another of his crew still thinking of Maggie. As soon as the men were settled, he would start the campaign. Flowers would be delivered to Monroe's flat daily. He'd found a gorgeous convertible Jaguar F Type for her. He'd have it delivered with a big white bow on top. It was dark blue and she'd look glorious driving it with the top down, her hair catching the glint of sunlight, streaming behind her as she drove.

Love letters. He'd composed one during a lull in the chaos. Hand-written. He had the ink-stained fingers to show for it. A letter would be delivered to her every day until she came around. Of course, if the bloody blasted curse was true, he'd have to do some fast-talking with Thorne or he wouldn't be around to wait her out. It wouldn't do at all to become a wraith. Not going to happen. He had to win back the woman he loved. He'd been the best of the best when he was human. As a pirate he'd negotiated more deals then he could remember, he was good at it and was positive he could offer Thorne something to make this ridiculous curse business go away.

Thinking about various inducements that might sway their aloof leader, he was so intent on his plans, he was startled when Fury burst through the doors of the great hall at a fast clip, straight for him.

"Dude. Something is seriously cocked up. I'm having difficulty sensing Maggie." The brown-eyed head spoke.

"What do you mean 'difficulty sensing' her?" Robert turned his head to look at the demon hound. All three heads fixed eyes on Robert.

"You're not the brightest one in the bunch are you?" Fury's tail thumped the floor. "Relax, Shadow Walker. In giving Maggie the ability to contact me, I can sense her. So the fact that I cannot, has me worried. You know, like the signal on your phone going in and out. At first I thought it was indigestion, I've never experienced this feeling before but it must be worry. We need to find her. Now."

"She's with Monroe, I'll call him." Robert's hand was steady. He looked down, thinking his entire body should be shaking. The fear was a live thing inside him, clawing and biting its way out. If he let it out, he'd be useless to her. Monroe's mobile rang and rang before dropping to voice mail. The monster within crawled up from his stomach to his throat, choking him. He called Maggie's mobile. She might be furious with him but she'd answer. Wouldn't say anything but she'd at least pick up. He couldn't remember ever wanting to hear her angry silence as much as he did at this very moment. Damn it to hell. Same as Monroe's, the wretched thing rang straight through.

"Neither one is answering." Strange. His voice was calm though inside he was screaming, bellowing her name.

"You look like you're gonna hurl. You okay?" The left head was peering at him. Robert waved him away, willing himself to breathe.

"Draken and I will search for her. Once I'm in the air, it may be easier to find her." The hound was padding out the door when he stopped and the middle head looked back. "Robert. We'll find her. I swear it."

All he could do was nod and watch him leave. His mobile rang shattering the silence. It was Jasper. "Robert. I got a call from one of my contacts. An old industrial building in Glasgow was blown to bits. It was a large farm." The Frenchman paused. "My guy didn't hang around, he didn't want to risk encountering any legal types. Before he departed he saw a black mangled Mercedes SUV. I had the plates run—Robert, it was Monroe's vehicle. I'm sorry."

"Did he see anyone? They might have gotten away before the building blew." A small fissure of hope sprung from his chest. It could all be a mistake.

"No one. If I find out more, I'll let you know. Is there anything else I can do?"

Thoughts spun through his brain. He threw them away as quickly as they formed. He needed his fucking powers back. A final thought settled in. If something happened to her, he would bargain with Thorne or find a way to escape the wraith realm and he swore, he'd hunt down those responsible and kill each and every one of them, not stopping until he came face to face with Solien himself. "If she's...help me destroy them all." He disconnected. The volcano within threatening to erupt and destroy anyone and anything in its path.

The wretched piece of plastic's shrill voice resounded through the room again. "What?"

"You've already heard." It was a statement, not a question from Fury. He had to know.

"Did you find them?" The silence seemed to fill the study sucking the air out.

"The authorities are on the scene. We can't get closer without revealing ourselves, the energy around the building is strange, it could remove our invisibility. There are two bodies on the ground near the blast radius." In muffled tones, Fury spoke to Draken before coming back on the line. "Robert. Draken overheard the emergency workers. A man and a woman, neither is responding. They're taking them both to hospital. We'll follow and meet you there."

Bloody sheep bollocks. "Fury—I can't dematerialize right now."

In any other circumstances his pause would have been funny. "I see. I'll send Draken back for you." Fury ended the call. Robert noted he didn't pretend and tell him everything would be fine.

Had he truly lost Maggie?

Was she dead?

ed...

❧ 42 ❧

C astle Gloom was a ruin. How was it possible? Hamish thought it would stand forever. Yet now, looking at his home, he was flooded with anger. Colin was to blame. He'd let the estate fall while Ravensmore was still standing proud.

Wandering aimlessly through the ruins imbued with memories, he noted the steps leading down to the dungeon. Well, well. It looked as if someone had been trespassing. There was fresh blood in some of the cells. Empty bottles and wrappers carelessly discarded on the stone floor. Oil in lamps replacing the ancient torches on the walls.

Hamish dematerialized to the last remaining tower. Looking out over his lands, he came to a decision. The castle would be restored to its former glory. Would be easy enough to find willing workers, he had plenty of gold now that he was working for Thorne. Colin didn't know Hamish had joined their little club; the god thought it would be a nice surprise for Colin. Hamish wasn't so sure. A great many years had passed but Colin would be as likely to kill him as welcome him.

They had unfinished business. Sitting with his back against the wall, he stared out at the loch, unseeing.

"What a lovely surprise. Hamish Campbell." Rawlins stood leaning on the crumbling stone.

"Rawlins? What the devil are you doing here?" Hamish started. He hadn't seen the English captain since right before his death. He'd learned a great deal this past year. Rawlins wasn't a Shadow Walker, his energy smelled and sounded different, he was a Day Walker. Hamish jumped up, pulling his gun from the holster.

"Really, guns? No need. Consider this a pleasant chat. It's been a long time since we've worked together." Rawlins narrowed his eyes. "I've been making use of your dungeons. Hope you don't mind. That is, until Colin ruined it."

"I wondered who had been here. What happened to my home?" Hamish couldn't keep the anguish from his voice.

"You've not seen Colin yet? No grand reunion?" Pausing, Rawlins kicked at a loose stone. "Thought so. Colin won't be so pleased to see you, I'll wager. As to your home—Colin kept the taxes paid, but that's it as far as I know. Gloom fell into shambles over the centuries until it is as you see it now. I believe he rather liked seeing your estate fall to ruin. Planning to live here, are you?"

Putting his gun back in the holster, Hamish decided Rawlins wasn't here for a fight. He was sharing information, and while Hamish was glad to get it, he couldn't help but wonder why.

"No, I've not seen Colin. I wanted to accustom myself to this world first...so much has changed." Hamish stared at Rawlins. In his human life they'd become partners in order to take Colin and Robert down. Rawlins had been a necessary tool of the times. It was surreal to see him now, hundreds of years later, both of them Walkers albeit on different sides. "Why do ye fight for the Day Walkers? I thought you liked winning?"

The English captain's laughter rang across the stone. "I *am* on the winning side. Your precious Shadow Walkers have too many blasted rules. Us, not so much, especially regarding draining humans which I do so enjoy." Rawlins turned to look at the loch.

"Consider this your one free pass with me. The next time I see you, I will kill you. No hard feelings. Dayne tends to take our heads if we let the likes of you roam about. Clear?"

"Crystal." Hamish looked hard at his once ally. "You didn't condone what I did to Colin or Robert. Guess I thought you might have picked the Shadow Walkers."

Rawlins paused. "You thought wrong." With that, his enemy dematerialized.

Letting out a breath he didn't need, Hamish thought about what had happened all those years ago. He'd betrayed Colin to the English, turning him in for smuggling.

He let his thoughts drift back. He'd hated Colin since they were boys so it was easy enough to turn him in to Captain Huntington. He remembered how hard it was to plunge the dagger in Colin's chest. He'd ruined his favorite jacket. For a moment Hamish felt something twist inside, almost like sorrow for his brother who was always kind to him, but he quashed it before the thought could take root.

Abigail. Once that evil shrew spent his gold, she had no further use for him. She had him murdered, planned it so she would be on a ship bound for the West Indies to marry a wealthy plantation owner. Hamish smirked. One of the first things he did was to find out what happened to that bitch. She never made it; the ship was attacked by pirates and said all perished. Rumor was it was Robert's doing.

Fading out, Hamish vanished back to the Shadow Walker realm to think. He needed a plan before facing his sibling. The odd thing was, Thorne had told him that except for him, every Shadow Walker relived their death with all present. Didn't matter they had passed on. It was like a moment captured in time and replayed. Hamish had no memory of these yearly occurrences and it made his head hurt to try and figure out how it made sense. He had to thank Colin—if he hadn't of pissed off Thorne, Hamish wouldn't be here.

Apparently Colin needed to be taught respect so Thorne

thought it a wonderful idea to bring Hamish into the game. He snorted. The more things changed, the more they stayed the same. Somebody was always angling for the next rung up the ladder. Though they were on the same side now. What would Colin say when he learned Hamish was one of them? Would his honorable brother spurn him yet again or would he want vengeance for Hamish murdering him?

DESTINED SHADOW

✥ 43 ✥

aterializing into his brother's throne room, Thorne idly looked around the ostentatious room. He noted the male fae chained next to the gilded chair, asleep. His brother was unwise to offend the powerful race. He could use this to his advantage. Allay with the four courts. He needed all the help he could get to win the coming war with his brother.

The air shifted around him. "Dearest brother, to what do I owe this great honor?" Dayne warily approached, a smile pasted on his face.

"Dayne. I thought it time to pay my brother a little visit. Are you at war with the fae?" He pointed to the man chained on the floor.

His brother scowled. "There's been no declaration of war. This one and a few others have angered me. I am merely teaching them a lesson in manners."

Translation. War was imminent. He'd need to move fast to broker an alliance. Thorne arched a brow. "That's one way to do it."

"What do you want?" Dayne watched him carefully as if he was a serpent about to strike.

"Leave the humans to themselves. Let them destroy the

world and each other on their own without your interference. I find it wearing to continue these petty skirmishes all because you want to rule. Can't you rule over one of the other realms?"

"I'm not sure what happened to you. The Thorne I know is a warrior. Not some rejected schoolboy who pouts for the next millennia. Fuck no, I won't let the humans be. They were created to be ruled and I mean to rule over them all."

He tried. So now he was clear in his mind to kill his brother. Not giving any warning, he shot a blast of blue energy at Dayne. It was met in the middle by a matching blast of red energy. His brother was fast, he'd give him that.

The air in the room swirled into gale force winds. Terya appeared and with a single gesture, the energy blasts vanished. She floated into the throne room in front of them both. Their mother was beautiful. Truth be told, she looked younger than either of them.

"Boys. Stop bickering."

Before he could defend his actions, she threw up a hand and trees sprang up around them. "You each have much to learn. Disappointment fills me when I see the two of you trying to kill each other. In our world, there must be balance. Hear me well— if one of you kills the other, you in turn will die."

He processed what she'd said. This was complete utter bull-shit. Dayne jumped in before he could.

"Mother, there has to be some kind of mistake."

Terya silenced both with a single flick of her wrist. "And to ensure you both understand me, not only will you destroy each other but in doing so, your realms will be destroyed with you." Birds chirped, frogs croaked and their mother vanished.

Dayne scowled at his brother. "Nice. Guess I'll have to find another way to kill you."

"Always a pleasure to have these little chats brother." Thorne dematerialized back to his realm to think of another way to accomplish his goals.

❧ 44 ❧

"**S**olien. Your greedy bastards cocked it up." Rawlins appeared at Velvet. Stalking through the dark interior to the corner booth where the demon was kicked back drinking long island iced teas. There was no one around, it was too early.

"Whatever are you going on about?"

"Do you have any idea what I've been doing all day while you're here enjoying a bloody drink? Colin and Jasper took out all of the men because they were going to steal treasure from Robert and his crew."

The demon's gaze sharpened. "Treasure. What treasure?"

Rawlins wanted to throttle the guy. "The old Knights Templar treasure was apparently under Rosslyn Chapel all these years. Robert and his crew stole it and divvied up the spoils. The man you had on the inside got greedy and decided his share wasn't enough. So he plotted with Bruce and all the men to take it. They hit the crew. Only they didn't count on Colin and Jasper showing up. Bloody Shadow Walkers cut them down without breaking a sweat."

He paused in his tirade as the waitress brought him a martini. Drinking it in two gulps, he slammed the glass down.

"Bring me two more." The girl scurried off to get him the drinks and he resumed. "Bruce and a large number of men went to Gwrych to try and take Robert on his own land. Foolish idiots. All are dead. But before one of them was killed, he got off a text. Do you know what it said?" Rawlins could feel his blood boiling. While he might not have approved of the farming activities, this...this would start an all-out war. He preferred to catch his enemy unaware. Not going to happen now.

Solien raked a glare across him. "You're spoiling my good mood. I've only taken a few humans today and I'm in need of more. Finish your tale and be gone."

Ah. The demon was still torqued he'd thought of the idea of buying a few fast food chains to feed the humans and Solien hadn't. Let's see what he made of this news. "The text said that Fury was helping the Shadow Walkers. He's turned. Can't you and Dayne control your pet? And that's not all. They had a bloody dragon with them."

He had the demon's attention now. Solien sat forward. "I should throw you into the wall for your insolence but then the authorities would show up and ruin my day. I'll deal with Fury, don't worry about that one." He leaned across the table, pale in the dim light. His hands gripping the wood as claws appeared out of his fingertips. "What do you mean a dragon?"

"A dragon. You know, big giant beast with wings who breathes fire." He rolled his eyes. The guy looked spooked. Interesting.

Solien sneered. "You will report to Dayne, fill him in on what's been happening. Then, find us more humans. We'll need to build our ranks back up. I'll look into this dragon story."

Dismissed, Rawlins knocked back the rest of his martini. He'd be lucky if Dayne didn't incinerate him on the spot when he delivered this delightful news.

One eye cracked open, and Maggie rolled onto her side, retching. Grass tickled her face. She sat up slowly, taking stock of her body. Everything seemed to be in working order though she had a bitch of a headache. Where was Monroe? She'd been thrown into a ravine and wedged between two barrels from the impact of the explosion. Debris fluttered on the air currents like some modern art installation. Sirens sounded.

Hauling her aching body to its knees she looked again. There. Concealed beneath some type of hedge, an arm stuck out. Pushing to her feet, Maggie staggered to the shrubbery.

"Monroe. Wake up. Can you hear me?" Pulling his arm, she half dragged him out. He had numerous lacerations on his body and a big bump on his head. His blond hair looked brown from all the dirt and was laced with twigs and leaves. Oh hell, she'd yanked him too far. With a grunt, he slid down to the bottom of the ravine with her.

"Fuck, that hurt." A baleful turquoise eye glared at her. "What the fuck happened?"

"Thank god you're alive. And to answer your question, we were blown up by Rawlins. A Day Walker."

Maggie staggered to her feet. The ambulance had pulled away, sirens blaring. Who did they have in the back? There wasn't anyone else there. She waved her hands to get someone's attention but the police were busy investigating the blast. Black metal caught her eye. "Uh, Monroe. Can you stand?"

Listing a bit to the side, he rested one hand on the ravine. She pointed. "I think that used to be your car."

"Fuck it all to hell and back. She was my baby. I'll kill the bastard for this." He was so angry and it wasn't humorous so why was she laughing so hard she was crying. Hysterical laughter making her stomach hurt.

"It isn't funny, Maggie." He sounded so upset. Her words came out in a jumble.

"I'm not laughing at you or the car. I don't have a clue why I'm laughing. Nothing is funny. We almost died." The laughter subsided into small giggles and turned to hiccups.

Monroe patted all his pockets, turning them inside out. "My phone's gone. Do you have yours?"

"No. My purse and phone were on the ground when the bomb or whatever it was went off. You must have been closer to the blast because you're shredded and I don't have a scratch on me." How was it possible she didn't have a mark on her? Even her headache was gone.

"Anyway we don't need a phone. I can get us out of here."

❧ 46 ❧

At the hospital, Fury changed into human form. The nurse on duty told him, well with a bit of a telepathic tinkering, the woman had a purse with her, identified her as Maggie. No last name. The man didn't have any identification on him. He already knew the car at the site was Monroe's. They were gone. He had to get to Robert.

Fury met them in the air in his raven shape, telling Draken to land. They took advantage of an empty parking lot. Changing back to his hound form, the middle head spoke. "Robert. The bodies were burned beyond recognition. The man didn't have any ID but it was Monroe's Benz. The woman...I'm sorry. Her purse was there, along with her mobile. Maggie and Monroe are gone."

Falling to his knees, he couldn't breathe. The volcano erupted, scorching his insides, burning everything away, leaving nothing but ash behind. Robert's soul split in two as he howled to the heavens. The only woman he'd truly loved was gone.

288

Monroe's arched eyebrow said it all. Whatever. "Stow it and listen. Fury gave me his name if I ever needed him. I think this definitely qualifies as needing him."

"Wait. Gave you his name. How does it work?"

She shrugged. "Beats the heck out of me." Climbing out of the ravine, she looked around. They'd been carried a hell of a distance by the blast. The field they were in was far enough that if the police weren't looking in this direction, they'd never see them or Fury. Wouldn't be able to hear them either. Not sure what to do, she took a deep breath, thought *Please help us* and let it rip. "Fury. If you can hear me, it's Maggie. Monroe and I really need your help."

Draken made a keening noise in the back of his throat. And as Fury told Robert he'd gladly help him destroy every last Day Walker, a voice called his name.

"It isn't possible. Robert. Draken. Follow me." He leapt into the air, changing into a raven and flew to answer Maggie's distress call.

Monroe searched the sky. "How long does it take? Shouldn't it be instantaneous—you call and poof he's here?" He was sitting down, his back up against a tree.

"I don't know, I've never done this before." She put her hand up to shield her eyes from the afternoon sun, sending up a prayer he'd hear her and appear. The realization she could have been killed today in the blast—all she wanted to do was see Robert, throw her arms around him and never let go. She'd been thinking about what transpired between them and maybe, just maybe she could see his side. A four hundred year old pirate was bound to have some caveman tendencies. For Robert, his protectiveness was a way to show he cared. She trusted him and most importantly, loved him beyond all measure. They'd have to set ground rules and he'd be making it up to her for a long time, but she felt forgiveness spread through her heart, warming her.

Leaning against the tree, holding on to Monroe's arm she waited. The stubborn man wouldn't let her look at his injuries, said they were just scratches but he could sure use a drink. He drank a lot. She'd seen enough alcoholics in her time to know he was a highly functioning drunk. A great guy who obviously had some serious issues to need booze to cope with life on a regular basis. Who was she to judge based on her past? She'd be there to help whenever he was ready.

The wind ruffled her dirty, matted hair and she swore she smelled the ocean. Looking to the sky, she didn't see anything yet but her gut told her the cavalry had arrived.

"They're here." Maggie pointed to the speck, growing larger and stood, moving out from under the tree, waving her arms to draw attention.

Fury landed first. One moment he was a raven, the next his usual form of hellhound. She ran to him, hugging each head, kissing the muzzle. "It worked. You found us."

The heads licked her face. The middle one speaking. "Maggie. They found your purse and mobile next to a woman's body.

There was a man as well. Both bodies were badly burnt. We thought it was you and Monroe. We thought you were dead."

Draken landed at that moment and her heart flipped over when Robert leapt from his back, running to her. He swung her up in his arms, kissing her. "I thought I'd lost you." He murmured into her ear. "I know you're terribly angry with me. Give me another chance and I'll spend eternity making it up to you...or however much time I have left. Please, Maggie."

Tears streamed down her face, she hugged him harder. "Yes." It was all she could get out without bawling like a baby and she refused to breakdown in front of an audience.

A throat clearing had Robert gently depositing her to the ground, his arm around her shoulders.

"About time. Pretty Maggie, we're so joyful you're alive." Draken rubbed his snout on her shoulder, chuffing into her hair. She hugged him back.

"Thank you, Draken. And thank you for bringing Robert to me."

They told the story of their ordeal and how Rawlins was the one who set off the bomb. There were no people there, they'd checked.

"The two of them must have been hiding or were already dead when the blast hit." Robert spoke softly, aware of what might have been. Monroe was standing, talking to Fury and Robert called out. "You said you couldn't sense her, what happened?"

Brown eyes studied him. "The blast of energy from the Day Walker temporarily severed my connection to her. I didn't want to make it too strong as other things can happen...though based on what I'm sensing, it's too late. Maggie is changed. Oops."

"Oops?" Maggie and Robert spoke at the same time. Draken and Monroe were looking on with interest at what Fury would say.

Red eyes looked into her soul. "It's only 'oops' if you are unhappy with the outcome. Maggie...did you wonder why you bear not a single scratch upon your body after being thrown from the blast into a field?" He went on without waiting for an answer. She couldn't have formed a word at that very moment if she had to. "You are human, and humans have a weak life-force. We boosted it so to speak."

The middle head with gold eyes finished the sentence. "What he means to say is, welcome to the club, you're immortal."

She blinked, mouth open. "What?"

A grin broke out across Robert's face, and Maggie thought she saw naked envy on Monroe's before he hid it and smiled as well.

"I don't understand."

Fury rumbled. "Don't try. Accept and enjoy the long life ahead of you." Stunned, her knees gave out. Robert caught her, chuckling.

"'Tis a great deal to take in. Give it time, milady."

Worry filled her. Time. Weren't they running out?

❧ 48 ❧

The last few days had been full of surprises. A car arrived to take Monroe back to Edinburgh. He'd scarfed down a late lunch on the way. Maggie was going to Gwrych with Robert for a long overdue chat. Her words, not his. She assured him she was still working with him and would be by to pick up her things. Fury and Draken left, bickering like two old biddies.

"Oy! Colin." The hard-headed Highlander ignored him turning the corner down a narrow street, walking arm-in-arm with his wife, Emily. Carrying a case of beer, Monroe cursed and moved faster. He might have been killed, should have been in all reality but he'd cheated death and was gloriously alive. What better way to celebrate life than to watch the Celtic match with Shamus. Better hurry, he didn't want to be late.

Catching up, he rounded the corner and spied Colin. He was leaning against the wall in the alley talking to Emily. Only it wasn't his wife. *What the hell?* Colin worshipped the ground his wife walked on. He'd never step out on her. Ducking into a dark entryway across the street, Monroe watched and waited.

Staring hard at Colin, Monroe's eyebrows shot up. He'd only had six beers today, wasn't close to being drunk and didn't even have a good buzz going. He shook his head and looked again. It wasn't Colin.

This guy was the spitting image of Colin but not. The man was a few inches shorter and his hair was cut short. A dark gray suit showed under his trench coat and Monroe swore he caught the outline of a shoulder holster. Who was he? Colin didn't have any family that Monroe knew of.

Pulling out his mobile, he dialed Robert. Before he could tell him, Robert jumped in. "Monroe. Everything OK?" The concern in his friend's voice caused him to tense up. Robert knew how much immortality meant to him. Had to know he was pissed at Fury for not giving it to him. The bloody hound had the nerve to spout some bollocks about destiny and finding one's own path. So not going there right now.

He took a swig from his flask and gritted out the words. "Fine. Look, I'm standing here in the city looking at a guy who could pass for Colin's twin. What gives, mate?" Monroe stole a look, yep, the guy was still there. Getting it on with the woman in the alley if their movements were any indication of what they were doing.

He heard a sharp intake of breath. "Are you sure?" Robert asked. "It's important."

"Snapped and texting the guys mug to you now." Monroe waited. Creative swearing answered him.

"Does he know you're there? Has he seen you?"

He took another look see, "Nope he's busy nailing some bird in the alley."

"This is bad. It's Colin's younger brother, Hamish."

It took a moment to sink in and another for his brain to catch up. "Wait a second. I thought he died like a million years ago. How is that even possible?"

"Blast if I know. Listen, don't say anything to Colin yet. He's got enough on his mind with the twins. I'll see what I can find out. Thanks for the info."

"Laters." Monroe hung up. Leave it to Robert to bring up the one thing he could do nothing about...his life-span. Rolling his shoulders to ease the knot of tension, he shoved the thoughts away. Focused instead on this latest bit of information. He didn't want to be part of that family reunion. Colin was cranky at the best of times, far be it for him to break the news his brother was back among the living after so many years.

Hamish sent the woman on her way as Monroe watched. The girl stumbled, looking a bit tipsy. Before he could step out of the darkened doorway, Hamish vanished.

Yep, some kind of Walker but Shadow or Day? Monroe was on the fringe of the Shadow Walkers thanks to Robert. The guy had saved his arse last year; Monroe would have died if Robert hadn't been there. The guilt over his girlfriend ate at him, even after ten years. The closure Robert provided by letting Monroe strike the fatal blow helped. Though each morning he woke he blamed himself. There should have been a clue or something he could have done. The responsibility weighed on him like a vest weighted with concrete. Her death was on him for not being there to save her. Killing the Day Walker who'd been respon-sible for murdering Alice satisfied his need for justice...the emotional issues he couldn't deal with. Made him squirm thinking about it.

After that day, Monroe's world shifted. Now he knew beyond any doubt, there were all kinds of beings wandering around and thanks to briefly dying, he could see them. He'd vowed to become a part of the Shadow Walkers, however he could. He helped them investigate, putting the resources of his department behind him to find out what he could. Well at least until they'd canned his arse.

Hurrying down the deserted street, the denizens tucked in for the cold night, he caught up with the bird. "Miss. Miss, are you OK?" The woman stared up at him and Monroe sucked in a breath. From his earlier vantage point and the way she'd been dressed, he'd have pegged her at twenty. But she looked late forties, easily.

"Oh, just tired I guess. Long day of classes. Must have been daydreaming, don't know how I ended up on this street."

"You should be more careful. Can I walk you home?"

"Thank you but you don't need to. My flat is two streets over. I'm fine now, really."

He watched her go. Classes. Bloody bastard had taken some of her energy, he'd swear to it. That was against the code of the Shadow Walkers. He must be a Day Walker then. Wished there was an easy way to tell the difference.

Reaching into his pocket to shoot a text to Robert about the woman, Monroe realized his cash was gone. Had he lost it? He looked down the street after the girl. Did she take it? Cursing, he looked at the time on his mobile and swore. He'd have to jog to make it before the match started. Picking up the beer, he ran for Shamus' flat, cursing the entire way.

❧ 49 ❧

T hursday, November 9th - *The last day of the curse*

BACK AT GWRYCH CASTLE, ROBERT STRETCHED. IT WAS EARLY morning. Afraid he'd almost lost her, Robert made rough, passionate love to Maggie. Afterwards, they'd cleaned up and come down to the library. Standing by the mantle, he watched Maggie dig into a bowl of pomegranate seeds. Unaware of the ticking clock, she had a glass of wine and a blanket wrapped around her. Watching her sitting on the rug in front of the fire, his heart jumped erratically. She was his.

What would happen in the next hour? Would it be business as usual or was it true and he'd be dragged away from her to exist as a wraith for all time? It would be a cruel joke for the gods to take him and curse her to be alone for eternity, knowing she was now immortal. Unwilling to break the moment, he contented himself with searing her image onto his very soul. Capturing her smell. Small things to hold on to when he was gone. In more ways than one he'd failed miserably.

"What? Do I have something on my face?" She looked miffed and he stifled the urge to chuckle.

"No. I was thinking." Always sure in battle and with his men, he was at a loss how to tell her what he was feeling. Best to get it out before he lost his nerve. Taking a sip of wine to steady his nerves, he shot a prayer to Terya, took a deep breath and began.

"I was wrong to keep the curse from you. At the time, I thought it would be easier to handle it myself and not give you something else to worry about. Instead, I created discord and mistrust between us. You had every right to be angry, to still be mad at me." Robert stopped. Gripping the thick wood of the mantle, he let the corner bite into his hand. Pain would clear his vision. Draining the glass of wine, he walked to the sideboard to pour another, for if he continued speaking, he'd break down and bawl like a babe.

'Twas too late and now he was going to lose her. Thorne would never bargain, he'd been a fool to think so, could see that now.

Turning back to her, he smiled seeing the pomegranate seeds forgotten, rolling across the rug. Maggie. His north star. Standing in front of him with a look of hope on her face. Gods, he was the worst scoundrel, about to crush the tiny light she still had within her. Not saying a word, she stood on tiptoe and kissed him. A gentle kiss, light as the finest silk across his mouth.

The sun broke through the uncovered windows as Robert looked at the clock. Minutes left. Cruel time. It stretched endlessly when bad things were happening but hours vanished in seconds when everything was perfect. Like now. Would he vanish when it struck ten? Would Thorne take him away or would something else—wraiths? Maggie would be frantic.

His knees hit the floor. Wrapping his arms around her waist, he held her tight. "Maggie, my fiery darlin'. I cannot bargain my way out of the curse. I know this now. If only I had more time. When you left...I came up with a grand plan to woo you back to me." Had he been punched in the gut? It felt like such. "Then I thought I'd lost you and my world shattered. Without you by my side, I didn't want to go on. I love you. Completely. Every star in the heavens is a declaration of my love for you. Can you ever find it within yourself to forgive me?"

Kneeling down in front of him to look him in the eye, her eyes shone with tears. "I love you. I've loved you since the moment you yelled at me for saving you from hanging. There's nothing to forgive. I forgave you when I realized I might have acted the same way if our roles were reversed. You showed me how to live again."

Fisting her hair in his hands, he pulled her to him, demanding, needing. Slanting his mouth over hers, he kissed her. With his kiss he told her how much he loved her, needed her, would miss her.

The first chime struck. Time was running out. "When the clock strikes ten, I will turn wraith." Leaning back, he looked up at her while she caressed his hair. "If you can find another to make you happy, take the chance and forget me."

Wild, she shook her head, greens eyes blazed. "Never. I will love you every day for the rest of my life." A sob escaped her and she trembled in his arms.

"Shh, my darling. Don't cry. Maggie, no matter how long it takes, I give you my solemn oath. I will find a way back to you."

The clock struck ten.

The air around them began to swirl. A silver and lavender mist filled the room, sparkling and covering them in iridescent shimmer. She clung to him. Resignation flooded him as regret flowed through his veins—the only part of this past week he didn't rue was *her*.

"Go on then, take me. I'll find a way back to her. Fuck your bloody curse."

Lightning crackled across the room and the lights winked out. The only illumination in the room came from the fire and the lavender and silver shimmer, dancing on the air like tiny fireflies.

"My, aren't we rather dramatic." Thorne stood before them in all his six foot seven glory, long silver hair floating around him, dancing with the lightning flashing in the room. Varying shades of blue tattoos flashed across his skin, seeming to change in the light from the fire. A fitted white tee showed off his huge muscled arms. Robert had to admit, he was a sight to behold.

"Nothing to say from either of you?" Eyebrows rose up into his forehead. "I'm speechless."

Maggie stammered. Robert looked around to see if there was anyone waiting to drag him off to the wraith realm.

"Cutting it rather close, weren't you?"

Incredulity filled his voice. "Are you telling me, we broke the bloody curse? How? We've not seen any sign." Keeping an arm around Maggie, they sat on the sofa as Thorne dropped into the chair facing them, looking quite pleased with himself. Robert wanted to punch him in the face. That would wipe the smirk off the unpredictable god's face.

Thorne leaned forward, elbows on his knees, fingers resting on his chin. "Some days dealing with all of you is a bit like herding cats."

The god stood and looked down at them. Robert tensed.

"What you wanted something more dramatic?" Thorne rolled his eyes. "Sometimes the most astonishing changes come from within. You were willing to sacrifice your very essence for Maggie. Though, by the way...if you had been condemned to the wraith realm...no one has ever escaped so it was folly to think you could have. Think on that, Robert. Now go—be happy." Robert and Maggie stood. Thorne slapped Robert on the back, kissed Maggie on both cheeks and before he vanished, called out to the air. "My brother's going to be incredibly pissed at you Fury...Great job. Come see me and let's have a little chat."

Robert stood there looking at the empty spot where mere seconds ago Thorne stood. "Rather a bit anticlimactic." He felt

like a schoolboy caught playing at monsters long after he'd
outgrown them. The lights blinked back on and a jolt of energy
hit Robert hard. Doubling over, he welcomed the pain as his
power flooded back into him. Gods, it was good to be whole
again.

Maggie wrapped her arms around him and held tight. "Don't
ever scare me like that again."

Wrapping her hair around his fingers, watching it slide
across his skin, he wanted to mark her, ensure she was his
forever but first... "You know my plans to woo you were quite
impressive if I do say so myself. Rather a shame not to
execute."

Her eyes sparkled. "I've never been wooed. Sounds like fun.
Do I get to send you on a ridiculous quest with treasure and a
dragon?" She paused and laughed. A fully, throaty laugh from
deep within. "Oh right. We already did that. In that case, I'd like
to be swept up the stairs and into our room where you ravish
me...you know, like Scarlett, in my book." Maggie batted her
eyelashes at him as he swept her up into his arms.

"My pleasure to oblige you and your bloody book. Are there
any other things in that book you might like?" He knew he was
leering at her but couldn't help it. She pulled a very prim and
proper look. "Oh, milord. Not in that book. But there is another
book I'm reading..." She squealed as he dematerialized to the
door outside their room. Cutting off her question as to why they
were in the hallway, he kicked the door open, strode across the
room, and threw her on the bed.

"How's that compare to your blasted book?"

"Why Robert Bartholomew are you jealous of a silly, ol'
book?" She simpered up at him. Instead of answering, he simply
arched a brow and dematerialized their clothing, chuckling when
she gasped. Covering her body, he kissed her, tracing her lips
with his tongue. Kissing the tip of her nose and eyelids. Each
kiss a benediction. His voice hoarse, he put his lips next to
her ear.

"I will spend eternity worshipping you, showing you how much I love you, my fiery north star."

Shivering in his arms, Maggie wrapped her legs around his waist, guiding him home. "You showed me how to trust, to hope, and to believe in love. Every day from now until the end of time, I'll tell you how very much I love you." Her voice broke and she gasped as he slid her knees up, thrusting deep, growling her name, over and over, bringing them both safely home.

F
riday, November 10th

THE NEXT MORNING, MAGGIE WOKE WITH A SMILE ON HER face. No more running. No more fear. Safe, secure and with the man she loved. What more could she ask for?

Robert came bustling into the room, already dressed. Disgustingly cheerful, he'd evidently been up a while. "Good morning, milady. I wondered if you were going to sleep the day away. Much as I'd like to stay in bed and lick every inch of your delectable skin, we have a very busy day ahead of us."

"Not sure what you're talking about." She stretched, sore in all the right places. Warm in bed, she planned to stay there until noon, reading and being lazy. It would be heaven. "I'm not getting up. In fact, I might stay in bed the entire weekend." Maggie grinned at him.

Robert was bearing a gold tray as he came over to the bed. There was a huge bowl of cut-up fruit and a cold Pepsi. "Oh, thank you. I'm starving." She sat up, pulling on his shirt. The smell of him enveloped her. Breathing in deeply, she decided she'd wear one of his shirts every day to keep his scent close to her. He was looking at her, a grin on his face.

"Do I look silly in your shirt?"

"Are you kidding? Methinks you should wear my shirt and nothing else all the time. But only in our bedroom. I don't want to have to kill every man in Wales for ogling you. So, my darling, you'll have to get dressed for I've a surprise for you downstairs."

In her life, surprises were never good. "What is it?"

He tsk tsked her. "Now darlin', it wouldn't be a surprise if I told you. Get dressed and meet me in the courtyard, I want to see your face when you come out. No peeking out of windows on the way."

"Aye, aye, sir." Mock saluting him, she laughed as he kissed her and squeezed her bottom. Pushing him out of the room, she took a fast shower, dressed and ran down the steps. Gareth was holding the door open. Rushing outside, scarf blowing behind her, she skidded to a stop. The most beautiful machine she'd ever laid eyes on was sitting in front of her with a big white bow on the top. Her hand flew to her mouth. "It's fantastic!" Running to Robert, she threw herself in his arms.

"I take it you like it, then?" A key fob dangled in front of her. "Shall we?"

Squealing, she grabbed it and popped the doors open. The delicious smell of a new car hit her. It was so luxurious inside. She'd never owned anything like this in her entire life. "It's a Jaguar F Type and a convertible. I pictured you driving down the road with your beautiful hair streaming behind you like a comet in the night sky."

"I love you and I adore the car." Leaning over to the passenger seat, she kissed Robert, licking his ear, satisfied when he let loose a growl. Sitting back, she touched every inch of the vehicle. Her sexy pirate cleared his throat. Turning to look at him, she sat up straight. He seemed—nervous was the only word she could come up with but it wasn't a word she'd use when talking about Robert. The man was supremely confident, ready for anything, never anxious.

A black box was withdrawn from the glove compartment. Now she was antsy. Opening it, she was stunned.

"The bracelet belonged to my sister, a very long time ago. The necklace, earrings and ring I found under Rosslyn. I never thought anything could compare to the beauty of these jewels... until I met you. I will cherish you for eternity. Would you do me the great honor of becoming my wife?" He'd removed the ring and was holding it out in front of her. The sapphires matched his eyes. As the man she loved beyond all measure sat in front of her, his heart on his sleeve, she thanked Fury, Draken, Thorne, and whoever else was listening for bringing them together.

"Yes. Yes, I'll be your wife."

Robert slid the ring on her finger. It was a perfect fit as if it had been made for her. Holding her hand out in front of her, she admired the ring. It was fashioned into flowers and vines. The vines were tiny emeralds, the flowers alternated between sapphires, rubies, and diamonds with a huge diamond as the center of the main flower. Running her hands down his chest, she saw a water spot on his shirt. He wiped the tears from her cheeks. "I love you, Robert."

"And I love you, Maggie." The next thing she knew, he'd popped them back into the bedroom. Before her was a beautiful white wedding gown, covered in tiny beads. It was worthy of a princess. "I don't know what to say."

"Say nothing and change your clothes, milady. We've nuptials to attend. And, what do you know, it's our wedding." He beamed at her, very happy with himself. Fury, Draken, Angus and the rest of Robert's men were her family now. Why wait?

"Let's get married."

Robert clapped his hands together. "Excellent. Colin and Emily are already here. She's been dying to talk to you."

Shyness filled her and she sank into the chair. "Will she like me?"

Robert knelt down in front of her. "How could she not, you're an amazing woman. Shall I send her in?"

Maggie nodded.

"Don't worry, love. I'm off to see to the final preparations." He held her shoulders and looked into her eyes. "I know we don't have natural family left but I hope you'll consider everyone here your family now. All of them wanted to help. They stayed up all night to prepare."

"When did you tell them? You just asked me." How had he done this without her knowing?

"Good thing about being a Shadow Walker, we don't need to sleep. So after I properly bedded you and watched you sleep, I snuck out of our chamber to make my plans. Rather enjoyed waking up the household. Do you know Draken is a bit cranky when he's unexpectedly woken up?" He laughed. "I'll see you downstairs." He walked to the door and ushered Emily in. "Maggie. Emily. Emily, this is my lady, Maggie. Now I'll leave you both to it." With a wink, he vanished.

"Oh, I've been dying to meet you. We have so much to talk about." Emily chattered on, helping Maggie dress, fussing over her hair and makeup. It was a bit of a blur and Maggie felt tears well up. "Did I say something?" Emily was looking at her with concern etched on her face.

"No. I was thinking how nice it would be to have a sister like you." She was almost bowled over when Emily hugged her tight.

"I had the exact same thought." Emily jumped around and then spied something that had her scurrying across the room. "You have cold Pepsi and ice. How fantastic." She poured them both a glass.

Maggie laughed. "Thanks to you, I'm addicted."

Emily led her over to the full-length mirror. "Breathtaking. Robert won't be able to take his eyes off you." She tapped her chin. "There's one thing missing."

Frowning, Maggie took stock. She was dressed, had her hair

and make-up done. Enough jewels to blind everyone, what could be missing?

Emily took her hand and slid a ring on her right hand. It was a large emerald, flanked by diamonds. "Where I come from, you need something borrowed. Please wear the ring."

Hugging her, Maggie dabbed her eyes so she wouldn't ruin all Emily's work. "Thank you."

How she found herself standing at the entrance to the great hall, she didn't know. Angus stood waiting. "Maggie, lass. May an old codger escort you down the aisle?"

"I couldn't think of anyone else I'd rather have, thank you, Angus." Taking his arm she walked into the great hall. All of Robert's men were there. She saw Monroe sitting next to Fury and Draken. She grinned thinking it perfect a three-headed hound and dragon were attending her wedding. She owed them her life and counted them friends. The room had been transformed. White flowers were everywhere, candles flickered, there must have been thousands, and every eye was locked on her. *Please don't let me trip.*

As she passed, Monroe smiled at her. Draken stretched his long neck out to her and chuffed against her hair. "Pretty Maggie. I wanted to walk you but I didn't fit."

Maggie patted his neck and hugged him. "It's okay. I'm so glad you're here, my friend."

Draken's eyes widened. "Friend? I've not had a friend before." He leaned over to Fury. "Maggie is my friend. If anyone annoys her, I'll eat them."

Fury's three heads smiled. "Not if we eat them first. She's our friend too."

Draken nudged Monroe. "Right. Maggie, you look beautiful. Draken thought you might not have time to get Robert a ring so he made one for you." Reaching in his pocket he pulled out a thick gold band. Oh my gosh, a ring. She'd completely forgotten.

"I'm so very grateful. It's perfect and I love it. I know Robert will as well." Kissing the dragon on the snout, she continued down the aisle.

Thorne was standing in front of her. This morning he looked human, his silver skin and tattoos hidden. Though with his silver hair she didn't know how anyone could think there wasn't 'other' in him.

Angus presented her to Robert. "I've a present for you after the wedding." Angus winked and took his seat. She was really getting married. Her. She'd given up on this dream as a child. Everything was perfect.

Robert held out his palm as Thorne took a silver dagger from his black Armani tux. Holding it up he intoned in a booming voice, "You pledge your blood and soul to this woman for all eternity?"

"I so pledge."

"You pledge to protect her from harm?"

"I so pledge."

"You pledge to sacrifice yourself for her?"

"I so pledge."

With that, Thorne sliced a deep cut across Robert's palm, the blood, flowing, dripping to the stone floor.

"Milady, your hand." Thorne nodded to her. A bit apprehensive, she presented her palm.

"Will you love him with your body and soul for all eternity?"

"I will."

The slice was quick and hurt. When Thorne placed her palm over Robert's, pressing them together, she felt the air around them shift. A tattoo of vines appeared on both of their wrists. Hers lavender and his dark blue. "By the energy of the blood this bond is consecrated."

Robert bent her back into a movie worthy swoon and kissed her. "I love you Mrs. Bartholomew."

Maggie laughed. "And I you, my pirate husband."

✦

THANK YOU SO MUCH FOR READING! I HOPE YOU ENJOYED Desired by Shadow. Next up is, Iced in Shadow, where Colin comes face to face with his murderer. I hope you love it.

IF YOU'D LIKE TO RECEIVE AN EMAIL ABOUT MY UPCOMING new releases, please join my mailing list. Visit my website, cynthialuhrs.com

ABOUT THE AUTHOR

Cynthia Luhrs spends her time out on the deck, looking into the woods, imagining what if. She writes women's fiction, time travel romance, contemporary romance, family sagas, paranormal romance, and thrillers. Readers say her books (well not the thrillers, those are gritty) are light-hearted reads to escape reality.

She lives in the mountains of North Carolina with two rescued tiger cats, has always been a reader, and is overly fond of sparkly flip flops and pretty pens. Though now that she lives in the mountains she's going to have to find fabulous boots, mittens, and hats!

Keep up with her on her website

- f facebook.com/cynthialuhrsauthor
- ⊙ instagram.com/cynthialuhrs
- BB bookbub.com/authors/cynthia-luhrs
- g goodreads.com/cynthialuhrsauthor